'Likely the next *Game of Thrones*, and the best book I've read in several years. Erikson, Martin and Rothfuss are going to have to shove over and make room at the bar. A gem. Not one likeable character in the swamp but I still became totally emotionally engaged. I can't think how to tone down my enthusiasm'

Glen Cook, author of The Black Company series

'Like Tarantino crossed with David Gemmell . . . Absolutely splendid. Shackle has come up with something really special here, and I enjoyed it enormously'

Peter McLean, author of *Priest of Bones*

'Hooked from page one, *We Are the Dead* rattles along with the pace of a runaway bullet train. Original, engaging, flawed but very human characters draw us into a world rent by war, a world of brutal occupation, tarnished honour and devastating magics. This is a powerful debut and Shackle is an author to watch'

Gavin Smith, author of *The Bastard Legion*

'A masterpiece of a story about hope, resistance and fellowship'

The Book Bag

'An adventure that's rich in darkness and bloodshed'   *SFX*

'*We Are the Dead* is a fantasy novel that is able to blend the modern trends of dark fantasy with the magical styles of the past' SF Book

'*We Are the Dead* is a staggering, marvellous and gripping fantasy debut that should be acknowledged alongside recent-ish excellent Grimdark debuts such as Ed McDonald, Peter McLean, Anna Smith-Spark and Dirk Ashton'   *Grimdark Magazine*

WE ARE THE DEAD

THE LAST WAR BOOK ONE

MIKE SHACKLE

This paperback first published in Great Britain in 2020 by Gollancz

First published in Great Britain in 2019 by Gollancz
an imprint of the Orion Publishing Group Ltd
Carmelite House, 50 Victoria Embankment
London EC4Y 0DZ

An Hachette UK Company

The authorised representative in the EEA is Hachette Ireland,
8 Castlecourt Centre, Dublin 15, D15 XTP3, Ireland (email: info@hbgi.ie)

11 13 15 17 19 20 18 16 14 12

A CIP catalogue record for this book
is available from the British Library.

ISBN (Mass Market Paperback) 978 1 473 22522 0
ISBN (eBook) 978 1 473 22523 7

Typeset by Deltatype Ltd, Birkenhead, Merseyside

Printed in Great Britain by Clays Ltd, Elcograf S.p.A.

www.gollancz.co.uk

For Tinnie, Dylan and Zoe

The Prayer of the Shulka

We are the dead who serve all who live.
We are the dead who fight.
We are the dead who guard tomorrow.
We are the dead who protect our land, our monarch, our clan.

We are the dead who stand in the light.
We are the dead who face the night.
We are the dead whom evil fears.
We are the Shulka and we are the dead.

We are the dead.
We are the dead.
We are the dead.
We are the dead.

We are Shulka and we are the dead.

I

Tinnstra

The Kotege

Tinnstra held the knife in her shaking hand. It was a small blade, easily stolen from the armoury, made of the best Rizon steel and razor sharp. Perfect for what she needed to do. Perfect for her little wrist, her small vein.

She sat in her room at the Kotege. It wasn't much, barely enough space for the single cot she was sitting on, a small writing table and chair by the window, and a fireplace, stacked with wood despite the summer heat. She told herself it was the temperature that made the perspiration run down her back, but that was a lie. It was the fear. It was the fear that made her hands shake. It was the fear that made suicide her only option, her only way out. The irony wasn't lost on her: the girl afraid to die was about to kill herself.

It was quiet outside. The evening meal was over, and most students would be studying or catching up on much-needed sleep. On a normal night, that's what Tinnstra would be doing as well, but this wasn't a normal night.

When Tinnstra arrived at the Kotege three years earlier, she'd never expected things would end this way. After all, boys and girls from only the best Shulka families were brought there from the age of sixteen to be trained, and Tinnstra came from the best family of all. Her father and mother and her three brothers had all graduated with its highest honours and gone on to distinguished military careers. No one had thought Tinnstra would be any different. No one had thought she was a coward.

Now there is no escape from the truth. No more pretence.

She looked down at her forearm. She knew where to cut – the Kotege had taught her that. Knowledge of human anatomy made better killers. Straight from the top of her forearm down to her wrist. It would hurt a little, but not for long. She'd pass out from blood loss before the pain got too bad.

A bell chimed the hour. There was no more time. They would be coming for her. She tightened her grip on the knife and tried to steady her hand.

The letter to her father lay on the table. Apologising, begging his forgiveness. He was on his way to Gundan in the north with the rest of her clan to fight the Egril. Maybe he was already there. By the time he learned of her death, Tinnstra would be nothing but ashes. She knew it would break his heart, but better that than disgrace his name. *No father should have me for a daughter.*

A sob racked her shoulders as she pressed the knife against her skin. *Not yet. Soon.* If only she wasn't so scared. She didn't want to die. There just wasn't another way out. Not that she could see.

Her heart pounded. Sweat stung her eyes and she did her best to blink it away, concentrating on trying to hold her trembling hand still. It would hurt more if she wasn't precise. And take longer to bleed out. She didn't want that. It had to be quick, painless, over.

The knife was cold against her skin, its edge sharp. All she had to do was push down and the blade would do its work. End it all. *Just push and cut.* And yet she couldn't make her hand do anything.

Her stomach lurched. Bile rose, burning her throat. She swallowed it back down, cursing her weakness. She had to do this. It was all she had left, her only path. She couldn't fail, not at this, too.

The rap on her door made her jump. 'Cadet Tinnstra, it's time.' A man's voice. Not one she recognised. One of the general's guards. She didn't reply. Hope fluttered for a moment that he might think her gone and leave her to do what she had to do.

He knocked again. 'Come on. The old man's waiting.'

There was no time to cut her wrist now. She moved the knife

to her heart, placed the tip against her breast. Death would be instantaneous. There would be no saving her. No last-minute dash to the infirmary – not even if the Shulka kicked her door down. She closed her eyes. Took another breath. *Time to die.*

The guard knocked again. 'Open the door, Cadet.'

She gripped the knife with both hands, but the shakes only got worse. Tears ran down her face. She couldn't do it. She had to do it. *Just push. By the Four Gods, push. End it all, you stupid fucking coward.*

The guard banged on the door. 'Stop pissing about. I won't ask again.'

Tinnstra dropped the knife. It clattered on the stone floor. 'I'm coming.'

She rolled down her sleeve, wiped her eyes and put on her cadet's tunic: dark black with silver buttons, all done up as per regulations, and brushed down. At least she looked smart, if nothing else. She might be the worst cadet, but she knew how to dress. There was no hiding the fact she'd been crying, though.

She sighed, unlocked the door, opened it. The general's guard stood in the doorway, looking as if he were one second away from putting his boot through the door. His breastplate was buffed so bright she could see her red, sore eyes gazing back. His helmet, with the blue plume running down the centre, identified him as Clan Mizu. Not her father's clan. Not her clan. She didn't know if that was a good thing or not.

'Come on. You're late.'

Tinnstra didn't move. She was too scared even to do that.

In the end, he reached in, grabbed her arm and dragged her out. He got her moving down the corridor with a shove and a grunt of disgust. Tinnstra knew how he felt. She felt disgusted, too. She thought of that small, perfect knife lying on her bedroom floor and wished she'd had the courage to use it. *Too late now. Another chance gone.*

They walked to the main stairs and went down, passing cadets returning to their rooms. She avoided all eye contact but knew they watched her, could hear the whispers. They all knew. Everyone knew.

The general's office was in the east wing. One long walk of shame. Tinnstra's cheeks burned the whole way, her legs so unsteady she was sure she was going to fall.

They passed through the central atrium with its long windows overlooking the parade ground. During the day, there would be at least one company of cadets in full battle armour out there, practising the Shulka's legendary phalanx formation: shields interlocked to form an impregnable wall, six-foot spears bristling outwards in a deadly hedge. They would move as one, forward, always forward. Two steps. Thrust. Two steps. Thrust. Organised. Efficient. Deadly. There was a reason why, for seven hundred years, no enemy had ever defeated the Shulka in battle. They were trained to be invincible. The best of the best. The bravest of the brave.

No wonder Tinnstra didn't fit in.

But am I wrong? Just because I don't want to die in some stupid battle? My life has got to be worth something. She glanced back at the guard. Why didn't he have the same fears? She knew the Shulka prayer, the vow they all took. It made no sense to her. *We are the dead indeed. Well, I'm not. I want to live.* No wonder she couldn't kill herself.

Two guards in full armour stood sentry outside the general's office. Sword on hip. Spear in hand. Eyes straight ahead.

The door opened. Now there was no escape.

'Go on,' said her guard. 'Best get it done.' She looked up at him, saw the sadness in his eyes. Maybe he had a daughter of his own. Probably praying she'd not turn out like Tinnstra. It was a Shulka's worst fear as a parent: to have a coward for a child.

She entered the general's office, wanting to be sick, struggling to breathe.

General Harka sat behind his desk, hands crossed. He was alone, thank the Four Gods. He watched her enter, saw her flinch when the door shut behind her. There was no smile, no greeting, no acknowledgement that she'd known him all her life. In that room, he wasn't her father's closest friend. He wasn't her godfather. He was the commanding officer of the Kotege.

And he scared the life out of her.

His hair was tied back into a queue and folded into a topknot, as was the style for Shulka, accentuating his sharp cheekbones. A candle burned on his desk, yet the light didn't find his face. Only his eyes glittered, but it was as if he were looking straight through her.

His office was simple. A banner hung on one wall – green with the sigil of the crossed spears of his clan, Inaren. His sword hung from a hook on the other wall. Designed to be wielded single-handed, the blade was some thirty inches in length, double-edged but best used to thrust at close range. A Shulka's spear was his or her primary weapon. A sword was for the wet-work done when you looked someone in the eye, in the madness that came after a phalanx had crushed the life out of their enemies and only the mopping up remained. Harka's helmet, gold to denote his rank of general with a green plume for his clan, sat on a table.

There was a map underneath the helmet; old, used, battle-worn. Jia took up most of the southern part of the continent, but to the north lay Egril, their old enemy. Only the fortress at Gundan separated *us* from *them*. She thought she could see bloodstains on it, covering part of the barbarians' territory. Fitting, really. There were no other landmarks – the Egril didn't welcome visitors or ambassadors. The Egril didn't care for trade. They only wanted what could be stolen. They only liked to kill.

A thousand years ago, when they still had all the magic of the world, the Jians had built the fortress across the pass at Gundan, stopping the Egril raids with thirty-foot-high walls and leaving them to kill each other instead.

Tinnstra came to attention in front of Harka's desk, eyes straight ahead, gaze skimming the top of his head, looking at nothing. At least she could do that well. He didn't tell her to sit or stand at ease. Nothing to make her comfortable. She didn't even deserve that.

He shuffled some paper on his desk though he didn't need to read her report. He knew already. Everyone knew. 'Cadet Tinnstra of Clan Rizon.'

'Yes, sir.' She squeaked the words out and prayed for the strength to hear what the general had to say.

'The first Shulka came from Clan Rizon,' said the general. 'Created to protect Jia once magic was lost from the land.'

'Yes, sir.' Her father had told her all the stories, all the myths, from the moment she was born. Of magic lost. Of how Gods became men, before becoming warriors. Today, magic only existed in the hands of a few mages who were as rare as snow on a summer's day. That's why the Shulka were needed.

'A proud house with a proud tradition,' the general continued.

'Yes, sir.' They were the king's favourites. The ones always called first to battle.

'Many, myself included, consider your father to be the finest living Shulka in the world today.'

'Yes, sir.' He was a legend, worshipped by all. People's eyes lit up when they heard Grim Dagen's name. Songs were sung of his exploits. Children pretended to be him when they played Shulka with wooden swords. Her father was everyone's hero.

'Your brothers all graduated from the Kotege with the highest honours.'

'Yes, sir.' They were perfection. Hard enough having a famous father, let alone trying to follow in her brothers' footsteps. Sometimes Tinnstra questioned how she could be related to Beris, Jonas or Somon. They were so like their father and mother, and so unlike her in every way.

'So, you can imagine how embarrassing that makes this situation for all of us.' He paused, shuffled some more paper. 'For me.'

'Yes, sir.' Tinnstra knew what was going to happen. *Get it over with. Just say the words. Please.* The knife waited. She could still save her father the shame.

Harka chewed on his lips as if he didn't like the taste of what he had to say. Tinnstra couldn't blame him. 'It's normal to be scared. Everyone is. It makes us human. But the training here at the Kotege is supposed to help you move past that fear.'

'Yes, sir.'

'Technically, you are one of our best cadets – with a sword and at Shulikan.' He pinched the bridge of his nose. 'But mastering the moves is no use if you're too scared to fight a real opponent.'

'Yes, sir.' By the Four Gods, did she know that only too well. She'd been taught the fighting stances by Grim Dagen himself. It was just a shame he couldn't give her his courage as well as his skill. Would her father have dedicated all those hours to her if he'd known she was a coward?

Harka looked at her, eyes full of disapproval. As used to that look as she was, it still hurt. She knew she should say more, explain herself, but she didn't have the courage even for that.

'Do you want to tell me what happened?'

The air caught in Tinnstra's throat. Harka had been there, had seen what she'd done. Everyone had. She didn't want to talk about it.

'Well?'

'The men we were fighting ... I saw the look in their eyes, the swords in their hands. I knew ... I knew they wanted to kill me ... and I got scared. I didn't want to be hurt or die. And I knew if I stayed there, if I fought ...' She faltered as tears sprang to her eyes. 'It was different from being in training, from any practice bout I've ever fought. I know I should've done better, been stronger. I know I should've believed in myself, but I—'

'You ran.'

'Yes, sir.'

'You abandoned your comrades and put their lives at risk.'

'Yes, sir.' Tinnstra felt sick. Talking about it brought it all back – the sand, the blood, the cries, the dead. She prayed Harka would say no more, but, like so many of her prayers, it went unanswered.

Harka sighed. 'We don't put students in the arena because we enjoy it or for entertainment. We do it out of necessity. We have enemies to the north who would see us dead or enslaved,' said Harka. 'The arena is the closest we can come to recreating the realities of war, to show what it is like to put your life on the line for your comrades, your clan and your country.'

Tinnstra nodded. She'd experienced that sensation well enough.

'The Egril have always hated us. Generations ago, they loathed us for our magic. They thought we were like Gods, and this they could not allow. But back then, we were able to build cities with a wave of our hands, fly through the air like birds, light a fire with a click of our fingers, fill our tables with food with just a thought. And we batted them away like irritating flies.' Harka paused for a moment, watching Tinnstra for a reaction. 'That hatred didn't disappear once magic left these lands. Now it's the responsibility of the Shulka, drawn from the noblest families, to defend all Jians and keep our land free. Those men and women who stand on Gundan's walls have stopped death and destruction raining down on us for generations.'

'Yes, sir.'

'It was bad enough when we fought random tribes, but this new Egril emperor – Raaku – has done the impossible and unified them all. Right now, camped one mile from Gundan, is the largest army we've ever faced. Reports put the numbers at tens of thousands.'

Tinnstra choked. 'But that's impossible—'

'No. No, I'm afraid it's not. The Egril are rattling their clubs, promising to kill us all. Your father is on his way there now with the whole of your clan to join Clan Huska. Ten thousand Shulka to face perhaps five times that number. Every single man and woman at Gundan must do their part. We can't have anyone … run away when the time comes to fight.'

Tinnstra remained silent. She could only think of her father, her mother, her brothers, facing thousands of Egril. *They will win. They have to. The Shulka always win.* But … She wanted to cry. She wanted to be sick. She wanted to run and hide. Hide until it was all over, and they returned safe and sound.

Harka moved the papers around. 'Out of respect for your father and your family, and as your godfather, I'm willing to give you one more chance – against the wishes of the other teachers, I must admit – as long as you can assure me that you'll deal with your weakness. Are you able to promise me this incident won't happen again?'

Tinnstra stopped breathing. All she had to do was say, 'Yes, sir.' Tell a small lie. But she knew it would only buy her respite for a short period. Then she'd be here again.

Truth was, the fear had always been there, bubbling away. She had hidden it well, almost convincing herself it didn't exist. But there had been no hiding that day. Not from herself or from the hundreds of spectators gathered to observe.

She'd dropped her spear and shield and run for her life, breaking the phalanx, putting her friends' lives at risk. All because she didn't want to die.

Better she got it over with. Put an end to all their misery. She would never be what they wanted her to be – what she'd been born to be.

'No, sir.'

He looked up, shook his head, looked down again. Found a piece of paper, picked up a quill, dipped it in ink and signed his name across the bottom. He blew on the ink, placed the paper back on his desk, looked at it once more, then back at her. 'Cadet Tinnstra of Clan Rizon, by the powers invested in me, I'm expelling you from the Kotege. There is a supply wagon leaving for Aisair in the morning. You can make your own way from there to your family home at Gambril. Your clan will, no doubt, take matters further.'

'What will they do?' asked Tinnstra. A single tear ran down her cheek.

'You'll be disowned,' replied Harka. 'Only Shulka may be part of a clan. You are not and never will be one of us now.'

'What will I be?'

'Nothing.' Harka's voice was cold as death. He held out the paper. 'Dismissed.'

Tinnstra stared at him, stared at the paper in his hand. If she took it, her life was over. All she had left was the knife in her room – but even that was a lie. She knew she didn't have the courage to kill herself.

'Tinnstra,' said Harka, his tone softening. His duty done, he was her godfather once more. 'Take the paper. It's for the best. It might not feel like it now but, one day, you'll look back and see this was the moment you were set free.'

'Free?'

'You can do whatever you want now. Not what your father dictates or what your clan expects. You have a role to play in this world. Take this opportunity to find out what it is. Start living your life.'

Tinnstra took the paper. 'Thank you, sir.' She went to salute, realised she didn't have to any more, and so smiled awkwardly instead and sniffed back another tear.

'Good luck.'

Outside the office, she stopped in the hallway, suddenly lost in a place that had been her home for three years. She didn't know what she felt – confused, scared, relieved. It was done. She was out. She'd never have to pick up a sword again. Or stand in a phalanx.

And it was true, what Harka said – she could go anywhere. Not back to Gambril, though. Perhaps she'd return there one day when she knew her father, her family, would be there, but not now. *I can go anywhere. Where no one knows who I am. Where I can be ordinary. Anonymous. I wouldn't be Grim Dagen's daughter. I'd just be me.*

She smiled. That was a beautiful thought. Maybe that was it. She wasn't a coward. She just wasn't a Shulka. She glanced over at the guards, still like statues, emotionless warriors. That was the difference. She had feelings. She wanted experiences. She wanted to do things, make something of herself. She didn't want to be a mindless killer.

The weight disappeared from her shoulders. Tinnstra set off for her room, almost floating. The sooner she was gone, the better. It was time to leave all the Shulka behind and get lost somewhere else. She was free. For the first time in her life, she was free. Thank the Four Gods.

No more hiding in the shadows not wanting to be noticed. Wherever she went next, she'd find out who she really—

The world exploded.

2

Dren

Kiyosun

Dren was having the time of his life.

It was late. He should've been asleep, getting some rest before a hard day on the boat, fishing with his father, uncle and cousin. But fuck that. His dad called it 'doing the right thing'. 'Being sensible.' Yeah, right. There was plenty of time for that when he was older. But right now? Dren had things to do. Mischief to make.

He sprinted along the rooftops, jumping the small dividing walls between buildings, scooting around the water towers, heart pounding, blood roaring. Feeling alive.

His cousin, Quist, followed on his heels, keeping up for a change. Dren grinned. Sleep could wait. They would both be knackered tomorrow, but he didn't care. Nor that they would be scolded by their fathers. Trouble was, those old men had forgotten what it was like to be young. They were too busy working to remember what fun was.

Dren loved running the roofs. Loved the freedom to move about the city unseen. Up there, he felt like the king of the world instead of some fisherman's son. Up there, he wasn't anyone's serf. He was a shadow, flitting past unheard and up to no bloody good.

The sliver of moon provided a little light – not that Dren needed it. This was his city. Dirty, sweaty Kiyosun. He'd lived here all his life and, apart from working on his dad's fishing boat,

13

he'd never left the city walls, not even to explore the mountains north of the city. Why would he? Everything he needed was in Kiyosun. Everything *anyone* needed was in Kiyosun. The port city was squeezed onto a spit of land at Jia's southernmost point and the docks, built over the deepest natural harbour in the country, worked twenty-four hours a day, with ships arriving from Meigore, Chongore and Dornway, bringing in everything from olive oil and wine to the fine silks all the rich women loved.

There were good pickings down at the docks if you were quick enough. Especially if you were clever enough not to overdo it. Take too much and you pissed people off to the point where they might try to stop you. Keep it small and no one could be bothered. Only idiots got caught stealing; only fools got their hands cut off for thieving. And Dren was neither.

Some said they'd forced enough buildings into Kiyosun to fill twice the available land, and Dren could believe it. When you're surrounded by water on three sides, you have to make do with what you've got, so everyone was packed in tight together. The buildings were squashed in rows along narrow licks of streets that were always rammed full of people. It took hours to walk from one side of the city to the other. Even late at night the streets were crowded. That's why the roofs were better for moving around. No one got in his way.

Even if someone was up there, having a drink or putting out the washing, they'd not stop him. They might give him a look to say he was mad or tell him to piss off, but none of that mattered. Dren would already be long gone. And, of course, he always had that little knife on his belt if things went south.

They approached the building's edge at speed. The six-foot gap to the next row stretched over a thirty-foot drop to the street, but Dren didn't slow down. Didn't hesitate. He powered straight ahead, pushing himself to run faster. It was a small jump onto the end wall and he launched himself up and over.

He loved this moment, suspended in the air, all but flying. Most people didn't have the nerve, the guts, the balls, to do a jump like that. But Dren wasn't scared of anything. It was all about the danger. The thrill. It made him feel bloody fantastic.

Too soon, his feet touched down on the opposite wall, then a little bounce and he was onto the roof, dropping into a roll, slowing his momentum before skipping back onto his feet.

Just like that. Easy.

He turned to watch Quist. His cousin's eyes were wide and bright in the moonlight, full of fear, but he jumped all the same, legs and arms flailing as he cleared the gap. Say one thing for his cousin, he was always up for it.

His landing wasn't as graceful as Dren's – more of a crash and a tumble – but it didn't matter how you landed just as long as you did.

'That doesn't get any easier,' said Quist, puffing out his cheeks.

'You need to lose some weight,' teased Dren, even though his cousin was whip-thin. No one grew fat hauling nets on a fishing boat all day long.

'Can't we go and get a drink somewhere? It's fucking hot out tonight and I'd rather not be sweating my balls off, running about up here.'

Dren slapped his cousin on the shoulder. 'It's Kiyosun. It's always fucking hot. At least it's cooler up here than it is down there.' He spread his arms wide. 'Feel the fucking breeze. You can breathe.'

'I can breathe well enough in a tavern, thank you very much,' grumbled Quist, but he got to his feet all the same. 'Sasha was asking after you.'

Dren's ears picked up. 'Was she?'

Quist grinned. 'She was.'

'And?'

'She said she'd be working at Old Man Hasster's inn if we fancied dropping by for a drink.'

Dren chewed his lip at the thought of a drink with Sasha. She was beautiful. The most beautiful girl in all of Kiyosun. Just thinking about her made his heart race.

'It's only a few streets away,' said Quist.

Dren glanced along the rooftops, his mind tracing the route to Old Man Hasster's place. Sasha would be serving drinks out front, getting plenty of laughs from the punters as the men fought for her attention. She could have whoever she wanted. But she wanted him. Well, he thought she did, at least.

Quist watched him, waiting to see if he was going to give in to temptation. Dren laughed. He was a smart lad. He knew just the right hook to dangle. Well, fuck that, too. 'We can go and see her after we've visited the Shulka. We'll have a tale to tell then.'

Quist shook his head. 'I'll say this one last time – this is a stupid fucking idea.'

Dren wrapped his arm around his cousin's neck, pulling him close. 'This idea is going to make us famous.'

Quist freed himself. 'I don't want to be famous. I don't want the Shulka knocking on my door with their swords out, ready to chop my head off.'

'Relax. That won't happen,' said Dren. 'Just think about how you're going to feel when everyone's talking about what we've done! *We'll* be the ones who made fools of the Shulka.'

Quist still wasn't convinced. 'You do realise they are the best fighters in the world, don't you?'

Dren nodded.

'No one's beaten them in battle. Ever.'

'I know that, too.'

'And they all carry swords and spears and enjoy killing people. People like you and me. Especially if they think we've shown them disrespect.'

Dren nodded again. 'And I know they take half what we earn in tax so they can go and play soldiers all day long. "The price of keeping us safe" and all that bollocks. Arrogant bastards. And we're supposed to get down on our knees and bloody bow as they walk past, otherwise they might cut our heads off. They think they're better than us just because they were born into the right fucking family.' Dren spat over the side. 'Well, they're not – and we're going to show them what we really think. I might only be the son of a fisherman but I'm just as good as they are.'

'All right, all right,' said Quist. 'Enough. I'm in. I told you I was. Just don't give me another lecture on the rights and wrongs of the Shulka. It's bad enough our fathers go on about it. The world is what it is.'

'Got your breath back?' asked Dren with a wink. 'Ready to go?'

'Fuck you.'

They set off again, feet flying across the flat roofs, jumping the gaps, moving on to the next building, the next row, heading west. They passed Dren's home, and he grinned. His parents were asleep in bed, thinking he was next door.

Sweat ran down his back, sticking his shirt to his skin. Quist was right. It was fucking hot. No stopping, though. It'd rain soon, anyway, so there wasn't time to waste. One big summer storm might fill up the city's water towers, but it would also ruin Dren's plan.

They crossed the last building and there it was – the Shulka barracks. They ducked down behind the end wall and peered over to make sure no one had spotted them, but – of course – no one had. It was all clear.

The barracks on the west side of the city were only three streets away from Dren's home, too close for his liking. Three ships were moored at the small military dock, in case some pirate was dumb enough to try their luck on passing trade.

Beyond the docks were rows of housing, the stables and a parade ground. Dren's father had said that over a thousand men and women were stationed there – the black-plumed bastards of Clan Huska. For a city short on space, the barracks took up a large chunk of what there was. Typical of the fucking Shulka. Let everyone else live like rats while they lorded it up.

A wall separated the barracks from the city but, like everywhere else in Kiyosun, the road running alongside was narrow enough to jump if you were of a mind to. Plenty of dark shadows for Dren and Quist to work in.

'It looks quiet,' whispered Quist.

'I told you – most of them have gone up north. Some trouble with the Egril again,' replied Dren.

'Bloody goat fuckers.' Quist spat. 'You seen all the Egril refugees around town? You can't go two yards without tripping over one of them. We should chuck them into the ocean. Help them move on. There's not enough room in Kiyosun for them all. Definitely not enough water.'

Dren ignored him. Quist liked having a moan as much as their fathers did. He climbed onto the ladder running down the wall. Huffing, his cousin followed, and they clambered down to the alley. It was full of shit and grime, cast-off junk and rotten food. Quist gagged but Dren didn't care about a little stink. Not if it kept everyone else away.

He uncovered the paint and brushes he'd stashed there a few days before, then handed a brush and a pot to Quist. 'You paint the cock as big as you can. I'll write the words.'

'We're going to get killed,' said Quist.

Dren chuckled. 'Not if we're quick. And come morning, everyone will see it.'

They ran across the road, keeping low, sticking to the shadows. Once there, they crouched and opened the clay pots of paint. It was red as blood, perfect for the ochre walls. Fucking Shulka. Cocksuckers, the lot of them.

Dren got to work, slapping the paint on, chuckling to himself. He had a good mind to hang around and watch the Shulka get their balls in a twist when they saw it. What a sight that would be.

He felt Quist's hand on his shoulder. Dren turned around. 'You finished—' The words stuck in his throat. It wasn't his cousin standing behind him. It was a fucking Shulka and he had his sword in his other hand. Quist was a few yards away, on his knees, another Shulka behind him, sword drawn.

'What the fuck are you doing?' growled the Shulka.

Dren dropped to his knees, not needing to act too much to look scared. 'Please, it was just a joke. We meant no harm.'

The Shulka looked at the wall. 'Doesn't look like a joke to me.'

'I'll clean it off. I promise.' Dren bowed his head, hating himself for cowering, but only too aware of the sword in the Shulka's hand.

'What do you think we should do with them, Caster?' the Shulka asked his comrade.

'The law's clear. They're serfs. Kill them,' said the other.

Dren looked up, saw the sword rise.

3
Jax

Gundan

Jax sat at his desk, wondering when the Egril would attack. He
was fed up with waiting and fed up with all the administration
he had to do in the meantime to keep an army at Gundan. He
wanted the Egril to just get on with the attack, so he could do
what he was good at – killing the bastards. And there were certainly enough of them out there waiting to be put in the dirt.

His mood wasn't helped by the fact it was so bloody cold in
Gundan, despite it being what passed for summer up north. How
he wished he was back in Kiyosun, enjoying some real warmth.

He threw another log onto the fire. The locals who worked at
Gundan thought him mad for keeping the fire burning, but he'd
spent enough years wet and cold on battlefields to know you
enjoy your comforts when you can.

Someone knocked at his door.

'Come in,' called Jax.

The door opened and his son, Kaine, entered, looking every
bit the perfect soldier of Clan Huska. Pride swelled in him. Hard
to believe the boy was already a captain. His spotless breastplate
sparkled in the firelight and he wore his black-plumed helmet
with the cheek protectors down, ready for war. 'Dagen's arrived
with his men.'

'Let's go and see him, then.' Jax picked up his sword and fixed
it to his belt.

'What about your armour?' asked Kaine with a tilt of his chin.

His breastplate was propped up against the wall. It was covered in a thousand scratches and small dents, souvenirs of a lifetime of action, but still had the gleam that only a professional soldier knew how to coax out. 'I think I'll survive without it. The Egril aren't about to attack this very moment.'

'You're the one who ordered every man and woman to wear one on duty.'

Jax smiled. The boy was right. He was always bloody right. Just like his mother. He retrieved his armour, slipped it on over his head and strapped it tight. 'Happy now?'

'Helmet?' There was a flicker of a smile on Kaine's lips.

'Don't think I won't have you whipped for insubordination just because you're my son,' growled Jax as he picked up his gold helmet and tucked it under his arm.

Kaine snapped to attention and saluted. 'Yes, sir.'

'Come on, let's find Dagen.'

They stepped outside into the early evening air. The sun had dropped behind the mountains, smearing streaks of red, gold and purple across the sky in its wake. As ever, the scale of the fortress never failed to impress him.

Gundan was more like a small city than a military camp. It had grown over the years, attracting all the things soldiers needed – places to eat, to drink, to gamble, to fuck, to fight, and all the people required to make them happen. There were homes for husbands, wives and children, stables, armouries, blacksmiths, carpenters … the list went on and on. There had been talk of sending all the civilians away when the Egril marched south, but the walls had not been breached in seven hundred years and that wasn't going to change now.

The battlements stretched five miles between the two mountain ranges blocking the valley that was the only route between Jia and the Egril. The main wall itself was thirty feet high. Jax could only wonder at the sweat, blood and tears that must have gone into building it all those centuries ago. It looked like it had been grown out of the ground in one solid piece of rock. There were no signs of bricks or joins on its surface, just smooth stone from one end to the other. The myths claimed it had been raised in a day by a single mage, but Jax didn't believe that. That was just nonsense to impress the locals. Certainly, none of the mages who still lingered on were capable of anything so impressive. Not even Aasgod, the Lord Mage.

Dagen waited on the parade ground with his Shulka lined up behind him. Another four thousand men and women to join the six thousand Jax already commanded at Gundan. It was madness. Even with the vast number of Egril in the valley beyond, Jax didn't understand why anyone thought he needed more help at Gundan. There wasn't an Egril alive he couldn't kill.

Jax put the thoughts from his head and marched over to his old friend. 'Grim Dagen himself! It's good to see you.'

'And you,' replied Dagen. 'How long's it been? Three years? Four?' The two men grasped each other's forearms. Dagen hadn't changed. He still looked bigger than a mountain Kojin. There were a few more wrinkles around the man's eyes but Jax had enough of those himself.

Jax laughed. 'Eight.'

'And it only took a few thousand Egril to get us together again.'

'I just hope you've not wasted your time coming up here. We have more than enough Shulka to deal with the savages.'

'Aasgod's worried,' said Dagen. 'I think he would've sent all the clans here if he could. As it is, he made me bring two of his mages up with me.'

Jax's back stiffened. He had no time for magic. 'What do we need them for?'

'He's scared of this emperor of theirs. He's even talking about Sekanowari.'

'He thinks this is the Last War? The man's mad.'

Dagen shrugged. 'His word carries a lot of weight in the court. People are listening. People are scared.'

'Raaku's no different from the rest of the savages,' said Jax. 'Maybe a bit meaner but that's all. This isn't the end of the world.'

'The Egril believe him to be the son of their God, Kage. That's why the tribes have united behind him.'

Jax scoffed at that. 'Nonsense. He's just using that to scare the bastards into following him and he's killing anyone who doesn't.

The refugees flooding through the wall are testament to that. He's committing genocide in Egril. Bodies everywhere.' He spat. 'And good riddance to them all. The only good Egril is a dead one.'

'I can't argue with that. I think Cariin's a fool to make us let them into Jia. It's hard to show mercy to any Egril when I've spent my whole life fighting them.'

Jax turned to Kaine. 'Get Dagen's men into their quarters and then fed. Let them have a good night's sleep and then start rotating them onto the morning's duty roster.'

'Yes, sir.' Kaine saluted, turned and marched away.

'Was that your son?' asked Dagen.

'Yes. I still find it hard to believe. It only feels like yesterday I was teaching him how to walk. How are your children? Have they taken their oaths yet?'

'My boys, yes.' Dagen motioned back towards his troops. 'Beris, Jonas and Somon are here with me, and my wife is leading the Second.'

'What about your daughter?'

'She's close to graduating at the Kotege. I have high hopes for her.' The man's pride shone on his face.

'Our children will be our greatest legacies.'

'That they will.' Dagan smiled. 'Do you want to show me the Egril?' He waved towards the battlements.

'Why not. There *are* a lot of them.' As Jax turned to lead Dagen to the wall, he noticed a man and a woman standing awkwardly to one side, out of place amongst the warriors. 'They the mages?'

'Yes,' said Dagen and waved them over. 'General Jax, may I introduce Hewlars and Matis.' Hewlars was a tall, thin man who looked like he was on the verge of crying. There was no colour to his sunken cheeks and his eyes darted everywhere as if expecting the enemy to suddenly appear and start killing everyone. Matis had more of a spark about her. She was small and compact with cropped dark hair. Unlike her friend, her face showed little fear. She held out a hand that Jax ignored.

'I'm not sure why Aasgod thinks we need you here, but in case there's fighting, don't get in the way of any of my Shulka,' said Jax.

'We are fully battle trained,' said Matis. 'We're here to help.'

Jax grunted, unimpressed.

'The general was just about to show me the enemy from the battlements,' said Dagen. 'Would you like to join us?'

'Thank you, yes,' said Matis, even though Hewlars appeared not to agree.

Jax led them across a courtyard and headed into the nearest tower. He made it a point to greet his troops as he passed them by. Even just a smile made all the difference. It was the least he could do if he was to send them out to fight for him and perhaps die.

They took the stairs to the parapets, climbing slowly as the steps curled around and around. A bitter wind greeted them as they stepped out onto the battlements and Jax wished he'd brought his cloak with him. Some summer.

The wall bristled with activity. Four thousand Shulka were on duty at any one time, each in full battle armour with sword at the hip, spear in one hand, shield on the other arm. Four thousand of the best men and women ever to bear arms, with more waiting down below in the camp, ready to be called on. Pots of boiling tar were positioned at regular intervals along the wall, to pour down on the first idiots to try their luck climbing up. Next to them were piles of stones to be dropped. Then there were archers with baskets of arrows waiting to be loosed. All in place to stop the enemy. Ready to start the killing. No matter what the Egril did, the Shulka were prepared.

Jax took them to the centre of the wall. 'There they are.'

'By the Four Gods,' said Dagen. The mages, too, stood open-mouthed and wide-eyed at the sight.

The enemy were over a mile away, camped out along the valley floor and on the hills to either side. Fires glowed in the darkness – so many that it looked like the whole valley was aflame.

'How many of them are there?' asked Hewlars.

'We estimate there's about thirty thousand of them. I sent spies in but only their heads came back, so I've not wasted any more lives trying to find out more.' Jax shrugged. 'It doesn't matter anyway. Five thousand, ten thousand, fifty thousand – none of them will get past this wall or our Shulka.'

'Do you think they'll attack?' asked Matis.

'They've not turned up just to chat, have they?' said Jax. 'Of course they'll attack. It's just a matter of when.'

As if in answer, the beat of drums started across the valley. *Dum. Dum. Dum. Dum.* On and on. Growing louder, faster. Then came the roar of the Egril soldiers themselves.

'What's happening?' said Hewlars.

Jax pulled his helmet on and fastened it. 'Looks like you arrived with perfect timing.'

The officers on the wall didn't need telling. They knew. Orders were shouted up and down the battlements as they prepared to face the oncoming attack. An alarm bell rang to warn the camp and call the reserves to readiness.

Jax was proud at the way the Shulka moved with calm efficiency and perfect discipline. No one showed the excitement they must all be feeling – that Jax certainly was. He'd got his wish after all. Time to start the killing.

'Shall I call my troops to the wall?' asked Dagen.

'Not yet,' said Jax, staring into the night. 'We have enough up here to deal with whatever they throw at us. Maybe in a few hours, we can bring in some fresh spear-arms.'

'A few hours?' whimpered Hewlars. 'How long will it go on for?'

'It's a fucking war,' snapped Jax. 'It goes on until one side's dead.'

Hewlars exchanged looks with Matis, making some unspoken plea.

'Get off my wall if you're scared,' said Jax. 'You can go and hide with the women and children in the camp. You'll be safe enough there.'

'We'll stay,' said Matis. She pulled a small vial out of her robes, uncorked it and drank the contents.

'Your choice,' said Jax, 'but keep out of the way. We have a lot of killing to do.'

4

Invasion

The wind brought a new sound to Gundan's walls. Jax knew it well but it still took him by surprise.

'Is that ... ?' said Dagen. He knew it, too. Every soldier did.

'They're marching,' said Jax.

'The Egril don't march,' said Dagen.

Jax didn't reply but Dagen was right. The Egril ran, they screamed, they died – but they didn't march. Savages don't march.

'What's going on?'

Jax turned and saw Kaine running towards them, shield and spear in hand. 'Are they attacking?'

'I expect the mages to ask stupid questions, not you,' said Jax.

'Sorry, General.' Kaine bowed his head.

'Don't just stand there – get into position,' ordered Jax. He sounded harsher than he intended but no one got preferential treatment. Something wasn't right, something that was bothering him. Nothing was happening the way he had expected – the way it always had.

He peered into the darkness. There were shapes out there, white dots coming towards them out of the black. What were they? He strained his eyes, leaning over the parapet as if another couple of inches would help.

'What can you see?' asked Matis.

They were men. Marching men. The Egril. And they were ...
Jax jumped back, shocked. 'The bastards are wearing armour.'

'The night must be playing tricks on your eyes,' said Dagen, taking Jax's place to look for himself. 'The Egril wear fur and hide, not metal.'

A screech silenced any further comment. Everyone flinched at the sound. It was unearthly, harrowing, as if the world itself had been wounded and cried out in pain. It dragged on and on, so loud it drowned out everything and made even the simplest of thoughts impossible. Louder and louder and then – it just stopped.

It took a moment or two for Jax's ears to stop ringing, to pick up the relentless stomp of the approaching Egril army again. Before he heard the screams come from the camp.

They all turned, no hiding their surprise. The screams were followed by the clash of steel on steel, shouts, orders, battle.

'What in the Gods' names is that?' said Jax. There was fighting in the camp. Where no enemy should be. Everything appeared normal from where he was but there was no mistaking the sounds of weapons doing their bloody work.

The world screeched again, and this time Jax saw it – a white light sparked on the other side of the camp. Then another to the west, and another, and another, all over the camp, and each time the noise grew louder still.

'They're gates,' said Matis, white-faced.

'What?' asked Jax, but the mage was already sprinting to the stairs. Others went to follow and Jax could see the discipline wavering across the faces of his troops. This wasn't what any of them expected.

'Stay in your positions!' he bellowed, pointing back out to the valley. 'There are enough Shulka down there to deal with what-ever it is. You've all got your jobs to do. There's a fucking army coming towards us, in case you've forgotten.' His words were enough to straighten their backs.

Sudden movement in the valley caught his eye. Something raced towards them out of the shadows, leaping and bounding over the ground, almost too fast to track.

'Archers! Shoot that thing,' he ordered.

Behind him, whatever was going on in the camp was getting worse. It sounded like a full-on war was being fought inside Gundan. 'Dagen, get down there. Find out what's happening and stop it as fast as you can.' Jax didn't bother watching his friend go. The man could deal with anything. He kept his eyes on the creature racing towards them instead.

Hewlars stood next to him, muttering to himself, wringing his hands together, worried as hell. Jax was about to tell him to get off the wall when the mage pulled a vial out of his robes and drank it. Whatever it was, it seemed to pick Hewlars up because he unclenched his hands and straightened his back. Jax nearly asked for a shot himself. There was an alien sensation inside his gut that Jax didn't like one bit.

The creature was thirty feet away, twenty, fifteen. Arrows arced down too slow to get anywhere near it. Still, it had the wall to deal with, and no way was it getting up and over that.

The creature had other ideas. When it was close enough, it leaped and ran straight up the side of the wall, all thirty feet of it. Not slowing, not falling.

There was no time even to shout a warning before it was over the parapet and on the battlements, roaring and snarling. In a blink of an eye, there were dead Shulka at its feet. Blood sprayed as it slashed with its claws, tore with its fangs. Moving so fast. A shadow, twisting, turning, killing. For the first time in Jax's life, he saw Shulka turn and run.

Hewlars managed to pull himself together enough to create a ball of fire in his hand. He drew back his arm to throw it, but the creature saw him before he could do anything more than that. It howled, blood and guts dripping from its fangs, its claws, before it leaped straight for the mage. No one had time to react before it was on him. Killing him. Ripping him apart, pulling his intestines out, his heart, his lungs.

It happened so quickly. Jax didn't react, didn't attack, even though the demon was right next to him. He just watched, disbelieving it all. None of this was possible. None of it made sense.

Kaine was quicker. He stabbed at it with his spear, but the creature was faster still. It snapped the shaft with a swipe of an arm and attacked. Another blow shattered his son's shield before it hit him with an ungodly force, sending him flying off the wall to the camp below. Kaine. His son. Gone. Just like that.

A dozen Shulka attacked behind a shield wall, using their spears to stab at the creature. The demon turned on them, slashing out at shield and spear alike, eager to kill the men wielding them. For each wound the Shulka scored, the creature took another life. More Shulka stepped in to take the place of their fallen comrades until the numbers worked, and they wore it down, cornered it, killed it.

Jax stared at the corpse. It was a monster. A demon! It shouldn't even exist and yet it had killed more than thirty Shulka, killed Kaine, killed the mage in a matter of minutes. None of it made sense. None of it.

He peered down into the camp, hoping to see Kaine, praying that he was alive somehow, that some miracle had saved him. But all he saw was heavy fighting. People dying.

There were men in white armour and skull masks battling Shulka, wielding scimitars and short spears. They moved with precision, well drilled, relentless.

They were the Egril.

And they were winning.

Tinnstra screamed as a ball of fire ripped through the atrium's window into the Kotege.

The blast showered Tinnstra with glass, threw her against a wall and knocked the air from her lungs. She landed heavily on her shoulder as glass and wood and stone rained down on her. Smoke filled the building and, over the ringing in her ears, Tinnstra could hear people screaming.

She pushed herself up on shaking arms, spitting blood and dirt from her mouth. Dead bodies lay around her, ripped into shreds by the explosion, but she'd survived. Somehow, she was alive.

Somewhere, a bell rang. The alarm. The Kotege was under attack.

Tinnstra got to her feet and staggered outside. She needed air, to catch her breath, to get her bearings, but it was chaos. Fires burned across the parade ground. A boy held his friend's body in his arms, crying for help. A girl crawled in the dirt, looking for a lost arm. Two students held bandages to the stomach of a fallen comrade, trying to stop his life leaking out from a terrible wound. Others ran in every direction, faces smeared with blood, dirt and dust. They called for help, guidance and commands.

Tinnstra stood there, watching the mayhem, frozen to the spot. Smoke bellowed from a hole in the wall of the west wing, near her room. Students and Shulka poured out of the main building, strapping on armour, putting on helmets, brandishing what weapons they had to hand. A boy, blood pouring out of a cut on his head, pointed skywards, shouted something, but it was as if he spoke another language, one she didn't understand.

Something flew high above them. A shape that flitted between smoke and shadow. It swooped down towards them. Fast, attacking. Tinnstra wanted to run but her legs wouldn't work. Whatever the creature was, she'd never seen anything like it. It was too big to be a bird. Then she saw arms, legs, a body. A man. No. Not human. Not that. It had hooked, leathery wings that stretched six feet in either direction. Bulbous eyes, glowing red with hate and fury. Skin like armour. A demon.

And behind it ... More of them. A swarm.

The demon roared. Tinnstra screamed.

Dren was going to die. He knew it. The fucking Shulka was going to kill him. The bastard was really going to kill him. He gritted his teeth and shut his eyes. But the sword didn't fall.

'What's that?'

Dren opened one eye, saw the Shulka staring back down the street. He turned just as a burst of light set the very air on fire, sparks flying in every direction. 'What the—' Then the air screamed and Dren had to cover his ears.

The two Shulka ran towards the conflagration, leaving Dren and Quist. They were halfway down the street when men detached themselves from the shadows. Six of them, dressed in rags, armed with short swords. The Shulka shouted at them, told them to drop their weapons, but the men stepped forward instead and buried their swords in the Shulka's guts.

For a moment, Dren didn't move. He couldn't believe his eyes

– no one attacked the Shulka – but then his brain kicked in and he stumbled to his feet.

All the while, the air was being torn apart, the gap growing wider by the second. On the other side of the rent, he could see an army waiting. Row after row of white-armoured troops with skull faces stared back at him, bristling with swords and spears and fuck knows what else.

'What's going on, Dren?' asked Quist.

'I don't know but we need to get the fuck out of here.' If only he could take his eyes off the rent.

The gap grew wider until it stretched from one side of the street to the other, until it was large enough for the soldiers to march through. There were so many of them, filling the street. An army. An invasion.

Too late, Shulka ran from the barracks, drawn by the screeching, wearing their bronze breastplates and helmets, carrying shields and spears. They didn't look so invincible now, not compared to the invaders.

The two sides raced into each other. Steel crashed against steel, Skull against Shulka. Blades rose and fell. Men cried out – in anger, pain, death.

'Don't move! Don't fucking move!' shouted one of Jax's men. There was panic in his voice, fear. Emotions a Shulka shouldn't feel.

An Egril refugee crouched on the wall – pale, sickly, dressed in rags, not looking like anyone to be feared. But whoever he was, he wasn't bothered by the Shulka's shouts or the spear that was being waved in his face. He moved his hand instead and everyone nearby collapsed as the screech erupted once more. Jax wanted to cover his ears and cursed his fucking helmet for getting in the way. His teeth felt like they were going to shatter from the noise.

A Shulka fell to his knees and vomited. Others crumpled, staggered back. Jax grabbed the parapet, remaining on his feet, but that was all he could do. Fighting was impossible.

The Egril mage worked his magic. Sparks flew from a flaming wound as the air was ripped open, the noise growing louder still.

The rent grew wider, revealing rank after rank of Egril. Jax realised this was *how they'd got in the camp, got past the wall.* The Egril in the valley were just a distraction.

The Egril charged. Most of the Shulka were still crippled by the noise and in no state to fight back. All they could do was die.

Jax screamed, trying to drown out the screeching with his own anger and fury. He snatched up a fallen spear and threw it at the Egril, not even bothering to aim. It hit one in the chest, but there was another to take his place. Hundreds more.

'Form up on me!' he screamed, but he might as well have shouted into the wind. No one heard him.

Jax drew his sword, dodged a scimitar and thrust his blade into a skull-face, relieved to see the bastard's blood was still red. Another came at him and he only just ducked under the man's wild swing. He slashed back but his sword skittered off the Egril's armour, so he threw himself forwards and battered into him with his shoulder. They both tumbled down and Jax made sure he came out on top. He rammed his sword up through the Egril's chin.

Jax reared back, gulping for air, and realised the noise had stopped. There was no sign of the white-faced mage, no sign of the rent that had allowed the Egril through. The enemy mage's job was done – the wall was full of Egril and they were killing everyone they could.

Something flew past his head, making him duck. Followed by another. And another. A swarm of them. Flying demons headed towards the camp. He watched them pass for a second but then another skull-faced warrior ran at him and the demons were forgotten as Jax fought for his life.

The warrior was good. He wasn't one of the mindless savages that Jax had spent his life killing. He was trained and trained well. His scimitar was more powerful than the Shulka sword, with a longer reach and greater weight, and his armour appeared to provide better protection while allowing maximum mobility. Superior to Jax's own armour. Armour he had almost not worn. What a slack fool he'd become.

Well, he could hate himself later. He had Egril to kill.

He traded blows with the skull-face in front of him, his arm shaking with the force of every strike. He leaned back as the scimitar slashed past where his head had been a heartbeat earlier and was forced to retreat as the blade returned for a second attempt.

Something hit the back of his head, sending him crashing to the floor. The world swayed as he rolled onto his back, not wanting to get stabbed from behind. His helmet was half-off, so he ripped it free and threw it at the Egril who'd clubbed him. His original opponent loomed over him, ready to hack downwards, but Jax thrust his sword straight into the bastard's groin and gave it a twist for good measure. Blood covered his face but Jax didn't care. It was well earned.

He sat up as the second man came at him again, but a Shulka attacked him from the side and, for a few seconds, Jax had no one to fight.

He staggered to his feet and looked up and down the wall. There was no cohesion to the fighting, just an endless series of individual battles and the losers left to litter the floor with their blood and guts. And most of the dead were Shulka.

Jax knew then that they'd lost, lost everything – the fortress, the wall, maybe even Jia itself. His Shulka must have known it, too, yet none stopped fighting. No one surrendered or ran. It was an honour to fight beside them, to die beside them. All they could do now was try and take as many of the Egril with them as they could.

He stabbed an Egril through the eye, ducked a wild swing from another and rammed his sword through the warrior's armpit. He kicked a soldier's legs out from under him before taking another blow to his head. The world spun and his vision blurred as warm blood seeped from the wound.

Tinnstra watched the flying demon throw a small object at the Kotege's main building. Time slowed for her as it fell, unable to move, unable to do anything except die.

Someone grabbed her, threw her to the ground, covered her with their body as the explosion ripped the Kotege apart.

'Are you all right? Are you hurt?' shouted a man. She opened her eyes, saw Harka over her. He'd saved her. He wore his sword, his breastplate, his helmet. 'Get a weapon. Quick.' He jumped off her, already shouting orders to others, gathering students and Shulka, mustering a defence. He urged the nearby students to form a phalanx, his voice full of desperation as they struggled to obey. But this wasn't a lesson. It wasn't even like the arena.

Everywhere she looked, white-armoured warriors with skull-faced helmets were hacking down everything in sight.

And these weren't battle-hardened Shulka the enemy faced. These were boys and girls yet to take the oath. So few against so many. Regardless, they tried to obey Harka, shields locked, spears out. The invincible formation. Not that the skull-faced warriors cared. They hit the phalanx in a wave, relentless, deadly, and swept the students away.

Tinnstra knew she should help, do something, anything, but fear held her firm. A warrior hacked down a boy not ten yards from where she lay. She saw his eyes as he died – full of shock and confusion. A girl cowered and begged for life, just as Tinnstra wanted to do, but someone stabbed her through the heart. There was no mercy to be had from these killers. No quarter shown.

And still more enemy soldiers crossed over from the burning rents, filling the grounds. She heard them shout, speaking a different language, not Jian. She knew it, knew the guttural tones. They were speaking Egril. But that couldn't be. How could Egril get this far south? Past the wall? Past the Shulka?

She stared at their well-crafted armour, each enemy soldier identical to the next, attacking in disciplined manoeuvres. These Egril weren't the mindless barbarians they were supposed to be. They were trained, professional, like the Shulka, but better. Deadlier.

The ground exploded, throwing her sideways. Tinnstra's head bounced against stone. Shards of masonry crashed down on her.

Another explosion destroyed the corner of the Kotege, showering her with more bricks and dust. Tinnstra's ears rang with the fury of it all as she tried to get her bearings, tried to see through the smoke. She looked up, dreading what she might find.

Demons. The sky was full of the flying demons with their bat-like wings. They carried Niganntan blades – six-foot spears with a single-edged sword at the head – and swooped down in unison, screeching, scything through anyone in their way.

A hand pulled her. 'Tinn! This way.' It was Jono. A student from her class. He held a sword in one hand, the tip bloodied. Cuts criss-crossed his face, his arms, his hands. There was blood on his shirt. Was it his? She allowed him to drag her to her feet and they ran, crouched low, back around the main building.

A demon flew overhead and threw another orb. It hit the ground and the world tore apart in a bright burst of fire and light, knocking Tinnstra flying again. She bounced off the ground, once, twice, three times. She could taste blood in her mouth, feel pain in her body as she lay in the dirt and rubble, surrounded by the dead and dying. She wanted to get to her feet, wanted to run far away, go anywhere, but her body refused to obey. She screamed and she begged and she pleaded to all the Four Gods, too scared to move.

Around her, both students and Shulka fought with whatever weapon they had to hand. A girl of no more than sixteen tried to swing a Shulka blade at an Egril. She gripped it with both hands wrapped around each another. She barely had time to lift it before the Egril took her head off. A Shulka charged in with his spear and stabbed the Egril through the back but five others fell on him before he could pull the weapon free. There were just too many of them.

She saw Jono trying to get to his feet, still holding his sword. Saw a demon flying in behind, closing the gap with every crack of its wings. She tried to warn him but her voice was gone. The demon raised his spear. The two-foot sword blade glistened in the firelight as it swept down.

Dren didn't wait to watch the Shulka die. He grabbed Quist and dragged him along until they were running back into Kiyosun, away from the massacre.

They'd barely escaped when he heard the flap of wings, loud in the narrow street. He hauled Quist into an alleyway as something flew past them. It looked like it had come straight out of the stories his dad used to tell him – about a demon who flew down from the sky to steal children who disobeyed their parents. The name came to his lips in a whisper. 'Daijaku.'

Quist watched the demon. 'It can't be. The Daijaku are just made-up stories.'

'What's that in its hand?' said Dren. Whatever it was, the creature threw it at one of the buildings before flying straight up into the sky.

The explosion knocked Dren to the ground before he had a chance to do anything.

He got back to his feet, swaying like a late-night drunk, and picked up Quist, saw blood pouring out of a cut on the side of his head. His cousin's eyes rolled around, unaware of where he was.

'Come on,' said Dren, dragging Quist forward. 'We have to get away from here or we're dead.'

It was chaos on the streets. People ran in every direction, pushing and shoving through the crowds, desperate to get away. Screams and shouts echoed down the narrow thoroughfares. There were cries for help from the Shulka and pleas to the Gods, both equally worthless. Dren had seen the mighty Shulka were only good at dying, and when did a God give a shit about anyone?

An explosion ripped apart a building on the corner of Rechel Street, bringing down half a dozen other buildings with it. The mass of people in front of Dren simply disappeared under the rubble and smoke. All dead in a heartbeat. Dren would've been dead, too, if he'd been half a second quicker. Flames sprang up around him, eager for the dry wood. It was Kiyosun's worst fear.

He heard more explosions ring out across the city from every direction. Relentless. Smoke billowed and the sky grew brighter as fires spread.

They staggered on, herded by explosions and flames. Dren looked back, saw the foreign warriors fill the street. Swords flashed out, cutting down anyone near them. Dren had never seen anyone die before but now it was everywhere, in every form.

'What are we going to do?' screamed Quist.

'I ... I ...' Dren didn't know. He stood frozen. He watched

a warrior cut down a woman with a baby in her arms and saw another murder an old man too slow to get out of the way.

'Dren!'

'They're going to kill everyone. *Everyone*. We've got to *do* something ... Help ...' But what could they do? They were boys and this was war.

'We have to get out of here,' said Quist. 'We have to run.'

'Yes.' Dren got his legs to move somehow. 'Let's go home—'

They ran. Through the chaos. Through the destruction. All Dren could think of was getting to his parents. They'd know what to do. They'd keep him safe.

They turned a corner and a skull-faced warrior appeared out of nowhere. He raised his sword, screaming something in a language Dren didn't understand.

Dren tried to stop, tried to turn away, but his momentum took him into the warrior and they clattered together, falling to the ground. The warrior grabbed at Dren's shirt but Dren swatted the hand away. He kicked out, panicking, felt Quist grab him from behind and haul him up. The soldier scrambled to his feet after him, reaching for his fallen sword.

'Let's go. *Now!*' screamed Quist. Dren didn't need telling twice.

The boys ran on, jumped a fence and cut down an alley, ignoring the shouts from behind. His home was close, the next street along. He'd find his parents. His father would know what to do. He always did. All Dren had to do was get to him.

They turned the corner. Dren saw his building on the other side of the street, saw his father leaning out of the window on the third floor, surveying the chaos.

'Father!' He waved, feeling the relief flood through him.

His old man heard his name, saw Dren and Quist. 'Dren! Quick!' He beckoned them forward.

Something buzzed past. A shadow. Dren looked up, saw the Daijaku, saw it throw something. 'No!'

His dad saw it, too, a second before the explosion. Flames rushed out, filling the street. Dren threw Quist to the floor, covered him with his own body, and screamed as his skin burned and his world died.

*

Jax stood covered in blood, surrounded by his dead troops, his dead Shulka. The fortress and camp were in flames, everything destroyed. An Egril came at him, swinging. Jax jerked his head back, but he was too slow, too tired. The blade sliced down but there was no pain. His heart was racing too hard to feel anything.

He hacked at the Egril, screamed how he was going to kill the man, but his sword was gone. All he accomplished was spraying the man's white armour with his own blood.

There was just a bloody stump where his right arm used to be. The arm lay on the ground, still gripping his sword. He had to find a doctor. A mage. Get it fixed somehow. But there was so much blood. Over him, over the ground, pouring from the wound. His blood.

Jax looked up, saw the Egril had moved on. He thought Jax was dead. Like the rest of the Shulka.

Then the world went black.

Tinnstra flinched as a shadow loomed over her. Another student, not a Skull. 'Get up! Get a weapon!' Tinnstra didn't move. *Couldn't* move. He shouted again. A curse, maybe. A plea. It didn't matter. A spear erupted from his chest and he spat blood all over her before collapsing on her, his weight heavy and dead. She screamed, kicked and pushed, desperate to get the corpse off her. To escape. She saw a demon come for her. It bared its fangs, wings flicking in and out. Its body was covered in a carapace with spikes jutting from its elbows and knees. Blood dripped off the spear in its hand.

She shut her eyes and screamed, waiting for pain and death. She could hear the sounds of battle, feel the explosions rocking the ground beneath her, but no spear fell. She found the courage to open her eyes, saw the demon dead and Harka battling three Egril where it had stood.

A sword lay near her hand. She could pick it up, help Harka, help her godfather, help fight back. He'd saved her. She had to help him. She knew she had to, but that wasn't who she was. She wasn't a Shulka. She was nothing.

She was a coward and she did what cowards do – she ran.

Tinnstra ran as fast as she could. She prayed to all the Gods to keep her alive, to forgive her for her fear. She left her friends, her clan, her life behind. Left them all to the swords of the Egril and the spears of the demons. Left them all to burn and die.

She ran through the woods and kept going, didn't look back. Branches slashed across her face, cut her hands, but the pain was nothing compared to what she left behind. She ran until she couldn't hear the screams or smell the smoke. She ran until her legs gave way and she fell to the ground, sobbing, battered, bruised but alive.

Six Months Later

DAY ONE

5

Tinnstra

Aisair

The priest began his prayer.

Tinnstra and the rest of the congregation sank to their knees. She mimicked those around her, brow furrowed, hands clasped together, lips moving along to the words that none of them, bar Tinnstra herself, could understand, seeking the approval of a God none of them had heard of six months before. A God quite happy to see them all dead. She watched her neighbours, her fellow Jians, wondering who really believed in this new foreign God, who was just pretending, and who was a spy for the Egril, looking for someone to betray.

It could be anyone. Betrayal was the only growing business in Jia these days. Pointing a finger and naming names could get you some food in your belly or even a few coins in your hand. Informing on a non-believer could keep your own head on your shoulders. *Better someone else suffer* was the new mantra.

Tinnstra tried to pray with more intensity. Only the devout were safe in the new world the Egril had created in Jia. Their new God was why the Egril had invaded, after all. Spreading his word, converting the faithless, the fallen. The Egril didn't believe in Alo, the God of Life, or Xin, the Goddess of Death, or Ruus, the God of the Land, or Nasri, the God of the Sea. To the Egril, the Four Gods were the False Gods, and it was their sacred duty to remove all trace of them from the world.

They'd reconsecrated the country's temples, cast out all sign the old Gods had ever existed and inserted Kage in their place. Mighty Kage, Lord of the Great Darkness. If you wanted to live, you prayed to him now. It was a law Tinnstra made sure she obeyed. Names were taken on entering the temple and names were checked off on leaving. Failure to attend resulted in death, if you were lucky. A drop and a dance in the city centre, left to swing in the breeze and rot in the sun. It said a lot about life in Jia now that such a fate was considered a good thing.

Still, most didn't want to die. Especially Tinnstra. So she turned up at her allocated temple, on the allotted night, gave her name – but not her clan – and knelt and prayed and stayed until she was allowed to leave. Then she got up and returned to the small set of rooms she now called home, safe perhaps for another night, another day. Still alive.

She dipped her head lower, moved her lips to the words with greater purpose. She believed in Kage, she told herself. Great Kage the merciless have mercy on her. *I believe, I believe, I believe*. She hoped Kage was watching if he existed, because she knew the Egril were watching from the corners and the alcoves and the dark places of the temple, watching for the non-believers, the traitors, the impure, the degenerates, watching for anyone who didn't fit into their new world.

More than a few of the congregation wore masks themselves, proclaiming their utter devotion to their new God. The Egril believed you only showed your true face to Kage so the wearing of a mask by a Jian was a very public statement of support for the invaders.

Each time she visited the temple, Tinnstra saw more and more Jians adopting the masks. She'd considered wearing one herself but the Jian rebels – the Hanran – were quick to punish anyone they found doing so. And Tinnstra didn't want that, either.

It was hot in the temple, despite it being winter. Suffocating. The Egril had bricked up the old temple's windows and the doors were firmly shut. The Great Darkness didn't like light, except from the sickly smelling candles that made her want to gag.

There was a statue of Kage at the far end of the temple, more beast than man, a monster with a missing eye and missing ear. He was a fighting God, a warrior God, eager for blood and slaves to tend to his every need in the Great Darkness. It was easy to believe he wanted to devour the world, but it was far harder to accept that such a monster had brought life out of the void. Not when he had the Egril send as many souls back there as they could.

'All rise,' said the priest, Kage's voice in the world. He spoke Jian, although his words were stifled by his accent and muffled by the golden mask he wore.

Tinnstra and the rest of the congregation did as commanded.

'We give thanks to Kage, Lord of the Great Darkness, for giving us life. We know that by serving him in this life, we will be rewarded when we return to serve him in the next. For we will stand by his right hand, and the faithless will be our slaves for eternity as the False Gods now serve Kage.'

The priest looked around the temple, at the faces gathered before him. Tinnstra forced herself to smile, as if every word brought her joy. *I believe, I believe, I believe.*

The priest stretched his arms towards the monstrous statue. 'As you sent my soul from the Great Darkness, so I will send it back to you.'

'As you sent my soul from the Great Darkness, so I will send it back to you,' repeated the congregation.

'As you gave me life, so I give my life to you,' said the priest.

'As you gave me life, so I give my life to you.'

An acolyte stepped from the shadows, a knife in one hand, a bowl in the other.

'As my blood nourishes me, so it will nourish you.'

Tinnstra hated this part the most. Time to make a donation. Time to make the oath. Still, it was a small price to pay to stay alive.

The priest placed the bowl on the altar before him. He bowed to the statue and then made a small cut on his thumb. A drop of blood fell into the bowl. The acolyte then bowed and offered his hand to the priest. Another cut, another drop.

Now it was the congregation's turn. People slipped from the pews and formed an orderly line in front of the priest. Tinnstra took her place, keeping her eyes down, watching the feet in front edge forwards, glimpsing others walk past, their duty done, eager to resume their lives back in the world.

She only looked up when it was her turn. The priest was before her, knife ready. She bowed to the statue of Kage and then held out her hand.

'Do you give Kage your blood?' asked the priest.

'I do.'

'Do you promise to serve Kage in this life and the next?'

'I—' The words almost caught in her throat, but she forced the lie out. 'I do.'

The knife flashed, nicking the skin on her thumb. A small cut, but deep. A drop of her blood formed and fell into the bowl, mixing with the blood already there. The sight always made Tinnstra feel sick, but she reminded herself it was a simple price for life. She had to force her legs to turn and march out of the temple. She concentrated on the light coming through the now-open doors, allowed it to draw her closer with the promise of what lay beyond. *Nearly there, nearly safe.*

She had no idea why she always held her breath those last few steps, but held it she did, waiting for a hand on her shoulder, a shout ordering her to stop. As she got closer to the exit, the pressure built inside her, the churning fear she knew so well. She'd not been convincing in her prayers. They sensed her doubts, her lies, her lack of faith. Someone had told them, pointed her out. The Egril would snatch her, make her disappear like they had so many others. She fought the urge to quicken her steps, pressed down the panic. *They don't know. They don't know. I'm safe. I'm safe.* She could see through the doors, see the streets of Aisair, see people going about their lives. Only a few more steps. The light fell on her and she could feel the cold, winter air. Through the doors. No one looked at her. No one stopped her.

She let out her breath and smiled. All that worry for nothing. She turned left and kept walking, head down. It would be dark soon, when the bells would ring for curfew, and she still had lots to do.

She'd come straight to Aisair after the invasion, after what had happened at the Kotege. It was the capital of Jia and the perfect

44

place to hide. The perfect place to create a new life. No one knew her as the daughter of a famous Shulka. In Aisair, she was just another scared girl trying to survive.

She crossed over Box Lane, then down Fassling Way. There were four Egril soldiers on the other side of the street, in their white armour and skull-faced helmets. Four Skulls. That's what everybody called them now. Skulls. Not to their faces, of course. No one spoke to a Skull unless they had a death wish.

The soldiers were hassling a woman. Tinnstra had no idea what for. She didn't care. *Better someone else suffer.* She just kept her head down and walked on.

It took Tinnstra another ten minutes to reach her destination: Salin Street, a small road off the far busier Edging Road, with only a half-dozen houses on either side. The corner building was nothing but rubble, destroyed by a Daijaku bomb. The other houses, though, were pretty much intact. They were still homes. Still lived in. All except one, halfway down on the left-hand side.

She'd spotted it a few days earlier when she'd been out walking. The broken door, the shattered lock. All signs the Skulls had come calling on whoever lived there. And if the Skulls called, ten times out of ten, they hauled off whoever lived there. And if the Skulls had them, they weren't coming back.

Of course, if the owners had gone, someone might've taken the opportunity to squat there already – that was how Tinnstra had acquired her own home, after all – but she hoped the place was still empty and ripe for picking.

She went up to the front door and knocked, her heart racing. Would anyone answer? *Please don't. Please be empty. Please. Please. Please.* Tinnstra had no idea who she was praying to. The Four Gods? Kage? Any God that would keep her safe. Being a coward meant that she didn't really care who was looking out for her as long as someone was.

No one came to the door. She sighed with relief. Luck was with her. She glanced up and down the street but no one was in sight, so she pushed the door open a crack and slipped inside.

The house was quiet and dark, illuminated by stray streaks of light filtering through the dirty windows. The only things moving were the specks of dust disturbed by her entry, the only sound the racing beat of her heart. Understandable – she was scared, after all. She always was when she broke into a house, but she reminded herself it was empty. Whatever danger had lurked there was long gone, taken to wherever the Skulls took the disappeared.

She moved quickly, expecting the warning bells for curfew at any moment. She had to be well on her way home by then. Anyone caught out after curfew got the drop.

She spotted a few nice things that a fence might buy, but there was no time to take anything to sell on the black market – Tinnstra needed money she could use straight away if she were to get food before curfew. She checked drawers, cupboards, boxes – anywhere someone could've hidden an ecu or a stater.

There was nothing downstairs, so she moved on to the upper floor. Three doors, three bedrooms. There was bound to be something in one of them.

She got lucky in the first room. Three ecus sat discarded on a small table next to the bed. She slipped the bronze coins into her purse, happy she'd be able to buy something to eat with that, at least.

Buoyed by this success, Tinnstra strolled into the next bedroom without a second thought. Then she saw the body and screamed. It was a woman. Or at least, Tinnstra thought it was. She didn't want to get too close to check. Decomposition had reduced the body to its most basic form, blood and organs staining the floor black as they'd liquefied. There was no smell and dust covered her body. She'd been dead a long time. Tinnstra turned and left quickly, unable to face the body, knowing all too well that the woman's fate could easily be her own one day.

The third bedroom had no occupants, dead or otherwise, nor any money tucked away in it, either. Three ecus was good but not enough, not really. She returned to the second room, knowing she should search it. All she had to do was ignore the corpse. Easier said than done. She felt faint just standing in the doorway. *Stupid girl. Scared of a dead body.*

But stupid she was, so Tinnstra backed away from the room, descended the stairs and left the house.

She was halfway along Edging Road before she calmed down and allowed herself a smile. She had some money in her purse once more. A small victory, but a victory nonetheless.

Her happiness lasted until she reached the baker's.

'How much?' asked Tinnstra, not believing what she'd heard.

The shopkeeper shrugged, looked away, embarrassed. 'It's one stater for the loaf of bread.'

'But it cost two ecus last week. And one ecu the week before that.' Tinnstra could feel the tears coming. She'd not expected this. Not at all. Not after all she'd gone through.

'What can I do? No one's got anything, so the price of what you do have goes up.' He peered over her shoulder into the street, looking as scared as Tinnstra felt. Satisfied, he leaned in closer, dropped his voice to a whisper. 'You know the Skulls take the best of everything, then the Weeping Men grab whatever's left for the black market. Between the Egril and the gangs, the rest of us get fucked. I'm sorry, but the prices are what they are. If you've not got the money, I can't help you.'

Tinnstra looked down at the bronze coins in her purse, counted them again for the thousandth time, counted the same sorry amount. 'I've got three ecus. That's nearly enough.'

The shopkeeper's mouth twitched as his frown deepened. 'You're an ecu short.'

'Please, please. I'll bring another ecu to you tomorrow if you let me have the bread today. I promise.'

He shook his head. 'If you have the money, go and get it now. I'm not giving anyone credit. You could be dead tomorrow, for all I know – or disappear like the others.'

Tinnstra glanced out through the window. The sky was darkening, the day all but done. 'I'll never make it home and back before curfew, let alone home again. Please, I beg you. I haven't got anything else to eat.' She let the tears come then, fast and furious, and quivered her lip as she stifled a sob. She knew how effective a weapon tears could be in a situation like this.

The shopkeeper stared at her, long and hard, probably thinking how pathetic she was, cursing his luck, but Tinnstra knew she had him. Sure enough, his shoulders sank and he shook his head again. 'I must be fucking stupid.' He picked up the loaf and put it on the counter. 'You owe me an ecu. I expect it tomorrow.'

'I promise.' With a sniff, Tinnstra reached into her purse, took out the coins with shaking fingers and dropped them on the counter next to the loaf. One rolled off and fell to the floor, so the baker had to bend down and pick it up. For a mad moment, Tinnstra thought about grabbing the loaf and the rest of the money and running for it, but her nerves got the better of her, so she waited for him to straighten up and hand her the loaf.

'Tomorrow,' he repeated, jabbing a finger at her.

'Tomorrow,' repeated Tinnstra, wiping a tear away with one hand and tucking the loaf under her arm. 'Thank you.'

'Get home quickly,' said the shopkeeper. He gave her a smile for free. They were all as lost as each other. All just trying to survive in the mad world they'd found themselves in.

Somewhere a bell chimed, telling her curfew was close and she still had too far to go. Fear fluttered in her stomach and she picked up her pace, eager to be behind her door once more. Not that it made any real difference since the Egril had invaded the country. The Skulls could come and kick her door down anytime. They didn't need a reason.

She could see the king's castle in the distance, all battered and scarred. The building was magic-made, raised in the heart of Aisair, and it towered above all. Word was that King Cariin was locked up in there with his family. She'd no idea why the Skulls had left him alive – they'd killed everyone else who represented any sort of threat. She hoped they weren't torturing him. She'd always liked Cariin. Tinnstra had met him a few times – when her father and their clan had been assigned to protect the royal family, they'd lived in the castle. Cariin was about fifteen years old back then and only a prince-in-waiting, but he'd been kind to Tinnstra, even though she was an annoying five-year-old.

Old Town circled the castle. According to the stories, the most powerful magicians had once lived in those streets, wanting to be close to the royal family in the castle. The buildings were magic-built as well and soared above the rest of the city, formed out of the very ground itself in a rainbow of colours. Each magician had sought to outdo the others, so no two buildings were alike. She still remembered the first time her father took her there to explore, how she'd run through the streets in awe at how they defied gravity, jutting this way and that. It was one of her happiest memories and it broke her heart to think of it now.

Of course, she'd not been to Old Town since she'd returned to Aisair. It wasn't safe. Rumour was the Skulls had taken everyone who lived there in a single night. Thousands of people just disappeared in a matter of hours. No one knew where they'd gone. No one dared ask. Tinnstra certainly didn't. The only things lurking in Old Town now were ghosts. There were probably rich pickings in the empty buildings but Tinnstra hadn't mustered the nerve to go and look.

She held the bread tight to her chest, petrified someone might try to steal it. The shopkeeper had been right to doubt her. She didn't have an extra ecu to pay him, and when she next found some money, she'd need it for more food, not her debt. She felt bad about lying to him, but that was the way of life in Jia now. You did what you had to. The baker wouldn't be so charitable the next time someone came in crying for food, but that wasn't Tinnstra's problem.

She looked up, saw gaunt faces with frightened eyes all around her. Everyone was in the same situation. Looking for food, avoiding trouble. Just trying to make it through the day, and through the night – staying alive any way they could.

Tinnstra recognised a few of the people still out and about, but she ignored them all. Kept moving. What would she say, anyway? Better to stay silent and not be noticed.

She turned into Ester Street. It used to be a beautiful little road with flower boxes on windowsills and colourful market stalls selling this and that. Now the only colour came from the Egril flags fluttering from every building, blood-red with one black eye – Kage's eye – watching all.

Everywhere she saw little scars from the night when Jia fell: a ruin that was once a home, a smashed window never repaired, scarlet-stained cobbles that no amount of rain would clean, another broken front door – she'd have to remember to come back and check inside.

A cold wind chased her, nipping at her flesh through her threadbare clothes. Snowflakes drifted past, announcing winter's arrival. As if they needed anything else to make matters worse. At least keeping warm wouldn't be a problem – she had plenty to burn. Who needed chairs when the only other choice was to freeze to death? Survival was all that mattered. Next time she explored a house, she'd look for something warmer to wear.

There was movement in the crowd ahead of her and Tinnstra caught a glimpse of black. She stopped in her tracks. A man was standing in the middle of the road watching a house at the end of the street. People swerved away from him, giving Tinnstra a clear view. Fear rippled through her, stealing the breath from her throat. *No. No. No.*

Her legs nearly gave way. Somehow, she staggered to a shop doorway, unable to take her eyes off the man. He wore the black uniform of the Emperor's Chosen, the elite of the Egril military. He had no need of armour. The baton hanging from a loop at his belt and the little silver skulls glinting on his collar were all the power he needed.

Even though a black mask covered his eyes and his white hair was cropped short, Tinnstra could tell he was young. Maybe not that much older than her. But that didn't make any difference. There was no mistaking the power emanating from the man. The danger. The fear. Of all the Egril's monsters, the Chosen were the worst.

Tinnstra had to get away.

Run.

She tried to enter the shop, but the door was locked. It rattled in its frame as the bolts held firm. Scared faces stared at her through the window, but no one came to help.

Behind her, the Skulls were setting up a barricade at the end of the road. There was nowhere to go. Nowhere to hide. She sank to her knees. She was trapped.

Dear Alo, God of Life, I don't want to die. Please protect me.

The street was now empty apart from the Chosen. Tears ran

down her cheeks as she watched. Prayers ran off her tongue – as if they could keep her safe.

She heard the wings next. Looked up. Saw the Daijaku swoop along the street. Four of them, demons all, black shapes cutting through white snow. All scales and talons and gleaming fangs, their wings spanned the road from one side to the other. The Daijaku of myth made flesh. Demons brought out of the Great Darkness to aid Raaku in his work. All but one carried a Niganntan blade. She stopped praying and started screaming.

The lead Daijaku had something in its hand. Something that glowed red and furious. A bomb. The creature threw it at the house at the end of the street and then the demons flew straight up and away.

Tinnstra had just enough time to close her eyes before the house exploded.

Wood, glass and stone rained down on the street. Tinnstra cowered in the doorway, not wanting to see how death would come for her. Her ears rang with the fury of it all. A wall of heat roared past, burning her skin as if the underworld had come to take Aisair. She choked on the smoke as it billowed past but still she kept her eyes shut. She covered her head with her hands and curled up as small as she could make herself.

Tinnstra had no idea how long she stayed like that, wrapped up in her ball of fear. It was only when she heard the pounding of her heart that she realised she was still alive. She opened her eyes, sobbing with relief. *I'm alive. I'm alive.*

The street was unrecognisable. Dust, dirt and debris lay scattered across the road. Broken beams and shattered doors. Shards of glass covered the ground. Bodies lay crushed by rock and stone. Only the ground floor remained of the building at the end of the street.

Squads of Skulls filled the road. The survivors were manhandled from the ruins into the street and pushed onto their knees, their hands tied behind their backs. Most looked half-dead already, bleeding from multiple wounds. Their blood stained the ground around them. The Skulls didn't care. They liked them that way. An array of weapons was thrown down next to them – swords, knives, bows. They were enough to get whoever was in that house the death penalty.

The Chosen watched it all. He stood unmarked despite the chaos, a smile on his lips. The sight of it chilled Tinnstra to her bones. The man was pure evil. Worse than any demon. She could only hope the Gods took pity on his prisoners and granted them a quick death.

The Skulls loaded the prisoners into the back of two caged wagons. Only then did the Chosen move. He circled each wagon, inspecting his catch through the bars. Always smiling. Satisfied, he signalled to the drivers to move off. The Skulls left with the wagons, forming an escort on either side – not that anyone would be foolish enough to try to stop them.

Once he was alone, the Chosen turned and headed back towards Tinnstra. She shrank into the corner of the doorway, tried to make herself small. Bit her lip to stifle her cries and begged all the Gods to keep her safe. *Please don't let him see me. Please. I want to live.*

For all the good her prayers did.

The Chosen stopped when he was parallel to her. Stopped and looked straight at her, as if he'd known all along she was there. His smile broadened, flashing white teeth. He tipped his head and saluted with two fingers. Fear crushed the air from her lungs. She could see the evil in his eyes. She could see he was death. *This is it. I'm going to die. Dear Gods, I'm dead.*

But the Chosen just laughed and strolled off. He knew she was no threat.

Tinnstra sat in the debris and the dirt, trying to catch her breath, stop her shakes. She couldn't believe she'd survived.

She sat there until the bells rang out for curfew. Time to be off the streets and death to anyone foolish enough not to heed their call. The bells didn't care about the trauma Tinnstra had just endured, the horrors she'd seen. There were no excuses, no pardons for breaking curfew. If a Skull stopped her, it would be the gallows – or worse. She had to get home.

Somehow, Tinnstra got to her feet and ran for all she was worth.

Her home was two streets away, a room on the third floor of a building much like the one she'd seen destroyed. She ran up the stairs, lungs burning, unlocked the door and rushed inside. She slammed the door shut, locked and bolted it, then dragged a chair across the room to prop up against it. Only then did she sink to the floor. More tears came. Chest-heaving sobs. Wails. She was safe but, by the Four Gods, it had been close. Too close.

It was then she realised she'd lost her bread.

DAY TWO

6

Yas

Kiyosun

It was a beautiful day in Kiyosun. A soft breeze brought the scent of the ocean from the harbour and through the narrow streets. Not a single cloud marred the perfect blue sky. The sun glistened off the ochre buildings, and the oppressive heat was gone at last. It was getting cooler in the way it only did in the south of Jia, when you dug out old coats to wear for a few months and looked forward to some rain, maybe enjoyed a fire for a night or two. They used to celebrate cold days in Kiyosun.

But not now.

Yas stood with her mother on the corner of the city's main square with her baby wrapped in her arms. At eighteen months old, she knew Little Ro wasn't much of a baby any more, but it was hard to think of him as anything else. He'd be standing soon. Already he could shoot off on his hands and knees and have everyone running after him. By the Four Gods, she loved him. He was the best thing she'd ever done. The only good thing she had left. And she didn't want to leave him. Not for a minute, not for a day.

Opposite, past the scaffolds, the Council House had been a grand old building once; a place of beauty and local government. Now it was a barracks and a prison; a place to be feared. If you went in there, you disappeared. No one *chose* to go inside. Not unless you were an idiot and had taken a job there. An idiot like Yas.

Her first day working as a cleaner for the Skulls. It wasn't the life she'd imagined, but the one thing she knew for sure was that life didn't give a shit about your hopes and dreams. If it did, the Skulls would still be in Egril, her husband would be alive and by her side, and she'd have money in her pocket and food in the cupboard. Not twenty-two years old, a widow, penniless and now a bloody cleaner for the enemy.

She shivered. She didn't want to go. Not into that building.

'You'll do fine,' said her mother. She reached for Ro but Yas couldn't give him up just yet.

'What sort of world is he going to grow up in, Ma?' she asked.

'What sort of world? How do I know? Six months ago if you'd asked me, I wouldn't have guessed it'd be like this, and I've certainly got no idea what's going to happen tomorrow.' Her ma gestured at the Council House. 'But what I think don't matter. It's now that counts.'

'Me and Rossi tried so hard – you know that. We thought Alo himself had blessed us when Little Ro came along. But now? Now I don't know. Maybe we were being selfish.' She brushed a tear from her face. She'd promised herself she'd not cry. 'What if something happens?'

'Tsk.' Ma shook her head. 'Why you thinkin' like that, eh? Stupid thoughts. You're there to do a job. The rest of it? They'll sort themselves out soon enough – you'll see. It'll all settle down one way or another. It has to.'

'I'm not sure we can wait. We can barely feed ourselves once a day and Ro's food's more water than meat.'

'That's why you're working.'

Yas glanced over at the Council House. It was like a mausoleum. All grey stone. Dead. 'In there.'

'Beggars ain't choosers, so they say. The Skulls are the only ones who got any coin, and that job pays two and a half staters. That's silver. Silver we need.'

'Some people could get nasty about me working in there. I'm no collaborator.'

'They'd be fools if they did. You're just doing what needs doing. No more than that. No more than anyone else.' Ma sniffed and squared her shoulders, eyes like stone. 'Your husband's dead. It's all very well he died fighting those bastards, but it's left us on our own.'

'You've seen the graffiti. And there was that girl two blocks down. Someone shaved her hair off and left her tied up naked on a street corner.'

'She was spreading her legs for the Skulls. You ain't intending to do that, are you? No? Then don't fret over what-might-be's. Right now, we need money for food. That's all you have to think about. This is the only way we'll get the coin – unless you want to go and do a deal with a Weeping Man?'

Yas shivered. No one wanted to owe those criminals anything. What was borrowed today had to be paid back thrice the next day and the Gods help you if you haven't got the money. They got their name because they marked their kills by inking a tear on their faces. 'You're right.'

'Now give us the boy and get gone. You don't wanna be late on your first day, do you? Eh?' Ma held out her arms again.

Yas kissed Ro on the forehead and he smiled back. By the Four Gods, he was perfect. She could see her husband's eyes, his smile in Little Ro. She missed him so much. If only Rossi was still with them. He'd know what to do.

The tears were coming again so she kissed her son one last time, breathed in his innocence and handed him over. 'Look after him, eh?'

'You think I'd just leave him to play in the street by himself or something? Of course I'll bloody look after him. Now get.'

'Right.' Yas brushed at her skirt. She felt sick. Looked again at the large, grey building with its iron gate and its iron railings. And Skulls. Skulls everywhere. Standing on guard. Walking around. And even more of them inside. 'Right. I'll see you tonight.' One more deep breath. A last look at Ro and then she was off, walking across the cobbles, pretending she didn't want to be sick. Her shoes clacked against the stone. Past the scaffolds, empty for once.

Yas kept her head down – she didn't need any disapproving looks – only stopping once she got to the main gate and handed her letter to the Skulls on duty.

'What you do?' asked one.

His accent was thick and muffled by the helmet and, for a moment, Yas didn't know what to say.

'What you do?' he repeated, angry now.

Finally understanding him, Yas blushed, feeling stupid. 'Sorry. I'm cleaning. A cleaner.'

'Raise arms.'

Yas did as she was told. Another Skull patted her down, searching for weapons. He shoved his hands into every crevice and lingered on her breasts, squeezing them just for the fun of it, watching to see how she'd react. Got up close to her face so she could see behind that mask of his that he was enjoying it. By the Gods, it made her angry. How dare they treat her like a bit of meat to be mauled? How dare they hurt her just because she needed to earn some bloody money? She wanted to tell them all to fuck off, knee the bastard in his balls and punch him in his smug mouth, but what could she really do except let them do what they wanted? She was powerless, and she hated that feeling most of all.

When he was finished, he nodded at the first guard to let her through. 'Put arms down.' The Skull thrust the letter back at her. 'Main building left, then right. Servants' entrance. Report there.'

'Thank you,' replied Yas, her cheeks burning. The guard hauled the gate open. She stood for a moment, staring at the Council House, hoping to the Gods that nothing worse waited for her in there. There was no going back once she stepped through.

'Move,' said the guard.

And, just like that, Yas stepped over the threshold. She followed the directions she'd been given and found the doorway at the bottom of some steps. A dog watched her approach and wagged his tail in hope of a treat. He jumped up, all big eyes and dangling tongue, putting his paws on her, but she pushed him to one side. 'Sorry. I've not got anything.'

She stopped again by the door and squeezed her hands into fists – once, twice, three times – before opening it and entering a busy kitchen. The smell of baking and meat cooking hit her, making her mouth water and her stomach rumble. She couldn't remember the last time she'd eaten anything that didn't smell half-rancid. People bustled in every direction, carrying pots and plates, stirring food over fires, watching ovens. Yas had never been in a kitchen like it – the room stretched back as far as she could see.

'Shut that bloody door,' shouted a large, red-cheeked woman in a cook's uniform. 'You're letting all the heat out.'

Yas stared at the cook, suddenly lost for words.

'Yes. I'm talking to you. You dumb or something?' The cook walked towards her, ladle in hand, looking like she intended to use it on Yas. The woman had to be six feet tall and towered over nearly everyone around her.

The sight got Yas moving. She closed the door, did her best to ignore the sudden feeling she was trapped, and hoped the cook wasn't about to clobber her with the ladle. 'Sorry. Yes. It's my first day.'

'Of course it is, otherwise I'd have recognised your sad little face.' The cook swapped the ladle to her left hand and held out the other to Yas. 'I'm Bets. I'm in charge here. You must be Yas.'

'Yes. Yas.' She took the offered hand.

Bets laughed. 'You don't sound so sure.'

'I'm definitely Yas. Sorry. I've not worked for a long time. Been looking after my baby.'

'I hope you mean a real baby and not some useless lump of a man. Enough women doing that these days.'

Yas looked down. 'My husband died the first night.' She didn't need to say any more than that. Half the city died the night the Egril invaded. She didn't need to tell Bets how Rossi hid her and Little Ro under the floor, or how, armed with nothing more than a kitchen knife, he tried fighting off the four Skulls who'd kicked in their front door. There wasn't any point telling the cook how her husband's blood dripped through the gaps in the floorboards onto her face, or how she then spent three hours staring into his dead eyes until a neighbour heard Ro crying and found them. 'He died.'

'We've only just met and I've put my bloody foot in it.' Bets patted Yas's shoulder. 'Sorry, love. Enough women suffering from that these days, too.'

'It's all right. I just need to work. Earn some money for food.'

'You're in the right place for that. You work hard and the Skulls – excuse me, the Egril, our wonderful lords and masters – won't mind you taking some leftovers home with you each night.' Bets winked. 'And I make sure there are leftovers.'

'That would be wonderful.' Yas suddenly felt some weight lift off her shoulders. Bets seemed nice, and if she got free food, she could save the money she was earning. Maybe taking the job wasn't such a bad idea after all.

'Now, if I remember right, you're doing a spot of cleaning for us, yes?'

Yas nodded.

'Good. I'd hate to be losing my mind at my age. Let me introduce you to the team down here.' Bets looked around the kitchen. 'Oi! Everyone! Can I have your bloody attention for a minute.'

Ten faces turned their way.

'This is Yas. She's going to be doing cleaning and fetching,' said Bets. 'Be nice to her, or I'll be having words with you.'

A chorus of hellos came back without much enthusiasm.

'That was pathetic. If we weren't so busy, I'd make you all do that again. Now, Yas, that long dribble of piss over there is Rib.' Bets pointed to a tall, thin man with a scruff of a beard by the main stove. 'If I'm not here, you listen to him. Rib isn't his real name, but it suits him better on account of the fact he looks like one. Kris is next to him, then you've got Baca, Lucin and Georga. They do all the cooking. Fucking terrible at it they are, but they're my boys and girls and I won't hear a bad word about them. There's Faul and Wisder on the pots and pans. A right pair of lazy arses they are, too.' Two young lads looked up again from the sink and nodded. They must've been all of sixteen, with spots and greasy hair. 'And finally, you've got the other girls like you – Helix and Samu – and Arga overseeing you all. Oi, Arga. Come over here.'

A thin-faced woman in a black dress and white apron scurried over. 'Yes, Cook.'

Bets pushed Yas forward. 'This is Yas. She's working with you. Get her set up and show her what to do – and try to smile, at least for today. I'm sure you can pretend to be happy for that long, can't you?'

'Yes, Cook,' replied Arga. She took Yas by the hand. 'Come on, then.'

Leaving Bets laughing, Yas followed Arga down a corridor into a small room with lockers on one side and uniforms hanging on a rail on the other. Arga took a black dress like hers and handed it to Yas.

'Get changed and leave your stuff in one of the cupboards.' Arga looked her up and down. 'I don't think you need to worry about anyone stealing any of it.'

'Is there anywhere to change that's ... private?' asked Yas.

'Oh yeah, we all use the governor's personal suite. He doesn't mind. Insists on it, he does. Likes the idea of us all being naked in there. Likes to watch, if you let him.'

Yas looked at her. 'You're joking, right?'

'Of course I'm bloody joking. You get changed here, in front of me. Unless you think you're special or something.'

'No. I'm not special.'

'Get a move on, then. We have work to do.'

The dress was uncomfortable, digging into her under her armpits and too short in the sleeve, which was not helped by the stiffness of the material.

Arga watched, shaking her head the whole time. 'What did I do to get saddled with you? I must've really pissed Bets off or something.' She grabbed Yas again and set off, a bucket with cleaning cloths in her other hand. 'We look after the offices on the ground floor and some of the living quarters on the first floor.'

They left the kitchen area and entered a chamber with a central stairwell. On the far side, two Skulls stood guard at a set of large oak doors. Arga didn't say anything, just started up the stairs. Yas had to tuck in behind her in the narrow stairwell.

'What's behind those doors back there?' she asked.

'Nothing good. Now I'm going to tell you the rules. Stick to them and you'll be all right. Don't and no one can help you. Got it?'

'Yes.'

'First rule: don't speak to anyone unless spoken to,' said Arga. 'If they do speak to you, just say, "Yes, sir," or "No, sir." They don't want a fucking conversation.'

'Right.'

'Second rule: don't look at them – ever. Keep your eyes on the ground. Last maid dumb enough to look at one of them got her eyes cut out. And you don't want that, do you?'

'No.'

'Third rule: don't get caught on your own anywhere. If you're lucky, they'll just rape you. If you're unlucky, they'll rape you and kill you.'

Yas stopped on the stairs, mouth open.

Arga turned and glared at her. 'What were you expecting? Bloody flowers and kisses? These are mean bastards we're dealing with and they hate us. Never forget that. If they could be arsed to cook and clean for themselves, they'd happily kill us all right now and be done with it. Got it?'

'Got it.'

'Now come on. Rule number four: don't be fucking late.'

On the ground floor, red Egril flags hung along the walls between giant arched windows and a grand central staircase curling to the left and the right, leading to the upper floor. Skulls stood guard by various doors while other Egril in grey uniforms and simple masks went about their duties. They carried no weapons, though, and she wondered what they did. She'd never thought that there might be Egril who weren't soldiers, but she had no doubt they were bastards all the same.

Arga pointed to the far end of the ground floor, to another corridor. 'We don't go down there. That leads to the interrogation cells. I don't have to tell you what happens there.'

Yas shook her head, mouth dry. What if there was some poor Jian in there right then? She shivered.

'We start every day by getting the fires going in each of the main rooms. Skulls hate being cold.' Arga led Yas past a sentry into a long room dominated by a table bigger than any she'd ever seen. A statue of a man with a scimitar in his hand towered over the room at the far end. 'This is the main meeting room.

They use this one the most.' Arga headed straight to the fireplace and began stacking logs in the hearth. Another Egril flag hung above it. There was a small flint box next to the bucket of logs and Arga started the fire. The sudden warmth felt good but Arga didn't let Yas enjoy it for long. 'Stop gawking. You've seen a fire before. We've got ten more rooms to do after this.' She threw Yas a cloth. 'Open the curtains and then wipe the table. It'll be a beating for us if they find any dust.'

As Yas wiped the table down, her attention was drawn again and again to the strange statue. A man in armour similar to what the Skulls wore, but more ornate. An amulet hung around his neck, shaped like the sun. The face was featureless, anonymous, a mask; only the eyes had any sort of life. Even though they were carved from stone, they seemed to be watching her, sizing her up, finding her worthless. 'Who's that?' she whispered.

'Who's what?'

'The statue. Who's the statue of?'

Arga rushed over, grabbed her hand and pulled her close, digging her nails into Yas's skin. 'What did I say about asking bloody questions?'

'You didn't say anything.'

'Well, rule number whatever-the-fuck-it-is – don't ask any questions,' snarled Arga.

'G ... g ... got it.'

'If you must know, that statue is of Raaku himself, all praise be to his name.' Arga hissed the words through gritted teeth. 'And don't you dare say, "Who?"'

Yas knew who Raaku was. Everyone knew who the Emperor of the Egril was. Her hands shook and her breath caught in her throat. This was the man who'd destroyed her life. The Egril worshipped him as the son of their god, Kage. The man who'd decided to wage war against all non-believers. The man who'd killed her husband. She stared at the statue with horror in her eyes. She wanted to run from it, never see it again.

Arga's nails dug in to Yas's wrist. 'Pull yourself together and get on with your fucking work or I'll go and tell Bets to find me someone else.'

'I'm sorry.' Yas started wiping the table again, ignoring the pain in her wrist. She kept her eyes down but could still feel the statue watching her. It was stupid, she knew that. It was just a carving. Nothing to be scared of. But she'd be lying if she didn't admit it was a relief to leave that room and move on to the next.

The girls continued to work and, for the next few hours, they didn't stop. It was the same routine in every room: make the fire, open the curtains, clean up the mess.

'You'll get used to it quick enough. First week's always the hardest,' said Arga.

'It's not too bad. My little boy's harder work.' Yas smiled. 'I was dreading coming in here. I thought it was going to be awful, but it's not. It's all right.'

Arga shook her head as if that was the stupidest thing she'd ever heard. 'Come on, we've still got work to do.'

They entered another room. 'The governor's office. Really we should do it first, but he likes a drink or two at night so he's always the last to start in the morning.'

Yas pulled the curtains open, letting the morning light in. A small desk was covered in papers weighted down with an empty decanter and a wine-stained glass. As Arga worked on the fire, Yas looked at the papers. The writing was spidery, hard to make out. There was a tally of food supplies, something on troop movements. Underneath was a report on the resistance, the Hanran. A list of names.

'What the *fuck* are you doing?' Arga was staring at her, a furious look on her face.

'Just tidying up,' replied Yas.

'It didn't look like that. Looked like you were fucking reading his papers.'

Yas shook her head. 'I can't read. Never been taught.'

'Well, don't even bloody look like you can. They think you're a spy for even one minute, they'll cut you down where you stand.'

The door burst open before Yas could say another word.

'Fuck. Fuck. Fuck.' The governor bustled in, red-faced, trying to tuck his shirt in around his fat stomach. Lord Aisling himself. 'Fucking rebels. They'll be the death of me.' He stopped when he saw the girls, brushed his grey hair back off his forehead. 'What are you two doing here?'

They curtsied. Arga said, 'Just making the fire, m'lord.'

'Then get on with it and clear off.' He waved a hand and sat down at his desk.

The two girls bent down to light the fire. A distant member of the Jian royal family, Lord Aisling had been liked well enough before the invasion, but after he'd turned collaborator, everyone's anger had focused on him as the one familiar face everyone knew. Yas had heard more than one person threaten to kill the man or pray that the Gods strike him down. In person, though, he looked like a sad old man.

'It doesn't take both of you to make a fire, does it?' Aisling called out. 'One of you fetch me some bloody wine to drink. How am I supposed to think without wine?'

Arga looked at Yas. 'I'll fetch it. You get this going. I'll be as fast as I can.' She stood up and scurried off, leaving Yas alone.

Someone entered the room as Yas opened the flint box. She kept her head down, remembering Arga's advice. She barely took a breath.

'Good morning,' said Aisling, his voice suddenly all deferential. A chair scraped back.

'Is it?' A woman's voice. Cold, brutal. 'So, it wasn't the Hanran that raided a weapons store last night, then?'

'Last night? Oh. I didn't know,' replied Aisling. 'I've just got in.'

'I want those responsible arrested today,' said the woman.

Yas fumbled with the flint in her hand.

'But how? We don't even know who they are,' said Aisling. 'We have some names, but—'

There was a crack as a hand slapped against skin. 'If you can't do it, I'll find someone who can,' said the woman. 'Perhaps you are unable to find the Hanran because you sympathise with them? Perhaps you're one of them?'

'No. No. No,' mumbled Aisling. 'Don't think that. I'll get it done.'

The woman walked out.

Yas heard Aisling sit down. 'Shit. Shit. What can I do? What can I do?'

Yas focused on the flint in her hand, struck it again and again, praying for a spark to catch. When one took, relief swept through her. She fed it, blowing on each little flame that came alive.

The governor walked over and stood beside her. She could see his feet but daren't look up.

'Stupid girl.' All weakness had gone from his voice. All kindness.

Yas didn't see the blow that knocked her to the ground.

7

Darus

Aisair

Darus Monsuta ran his fingers over the knives splayed across the table. Collected through the years, each one was beautiful in its own way. Special. They glistened in the torchlight as they vied for his attention, sparkling with promise, whispering with delight.

He picked up a vicious-looking stiletto he'd taken off a foolish cutpurse in Tursconia in Northern Egril. He'd been twelve years old. The knife was beautifully sharp. It had barely left a mark as it slipped in and out of the thief, puncturing him a dozen times before the first spot of blood even showed. Darus shivered at the memory. *Delicious.*

In the six months since the invasion, Darus had been having the time of his life. An endless supply of rebels and sympathisers to try his knives on. He had two guests at present. One was a Shulka warrior, tied to a chair in the middle of the room. A big brute of a man, with one eye swollen shut, a bloodstained gag in his mouth and a belly full of righteous fury. He'd been captured during the raid in Ester Street, and now Darus had him stripped to the waist, all ready and waiting to be questioned. Someone had already been to work on the man. No matter, there was enough left for him to enjoy. He intended to slice away the man's honour and dignity one strip at a time.

His other guest wasn't a prisoner, unfortunately.

Bored, his sister lounged in the room's other, far more comfortable chair. He'd rather have been alone – he'd certainly not invited her to join him – but that never stopped Skara.

'Just start cutting already,' drawled Skara. She looked, much to Darus's disgust, so very similar to him: tall and lean, with a sharp face and ice-blue eyes. The same silver hair, despite their youth – she wore hers long and tied back while his was cropped close to the skull.

Skara was dressed, as he was, in the Chosen's plain black uniform, their rank marked only by silver skulls pinned to the high collar beneath her mask. Darus was bare-faced and he hoped Kage would forgive the indulgence, but he wanted the Shulka to know who'd killed him. He wanted his face to haunt the man for eternity as Kage's slave in the Great Darkness.

'Come on, little brother. Don't be shy.'

Little brother? By Kage's infinite fury, that pissed him off – and Skara knew it. She was jealous of him. She was the elder, but it was *he* who'd been chosen by Raaku first. It was *he* who'd been in the vanguard that entered Jia first. It was *he* who'd sent over three hundred souls to serve Kage. *He*, Darus Monsuta, who'd earned the glory for their family name. He deserved a damn sight more respect than being called little brother. 'Why are you here again?'

'Just keeping you company. I'd hate for you to be lonely.'

Skara delighted in ruining these moments. He loathed the way she was always there, leeching off his accomplishments. Some days, he even thought she'd followed him into the Chosen just to annoy him. Granted, she was a more than adequate killer, but she and her axe had no style, no finesse or subtlety, not like he did with his knives. Her methods were functional, whereas he was a *master* at his work.

Keep calm, he told himself as he twirled the stiletto between his fingers. He wandered over to his sister. 'Some things shouldn't be rushed.' The Shulka watched each step and Darus's skin tingled as the soldier's breathing grew more haggard behind the gag. *Delightful*. Darus bent down and kissed his sister's forehead. 'Some things are all the more exquisite for waiting.'

Skara laughed. 'Do you tell yourself that every night when you go to bed alone?'

A flick of his fingers and the knife was an inch away from her eye. 'You should never make fun of a man with a knife.'

'Unless you have a bigger one of your own, little brother.' *Tap, tap, tap.* Her hunting knife rested against his thigh.

'Quite.' Darus stepped back, angered by Skara's smug expression. She was always so impressed with herself. But she was not as clever as she thought she was. They might look alike but she'd never be his equal.

Darus stepped back and turned his attention to the Shulka. A shame it wasn't his sister in the Jian's place, squirming beneath his touch. She'd not think herself so special then. One day, he'd find out how long she could last before her cries filled the room. *One day.* He could quite happily be the only Monsuta in the world.

He winked and the man knew his moment had come. The Jian strained against the ropes, but they had no give in them. He pleaded and begged but the gag stifled his words. Tears flooded his eyes but they were wasted on Darus. It was all too exciting.

With a smile, Darus removed the gag. They were playing a game now. There was an etiquette that had to be followed.

'You bastard,' spat the Shulka.

'Only in spirit.' Darus chuckled. 'Are you feeling brave?'

'Fuck you!' screamed the Shulka. He thrashed about in his chair, straining against the ropes, rocking the chair back and forth.

'So charming. So eloquent.' Darus darted in with the blade. The first cut was small, a simple nick on the shoulder. A sting. A taste of what was to come. It took nearly two seconds for the blood to even appear, so red against the Shulka's white skin.

The Jian gritted his teeth and stared at Darus with hate in his eyes. *Perfect.* The second cut went deeper. The third longer. Darus didn't speak, for this wasn't about asking questions. The Shulka spat and cursed, trying to be so brave. If only he knew what was to come.

Skara impatiently tapped her foot behind him. *Bitch.*

Darus lost his concentration. The knife opened up the Shulka from hip to hip, a jagged smile bleeding red, deeper than he intended. The warrior screamed so Darus stabbed down, burying the knife to the hilt in his knee, just for the fun of it. The scream

71

grew louder, echoing off the walls, almost loud enough to drown out Skara's annoying tapping. It was no accident – she knew she was spoiling his fun, but he wasn't going to give her the satisfaction of knowing how much it infuriated him. *No.*

He forced himself to keep his attention on the Shulka. The man begged for mercy, pleaded with Darus to stop, but he might as well have asked day not to become night. This was what Darus loved. He played with the pain, teasing and tormenting. Darus cut and sliced and stabbed, flowing around his darling prisoner, turning the Shulka's body into a map of blood-red lines. Even Skara sat up to watch. When it came to pain, Darus was a master.

The Shulka was less impressed. He fought against his restraints, roared and screamed, cursed and spat, jerked and twitched, but it was all for naught. There was no escape from the blade. None. And Darus never tired.

He stopped only when the Shulka passed out. There was no point torturing an unconscious man. Death waited to take the Shulka to the Great Darkness, but it wasn't this man's time to go. He wasn't that lucky.

Darus straddled the man's lap and slapped him awake. The Shulka squirmed beneath him, jerking his head away from Darus, as if escape was possible. 'Please, please, stop, let me go. I don't know anything. I'm just a soldier. I just do what they tell me. Please.'

Darus loved this part – when a prisoner fished for hope they could still escape. Still survive. It was time to dispel that fantasy, that folly.

'My darling man. Don't think there's going to be any quick escape to the Great Darkness, or that you will have the honour of dying before I can break you. It really is foolishness to think that.' Darus paused, savouring the moment, the fear in the man's face, the way his lip trembled. 'Did you know that my sister and I are the Emperor's Chosen?'

The Shulka let out a sob. 'Y... Ye ... Yes.' He glanced over to Skara, as if she was something for him to be worried about.

'Look at me.' Darus used his knife to push the man's face back so their eyes met. 'It's not just a rank or some division of the mighty Raaku's army. It literally means we were hand-picked by the Emperor himself to serve him. Why were we selected? Because we have Talent – an affinity for magic that has survived the generations, hidden away, waiting to be free. Almighty Raaku sensed it in us. He understood the potential of what we could do and the magic that only he could awaken.'

Darus saw the man's fear and confusion at his words and leaned closer until his voice was a breath in the man's ear. 'He took me, bathed me in Kage's holy waters.' He stabbed the man in the leg, twisting the blade. The Shulka screamed, eyes bulging. 'Imagine that pain multiplied a thousandfold and you would not even be close to what I had to endure as he remade me. But afterwards? Afterwards, I was so much more than what I once was.' He shuddered at the memory. 'What a glorious moment. To stand before Raaku himself, feel his touch. To be reborn.'

He pulled the knife from the Shulka's leg and held it so they both could watch the blood drip from the blade. One, two, three drops fell. The Shulka panted through gritted teeth, trying to control the pain.

Darus lowered the knife and held up his open hand. 'Let me show you what I can do.'

He gripped the man's face and let his power flow out. The Shulka convulsed beneath his touch but Darus didn't move. He kept his hold on the man's face and slowly, ever so slowly, the multitude of wounds across the Shulka's body closed until they had all disappeared. Only then did he release his grip. 'There you go. All better.'

'What ... what did you do?'

'Magic.' Darus wriggled his fingers in front of the man's face. 'That was just a taste. For you to truly understand what a wonderful gift I have, I'd like to show you a better example of what I can do.' Darus stood and walked over to his knives. He took his time. He wanted something that would make an impact. He picked up a meat cleaver, felt its weight. *Lovely*. He returned to the Shulka and ran the blade's edge across the man's biceps. 'I could, if I wanted to, cut your arm off.'

The Shulka sucked in lungfuls of air. 'Please, please. I don't know anything. I really don't.' He couldn't take his eyes off the cleaver.

'Oh, don't worry. I'm not in the mood to do that.' He squirmed and flinched as Darus rested the blade on the back of his thumb. 'Now this – this is perfect. Effortless, almost ...' Darus pressed down. Blood blossomed around the blade as it bit into the man's skin and, with an extra push, Darus severed his thumb.

The Shulka screamed. *Perfection*. So brave at the start, so broken at the end. The mighty always fall the furthest. He put the meat cleaver down on the table and straddled the Shulka's lap once more, so their faces almost touched. Darus stared into his eyes. There was so much intensity of emotion on display – the fear, the agony, the hate, the hope, the despair. Darus loved it all. There was no purer relationship than that between torturer and prisoner. He could feel Kage's might working through him as the Great Darkness waited for another soul to claim.

'Here we go.' Darus wrapped his hand around the bloody stump. Blood stained his fingers as he worked his magic. 'I've not experienced it myself, although I'm told this isn't the best of sensations. But you're a brave boy, aren't you? You're a warrior, a fighter. You can handle pain.'

The Shulka couldn't. He bucked about, panting, screaming, weeping as his thumb grew back. *Exquisite*. It was everything Darus wanted and so much more, right up until the Shulka lost control of his bladder. Darus leaped off his lap.

'My dear man, why would you do that?' he hissed.

Skara laughed her head off, enraging Darus further.

The small knife was in his hand once more and he stabbed the Shulka in the gut. Again and again and again, twisting the blade with each incision. Stab, stab, stab. Blood soaked his uniform but he didn't care. Blood was always well earned. Blood was *glorious*. He imagined it was Skara there, receiving his knife. A good stabbing would certainly stop that annoying laugh of hers. Oh, how he wanted to see her die.

The Shulka turned white and his head dropped to one side. He coughed crimson. The Great Darkness called. But Darus was true to his word. There was no easy death to be had. Not in that room. Not with him. Once more, he touched the Shulka. Once more, the wounds healed. Even the Great Darkness needed Darus's permission to take the Shulka away.

The Jian convulsed as his injuries healed, as air found his lungs and his heart beat once more.

Darus grinned. This was happiness. Bless Raaku for choosing Darus, for his gift. Bless Raaku for sending him to Jia to do his will.

'I think he's trying to say something,' said Skara, peering over his shoulder. 'A name, perhaps?'

Darus hated how she hovered, getting a thrill off his work. 'Perhaps it's one of his Gods.'

'At least cut his tongue out so we don't have to listen to his gibberish any more,' said Skara with a sniff.

His tongue. *Of course. Wonderful.* He grabbed the Shulka's jaw, forcing it open.

'*Aasgod!*' screamed the Shulka. '*Aasgod!*'

'Aasgod can't hear you, my dear boy,' said Darus.

'I know where he is. I know where Aasgod is.'

That stopped Darus. He stepped back, ran his eye over the wretched creature. Was it a lie? A last ploy to live? *No.* Darus didn't think so. They were well past that part of the game. 'Aasgod – the Jian's Lord Mage?'

The Shulka nodded desperately. 'Yes, Aasgod. I know where he is.'

Skara's obvious excitement infuriated him. Even she knew what a catch Aasgod would be. Not only was the Lord Mage rumoured to be as powerful as Raaku but also he led the Jian resistance – the Hanran. The rewards for his head would be immense. Raaku would honour him. He could finally leave his sister behind and stand at Raaku's side, favoured above all. He could see it now. The triumph in Egril. His name known throughout the Empire. His name, not his sister's. Oh, how Darus would *love* to cut the Lord Mage open.

'Where is he?' said Skara, her eyes burning bright with excitement. 'Where's Aasgod?'

'You'll let me go if I tell you?' said the Shulka.

'Of course, dear boy,' replied Darus. He made a show of putting the knife away. 'Of course. Nothing is more important than the capture of Aasgod. Give us a prize like that and you'll go free.'

The Shulka hesitated and then Darus saw him accept the role of traitor. Grasp that last straw. Some people would sacrifice their own mothers to stay alive. So much for Shulka honour. 'He's here in the city.'

'It's a big place. Where exactly in Aisair?' asked Skara, running her hand down the man's cheek.

'I don't know,' replied the Shulka, eyes flicking between the two Monsutas. 'But I know where he'll be tomorrow.'

'Delightful,' said Darus. He bent down so only he could hear the Shulka's betrayal. The man's breath was warm in his ear.

'What did he say, brother?' asked Skara. Always so eager.

'Oh ... Just this and that.' Darus produced the knife once more. 'Now, where was I? Oh yes ...' And he cut the Shulka's tongue from his mouth. There would be no more confessing.

8

Yas

Kiyosun

Yas flinched as the gate clanked shut.

'How was your first day?' said the guard, staring at her bruises. Yas didn't turn around. She had nothing to say. She just wanted to get home to her little boy. Forget her awful day. She headed off past the scaffolds and across the square.

She ran her tongue over her split lip, winced as her ribs sent a stabbing pain shooting through her. The governor had given her a good beating. The bastard. So much for feeling sorry for him. Not even the thought of the food in the basket Bets had given her made Yas feel any better. Still, she was alive, walking. It would take more than some fat, drunk man to break her.

Several streets later, someone fell in beside her. Too close for it to be an accident. She kept her head down, ignoring whoever it was.

'Hello, Yas,' said a woman.

Yas looked then. She couldn't help herself. She didn't recognise the woman. Tall, lean. Shoulder-length hair. Pretty in a hard way. She knew the look. A Shulka. 'Do I know you?'

'We've not met before. My name's Kara.'

Yas kept walking.

'How was your first day at work?' she asked, undeterred.

Yas walked faster but Kara kept pace.

In the end, Yas had enough. She stopped and faced the woman down. 'I don't know who you are or what you want, but I'm not interested – whatever it is. Now piss off, I want to go home.' She started walking again, eager to put some distance between them.

'I expect Little Ro has missed you,' said Kara.

That stopped Yas dead. She turned, fists clenched. 'How do you know my son's name? How do you know my name? Who are you?'

The woman smiled, ignoring Yas's aggression. 'I told you who I am. My name's Kara. I want to be your friend.'

'I don't need any more friends.'

'Everyone needs friends – especially now.' The woman paused, glanced around. 'We should probably keep walking. Standing here will attract the wrong type of attention.' The woman tilted her head in the direction of Yas's home. Another thing she shouldn't have known. 'Shall we?'

She was right. Whatever Kara wanted, it wasn't worth getting picked up by the Skulls over. They passed the church to the Four Gods, burned out and destroyed by the Egril. At least the priest's body was gone now. They'd left his corpse staked out in front of the church for months before someone took him away. 'I'm still not interested.'

'Who gave you the bruises?'

'It's none of your business.'

'Not great getting beaten up on your first day.'

'I figured that out for myself.'

'Can't be easy going working for the Skulls. Not after what happened to your husband.'

The knot in Yas's gut grew tighter. Thoughts flashed through her mind. Her husband dying. His blood dripping on her, onto Little Ro. 'Nothing in life's easy.'

'True. But taking money off the enemy—'

'What about it?' said Yas.

'Some could say it was blood money.'

Yas shook her head. So that's what it was all about. The woman didn't like her working for the Skulls. It was the last thing she needed. 'Just because I'm working in that place doesn't mean I'm a sympathiser, okay? I hate those bastards. I hate what they're doing. I hate that they're here. They killed my husband – as you

78

just bloody reminded me. But unless you've got food or money for my family, I need the work. So, go give some other fool a hard time and leave me alone.'

'I'm not trying to give you a hard time, Yas,' replied Kara. 'On the contrary, I'm glad you're working at the Council House.'

'Well, you're the only one because I'm not.' Yas stopped when the woman's words sank in. 'Why do you care?'

'I've been hoping to make friends with someone who works there.'

'Why?'

'I have other friends who'd like to know what goes on inside from time to time.'

Everything clicked into place. How could she've been so stupid? 'You're Hanran.'

'We should keep walking.'

'You are, aren't you?'

'I am. You are. We all are. Every Jian is, whether they know it or not. It's our Gods–given duty to resist the invaders.'

'My duty is to my family. I'm not a Shulka. This isn't my fight.'

They crossed a road and turned east. There was no hesitation on Kara's part – she knew where they were going – and Yas didn't like that one bit.

'It's everyone's fight,' said Kara. 'Don't you want Little Ro to grow up in a free country where he's not going to get hanged for being in the wrong place at the wrong time?'

Yas shivered as she thought of the scaffolds and her son. 'Yes. Yes, I do.'

'Then help us. You won't have to do anything that would put you at risk – just keep your eyes and ears open. There'll never be any connection to you.'

The two women joined the checkpoint queue on Houseman Street. They waited silently while the Skulls took their time ex-amining papers, looking for trouble, their hands never far away from the hilts of their swords. Yas hated the sight of them – hated the way they'd ruined everything she'd ever cared about. And now she was working for the bastards. What a mess.

Yas didn't wait for the Shulka after being waved through. She stalked off, hands thrust in her pockets, head down.

Kara caught up with her two streets later. 'What've they got you doing in there?'

Yas sighed. 'I clean the offices and some of the living quarters. Then we serve lunch, and for the rest of the day, I do odd chores here and there. For that, I get two and a half staters a week, a bag of free food and a kicking from the governor.'

'The governor beat you?'

'I was cleaning his office and some Egril officer bitch came in and gave him a bollocking in front of me, so after she left, he put me in my place so he could feel better.'

'Bastard.'

'He's an old man. He got tired before he could do any real damage.'

'What was his office like?'

'A mess. Papers everywhere. He drinks. A lot. The Skull woman wanted him out arresting Hanran members.'

'Did they say who?'

'I don't think they know who they are. Not really.'

'No doubt they'll go and arrest the first people they come across. The Skulls don't care as long as they've got Jians to string up. We need your help. We have to stop them. Innocent people will die. None of us are safe. None of us.'

They walked in an uncomfortable silence. Yas wanted the woman gone; her day had been bad enough as it was. They turned a corner and Yas sighed with relief on seeing her home.

Kara grabbed her arm. 'Will you help us?'

'No. I told you already – I've got my family to think about. They only have me to look after them.'

'Think of them, Yas. Do it for them.'

'How do I even know you're Hanran, eh? This could all be a trap – a test to see if I'm loyal. You could be working for the Egril.'

'I can assure you, I'm not.'

'Either way, I'm not doing it. Leave me alone. Find some other fool.'

80

'There is no one else. We need you.'

Yas looked up at her home. A candle flickered in the window. Her ma and Little Ro were waiting for her. Safe. No way was she going to jeopardise that. 'For the last time, leave me alone.'

Kara squeezed Yas's arm. 'At least think about it.'

Yas yanked her arm free. 'Piss off.'

'Okay. I'll see you around.'

Yas watched her leave, feeling both furious at the woman's intrusion and guilty that she'd done the wrong thing. Kara had a point – a good point. There were no civilians in this war. Just Jian against Egril. They'd all be fighting sooner rather than later.

Ma was by the window with Little Ro in her arms when she walked through the door. Ma put a finger to her lips. 'He's only just fallen asleep.'

She set down her basket of food and went over, shedding her coat on the way, eager to see her boy. His lips were puckered and he was frowning a little, as if being asleep took concentration. She kissed his head and breathed in that wonderful smell. Pure innocence.

'What happened to you?' whispered her mother, turning Yas's face so she could see the bruising better.

'Nothing important,' replied Yas, pulling free so she could focus on Ro. Seeing him made her feel better. He was everything and she'd do anything to keep him safe.

9

Dren

Kiyosun

'You have to be patient,' said Dren. Falsa sat curled up on the roof, watching him, her eyes full of admiration. This was her first time out and she was buzzing. Dren basked in it as he continued his instruction. 'You think you need to get all worked up, feel red-hot anger bubble away inside you – but you're wrong. You need cold cunning.'

Falsa nodded as if she knew, but she was just a kid. She knew nothing, of course, not at her age. She couldn't have been more than twelve years old. A scamp of a thing and perfect for what Dren wanted. No Skull would expect Falsa to knife them in the back. He just had to make sure she had the spine to do it.

He sat with his back against the side of the water tower, enjoying the chill that came through the wood. 'First of all, you find out where your target's going to be. Once you have the location, you check it out. Get to know it better than your own home. You're looking for one spot in particular. Somewhere dark and quiet. Somewhere close enough to strike from and, most importantly, somewhere you can easily escape from.

'Once you've found a spot, you disappear. Avoid the place like the plague, just in case someone else is watching it, too. You don't want to give anyone any warning that something's up or get yourself reported to the Skulls.'

Again, Falsa nodded, a bright smile plastered over her baby face.

'On the day you gonna do it,' continued Dren, 'you get there early, way early, so fucking early that even the birds are still asleep, and you hide and you wait. I'm talking about waiting for hours, not a few extra minutes. Your hiding place might be cramped, hot, sweaty, smelly – it don't matter how bad it is, you suck it up and wait. Sometimes it can get so bad, you'll think you can't even breathe, but still you wait. Right until your target turns up. That's the best moment. You're watching them and they don't know you're there. They don't know they're an inch or two from dying. You watch, you wait until they're close enough to touch ... and then you strike.' Dren stabbed forward with an imaginary knife.

Falsa jumped back like the scared little rabbit she was. She giggled to cover her nerves. 'That's why we've been waiting up here so long.'

Dren stopped himself from groaning and forced a smile instead. It helped to make the new ones feel good. Kept them keen. 'Yeah, that's right. You see – you're getting it.' Falsa smiled, proud of herself.

They'd been on the roof since first light, staying out of sight of the Daijaku and the Skulls. Eight hours thinking about the men they were going to kill, going over the plan, looking for faults, imagining success. Eight long hours stuck on a roof with a kid who had nothing worthwhile to say. He patted her knee. 'It won't be long now, though. Not long at all.'

It was a beautiful evening in the city. The part of him that could still appreciate it shrank a little more each day, but for now, it was still there. An array of colour washed over the sky, reds, golds, oranges, purples and every shade of blue, above the shimmering sea with its salty tang that always made Dren think of his father.

What he'd give to be out on the old man's boat now, working the nets with him, his uncle and his cousin. Stupid, really, he'd always moaned about it, putting in a half-arsed effort more often than not. They'd take the boat out while it was still dark and work the Meigore Channel to the east of Kiyosun. The seas were rich with grouper, sea bream, mackerel and tuna, and they always returned with bulging nets. They'd drop the catch off at the wharf with the Haslis brothers, who'd then sell the fish on across the city. His dad and uncle would haggle with the brothers, all mock indignation one minute and then backslapping laughter the next. It never seemed to affect the price much and everyone left happy.

Their fathers would take Dren and Quist down to Naas's inn and they'd all get stuck in to some meat pies and have a drink. He smiled. Those were happy days for sure, but the best ones were when it was just him and his dad on the boat. He'd sit by the tiller, chatting away, staring at the horizon, wondering what lay on the other side of that big ocean.

Maybe one day, he'd get a boat of his own and sail out of Kiyosun, leave the whole rotten place behind and find out. Go somewhere new. See the world. It would be nice to escape. One day he would.

Just not right now.

He shook the thoughts from his head. Now wasn't the time to get all sentimental. Only fools did that. Weak people. Not Dren. Not when he had things to do. People to kill. The Skulls had murdered his parents, destroyed his city. He couldn't walk away. The bastards would pay a fucking heavy price for messing with his city.

The sun draped its last rays over the rooftops, poking out here and there between the forest of water tanks. Most of them were near empty. It'd not rained in months. For a city surrounded by water on three sides, it seemed ridiculous that running out of drinking water was a serious problem, but it was what it was. You can't drink the ocean, after all.

Not only water. Food was scarcer than a virgin in a brothel. It'd been two days since the couple of mouthfuls of half-rotten meat he'd scrounged for his last meal. The farms had little to spare. Not after the Skulls had taken their cut. Greedy fuckers they were, too – worse than the Shulka had been. Now the stray cats and dogs were mostly gone, it'd be the rats' turn next.

However, Dren wasn't eating anytime soon so he focused on the Skulls instead, let that hatred fill him up. The rats could wait.

He checked his weapons again: a curved knife tucked behind

the back of his belt beneath his coat, and a nasty sliver of a blade in his boot. Possession of either would see him hanged but Dren didn't care. What were two more crimes added to the long list of things he'd already done? They could only kill him once. And they'd have to catch him first before they could do that.

The sun dropped lower. Nearly time. If Falsa's information proved to be good ... He glanced over at her. He could tell she was thinking the same thing. Probably saying a few prayers, hoping she'd not wasted anyone's time. And so she should. Dren would be pissed off if this was all for nothing.

He eased himself up and moved in a crouch to the edge of the roof. He took his time, doing nothing that would draw any attention from the ground or the sky. He wasn't scared of much, but those winged Daijaku bastards got him nervous.

He peered down at the street. Empty. Too close to the curfew even in this part of town for folks to still be out and about.

The Egril had claimed the district of Brixta. Their red flags fluttered from every rooftop and their headquarters was only three streets away on Monmouth Street. The Council House stood out as the tallest building, now a monument to the Skulls' control. It had once been a grand old building with its domes and turrets and all those bloody stone gargoyles. Now it was the place where innocents were tortured and killed.

It had taken time to fight back, but Dren had done it. The Skulls might have the numbers but Dren and his friends had the shadows and the night. They made sure the Egril paid a dear fucking price for every minute they remained on Jian soil – in his city.

They'd certainly done more damage than the Shulka had managed. So much for being the best warriors in the world. Dren was glad they were all dead. This was *his* war now.

The sound of laughter snapped Dren back to the present. You didn't hear much of that in Kiyosun any more. He peered over the ledge and there they were: three of them, just as Falsa promised. He gave her a smile, gestured for her to join him. She was shaking but didn't hesitate. *Maybe she's got some bones after all.*

He put a finger to his lips and pointed. The men were Egril, all blond hair and square jaws with an air of superiority that made killing them so enjoyable. They wore half-masks, but they were definitely soldiers. Off duty and out of armour. Still armed with those bloody curved scimitars, though. No Egril soldier went unarmed in Kiyosun. They might have won the invasion, but they hadn't won the occupation. And they never would. Not if Dren had any say in things.

He checked the skies again. Better safe than dead, as they say. Nothing. He smiled. Time to kill.

The soldiers strolled along the street as if it was just an ordinary evening anywhere in the world. Three friends out for a good time.

The soldiers took a table outside Old Man Hasster's tavern and moved their seats so they had a good view of the street, being careful like good little soldiers. Bad luck for them, they didn't have the sense to look up.

They shouted at a pair of women walking past in the opposite direction, throwing out lewd comments and invitations to join them. The girls shied away, visibly shaken, and Dren was happy to see them walk on, chased by more insults from the Skulls.

Hasster hurried out, making a fuss over them, lighting candles for the table, giving it a good wipe, all but bowing to the bastards and kissing their arses before scurrying back inside to get their drinks. It was disgusting. Dren was glad Sasha was no longer alive. Had she still been working there, Hasster would've tried to get her whoring for the enemy without a second thought.

But Sasha wasn't there and Dren didn't want to think about her. He didn't like to think about what might've been. He wouldn't see her smile again or share a joke with her. She'd died that night when other worthless fuckers had lived.

Ten minutes later, the second part of Falsa's information came good. Three girls appeared and joined the soldiers. Good Jian girls who should've known better. Dren could feel his temper rise. Drinks were brought out and soon everyone was laughing and joking like they didn't have a care in the world. The girls even attempted to speak Egril. All grunts and growls. A pig's tongue. *What whores*. Dren's anger flared. He hated collaborators as much as he hated the Skulls. Maybe more. You didn't see the

Skulls betray their own kind, after all. And yet, Jian girls seemed more than happy to open their legs for a free meal.

Dren had seen enough. Signalling for Falsa to follow, he ran over to the other side of the roof and clambered down the ladder to the alley below where Quist waited with Lia. His soldiers. Dressed in rags, armed only with their fury. Lia held the baby, all wrapped up and out of sight.

'They're here,' said Falsa before she'd got her feet on the ground.

Dren squeezed her shoulder. 'As you said they would be.'

'So, we're on.' Quist was fifteen, all thin and wiry. Any fat had long dropped off him. Hair cut down to the scalp like Dren's. The boy was calm, but then again, this wasn't his first time. Quist was Dren's right hand, his cousin, his best mate, and a mad-dog killer. Dren bloody loved him.

Dren nodded. 'We're on.'

All three turned to Lia. She was silent. No excitement in her eyes. No calmness in her manner. She hugged the bundle of rags tighter to her chest and shuffled her feet. Twitching. It was no surprise. Lia was older than the rest of them, but she had the hardest job to do. The impossible job.

'Are you okay?' asked Dren.

Lia looked away and chewed on her lip to stop it quivering. 'I don't know.'

'You can't back out now—' Falsa jabbed a finger at Lia but Dren stepped in, holding up a hand. Now wasn't the time to get emotional.

Dren turned Lia's chin so their eyes met. 'You can do this.' He kept his voice soft, reassuring. 'Best not to think too much about it. Just be quick. Walk up to the table. Say you need money for food for the baby.'

'I'm scared.'

Dren leaned in. 'It's okay to be scared. I'd be amazed if you weren't. There's not been a day since the Egril invaded that I haven't been petrified.'

'How do you do it? How do you keep on?' Lia's voice quivered and cracked.

'My hate is stronger than my fear. Remember what these bastards did to your family. To your husband.' He wiped a tear from her cheek. 'To you.'

That got a nod from Lia. She sniffed her tears back.

Dren kept his voice calm and quiet but firm. 'Jia was an amazing country once. Before they came. Everyone had food. Homes. The Shulka were a pain in the arse but we were used to them. Then the Egril turned up, killing and raping, stealing and destroying. And now all we do is bury our loved ones and watch everyone starve and suffer. That's no way to live.'

'I know, but—'

'There are no buts. We have to do this. We have to make them realise that there will be no victory in Kiyosun. After what they've done ... All because they want us to worship their fucking God. It's not right.'

Lia dropped her head and nodded.

'I'd go do it myself, but I'd never get close enough. They see me and they'll know I'm trouble. Same with Quist. But you ... All they'll see is a mother with a hungry baby.'

She looked at the bundle in her arms and there was no stopping the tears this time. 'My baby ...'

'Think of your baby,' said Dren. 'Those bastards stopped her from having the life she was meant to have.'

'I'll do it,' said Lia.

Dren didn't wait. He took her hand in his and turned it over. His knife flashed out, quick as you like. A kiss of a cut. A drop of blood.

Lia bit her lip. They watched her blood seep out.

'Good girl,' said Dren. 'Now, best get it done.'

'Come on,' said Quist. He wrapped his arm around Lia's shoulder. 'I'll walk you to the corner.'

She checked the bundle in her arms again. Sniffed again. Pressed her hand against her chest to hide the cut. Quist looked worried but Dren could see she was going to do it. *Thank fuck for that. Better she does it of her own free will than be coerced.* 'I'm proud of you, Lia. May Xin reunite you with your family in the next world.' Dren didn't believe in that religious claptrap.

Jian Gods, the Egril God – as far as he was concerned, it was all a load of shit, but he knew the words made people feel better, especially now.

'Thank you, Dren.'

Dren gave her a final kiss and then Quist led her away.

Falsa bounced up and down next to him. 'I can't believe it. I can't fucking believe it. I thought she'd cracked. No way did I think she was going to do it. No way.'

'Have some respect,' said Dren, with a look that told her exactly what he'd do if she didn't shut the fuck up. The girl got the message.

'Sorry.' Her excitement was gone, replaced by a fear of her own. A fear of Dren. *Good.*

He shook his annoyance away. She'd learn. More blood under her fingertips would help. 'It's okay. It's just ... none of this is easy. You gave us great information, but if the Egril had found out, they'd have killed you for it. They'd kill all of us for knowing it. Not quickly, either. So, it's okay to be scared or have second thoughts. That's how we stay free.'

'I'll do better.'

'Of course you will.'

Quist ran back to join them. 'She's on her way.'

Without a word, Dren began to climb back up to the roof. The others followed.

'Hey, Dren!' Quist called.

'What?'

'Isn't it your birthday today?'

Dren stopped. So it was. He was sixteen.

10

Hasster

Kiyosun

Hasster pushed his way through the swing doors into the kitchen, empty plates balanced in both hands. His wife, his precious Ara, was scrubbing a pot by the window. 'They want more food.'

The pot slipped but Ara caught it, caught herself. 'There's not much left, only—'

'Ours. I know.' Hasster put down the plates and wiped his brow. By the Four Gods, he was sweating like a madman. His heart raced. 'Keep a small bit for us. So Jonas has something to eat, at least. We'll have to give them the rest.'

'Will they pay us for what they've eaten, at least?'

He glanced towards the doors, sick to his stomach. 'I doubt it.'

'But how will we get more supplies? They can't do this to us.'

'Can't?' Hasster laughed. Better to laugh than to cry. 'They can. They do. It's we who can't. We who have to make do.'

'Tell them there's no more. They'll understand. The whole city's on rationing.' The words spewed out, but he could tell even Ara didn't believe what she was saying. 'Tell them no.'

'And they'll kill me if I do. Or kill you. Or – may Alo above protect him – Jonas.'

'Not our son,' replied Ara, her voice breaking. They both looked up to the ceiling, as if they could see through it to where their beautiful boy slept.

'You know they would. Without a moment's hesitation. Or they'd take us to wherever the disappeared go.'

'The disappeared?' Ara slumped, defeated. 'Tell them the food will be with them in ten minutes.'

'I will.' Hasster turned to leave, feeling helpless, wanting to throw up.

'Give them another bottle of wine,' Ara called after him as she set to work once more.

Hasster paused by the swing doors. Took a deep breath. He wished he was as strong as his wife. 'I will. And pray they choke on it,' he whispered under his breath. One last wipe of his brow, then he found his smile again and stepped back into the tavern.

It wasn't a big place. A city as crowded as Kiyosun didn't allow for much room, but it was enough. Enough for him to be proud that it was his. He didn't care that it was run-down, or that the furniture had seen better days. It was his. Hasster had hoped that one day he'd be able to pass the inn on to his son, but not now. All because of the soldiers outside. No locals drank there any more because it was seen as an Egril inn, and once all the food and wine were gone, Hasster wouldn't even have that business. His tavern was ruined.

At least Ara and Jonas were safe. They were the only things that mattered now. Keeping them alive. One day at a time. He would worry about tomorrow when it came. There was nothing else he could do.

He picked up another bottle of wine. The Egril could have the rotgut now they were too drunk to know any better. The few remaining quality vintages, bought from Meigore back when ships actually came to Kiyosun to trade, were for when he really needed to barter his way out of trouble.

'My friends!' Hasster swept his arms wide as he walked outside, projecting joy he didn't feel. 'Ten minutes. My good wife promises she'll have your food ready in just ten minutes.'

'Thank you, Hasster,' said the soldier to the left, with a girl on his lap and his hand up her skirt. 'You treat your customers well.' The white mask covered the top half of his face, but it didn't hide the lust in his eyes.

'That's what I'm famous for,' Hasster replied, filling their tankards, trying to ignore the second soldier as he forced his tongue down his girl's throat, smothering her cries. Thank Alo, the Precious One, Hasster only had the one son, and that dear Ara was too old for the Egril's attention.

The third soldier, younger than the others and fresh-faced, at least had the decency to look embarrassed by his friends' behaviour. His girl sat by his side, grateful that she wasn't being mauled, too. The soldier put his hand over his tankard before Hasster could pour him more wine. 'I'm fine.'

The second soldier broke away from his energetic kissing. He shouted at his comrade in their own language, stabbing his finger towards the boy. Hasster didn't understand a word and was glad of it. The girl on his lap tried to stand up, but he yanked her back down and shouted some more.

The third soldier removed his hand and Hasster filled his tankard, blushing with shame.

He saw the girl approaching when he straightened up. Heading straight towards them. Crazy to be out so close to curfew. Especially with a baby in her arms. 'Can I help you?' he called and stepped around the table. Better to keep her away from the soldiers.

'I need money. Money for my baby.' Her face glistened in the lamplight, wet from all her tears. 'She needs to eat.'

'I'm sorry,' replied Hasster, holding up both hands. 'I think you should go home. It's late.'

'My baby needs to eat.' The girl didn't slow down, didn't look at Hasster. Her eyes were locked on the soldiers. She spoke only to them. 'Just an ecu.'

Hasster tried to catch her but she swerved past him. 'Please, miss,' he begged. 'Don't disturb my customers.'

The girl reached the table. 'Please. Just some money. Anything. My baby is hungry.'

'Piss off,' said the first soldier.

She held out her hand but the second swatted it away. 'Fuck off back to your slum.'

'Please, miss,' said the third, rising from his seat.

'I'm sorry, sirs,' said Hasster. He grabbed the girl's shoulders, tried to guide her away from the soldiers. 'I'll take her inside.

Nothing to bother yourselves with.' He pushed the girl, but she was stronger than she appeared and he only managed to turn her head so their eyes met.

Hasster's blood turned cold. She was no beggar. Then he saw her bloodied hand. 'Please. No. My family is inside—'

The girl thrust her hand into the bundle she held.

And the world exploded.

11

Tinnstra

Aisair

Tinnstra woke up with a hand pressed against her face, smothering her cry. Someone was in her bedroom.

A face leaned in. Beris, her brother. Her dead brother.

'Don't shout,' he said. 'It's me.' He paused for a moment, making sure she was calm before withdrawing his hand.

Tinnstra scuttled back until she was pressed up against the headboard with the sheet pulled up to her neck, as if that would protect her somehow from the ghost before her.

'Beris?' It was a stupid question but the only one she could ask. It was obviously him. It had been nearly a year since she'd last seen him and six months since he'd died, but he hadn't changed. He was still big and tall and looked so much like their father. Like the perfect Shulka warrior.

Beris sat down on the bed, grinned. 'Tinn, it's good to see you.'

Tinnstra stared at him. She wanted to scream but lacked the courage. 'You're dead. You died in the invasion.'

A little shake of his head.

'You died in the invasion, fighting the Egril at Gundan.'

'I got away.'

'No. You're dead.'

Beris took her hand and rubbed it gently. His touch was warm and she could feel the callouses from years of combat training. He was real. He was alive. 'I escaped. I've been in hiding since the surrender.'

Hope flared in her heart. 'What about Mother and Father? Jonas? Somon?'

'I'm sorry,' replied Beris. 'As far as I know, I'm the only one who survived.'

'By the Four Gods. May Xin protect them all,' sobbed Tinnstra. She wrapped herself around him as best she could – he was so much bigger than her. Stronger. She held him tight, feeling his heart beat, his chest rise and fall. She cried into the crook of his neck, just as she had when she was a child. She didn't know what else to say. Her brother was *alive*.

'Hey, Tinn. It's okay,' he whispered in her ear. 'I'm here.' He stroked her hair and let her cry.

They eventually moved to the living area. Tinnstra lit one of her last candles and heated up a small pot of water. Beris watched her silently, this new life of hers. It was a cold night and her fire was barely able to boil the water, let alone warm the room. She hesitated, and then added the last of her tea to the pot. Beris was worth it. A lack of tea would soon be the least of her problems, anyway. She looked over at him, still unsure whether to trust her own eyes. 'How did you find me?'

'Some Shulka were hiding out in a house on Ester Street,' replied Beris. 'One of them saw you a few weeks ago, recognised you, followed you here. They passed me your address when I arrived in Aisair.'

Tinnstra's breath caught and nausea rose in her stomach. 'I was near there yesterday. I … They …'

'I know,' said Beris. 'I know what happened.'

The fear hit her. 'They know where I live? They'll talk … They'll tell …' She looked to the door as if the Skulls were about to kick it in. How could she have been so careless? To be followed and not notice? She would move tonight. It wasn't safe.

'Don't worry,' said Beris, sensing her panic. 'Only one of them knew and he wasn't captured.'

'Oh.' His words did not comfort her. Danger had found her again. Her own brother had brought it to her home. She remembered the dead woman in the abandoned house. *That could be me. How long do I have before they come? Should I run now? Dear Gods, what should I do?*

95

Beris watched her, smiling as if everything was all right with the world. But it wasn't. Not now. She finished making the tea with shaking hands and gestured to the small table in the corner. 'Please, sit down.'

Beris froze, suddenly uncomfortable. 'You have a statue of Kage.'

Tinnstra had forgotten the small idol in the centre of the table. Kage. The Egril God and master of the Great Darkness. An ugly God for a vicious race. It looked more like a monster than a man. 'I don't believe, if that's what you think ... It's just ...' She glanced at the door, feeling guilty, feeling scared. 'The Egril ... You know they make us worship him and ... if anyone comes here, I want them to believe that I believe ...' She took a deep breath, picked it up and placed it on a shelf.

'It's okay, Tinn. I understand,' said Beris.

'I didn't want to give them any excuse—'

'Tinn, it's okay. Sit down. Drink some tea.'

'I—' She stopped herself. Somehow, Beris made her desire to survive feel like a bad thing, a selfish thing.

They sat together, their shoulders touching. It was still difficult to accept he was alive and not some dream she'd wake from. 'I've missed you so much.'

'I've missed you, too,' replied Beris. 'I wish I could've come and seen you sooner.'

'Where've you been? What've you been doing?'

'After Gundan fell, a few of us managed to get away. We hid in the mountains outside Selto. We thought we'd rejoin our clans and continue to fight, but the Egril have these creatures called Tonin – they were opening gates up everywhere, moving whole regiments wherever they wanted. We never had a chance. The whole country fell in eight days. *Eight* days.'

'I didn't think there such monsters in the world,' said Tinnstra.

'None of us did. We were too arrogant. We thought we were invincible. We'd beaten the Egril every time they'd come at us before.' He poured tea into their cups. 'And after we surrendered, we were stupid enough to believe no one else would die. We were wrong about that, too.'

'So, it's not just in Aisair ...'

'It's across all of Jia. They're not giving us a chance to regroup. They came for the rest of Aasgod's mages first and anyone else with potential. The city leaders who didn't agree to work for the bastards were the next to disappear, then any able-bodied man the Egril thought could pose a threat of any kind. After that, it was the priests, the teachers. It just goes on. Every day they find an excuse to grab someone else. We don't know if they're executing them all or taking them away somewhere. We don't know anything.'

'They've been hanging a lot of people in the city square. Every day. And I've heard stories ...' *Torture. Mutilation.*

'More people are disappearing than we can keep track of. The prisons are full, but even so, the numbers don't match up – we have no idea what they're doing with them.'

'I wish they'd left us alone.'

'They say it's because we worship the wrong Gods.' Beris tilted his head towards the idol on her shelf. 'Raaku claims he's descended from Kage, and he's conquering the world to cast out all the False Gods.'

'Is it true?' She glanced at the statue, nervous. She'd been to Kage's temple, listened to the priests, begged for her own Gods' understanding and forgiveness while she was there. Had she been wrong?

'I don't know. Maybe it is, maybe it isn't. He's getting his power from somewhere. And it sure doesn't feel like our Gods are looking after us right now, does it?'

Tinnstra shivered. She didn't want to think about any of it. Her imagination was more than capable of making everything worse. 'How long have you been back? Why didn't you let me know you were alive?'

'I've been here for a few weeks but it wasn't safe to get in contact. I didn't want to give anyone an excuse to snatch you. Someone could've told them who you are – who your family was. Seeing me would've been the final straw.'

'I'm no threat to them. I follow the rules. I go to the temple. I don't go out after curfew.'

'You're the daughter of Grim Dagen, one of the most famous

Shulka warriors Jia has ever known. That's enough to make someone fear you.'

'People don't know that's who I am.' Tinnstra hid her sad smile by looking down into her tea. She couldn't meet Beris's eyes. She couldn't tell him the truth. How she'd actually been happy not to have her father's name weighing heavily on her shoulders. The truth felt too much like betrayal.

'Father used to say you were the most gifted of all of us with a sword,' said Beris, trying to make her feel better. 'He was proud of you.'

'I'm not a fighter like he was. Like you are. I'm sorry, but I'm not.' Should she tell him the truth? That she was the disgrace in the family? The one who'd got kicked out of the Kotege? The coward amongst heroes? *No, I'm not brave enough for that.*

'Do you still practise Shulikan?'

'Every morning when I wake up. Just like Father taught us. Not with an actual sword, though. No one has weapons now.' She sipped her tea. 'I don't know why I bother. It's not like I'll ever fight anyone, but ... It helps me feel close to him. I can hear him as I go through my positions, correcting my stance or scolding me when I get things wrong. He was always so patient.'

Beris smiled. 'Only because you were so good at it all. He used to be tougher with me, Jonas and Somon. We'd be covered in bruises by the end of our sessions.'

'I never saw it like that. I thought he didn't believe I was good enough to push me harder.'

'We were all jealous of your talent, Tinn.'

'It never felt that way to me.' Tinnstra finally looked up and met his eyes. She didn't want to be talking about any of this. It still hurt too much. She could still hear General Harka – her own godfather – tell her that she was nothing. He'd been right, too. 'I was never brave like you. I never will be.'

'Tinn.' Beris's voice was soft but there was something in it that frightened the life out of Tinnstra. 'I need you to be brave now. I need your help.'

'What do you mean?' Already the dread was building. She wasn't going to like what he had to say.

'I'm Hanran, Tinn.'

'No.' Tinnstra felt sick. Unsafe. 'Don't say any more. I don't want to know any more.'

'I am. The Hanran are everywhere. In every city. Growing by the day. Some of us are Shulka. Some of us are just ordinary people who want to fight back against the Egril. People like you.'

'Not like me. I wouldn't do such a thing. The Egril are here. They won. They're in charge. Fighting them is suicide.'

'It's not, believe me. It's difficult and dangerous but not impossible. We will win. Something's happening tomorrow that will change the war. Change everything.'

'Change the war?' Tinnstra shook her head. It was all madness. What didn't Beris understand? 'There is no war. We surrendered. It's over.'

'Nothing's over,' said Beris. 'The war's only just begun. And today ... I can't tell you any more, but I need you to come with me. Now.'

'No. This has nothing to do with me.' Tinnstra pushed her chair away from the table. She couldn't bear being so close to Beris. She wished he hadn't come back. Wished he'd stayed dead. 'Even if I could help, it's still night. The curfew is still in effect. We're not allowed out. If we get caught, the Skulls will hang us.'

'We'll avoid any patrols. We'll be safe.' He reached out for her hand, but she kept it tight against her chest.

'No,' said Tinnstra again. She stood up and turned her back on Beris. She didn't want to see the disappointment in his eyes as she let him down again. But she was the coward, the frightened one. He wouldn't have asked if he knew. 'You can stay here for the rest of the night, but it's probably best if you leave once the sun's up.'

'Tinn, you know I wouldn't ask if I had any other choice, but there are lives at stake here.'

'I don't want mine to be one of them.'

Beris got up and walked over to her. Put his hands on her shoulders. 'No one's going to be safe. Not even you, hiding away in this room for the next how many years. They'll come for us all eventually.'

Tears ran down Tinnstra's cheeks. 'I'm not a fighter. I'm not like the rest of you.'

'I don't need you to fight. I need you to carry something for me – that's all. It'll be easy. I promise. You'll be safe.'

Tinnstra put a hand over one of his. Beris always made the world a better place. He always managed to banish the demons lurking in the shadows of her mind. When she was younger, she'd look at him, look at the others, and wonder how she could be a part of the family when she was so different. If only she had a fraction of Beris's courage. 'You don't know what happened at the Kotege. If you did, you wouldn't ask for my help.'

'I heard about the arena. You're not the first to fail that test.'

He knew. Dear Gods, he knew. Shame burned her cheeks. She dropped her head. 'I was the only one of Father's children to run away. The only one to have a whole stadium laugh at her.'

'Please, Tinn. I need you.'

Tinnstra closed her eyes. 'There must be someone else.'

'There isn't. If you do this, then we have a chance to get rid of the Egril. You won't have to hide here, worrying how you're going to eat or stay warm or being scared every time someone knocks on the door. Things can go back to the way they were. Before the monsters walked the streets.'

By the Four Gods. Tinnstra wanted to be sick. She wanted to get back into bed and pull the covers over her head until this whole nightmare was over.

'Please,' said Beris. 'Then I'll leave you alone.'

'I want to but I'm scared, Beris.'

'I'll look after you. I promise. Nothing will happen to you.'

It was madness. She had a life. She was safe. She should tell him to leave. Then she remembered a woman who had no life, rotting in an abandoned house, dead for no reason except she was born in a country that worshipped the wrong Gods. She remembered her friends, slaughtered at her school, all their potential snuffed out in an instant. And then there were her mother and father, her brothers. Didn't they all deserve vengeance?

Tinnstra sighed. 'I'll do it.'

DAY THREE

12

Tinnstra

Aisair

'The Skulls will hang us,' whispered Tinnstra. 'And if we're lucky, that's all they'll do.' She knew she was panicking but couldn't do anything about it. Fear was all she had. She wanted to turn back, go home, forget all about her brother and his mad plans. But returning home would be just as dangerous.

'No one's going to die today,' replied Beris. They crouched in an alley off Basket Street, tucked in the shadows. They'd been there for nearly an hour, waiting for a signal. For her, it had been hell. An hour in the bitter cold, hiding amongst the refuse, trying not to gag on the stench, jumping at the slightest noise, petrified that a Skull patrol would find them, cursing her brother for getting her into this mess.

Beris, on the other hand, appeared calm as a man could be, undisturbed by the smell, the cold or the Skulls.

There was a glimmer of light in the pre-dawn sky as the black turned bruised blue, but daybreak was still too far away for her liking. She warmed her hands under her armpits and wondered for the thousandth time why she'd agreed. 'I still don't understand. I'm not a Shulka.'

'I need you because you're *not* a Shulka. I can't do this without you.' Beris squeezed her hand. 'Now be quiet. It's nearly time to move.'

They were thirty minutes' walk from Tinnstra's home, but they might as well have been in another world. Basket Street and the surrounding roads famously housed rich merchants and minor nobility. From what she could tell, somehow not one had suffered in the invasion. No bombs had fallen to ruin their beautiful facades or destroy the lives within. She couldn't think of too many neighbourhoods that could say the same. However, Tinnstra doubted that even the distinguished residents of these houses had been left unscathed. The Egril purges afterwards had affected everyone. Not even the rich escaped the Skulls' notice. *A good neighbourhood to search later – if I don't get arrested now.*

A flash of light broke the darkness for a heartbeat. 'Come on.' Beris was off at a sprint before she could reply.

Tinnstra hesitated. She'd rather stay where she was, out of sight and as safe as she could be, and wait for curfew to be over. But even she knew that wasn't an option. After checking the street was still empty, she forced herself to stand and ran after Beris.

He was waiting for her by a door halfway down the street. When she reached his side, he rapped on the door – once, then twice in quick succession, paused then knocked once more. A crack opened, just wide enough for a pair of eyes to see who was there.

'We are the dead,' said a man's voice in hushed tones.

'Who face the night,' replied her brother, finishing the line from the Shulka prayer.

The door opened and Tinnstra followed her brother inside. It closed behind her and she found herself in darkness once more, her fear pressing down on her, making it hard to breathe.

Something cold touched her throat. A knife. A hand clamped across her mouth, stifling any noise. 'Who's this? You were supposed to come with Gera.'

Beris turned around. His face hardened when he saw the knife at Tinnstra's throat. 'Easy, Pet'r. Put the knife down. She's my sister. She's helping me out. I cleared it with Harka.'

The knife bit into her skin. Her legs went weak.

'No one told me,' said the man, sounding scared.

'The Skulls picked up Gera,' replied Beris, 'so we need another girl for the checkpoints. Now put the knife down. I won't ask you again.'

Tears welled up in Tinnstra's eyes. She was going to die. Her throat cut open by someone on her own side. She quivered and shook. She didn't want to die.

Then the hand and the knife were gone and Tinnstra's legs gave way. Beris rushed over, held her upright. 'By the Four Gods, Pet'r,' he hissed. 'Do you think I'd bring just anyone along?'

Pet'r stepped away, slipping the knife behind his back and out of sight. 'There's too much at stake to be taking any chances. The Skulls are fucking everywhere. They know what we're doing before we do.' He flicked his eyes over Tinnstra and she could tell he didn't like what he saw. 'She got the bones to do this?'

'Yeah, she has,' said Beris. Tinnstra knew he was the only one in the room who thought that.

'Your funeral,' said Pet'r. Then a worried expression clouded his face. 'Did Gera know about this place?'

'No,' said Beris. 'Only me.'

'Thank the Gods for that. Come on, he's expecting you.' The man headed upstairs without waiting for them.

'He has a knife,' said Tinnstra. 'If the Skulls come here, we'll all hang.'

'If the Skulls come here, we'll hang anyway. A weapon's the least of our crimes.'

'I can't do this, Beris,' said Tinnstra. 'I want to go home. I'm not the right person for this.'

'Don't worry. Everything will be fine. We'll be gone soon enough.'

Tinnstra followed Beris to the third floor, where light spilled into the hallway through a bedroom doorway. Inside, Tinnstra's eyes took a moment to adjust to the bright illumination. It was a cramped space with shuttered windows, a single bed in the corner on one side, a night table next to it.

A small man was bent over a desk in one corner of the room. He didn't look up as they entered, engrossed in his work. He had a pair of magnifying glasses perched on the end of his nose and a quill in his ink-stained hand, and the desk was surrounded by letters. He was copying the text from one of them onto blank parchment.

'The couriers are here,' said Pet'r.

'Nearly done,' he replied. 'Take a seat if you want.'

Neither Beris nor Pet'r moved, so Tinnstra followed suit despite wanting to collapse onto the bed. Taking a step closer, she saw that he was copying an Egril letter of travel, giving the bearer permission to move from one part of Jia to another. *By the Four Gods, no. This is treason. If the Skulls find out, they won't just hang us. There'll be torture – and worse.*

She looked over at her brother, panicking, but he signalled her to stay quiet. *How can he be so calm?* A surge of anger rose then, almost enough to displace the fear. *How can he do this to me? I was safe before he came back. I had a life. He's killed me now. My own brother.*

'Finished!' said the man. He blew over the ink to dry it and waved the paper back and forth.

'May I have a look?' asked Beris, stepping forward.

The man beamed with pride. 'Certainly.' He handed over two sheets of paper. 'The original letter and the forgery.'

Beris held them side by side as he examined them. 'They look identical.'

'Of course they do! What would be the point if they didn't?' The man leaned back in his chair. 'I'd hardly be able to call myself the best forger in all of Jia if that were the case.'

Beris passed the letter to Pet'r, smiling. 'It's perfect.'

'And the others?' asked Pet'r.

'All as promised,' replied the forger. He gathered the papers together then spread them all out in a single line. Seven forged travel permits.

Pet'r returned the last one to the forger. 'Well done, old man. Well done indeed.'

'My pleasure.' The man placed it alongside the others. 'Just need to apply the seals.' The man rummaged around the desk for something, then stood up and patted his pockets. 'Now, where did I put it? Ah, yes,' he said as he reached his waistcoat pocket. He hooked his finger in, pulled out a gold ring and smiled at the others. 'Wouldn't have done to lose this. Not after what we had to do to get it.'

He held a red wax stick over a candle. As it warmed up, it dripped onto the first letter at the bottom, next to a signature. The man then pressed the ring down into the wax. He repeated the process until they'd all been stamped. 'You'll be able to get whoever you want past any Egril checkpoint now. No Skull will question this.' He held up the ring. 'This is the sigil of the office of Emperor Raaku himself. Don't ask me where I got it.' The ring disappeared back into his waistcoat pocket.

Beris crossed the room in a couple of strides and shook the man's hand. 'I don't know how to thank you.'

'Just get the king to safety,' replied the old man. 'That's all the thanks I need.'

The words stunned Tinnstra. 'The king?' She looked from Beris to Pet'r to the old man and back again. 'Cariin? Cariin the Gentle?' As if there was another king of Jia ... Cariin had only been king for five or six years since his father King Roxan died, but he was as well loved as Roxan the Wise, his family adored. He'd promised the start of a new golden age of poetry and art and science. It all sounded wonderful before the Egril showed them how stupid that was.

'We're going to free him and his family,' said Beris.

'No.' This was getting worse by the second – weapons, forged papers and now an attempt to rescue the king?

'We'll talk downstairs,' said Beris, grabbing her hand.

'What have you dragged me into?' said Tinnstra when they were back in the living room. 'King Cariin and his family are locked up in Aisair Castle. The Skulls will never let them out, forged papers or not.'

'Do you know who Aasgod is?' asked her brother.

Tinnstra nodded, took a deep breath. 'I met him once with Father.'

'He fled across the channel to Meigore after the invasion but he's back now. The queen's brother is Sitos, the King of Meigore, and he's promised Aasgod that if we can get Cariin, his sister and their children to safety, he'll help us fight the Egril.'

'Why would he do that?' asked Tinnstra. 'If the royal family is safe, why would Sitos care what happens to Jia?'

'Because he's not stupid,' replied Beris. 'Once the Hanran are destroyed in Jia, Sitos knows the Egril will conquer Meigore next. Better to fight them here in Jia than in Meigore.'

'But how are we going to free Cariin?'

Beris smiled. 'We don't have to do anything. Aasgod is going to break Cariin and his family out of the castle tonight. Our task is to meet them at a safe house somewhere in the city and give them the letters. Others will then help them get away.' Beris paused, let his words sink in. 'That's it. You can go straight home afterwards. No one will know you've helped.'

Tinnstra pulled a chair over and sat down, so very tired. 'But why do you have to get involved? Why do you have to get *me* involved?'

'Because I'm a Shulka and I will be until the day I die. Because I can't sit around while innocents are murdered. I took an oath to protect my king and my country, and that's what I'll do.' Fire burned in Beris's eyes, an utter conviction that what he was doing was right and the belief that he would succeed.

We are so very different, Tinnstra thought. 'I didn't take the same vows. You should've told me what you're planning to do.'

'You would have said no if I'd told you.'

Anger flared inside Tinnstra. 'With good reason. This is suicide.'

'It's not. Trust me,' replied Beris.

'Why not just do it on your own? Why do you need me at all? I'm not a Shulka. I'm not a Hanran. I'm not brave like you. I'm not like any of you.' Tinnstra's head dropped. All the wishing in the world couldn't change who she was. A coward.

Beris touched her cheek. 'I need you because you're not like me. The Skulls see me and recognise a Shulka. They always search me. If I carry the letters, they'll find them. But you don't look like a threat. You look like a scared girl. They'll never search you.'

Tinnstra stared her brother in the eye. 'But what if they do?'

'I told you – I'll protect you. I promise.'

13

Jax

Kiyosun

Jax peered through the window again, fingers rapping against the glass as though he could call the sun to rise faster, and with it an end to the curfew. It should've been up already. He needed to be out there, investigating what had happened. He hated not knowing.

'Glaring out of the window every five minutes won't help.' His son, Kaine, sat in his wheelchair with that patient smile of his. A familiar pang of guilt hit Jax. If he'd not been so confident up at Gundan, if he'd been better prepared . . .

He let the curtain drop, feeling foolish, and scratched the stump where his right arm used to be. 'I know. It's just . . . I'm going mad, trapped in here. The bomb went off before bloody curfew . . .' Ten hours stuck in a small room at the back of a carpet shop that didn't even sell carpets any more. He was the second-highest ranking officer in the Shulka army, the leader of the Hanran in Kiyosun, and yet he'd never felt so helpless in his life.

'We don't know it was a bomb,' said Kaine.

'What else could it be? We've heard enough of them by now.' Impatient, Jax glanced at the window. 'It has to be the kids. *Again*. Disobedient little shits.'

'You're not their general, Father – they're not Shulka. And they refused to join the Hanran. They have no clue about following orders.'

'Don't you think I know that?' Jax waved his stump at his son, his voice rising. 'This is the last thing we need. The last thing. I'll wring that little shit's neck when I next see him.'

'Dren and the others just want to fight.'

'And I don't? I want to get my sword and go out and gut as many of those faceless bastards as I can, but it's about winning the war, not cheap thrills and petty revenge.' Jax slumped down on a bench, forcing himself to be calm. 'They're just chaos and mayhem, lashing out whenever they can. They don't understand that there'll be consequences. More Skulls on the streets. Mass arrests. More hangings. We could end up losing everything because of that kid.'

Kaine wheeled himself over so he was next to his father and squeezed his hand. 'The Egril won't win. We won't let them.'

'I wish I could be as sure as you.'

'Once the king is safe—'

Jax held up a finger. '*Ssh*. Don't say another word.'

'They're not listening, Father. Not here.'

'How do you know what they can do? I don't. We didn't know they had bloody monsters that could open windows in the very air itself so their army could appear miles behind our defences. We had no idea their bastard Emperor Raaku had somehow got hold of thousands of demons to wreak havoc on us. We still don't know how he fucking did any of it. So how are you sure they can't listen to what we're saying right now? There could be a squad of Skulls on their way to arrest us.'

'Father, calm down. You're being paranoid. We'd already be in prison by now if they had that sort of power. We've done more than talk already and we're still free.'

'What was it Harka used to say? "Just because I'm paranoid, it doesn't mean they're *not* out to get me." He had the right idea.'

'The sun'll be up in a minute. Why don't we pray? We've not done that in a while. It'll do you good ... do both of us good.'

'It doesn't feel right any more. Not after what happened. Not now we're hiding like rats in a storm. What use are our oaths now?'

'Seems to me there's no better time.'

Jax looked at his son, proud of the man he'd become. Still strong despite everything. He was so much better than Jax. He had all his mother's best qualities and none of his worst. 'Very well.'

He knelt beside Kaine.

'We are the dead who serve all who live. We are the dead who fight. We are the dead who guard tomorrow.' The words filled the room. 'We are the dead who protect our land, our monarch, our clan.' The oath was a part of Jax, burned into his very soul, taught to him by his father and passed on to his son. A source of strength to them all. A secret prayer known only to the Shulka.

'We are the dead who stand in the light. We are the dead who face the night. We are the dead whom evil fears. We are the Shulka and we are the dead.' The Shulka. The best of the best, experts in all the martial arts. Each and every one of them taught to consider themselves already dead, their lives given to protect all those who lived in the blessed land of Jia from any and all threat. This core belief gave the Shulka their strength. A man who is already dead has no fear and can act without hesitation to vanquish even the most fearsome foe. For all the good it had done them when the Egril had invaded.

'We are the dead. We are the dead.' Their voices became one, giving the other strength. 'We are the dead. We are the dead.'

Jax tried to find the confidence he'd once had. When he was a warrior. A man. 'We are Shulka and we are the dead.' Jax closed his eyes, remembering the funeral pyres. They were the dead all right. So many fine soldiers lost ... How could they beat the Egril now when not even their best had been good enough?

'I think the sun's up, Father.'

Jax opened his eyes. A glimmer of light slipped under the curtain, marking the floor. 'Right.' He stood up, took his jacket off the peg and put it on. The right arm was already pinned so his stump slipped in easily. 'I'd better go and see what's happened.'

'Be careful, Father.'

'I always am.' He smiled at his son. 'Stay safe.'

'I'm not going anywhere.'

'Right.' He loosened his shoulders. 'Still don't like not carrying a sword.' He paused, then lifted his stump of an arm. 'I'm not used to being unarmed.' It wasn't the best joke, but the best Jax could manage.

His son had the grace to laugh all the same. 'Take your staff. They can't say an old man like you doesn't need one.'

Jax smiled. 'I love you, son. Your mother would be proud of you.'

Kaine waved him off. 'Get out of here before you embarrass yourself.'

Jax hesitated, was going to say more but stopped himself. Kaine was right. He was enough of a fool already. The boy knew how Jax felt about him. There was no need for any more words.

Staff in hand, he stepped out into the street and closed the door behind him. He paused for a moment, trying to find the courage the prayer hadn't rekindled. How was he supposed to lead a resistance against the Egril if he couldn't even keep a bunch of street urchins in line? They just saw an old, one-armed man who'd fucked up once already. He couldn't blame them for that. It was true.

He felt every one of his years pressing down on him. If only there was someone else who could take his place, he'd happily give up the responsibility. But the fact was, it was down to him. He sighed.

The sun had barely cleared the rooftops and yet the street was already busy. With food in limited supply, no one was willing to risk waiting to try and buy what little there was. People pushed past Jax to join the queue at the baker's, while others surged towards the market square for when the farmers arrived with a few vegetables to sell. Each day, the prices went up as supplies dwindled. It was not uncommon for fights to break out over a handful of carrots, even between people who'd known each other for years. Friendship had become a luxury few could afford. He watched their scared faces, avoiding eye contact. No one spoke. Everyone was too busy trying to survive.

It had turned colder over the past few days, though nothing like his months on duty at Gundan. Cold had taken on new meaning up there. Even in the throes of summer, it was bloody freezing. Jax had hated every moment, yet now, given half a chance, he'd happily go back, as long as he was there with his Shulka, behind the battlements, staring down on the enemy with both his bloody arms and Kaine back on his feet.

But no, he was in Kiyosun with only one arm and a crippled son. And the Skulls were here, too.

The Egril flags hanging from the buildings were a constant reminder. House owners flew them out of a desire for self-preservation rather than as a demonstration of loyalty to the invaders. Even so, Jax hated the sight of them. He'd love to rip them down and clear the whole city of them.

He cracked his neck from side to side, trying to get rid of the tension. Better to concentrate on important matters. Flags were just flags.

The central district, Risenn, hadn't suffered as much as its neighbour to the west, Toxten, but it hadn't emerged unscathed, either. The streets throughout Kiyosun were barely more than a cart-width across with terraced houses on either side, all showing scars from the fighting. The odd burned-out home gave the early morning sun an opportunity to reach the ground, but the rest of the street was still in shadow.

Jax hadn't walked far before he saw his first Egril of the day – a squad of four Skulls stationed on the corner of Houseman Street and Carsta Lane. He still couldn't believe the Egril were so well armed and armoured. He'd spent his life fighting leaderless tribes who only cared about raiding and raping south of the border. He'd never lost a battle against *those* barbarians. Then they turned up looking like a proper army with tactics and leadership and that fucking white armour of theirs. And with magic and demons. He still didn't understand how it'd happened. They must have been preparing for the invasion for years – decades – without the Shulka realising. The Jians should've had spies exploring the Egril lands. They should've questioned the refugees as they came south and gathered intelligence about what was happening north of the border. They should've restricted the numbers of Egril wandering into Jia without so much as a by your leave. They should've done anything other than just sit behind their high walls, feeling superior, feeling safe.

As a military man, he could only admire how well designed the Egril armour was, providing maximum protection while allowing almost total freedom of movement. Everything was in sections. The chest armour was made from a series of plates, little oblong-shaped pieces of steel linked by strips of leather. A direct strike against it might destroy a single plate but the rest would be unharmed. The armour wouldn't stop an arrow from a longbow at close range, but no one had those to hand any more.

Extra protection was provided by a neck curtain of jointed metal, while shoulder guards made from small plates laced together with silk braid allowed for ease of movement. Even the thighs were covered by a combination of chain mail and plates to keep the lower body safe. The armour made the soldiers far bulkier but they could fight unhindered.

Their helmets extended at the sides and back, overlapping the shoulders and neck, minimising weak spots, finished with a face mask shaped like a skull, designed to terrify the enemy.

And then there were their swords. The Egril used to fight with whatever they'd managed to steal – the odd stolen Shulka sword, or rusted, blunt hunks of metal that were part axe, part blade. They didn't care as long as it did the job. He remembered one battle when the barbarians had been armed with jawbones from some animal or other. But this lot? They had scimitars. Well-made long, curved blades that sliced open the Shulka like paper. And they knew how to use them. He'd not even noticed the loss of his arm at first. And only Alo knew why the blow to his face had grazed him rather than splitting his head in two. He scratched the scar. More days than not, he wished it had killed him. He'd rather have died than see his country fall to those scum.

Maybe Raaku really was the son of Kage. Maybe he was just the meanest bastard who had ever been born. Maybe if Cariin hadn't been so set on building his libraries, listening to his symphonies and contemplating his navel, he might've taken Aasgod's warnings more seriously. But then again, no one other than Aasgod had taken the Egril threat seriously. Jax certainly hadn't. They had Gundan and he believed the Egril would never get past it. It had stopped them for a thousand years, after all. The irony wasn't lost on him that they had literally opened the door to the bastards, allowing their 'refugees' to walk into Jia out of some kind of misplaced sympathy. But no, Cariin had to do the right thing and save them from persecution.

They had been so fucking arrogant and paid the price. Well, that wouldn't happen again. Not on Jax's watch. He'd never underestimate them again.

The Skulls watched him walk by and Jax leaned on his staff, exaggerating the stiffness in his limbs as he shuffled past.

As he neared the Brixta Quarter, the number of Skull patrols and checkpoints increased, just as he'd feared. The bombing had brought them out like cockroaches. Bags were searched. People patted down. Jax saw one man being taken away because he had a set of kitchen knives on him.

Jax hated the Skulls. Always had, always would. The urge rose again to attack them, spill some blood, save the cook from his fate, but he forced it down, glad he wasn't carrying his sword. Discipline won wars. Control. He had things to do. He moved on, cheeks burning with shame.

The bomb site was easy to find. Old Man Hasster's place was still smoking even though the fire had been put out. The Skulls kept everyone half a street away but Jax could see the devastation well enough.

Someone stopped next to him. 'Not a pretty sight, is it?'

Jax glanced out of the corner of his eye and returned his attention to the ruined inn. 'Hello, Monon.'

'Jax.' Monon was Shulka, lean, and still had the posture of a fighting man. And with all his limbs, he was doing better than Jax.

'Have you been here long?' asked Jax. The explosion had shredded the front of the building and taken out most of the first floor. The second floor looked close to collapse.

'Long enough.'

'How many died?'

'Ten. The bodies are over there. Three Egril soldiers. Four local girls. Hasster. His wife. And his son. The poor kid was asleep upstairs. Hopefully he didn't know anything about it. He was only four years old.'

Jax saw them then. The bodies lined up, burned beyond recognition. The Egril would give their own dead proper funerals but they'd just toss the Jians into the furnaces at the back of the Council House. 'Shit. Seven of ours just to kill three of theirs? Madness.'

'To be fair, one of the dead was most likely the bomber so I'm not sure she counts, but yeah ... it's fucked up. We shouldn't be doing the Egril's job for them.'

'Dren and his gang?'

'I don't know for sure but I reckon it was. It definitely wasn't one of ours gone rogue. We haven't got any bombs.'

'Something else we need to sort out.'

'Yeah, it's on the list.'

'The Skulls said what they'll do?'

Monon sighed. 'Not yet. But it'll be bad.'

'It always is.' Jax felt sick. This wasn't how wars were supposed to be fought. Where was the honour? 'Arrange another sit-down with Dren. Hopefully we can talk some sense into him this time. He can't carry on like this.'

'I'll see what I can do. I wouldn't put any money on it working, though. Dren would set the world on fire if he could be sure of killing a few Skulls.'

'Leave word at the shop when it's done.'

'I will.'

'Any progress getting someone inside the Council House?'

'Kara's hopeful.'

'Good. We've been blind in there for too long.' He glanced at Monon. 'We need to find out where they keep the Tonin. If we can, we've got a chance to remove one of the Egril's greatest advantages.'

'Even now?' asked Monon.

'Especially now.' Jax took one last look at the wreckage, shook his head at the waste of it all and turned to leave. 'It'll be better for us if they can't bring any reinforcements here.'

Monon held him back with a hand. 'The king and his family will be leaving soon. They'll be here in four days, all being well.'

'They have to be here then. The only reason the Meigorians

are willing to risk the crossing is because it's the night of the new moon. They won't come back if we miss the pick-up.'

'I know but it's damn tight.'

'The gate still secure?'

'Some of my lads are watching it. They've not seen any Skulls.'

Jax glanced at his friend. 'If we lose the gate, all hope's gone.'

Monon nodded. 'You can count on us.'

'When they come through, make sure you've got plenty of bodies to escort them here.'

'It's all organised. I've not told anyone who we're expecting. I'll save that surprise for when they turn up.'

'May the Four Gods look after us all.'

Jax walked off, leaning heavily on his staff, hating the fact they were relying on magic to make their plan work. The gates were scattered across Jia, hidden beneath secluded temples, and allowed people to travel instantly from one part of the country to another. Journeys that would take weeks or months by road could be made in seconds. It was old world magic and their existence was a closely guarded secret, even amongst the Shulka, and yet the Skulls had seized most of them after they invaded. No doubt, some traitorous little shit had helped them. But thank the Four Gods, they'd missed some. They'd missed the most important one.

He glanced up at the mountain overlooking the city. As long as that gate remained free, the Hanran had a chance.

14

Yas

Kiyosun

Ma had stayed at home with Ro. Yas didn't want the company as she made her way to work. There was too much to think about – too much to worry about. She yawned. Sleep hadn't come easy. Hadn't come at all, really. *Bloody Kara*.

How dare Kara ask her to spy? Yas hated the Egril, no doubt about it. She'd be more than happy to see the back of them, but she couldn't do this! She'd got beaten up while lighting a fire, for the Gods' sakes. She'd be dangling from the scaffold before she knew it.

She stopped when she smelled the smoke in the air. Her stomach lurched and she felt sick. On the street around her, everyone looked even more scared than usual. There'd been a fire in the night. Another bombing, no doubt. More dead. It felt like there was one every day now.

She wanted to turn back, go home, shut her door and forget about the world, but that wasn't an option. She didn't have the luxury of hiding away. She took a deep breath, ducked her head down and marched on, cursing her luck every step of the way.

A few streets away from the Council House, she saw the smoke. She had friends in that neighbourhood. Good friends. She dragged her feet the last few yards – as if that would help. Turned the corner and there it was – the bombed-out ruins of Old Man Hasster's tavern. The front gone, as if a giant hand had just clawed it away. A few people were milling about while the Skulls did their best to move them on. Bodies lay along the pavement. Ten of them, including a tiny one, *Hasster's son*, all black and charred.

Yas was barely aware of walking the last few streets to the Council House. She felt sick, sad, angry – a thousand emotions bombarded her.

As long as the Egril were in Jia, things would only get worse. No one was safe.

There were extra guards on duty at the gate. They were pissed off and took turns to search and grope her, cursing her at least a dozen times all the while. She closed her eyes and tried to ignore it, and thought of the money she needed. She could put up with anything if it meant little Ro got food in his belly. There was nothing she wouldn't do to keep him safe.

A final shove in the back pushed her through into the grounds.

Bets was by her side the moment Yas entered the kitchen. 'Wasn't sure if you'd turn up today. Not after what happened yesterday.' The cook examined her split lip and bruises. 'I'm hoping it looks worse than it is.'

It was as bad as it looked but there was no point saying anything. 'I'm okay. Thanks for the food.' Yas hadn't eaten a thing, just watched Ro and Ma tuck in.

'There'll be plenty more where that came from,' said Bets. 'Just keep your nose out of trouble today.' The cook spotted Arga coming through the far door. 'Hey! Come here.'

Arga scurried over. 'Yes, Cook?'

Bets locked her arm around Arga's neck and pulled her forward. 'I thought I told you to look after Yas yesterday?'

'I only left her for a minute to get the governor some wine.'

'What's the bloody rule? Eh?' Bets rubbed her knuckles into Arga's head. 'Never be on your own with them. Remember?'

'Aye. I do.'

'Don't bloody let it happen again.' Bets let go of Arga and the cleaner staggered upright, red-faced and pissed off.

'I won't.' Arga glared at Yas.

Yas mouthed, 'I'm sorry,' at her, but it didn't make a difference. In the changing room, the two girls dressed in silence.

By the stairwell going up to the ground floor, a squad of Skulls waited to go out on patrol, armoured up and checking weapons. 'Smile for me,' said a Skull as he spotted her. His accent was thick, which made the words sound even cruder, threatening.

Yas dropped her head as she tried to squeeze past.

A hand grabbed her backside, another cupped her breast. A Skull mask leered in her face. Yas's cheeks burned as she kept moving, pushing her way through the throng. Others joined in with cheers, shouting in their own tongue, laughing and grabbing at her.

A shout made the Skulls stop instantly. Another Skull marched towards them, shouting in Egril as he approached. They all stepped back, away from Yas and Arga, heads bowed.

The new soldier stopped in front of the two women. 'I must apologise for my men's behaviour,' he said.

Yas had no idea what to say so she said nothing. Arga did likewise.

'I am Polemarch Raxius,' he continued. 'If anyone troubles you again, tell them my name. We are here bringing the true faith to the fallen, not falling into disgrace ourselves. We are Egril, not animals.'

Still the women said nothing. Yas kept her eyes on her feet. They both knew you could never trust a Skull.

'Get on with your duties,' said Raxius after a few more moments' silence.

'Thank you, sir,' said Arga and they both stepped backwards, keeping their heads bowed.

Once they were inside the stairwell and out of the soldiers' sight, Yas slumped against the wall and took several deep breaths. Her hands shook as she brushed at her dress, trying to settle herself.

'Bloody monsters,' Arga hissed. She tried to adjust her dress but there was no hiding the rip in it. 'You all right?'

'I think so. I'm glad that Skull Raxius turned up. Who knows what could've happened otherwise.'

'Fuck him,' said Arga. 'He'll probably be hanging some poor fool in a few minutes.' She shook her head. 'What a way to earn a bloody living, eh?'

'I'm starting to think it's not the best job I could have.'

'Bet yer thinking you should've stayed at home with the kid.'

'Something like that,' said Yas.

Arga brushed the front of her dress one more time. 'Come on, let's get on with it.'

They started in the meeting room with that bloody awful statue of Raaku. Yas had to force herself over the threshold. It was just a bit of stone. Nothing to be scared of and certainly better than being groped by the Skulls. Still, it unnerved her, like it knew what she was thinking. Like she was being watched.

Arga tended to the fire while Yas opened the curtains. The view of the scaffolds churned her gut up some more. Everywhere she looked, there was another reminder of what was at stake. It was easy for Kara to talk about doing the right thing, of making a stand, but it was Yas's neck on the line. Little Ro had already lost his father. He didn't need to lose his mother, too.

'Is it always like this?' asked Yas.

Arga looked over. 'Like what?'

'Getting groped, beaten up, abused.'

Arga didn't have to think about her answer for long. 'Pretty much. With some hard graft in between all that good stuff.'

'How do you do it? How do you come in every day, knowing what's going to happen?'

Arga laughed. 'Ain't got no choice – just like the rest of us. Look, it's a shitty job for shitty people, but it helps us survive the mess the world's in right now. And the people I work with are good folk – apart from you, of course.' She smiled. It was the first sign Arga had given that she didn't hate Yas and it lifted some of the gloom.

They moved on to the next room. 'It's easier if you just follow the rules.' Arga counted them off on her fingers. 'Don't speak, don't look, don't get caught on your own, don't be late and don't ask questions. They've done me all right.'

Yas tongued her split lip. She didn't mention that it was Arga who'd left her alone to get beaten up yesterday.

When they reached the door of the governor's office, Yas hesitated.

Arga saw her stop. 'Come here, you. Don't be soft.' She yanked Yas into the office. 'The sooner we get it done, the sooner we get out of here.'

The room was the same as yesterday, a dark, cold mess with a sour odour of old wine and misery. And no sign of the governor, thank the Gods above and below. There was a bloodstain – her blood – on the floor by the fireplace. Two empty bottles sat next to the desk. Another by the chair near to the fire. And only the one glass. The man had worked hard again at his drinking the day before. Yas hoped he woke up feeling like shit.

Arga went to work on the fire and Yas wandered over to the desk. She felt guilty doing it, probably looked it, too. If anyone caught her gawking, she'd be done for and no mistake. But his lordship's papers were right there, scattered over the desk, even more than yesterday. Her heart raced as she shifted through them as subtly as she could. A voice in her head told her to stop, back away, leave it all alone, but she couldn't help herself. It was as if Kara had put a spell on her. Maybe she was just mad. It would explain everything.

Yas found the list of Hanran members and picked it up without thinking about it. Folded it. Once. Twice. Three times. Nice and small. She slipped it inside her dress, under her breasts, then straightened the rest of his papers into a neat pile and tried to act as if she hadn't done something so suicidally stupid.

As they left the office, Yas saw the governor stalking towards them, shouting at some aides. She coloured up, all but stopped in her tracks. By the Gods, she couldn't feel more guilty if she tried.

'Thirty people!' screamed the governor. 'They want thirty people hanged tomorrow. Have we even got that many in the cells?'

'We'll find them,' said one of the aides. 'Somewhere.'

Aisling didn't even look at Yas as he walked past. She didn't even exist.

'You finished gawping?' asked Arga. Yas nodded. 'Then move yer skinny arse. We've still got rooms to clean.'

15

Tinnstra

Aisair

Tinnstra and Beris spent the rest of the day at the house on Basket Street. Six of the travel papers were hidden in the lining of her coat, and they each carried one in a pocket in case they were stopped.

Those passes gave them the freedom to go *anywhere*.

For one mad moment, Tinnstra thought about running, leaving her brother and everyone else behind, to find somewhere she could hide away from the world, where it didn't matter who ruled whom. But even if she found the courage, where would she go? The Egril had conquered everywhere.

They left the house an hour before curfew. The documents pressed against Tinnstra's back with each step, reminding her of the danger she was in. Her legs felt weak and she struggled to breathe. *What am I doing? I've gone mad. This isn't right.* She glanced over at Beris as they turned into Market Way. *How can he look so calm – like he doesn't have a care in the world – when all I want to do is vomit?*

The cobbled street was lined with terrace houses, built from wood and brick with beautiful glass windows. The best of Aisair. Old money. Any damage from the invasion had long since been repaired. The blood-red flag of the Egril flew throughout the neighbourhood. They were becoming more commonplace. It broke her heart, but it kept people safe.

'Hard to imagine only six months ago, Aisair was a place of

123

learning and culture, the envy of the world. Every building a work of art,' said Beris. 'Now look what they've done.'

'I wish things could go back to the way they were,' said Tinnstra.

'Only we can make that happen, Tinn. Don't you see?'

Tinnstra tried to find her anger, to draw some strength from it, but her fear was stronger, and had been with her longer. *I don't want to make anything happen. I just want to stay alive.*

'We have to get to an inn called the Crook'd Billet,' continued Beris, 'near the Butchers' Quarter. Tinn, *listen* to me. It's important.' He spoke slowly and clearly. 'In the kitchen, there's a trapdoor. Go fifteen paces and you'll find a lever. That opens up a tunnel. Follow the tunnel as far as it goes. That's where the others will be.'

Tinnstra hugged herself, trying to stay warm. Her eyes darted everywhere. She saw suspicion in every face, danger in every doorway. *I should be at home. Safe. I'm not a rebel, a fighter. It's madness to think otherwise.*

Beris caught her elbow, turned her around to face him. 'Are you listening? You need to know where to go and what to do.'

'You'll be with me, won't you?' replied Tinnstra. 'I'll just follow you.'

'I will, but ...' Beris hesitated. 'If anything happens, you must go on without me. You need to know what to do.'

Tinnstra nodded, more scared than ever. She didn't want to think about what could happen. 'I understand. Crook'd Billet. Trapdoor in kitchen. Follow the tunnel.'

The answers satisfied Beris and they continued on their way. 'There will be a guard in the tunnel. He'll say, "We are the dead," and you'll reply, "Who face the night." *Don't* get it wrong.'

'I *know* the oath.'

'This isn't a game, Tinn.' They crossed Harris Avenue and headed towards the capital's main square, next to the courthouses. 'Once we get to the safe house, we hand over the travel documents and then we leave. Back the way we came. There's a room upstairs at the inn where we'll stay for the night. We'll move again in the morning, once curfew is lifted.'

'And you never ask me to help you again.'

'If that's what you want.'

'It is,' replied Tinnstra. They turned into the square. 'I don't want to end up—' She stopped. Her mouth dropped open.

The three bodies dangling from the scaffolds in the centre of the square were more than enough to make her point. They twisted in the wind, the scaffolds groaning with each turn.

'Better than yesterday,' said Beris. 'They had six Jians dance the last jig.'

'I can't do this,' said Tinnstra. 'We'll end up like them. We will.' She turned to head back home, get far away from the dead, but Beris caught her by the elbows, held her firm.

'We won't.' There was such conviction in his voice. She almost believed him.

'Yes, we will. Better to submit. Accept the Egril are our rulers now. Accept them and we survive. Come with me. We can make a life that will work. It won't be that bad.'

'Look at those bastards,' said Beris, nodding towards the squad of Skulls guarding the scaffold. They looked like demons from the underworld. 'They keep the dead swinging. Just to warn us to behave.' The Skulls laughed and joked amongst themselves while everyone scuttled past, eager to be anywhere but there. Tinnstra didn't blame them. She wanted to run, too.

'Please, Beris,' she pleaded. 'Let's turn back. Someone else can take the risk.'

'There's no turning back. It's not about just trying to survive. Those souls on the end of those ropes probably weren't even Hanran, but the Egril killed them all the same. It's been six months since Cariin surrendered, and in that time, the Egril have murdered thousands of us – and that's just the ones we know about. How many more have simply disappeared? We don't know where they've been taken, whether they're alive or dead. And in the end, the Egril will come for all of us. *All of us*, Tinn. There is no place we can be safe, no new life we can build. There can be no peace while they're on our soil. The fight will find all of us, one way or another. There's no hiding from it.'

Tinnstra glanced over to the scaffolds. *Beris is right – I know he's right. But why does it have to be me that fights? Why can't I hide a bit longer? It was working. I was getting by.*

'Beris ... I want to help, but—'

'There is no one else. I need you.'

She closed her eyes. By the Four Gods, she hated Beris for doing this to her, for giving her no choice but to carry on. 'Fine. I can do it. I can do it.' She didn't know who she was reassuring, Beris or herself. Or if either of them believed the words.

Tinnstra picked up her pace, keen to leave the square, but Beris took her hand, held her back. 'Don't rush. You'll draw attention to us.'

'Sorry.' She forced herself to slow down. Her heart pounded and her fear was a hard knot in her gut. She felt disconnected from the world, as if she were watching someone else walk towards her doom. She wasn't any good at this.

Beris was born to it. He was only two years older and yet he was everything Tinnstra wasn't.

When she'd joined the Kotege, Beris was already making a name for himself. The legendary son of the legendary father. Everyone was in awe of him – the way he fought with the sword or with his bare hands, his tactical acumen, his speed and endurance in the races. It was hard enough joining with the weight of her family name on her shoulders, but Beris's success made it even more difficult – and made her own failure that much more spectacular. Everyone had expected her to be just like her brothers, her parents. Not to run at the first sign of danger.

That's all I do – run. I ran from the arena and I ran from the Kotege. And I've been running ever since. Maybe it is time to stop and make a stand. Beris is with me. He'll keep me safe. 'I can do this.'

Beris squeezed her hand. 'I know.'

They cut left, down Hawkers Lane and across into Meadows Way. Walked along Seeders, then over to Lastings. Their parents had been stationed in Aisair when Tinnstra and Beris were children, while it was their clan's turn to guard the royal family, so they both knew the streets well. The familiarity of their route and Beris's company helped ease the knot in her stomach. If she didn't think about what they were doing, she almost didn't notice the fear.

The colourful buildings of Old Town loomed over the rooftops, once a beacon of Jian greatness. It used to be a thrill to go there, to see how the buildings defied all of the world's natural laws. Now their rainbow hues looked muted, soiled by events, their glory faded.

She recognised an empty store at the end of Meadows Way. It'd been a baker's, back when they were children. 'Look,' she said. 'Do you remember drooling over all the cakes and pastries?'

'We used to spend all day there. The baker would give us a handful of boiled sugar treats,' replied Beris. 'I think he did it to get rid of us rather than out of any kindness.'

'I used to take my time with them, sucking them until they melted in my mouth.'

'I crunched them as fast as I could. Mother used to say I'd break my teeth.'

The bakery was empty now, windows smashed, door missing. Dead. Like so much of Aisair.

'We'll get them back one day,' said Beris. 'Rebuild what we've lost.'

Tinnstra looked at her brother, tried to smile. She didn't believe it, but she was glad he did.

They moved on and turned into Temple Street. The once-beautiful church buildings were nothing but burned-out shells now. The Egril ensured there was no more worshipping the False Gods in Jia. She knew secret prayer meetings still took place in dirty cellars and dusty storerooms throughout the city, but she'd never sought them out.

She shivered as she walked past the ruins, feeling guilty for abandoning her faith, but she told herself it didn't matter where she prayed or what she said. She still believed in the Four Gods in her heart.

But worse awaited ahead. A barricade blocked the street where Skulls were examining people's papers. There was a guard's hut too and Tinnstra could see people moving about inside.

Beris pulled her up. 'You go first. I'll follow on behind.'

'Our papers are good, aren't they?' Tinnstra hated the nervousness in her voice but she couldn't help it.

'Relax. They're perfect. The Skulls won't give them a second glance. Just act natural. Just like we talked about.'

'What about if they search me? What if they find the other letters?'

'They won't search you. You don't match any description of anyone they're looking for. Even if they do check, they'll get you to open your coat, nothing more. Remember, they're looking for weapons, not paper. They'll never check the coat itself.'

'Okay. Okay.' Tinnstra took a deep breath. She wanted to throw up. She glanced at the Skulls and thought about running. But Beris held on to her and she could feel the strength in him. As she turned to face him, he kissed her, quickly, on the cheek. A spot of warmth on her cold skin.

'That's for luck,' he said. 'Not that you need it. I'll meet you in Aster Road.'

She felt his eyes on her all the way to the checkpoint where she joined the queue, keeping her gaze downcast. Everyone knew what to do. Look at no one. Speak to no one. Do nothing to be noticed. Survive.

There were four Skulls, armed with scimitars and spears. There would be no mercy from any of them if they found the forged papers. She took another step forwards as they let someone else through. It wasn't too late. She could turn away, pretend she'd forgotten something, do anything but walk up to the Skulls. But then a man and his son fell in behind Tinnstra and the moment passed. She was trapped. Beris took his place in the queue after them. It helped knowing he was nearby.

Tinnstra took another step closer. Three people remained in front of her and the Skulls were taking their time. She wrapped her arms around herself to fight the cold wind. Even the weather seemed to have turned against them.

The Skulls waved a woman through. Two to go. Then it would be her turn.

The door to the hut opened and a man stepped out, and another wave of panic hit her. A Chosen.

The man watched the queue, lightly tapping his baton against the palm of his other hand. Ice-blue eyes shone behind the mask, pale skin, jet-black hair cropped short, as was their fashion – in another world, one would say the man looked ordinary. But Tinnstra knew better. Knew what cruelty lay in his heart. Knew the power contained in his baton.

Two old women hobbled through and then it was Tinnstra's turn. She handed over her papers with shaking hands and waited. The papers were good, she told herself, made by the best forger in Jia, but still the fear niggled away at her. Even with legitimate paperwork, the Egril needed no real excuse to snatch you away to a dark dungeon somewhere. Just the thought of it was enough to make her breath catch. If only Beris had chosen someone else to help him with the mission.

The Skull took his time examining her papers. Tinnstra kept her head down. Submissive. Showing that she was conquered. At least that was easy. It was about the only thing that came naturally to her.

The Skull handed her papers to the Emperor's Chosen and Tinnstra's heart sank. With his baton tucked under his arm, he glanced at the papers and then at her. She could feel his eyes running over her and prayed he'd not see a threat. How could he? Time stopped. In her mind, she died a thousand times. Slowly. Painfully. In all the ways the Egril loved.

The Chosen stepped closer, placed his hand under her chin and raised her head. His touch was cold, like a dead man's. So different from Beris's. She kept her gaze cast down, but her body shivered at his touch, betraying her fear. Tears welled up in the corners of her eyes. What powers did he have? Could he read her mind? Sense her guilt? Did he know what was happening? What she and the others were doing?

The man pursed his lips and squinted. Still he didn't remove his hand. He knew. It was over. This was it. Tinnstra thought about running knew she wouldn't get far. Her stomach lurched. She could feel an itch burn through her mind. She was going to die.

'Come on, you bastards. I've not got all day,' snarled Beris. Tinnstra flinched at the sound of his voice but it got the Skulls' attention. The Chosen's, too. His hand went from Tinnstra's jaw to his baton.

'Silence,' said a Skull, jabbing a finger towards Beris.

Beris stepped forward. 'Think I'm afraid of you? This is my country, not yours. Why don't you piss off back to where you came from – leave us all alone. You're not wanted here.'

Beris, no. Don't do this. Please don't.

'Walk away, citizen,' said the Chosen. His accent made the words sound like gravel. A man used to being obeyed. 'Now.'

'Okay, okay, as you say.' Beris held up both hands in surrender. Bowed. 'Didn't mean anything by it. You're in charge.' He turned as if he was going to do what they ordered, do as Tinnstra prayed he would. Took a step. Took another. Tinnstra held her breath as she urged him to keep going. But he stopped. Shook his head. 'Nah. Fuck that.'

Beris swung back around and charged straight at the Chosen, fist already in motion, screaming. As fast as he was, the Chosen's baton was faster. A blast of yellow light shot from the end of it.

16

Dren

Kiyosun

It was midday and Dren hadn't slept.

It was hard enough on a normal night. His home now, after all, was nothing more than a collapsed water tank on top of a ruined building in a demolished part of town. His roof was the sky. His bed was the tank's half-rotten wooden floor, his pillow an old coat that wasn't even fit to burn. Of course, his stomach didn't help, either – growling and grumbling about how empty it was. But it could complain all it wanted, there was no food to be had.

His home was a shit hole. He knew that. He wasn't stupid. But that was only because the Egril had come and dropped their fucking bombs. Before that, it had been a proper home, where he was born, where he'd grown up. If he half-closed his eyes, he could imagine the roof as it had been; his mother hanging the washing while his dad sang songs to amuse them all, cooking fish from that day's catch over a small fire and Dren running from one to the other, laughing, stealing hugs. He'd be fucked if he was going to leave now. Their spirits remained, clinging to the bricks and the stone. It was his home no matter what state it was in, and he'd kill anyone who tried to make him leave.

But even if he'd been lying in a comfortable bed with a full belly, surrounded by four walls and a roof, he still wouldn't have slept. Not after a mission. Every time he closed his eyes, he saw the explosion. The ball of fire engulfing Lia, Hasster, the Egril.

Heard the screams after the bomb went off. The smell of roasting flesh – so like pork – and the flash of heat in the air. It had been over so quickly, yet it lasted for ever in his mind.

He pretended to the others that he was used to it. That it didn't bother him to watch one of his soldiers blow themselves apart. But no, he wasn't used to it. Not even close. Just thinking about it made him want to go and puke in the corner.

So, there was no sleep to be had despite the fog in his head and the exhaustion in his bones.

Dren curled up in the shadow of the water tank with his arms wrapped around his legs. The only thing to do was wait the day out and hope he'd nod off sooner rather than later.

At least there was the satisfaction of killing the three Egril and the collaborators. Next time a traitor felt happy to take Egril coin, they would remember what happened to Hasster and know the consequences.

The Shulka might have surrendered but Dren would show the Egril that there was still a man in Jia with the balls to fight back. He glanced over to the other side of the roof, to his neatly stacked collection of Skull helmets. Proof of the good work he'd done.

Those Egril bombs were wonderful things. He didn't like to admit how much of a difference they made. He and Quist had found them by chance when they were out scavenging. They'd jammed up a street as an Egril baggage train came through, hoping to steal some food or something worth selling. While the Skulls were trying to clear the road, Dren and Quist had darted in and lifted a crate off the back of one of the wagons. They'd been pissed off at first when they opened it and found the black orbs, each only slightly bigger than an apple, nestled in the straw. Quist was for dumping the box, but then Dren remembered the Daijaku and he knew what they were. Bombs. And suddenly their theft wasn't a waste of time after all.

It had taken a while to suss out how they worked. The metal orbs looked solid but they could feel liquid sloshing about inside. The boys had experimented by throwing them against an old ruined wall, but the orbs hadn't even shattered, let alone exploded.

They discovered how to activate them by accident. Little

Bruno had cut his hand jumping a fence and tried to act tough, even though it was obvious to everyone he was desperate to cry. What six-year-old wouldn't? When one of the other kids took the piss, Bruno had picked up one of the orbs with his bloody hand and thrown it at his tormentor. The explosion had killed five of them.

They'd immediately locked the orbs away and kept them guarded. Until the guards started getting sick. Real sick. It started with coughs, then moved on to shitting blood and vomiting puss. Then death. The Daijaku might be able to handle the orbs without a problem but humans not so much. Dren and Quist, wearing gloves and scarves for whatever protection they afforded, had hidden them for a third time. Buried them deep where no one else knew. Now they only dug them up when they needed them, and only the one doing the run was allowed to touch them with bare skin. Getting sick wasn't a problem if you were on your way to kill yourself.

'Dren!' It was Quist. His head poked up through the hole in the roof, a big smile plastered across his face. 'This is your lucky day.' His hand appeared, holding a small sack.

Dren jumped to his feet. 'Food?'

Quist hauled himself up. 'Why? Are you hungry?'

'Starving.' Dren grabbed at the bag but Quist swung it out of reach.

'Who's got the magic?'

'Come on.' Dren's mouth watered at the thought of eating. His stomach ached. 'Stop mucking about. Give it here.'

'Not until you answer the question. Who's got the magic?'

Dren snatched out again but his friend danced away, laughing. 'Come on, you bastard. Stop pissing around. I'm hungry.'

Quist put his hand to his ear. 'I'm sorry. I didn't catch that. Did you say you're hungry?'

'I'm hung-ger-ree,' said Dren, dragging out every syllable. 'I'm really, really hungry. I'm starving.'

'So who's got the magic?' asked Quist again.

'You do.' Dren gave in, laughing with his friend. 'You've got the fucking magic.'

'That's all I wanted to hear.' Quist dropped down on the floor, shoved his hand into the sack and pulled out a loaf of bread. 'Now get stuck into that.'

The boys ripped the loaf in two. It was still warm from the oven. Dren couldn't remember the last time he had fresh bread. It tasted amazing.

'Don't rush,' said Quist, crumbs falling from his mouth. 'There's this as well.' He produced a joint of ham from the sack. 'And this.' A bottle of wine followed.

'Where the fuck did you get all this?'

'The Egril have some officers stationed in a house on Warren Street. All the bastards were called out because of our little present from last night, so I nipped in through a back window. Helped myself, as you do.'

'You're mad but you've got the magic.' Dren sank his teeth into the ham. Juice ran down his chin as he tasted flavours he'd long forgotten. 'You're lucky you weren't caught. The Egril would've strung you up if they'd nabbed you.'

'They'll string you up for bloody breathing the wrong way.' Quist pulled the cork out of the wine bottle with his teeth. 'Nah, they're not good enough to catch me.' He glugged the wine and followed up with a belch. 'Nice.'

Dren wiped his mouth. 'Let's get the others. Better we share it. It wouldn't be right to eat it all ourselves.'

Quist looked at him, like he was expecting a punchline. When it didn't come, he shook his head. 'Nah, this is ours. My treat for you. Let the others go on the rob. Let the others risk the drop.'

'You know it's the right thing to do.'

Quist jabbed his finger at Dren. 'No. No. No. It's ours.'

That wouldn't do at all. Dren lowered his voice, looked his friend in the eye. 'Get the others.'

He could see the message finally sink into Quist's thick head and his cousin backed down. He put the food and wine on the floor and stood up. 'You better not eat it all while I'm gone.'

He laughed. 'I won't. I promise.'

Quist walked over to the stairwell but stopped before descending. 'What the fuck are you doing here?' he called down.

Dren was beside him a second later with one of his knives in his hand.

'All right, Dren, Quist,' said Monon from the top of the stairs. 'Just the two people I was looking for. Got time for a quick word?'

The Shulka was all smiles, and the one thing Dren had learned pretty damn early in life was never trust a smiling Shulka. It didn't come natural to them, not by a long shot. It probably meant someone was about to get their head cut off. Well, it sure as hell wasn't going to be Dren. 'What do you want?' He kept his knife out to show what he thought of the man's visit.

'Boys,' said Monon. 'I'm just here for a chat. No more.'

'You can talk from there,' replied Dren and spat over the edge of the roof.

'I'd rather not have the whole neighbourhood hear, if that's okay with you.' Monon showed the insides of his coat. 'I'm not armed.'

'Only because the Egril would have your balls if you were,' said Quist.

'You make a good point there.'

Dren stared at the Shulka. He didn't want him in his home, didn't want to talk to him at all, but he didn't see he had much choice. 'Come on up.'

Monon hauled himself onto the roof and Dren waved him into the water tank, following behind. No way was he going to turn his back on a Shulka.

'What's this all about?' Dren said once they were all seated. His knife lay an inch from his hand.

Monon nodded at the food. 'Looks fresh.'

'It's not for you. I ask again – what's this all about?'

'Jax wants to meet.'

'Why would I want to meet that one-armed bastard?'

'You know why.'

'No, I don't. Enlighten me.'

'I've just come from Hasster's. I take it that was your work last night?'

Dren sniffed. 'Don't know what you're talking about. I've not left my cosy little home here in days.'

'Let's not take each other for fools. Someone bombed Old Man Hasster's place last night. Now, I know it wasn't my crew because we haven't got any bombs – so that just leaves you and yours.'

'Nah, it doesn't,' replied Dren, smiling. 'Could be anyone. An unhappy customer, or maybe he'd got behind in payments to the Weeping Men, over an unpaid loan or something. Definitely not us kids from Toxten. Got enough trouble trying to find something to eat.'

'You seem to be doing all right for food,' said Monon, waving at the ham and bread. He looked around the ruins, acting like he didn't have a care in the bloody world. 'It wasn't the Weeping Men. They'd have broken his legs or cut an ear off. They don't do suicide bombings, not with the money they're making with the slave trade and all the other things people need on the black market.'

Dren shrugged. 'I'm all out of ideas, then. Sorry.'

'Let's not play games.' Monon brushed some dirt off his knee. 'You killed a lot of people last night. More of us than them.'

'Again – I didn't kill anyone last night, but whoever got caught up in the bomb shouldn't have been there. Hasster shouldn't have been fawning over the Egril. The girls shouldn't have been fucking the Egril soldiers. You reap what you sow.'

'Everyone's just trying to survive day by day. Hasster had a family to think of.'

'He sacrificed them when he opened his door to the Skulls,' said Dren. 'He'll get no sympathy from me. Whoever killed the collaborators deserves a medal, if you ask me.'

Quist thumped his chest. 'Too right.'

Monon leaned forward, acting like he was talking to a pair of lads who were soft in the head. With no fucking respect. 'The bombings do more harm than good. The Skulls are arresting people for no reason whatsoever now. They'll hang them all. Because of what you did.'

'And how's that different from any other fucking day? They hang some of ours, we kill more of theirs. At least this way they know there's a price to pay. We make the cost high enough and they'll fuck off out of our country.'

Monon shook his head. 'It doesn't work like that, kid.'

'Then how *does* it work? We just sit back and accept being conquered? Kiss their backsides and do nothing? Is that the great Shulka master plan?'

'No one likes this situation. Things are happening. Things you don't know about. Missions that we can't risk your actions jeopardising.'

Dren was astonished at the arrogance of the man – coming to his home and telling him what he could or couldn't do. 'Missions? Is that what you call sitting around doing fuck all? A bunch of has-beens – a bunch of fucking old men – too scared to say boo to a Skull?'

'There's a lot going on that you don't know – can't know. You have to trust me on this.'

'Never trust a Shulka, that's what my dad used to say and he was fucking right.'

'Dren ...' said Monon, getting that look his father used to get when Dren found himself in trouble again. 'Don't be like this. Don't make it difficult. You don't want us as your enemy as well. We should be on the same side.'

'Same side?' Dren spat the words out. 'When have the Shulka ever been on our side? You treated us like dirt for centuries, swaggering about thinking yourselves fucking better than the rest of the world. Lording it over us serfs. Taking our money. You lot have always enjoyed being the ruling class. Truth is, there's not much difference between you and the Egril.'

'Our duty is to protect the common people of Jia. We devoted ourselves—'

'There you go,' shouted Dren. 'That's what you think of us – "common people". Over the years, how many of us "common people" do you think the Shulka killed because of some perceived slight to your honour? Maybe some poor fool didn't bow quickly enough or low enough as you passed them in the street, and then out came the sword and another one of the "common people" was left dying in the street.'

'You're exaggerating.'

'Fuck off.' Dren stared the bastard down. He wasn't afraid of

137

him. 'Do you know that the night the Egril invaded, one of your bloody Shulka was about to cut my head off? Just because he couldn't take a fucking joke. You ask me, I'm glad the Egril put you smug bastards in your place. Not feeling so high and mighty now you're begging for scraps like the rest of us, are you? Same side? I spit on your fucking side. The Shulka, the Weeping Men, the Hanran, the Egril – you're all the same to me. You're all out to fuck the "common people".' He stood, the knife in his hand, fired up enough to hope the Shulka would do something stupid. 'You should leave now.'

Monon got to his feet in a leisurely fashion, pretending he wasn't scared of Dren. He brushed some dust off his trousers, like he'd all the time in the world. 'Dren, we need to work together if we're going to beat the Egril, not fight each other.'

'We don't need anything. My people will deal with the Egril – count on it. You just go back to whatever hole you crawled out of and wait there till it's all over.'

'Jax still wants to meet.'

Dren jabbed the knife in Monon's direction. 'Tell him to fuck off.'

Monon walked to the stairs. 'Jax won't like that.'

'I don't give a shit what he likes. Tell him the past was his and he fucked it up. The future belongs to us now. And we'll do what we want.'

Monon laughed. 'I look forward to seeing you tell Jax that to his face.'

'Feel free to tell him where I live.'

'He knows.' And with that, Monon was gone.

'Are you sure that was wise?' asked Quist once they were alone. 'We've got enough going on without picking a fight with the Shulka.'

'They had their chance. How many Egril have we killed? Huh?'

'I dunno. Twenty, maybe? I stopped counting.'

Dren grabbed Quist's collar and dragged him over to the stack of helmets. 'I've kept a helmet for every head we've taken.' He kicked one, sent it rolling across the floor. 'Thirty-four skulls we've killed. Thirty-four! Just us. So why do we need the Shulka's or the Hanran's permission to carry on? Fuck them. We're just going to keep on killing Skulls until they give up and go home. If the Shulka get in the way, we'll just add some more crosses to the board.'

'Hey, it's all good to me, Dren.' Quist stepped back. 'I'll go get the others. Better not waste the food.'

'Sure.' Dren ran a finger over the top of the helmets. He wouldn't have a problem killing Jax if he had to.

17

Tinnstra

Aisair

The blast picked Beris off his feet and threw him back ten yards. He hit the ground and bounced, once, twice, before sliding to a stop. Smoke drifted from a hole in his chest. The air stank of burned flesh. Beris's leg twitched and then went still. Tinnstra watched her brother die and still couldn't believe it. Not Beris. Perfect Beris.

He never had a chance. Not against a Chosen. Her brother was dead. Beris was dead.

Dear Gods, no. No. 'Noooooooooooooooooo!' She howled the word, let it burst from her gut with all the fear and horror that she'd kept inside herself for six months. Her throat strained with the agony of it. *How could they kill Beris? I only just got him back.*

A Skull grabbed her arm and slapped her. *Hard.* 'Shut it.'

The pain only made her tears come faster.

The Chosen turned and faced her. There was nothing in his eyes. No emotion. His baton crackled in his hand, ready to be used again.

That threat pierced her anguish. She got the message. *Shut up. Survive. Get away.* Tinnstra swallowed her cries. She gulped for air with tears and snot streaming down her face. She tried to take a step back, away from the Skulls, the Chosen, her brother, but the soldier held her firm. They weren't letting her pass. *Shit, they're going to arrest me. Beris died for nothing.* She looked again at his charred body, bile rising. At least his death had been quick.

Hers would be slow, painful. *By the Four Gods ... I don't have his strength.*

The Chosen held her papers in his other hand. He looked at Tinnstra, then to her letter of passage, before returning it to the guard and dismissing her.

Tinnstra stood staring at him in shock.

'Move,' said the Skull in his thick accent, offering her the letter, but the words didn't sound right to her ears. Didn't make sense. Move along? They were letting her go? Beris had just died and they were letting her go?

He thrust the paper at Tinnstra and pushed her on. She took hold of it, squashed it against her body to stop herself from dropping it. Somehow, she forced her legs to work and stumbled forwards a step, then another, then another. As she passed the barrier, she expected to be called back at any moment or feel a spear stab into her. It was the sort of thing an Egril would do, after all. But each step took her further away and no one called out to her and no spear was thrust into her body. And so she walked on, leaving Beris dead in the street, smoke drifting up from his body.

In Aster Road, out of sight of the Skulls, she stopped and threw up all over the street, vomit burning her throat. Tears ran down her face as she sobbed. She pressed her hand against her cheek where Beris had kissed her as if that could keep him alive. But dead he was once more. And he'd died for her. May Xin cherish him for eternity, but she wasn't worth his sacrifice.

'Are you all right, love?' asked a man. Tinnstra looked up at him with wet eyes and pain in her heart. She didn't think she'd ever be all right again, but she nodded at the man and waved him on. *You can't trust anyone.*

Tinnstra wiped her eyes and spat the taste of sick out of her mouth. What was she going to do now? Everything inside told her to run home and hide. But to do that, she'd have to pass the checkpoint again and the Skulls would never understand why she'd returned. She couldn't stay where she was, either. Not with the forged letters on her. She needed to get rid of them.

She stumbled on, trying to suck down the pain, looking for

somewhere to dump them. It was for the best – just throw them away and then pretend nothing had happened.

Except Beris was dead. He'd died for her, to save Tinnstra so she could deliver them, to help save the king. If she threw them away, then Beris would've died for nothing. If only he'd realised his life was worth a thousand of hers.

She walked down battered streets past war-scarred buildings, crying all the way. Luckily, so late in the day, there was hardly anyone to see her. Not so close to curfew. Sensible people hid away behind locked doors and shuttered windows, grateful they had made it through another day alive.

The curfew bell rang out as she reached the Crook'd Billet. A battered old sign rocked in the wind, just legible enough to tell Tinnstra she was in the right place. The front of the inn was boarded up, though. It hadn't done any business for a long time.

Tinnstra tried the front door. Locked. Down the alleyway to the right of the inn, she found a side door. It opened with a clunk. She hovered on the threshold, even now unsure if she could go any further. *It's just another empty building. I've been in dozens. It's nothing to be scared of.*

Then the curfew bell stopped its toll. Silence filled the air around her. She had no choice. She had to get off the street. It was death to be outside.

She stepped into a gloomy taproom. No one else was there. Dust swirled around her, caught in the light that sneaked through gaps in the boards covering the windows.

The inn would've been a lively place six months ago, a place where the locals met after a hard day's work to share a joke or two, but now it was empty. The barrels had long since run dry and customers were a distant memory. All that remained of its past glories were the faint smell of stale beer and a few knackered tables and chairs covered with a layer of dust.

Tinnstra sat down on a stool to catch her breath and clasped her hands together in an attempt to stop them shaking, but it was a hopeless task. Bile rose in her throat once more, but she swallowed it down. *I'm alive. I'm alive.* That was something at least.

Weak with relief now she was safe inside and out of sight, all she wanted to do was curl up in a corner and grieve.

If only that were an option. She needed to find the Hanran. Hand over the papers. Even though Beris was dead, she could feel her brother beside her, urging her on, begging her not to give up, not to let him down.

Tinnstra got to her feet and dragged herself to the other side of the bar. She found three sacks hidden there. One was stuffed with travelling clothes of varying sizes. The others contained water skins and some cold meats and bread. Her stomach rumbled at the sight of the food, but she closed the sacks up once more and left them where she'd found them. They weren't hers.

The kitchen was just as cold and abandoned as the taproom. Ashes were piled in the centre of the fireplace and spiders' webs provided the only decorations. It took Tinnstra a few moments to find the trapdoor, which was half-obscured by a table full of stacked plates and bowls. She carefully manoeuvred past the table, not wanting to send the whole thing crashing down, and then hauled the trapdoor up. Its rusted hinges groaned as it opened, setting Tinnstra's nerves aflame once more.

She froze, listened, prayed. But no one heard or came to investigate. She was alone. *Silly girl*.

A ladder disappeared into pitch blackness below. She searched around for a lantern or a candle but found none. She'd never liked the dark. As a child, she'd woken her father up every night, petrified of the monsters she thought were out to get her. He'd smile and take her back to bed, telling her all the while that there were no such things as monsters any more. How wrong he'd been.

The hole in the floor stared back at her. Only the Four Gods knew what she was going to find down there. The darkness hid every fear she'd ever had. What if the Egril were waiting for her? What if it was all a trap?

She shook her head. She was nineteen years old. How could she be afraid of the dark? With a deep breath, she climbed down, taking her time, feeling for each step with her toes.

She debated propping the trapdoor open to let in some light at least, but she didn't want to leave a trail in case the Skulls searched the inn. Common sense told her it was a ridiculous fear. No one had been in the inn for months. Except the Hanran. And the Skulls were looking for them. So maybe it wasn't such a silly thought after all.

Once the trapdoor was shut above her, there was only the dark and the sound of her panting breath and the feel of her pounding heart.

Stepping from the ladder, she ran her hand along damp stone as she moved deeper into the room until she reached the far wall. The cellar was only twelve feet long. There had to be another way out, a door she'd yet to find. She continued feeling her way along the wall, counting each step as Beris had told her. When she reached fifteen, she found a small hook just above head height. She pulled on it and a door cranked open revealing a tunnel on the other side lit with torches. The sudden glare blinded her for a moment, and she had to shield her eyes until they adjusted. She stepped through, grateful she had light to see by. Her journey must be nearly over.

She followed the tunnel as it twisted and turned, confusing her sense of direction. Tinnstra tried to keep track of her progress by picturing the map of Aisair in her head but she soon had no idea where she was in relation to the city above. Panic hit her hard. She didn't want to do this. Each step became more difficult to take, fighting her fear to get her legs to move. She kept looking behind her, scared that someone might be following her, yet wanting to turn back at the same time.

She rounded another corner and cried out.

A giant of a man stood next to a chair, a Shulka sword in his hand. She shrivelled under his gaze.

'We are the dead,' he said. The code Beris had told her about. The Shulka prayer.

'Who face the night,' she squeaked back.

He nodded and stepped to one side. 'The others are waiting just ahead.'

Tinnstra stared at him in awe. He looked everything a Shulka was supposed to be. She felt so weak in comparison, so unworthy. 'Thank you.'

The Shulka bowed. 'We are the dead.'

'May the Four Gods keep you safe,' replied Tinnstra. She knew that wasn't the correct response, but she was no Shulka. She hurried down the tunnel, too scared to look back, not wanting to betray her weaknesses.

The tunnel grew narrower and lower with every step, eventually forcing her to crawl on her hands and knees. The walls and floor were hewn out of the rock as if dug by some strange creature. The rough edges dug into her and scratched her. The torches were only placed where space allowed now, creating pockets of shadow between them for Tinnstra to crawl through. It became harder to breathe, adding to her discomfort and claustrophobia. Every obstacle brought a temptation to stop, but turning around was impossible. Only forward. She hated Beris for putting her there and felt guilty for doing so. She should've been at home, not caught up in a mess she had nothing to do with. Yet he'd given his life for hers and that debt helped push her on.

She was soaked with sweat and gasping for air when she reached what looked like the final chamber. The room was larger, high enough to stand in, thank the Four Gods. It joined with other tunnels that led off elsewhere in Aisair, and for a moment, Tinnstra panicked that she was supposed to take one of them. Then she saw the stairs and the steel trapdoor that waited at the top of them. *Please let this be the end.*

Her strength all but gone, Tinnstra struggled up the steps. She pushed the trapdoor; it swung open easily enough and light spilled down towards her. She clambered up into the room above.

A sword swept down, stopping an inch from her face. 'Who are you?'

She froze, stared at the tip of the blade, too scared even to look at who was holding the sword. 'My name ... My name is Tinnstra. I'm Beris's sister.'

'Where's Beris?'

'He's dead.'

'Step back,' called out another man. 'Let the girl stand up. I'll vouch for her.'

Tinnstra recognised the voice. She'd known it all her life. She looked up as the man who had confronted her stepped back, and there he was, pushing his way towards her. General Harka. Her godfather. Alive! She'd not seen him since that day at the Kotege when ... Her eyes fell, full of shame and guilt. When he'd expelled her, and she'd run away while he fought single-handed against the Skulls.

He'd aged in those six months. Heavy lines etched his face and his cheekbones were gaunter than ever. He wore his hair long about his shoulders and grubby street clothes had replaced his uniform. He looked so uncomfortable, trying to not look like a Shulka. He still had his sword, though, slung over his back, despite the law forbidding anyone other than Egril to carry weapons of any sort.

She looked around the room. Harka wasn't the only one flouting that law. There were about twenty people in the room and all of them were armed. All ready for war.

Harka helped her up. 'It's been a long time, Tinnstra,' said the old man. 'I must admit, I wasn't expecting to see you. I'm glad you're alive.' There was genuine affection in his voice.

Tinnstra bowed, her cheeks flushed. 'Beris asked me to come.'

'I see,' replied the general. 'I take it he ...'

'He died, sir. We were stopped at a checkpoint. A Chosen inspected my papers and I thought he was going to arrest me. Beris must have thought so, too. He attacked ... he attacked the Chosen ...' The words tumbled out of Tinnstra, as did the tears. She tried to stay composed but it was beyond her.

Another woman rushed over. Tinnstra recognised her as well – Major Majas. A tall, handsome woman, she kept her dark hair cropped short. A scar, old and faded, ran from her ear to her chin. 'Where's Beris?'

Harka shook his head. 'Dead. They encountered a Chosen.'

'What about the papers? The letters of travel?' replied Majas.

'I ... have them.' Tinnstra shrugged off her coat and held it out. 'The papers are hidden in the lining. One was lost when Beris died.'

Harka placed a hand on Tinnstra's shoulder. 'You've done well. What happened with the Chosen? Was there something wrong with your papers? Is that what gave you away?'

'I don't know,' replied Tinnstra. 'I don't even know if they suspected anything. The Chosen just held my face. It felt like something was crawling through my mind.'

Harka glanced at Majas. Something unspoken passed between them that made Tinnstra feel even more scared. 'What is it?'

'The Chosen might've been a mind-reader,' replied Harka.

'A mind-reader?' repeated Tinnstra.

Majas nodded. 'How much of our plans did you know?'

'Beris ... Beris told me how to get here.' Tinnstra felt herself shrinking under the scrutiny of the two Shulka leaders. 'And what you're planning to do.'

'*Shit.*' Majas looked like she was ready to kill Tinnstra. 'We're fucked.'

'We don't know that,' replied Harka. 'We can't be sure.'

'Did they let you go or did you escape?' asked Majas. 'Think, girl.'

Tinnstra took a step back. 'After the Chosen killed Beris, he returned my papers and told me to go. The Skull actually pushed me on my way.'

'Why would he do that?' Majas screwed up her nose as she spoke, as if she were already disgusted by the answer.

Tinnstra didn't want to reply. Her cheeks grew red as she glanced around the room, looking anywhere to avoid Majas's scrutiny.

But Majas wasn't going to let her off that easily. 'Well?'

'I was too scared to move.'

'By the Gods,' hissed Majas.

Harka stepped forward, separated them with his arm. 'Go easy on the girl. She's not one of us.'

'I'm sorry,' replied Tinnstra. 'Look, just take the letters and I'll be on my way. I never wanted to get involved in the first place.'

Majas shook her head. 'You're not going anywhere, girl. Not till this is over one way or another.'

'What do you mean?' asked Tinnstra. 'I've done my part. I brought your papers here. I want to go.'

'We can't take the risk,' said Harka. 'You know too much. As

147

it is, the Egril may already be on their way.' He turned to Majas. 'Double the guards outside. If the Four Gods are with us, the king and his family will be here soon and we can be gone before this place is discovered. We have the letters. If we move quickly, we can still get everyone out of the city. The wagons are ready in the stables in Garrett Street. Then it's four days to the gate. We can still keep to the plan.'

Majas bowed. 'We'll get it done.'

Tinnstra watched Majas leave, feeling more lost than ever. '*Please*, Beris promised that I could go once I gave you the letters.'

'Just wait, Tinnstra. Try and get some rest,' replied Harka. 'You can be on your way soon enough. I'll send someone over to get the papers in a minute.'

He left her clutching her coat, so she retreated into a corner and slunk to the floor. Better to get out of everyone's way and hope it would all be over soon.

Tinnstra glanced around at the other people in the room. She recognised Mother Rosina. The high priestess of the Four Gods was one of the Egril's most wanted. She was short but broad of shoulder, with dark hair pulled back into a ponytail, revealing shaved sides. Tattoos of holy scriptures ran from under her chin, down her neck and into her heavy woollen robes, showing her primary allegiance to Alo, the God of Life. The Egril would pay a year's worth of gold for her head. She looked Tinnstra up and down as Harka spoke to her, disappointment plain to see on her face.

A man stood next to Rosina and, for a moment, Tinnstra thought he had paint on his face, but a second glance told her otherwise. They were tattoos like the priestess's, but his weren't in honour of the Four Gods. The man had teardrops inked on his cheeks. Many, many teardrops. He was a Weeping Man.

A shiver ran through Tinnstra. The Weeping Men were the sworn enemies of the Shulka. They were the organised criminals who controlled the illegal slave trade across Jia, as well as operating as money lenders, smugglers and much worse. They were the only ones who'd thrived since the invasion. They'd taken control of the black-market trade in food. When people were starving, a carrot was worth a month's salary. She'd heard tales of people willingly sell themselves and their families into slavery for the promise of regular meals and protection from the Skulls and the Weeping Men had taken advantage of that desperation. But fall foul of the Weeping Men and there was a good chance you'd get your throat cut. They marked each kill by inking a teardrop on their face. And that man with Rosina was covered in them. *Dear Gods, what am I doing here?*

A young woman with an eyepatch approached, startling Tinnstra. 'I've come for the letters of travel.'

'Here ...' said Tinnstra. She offered her coat to the girl.

The trapdoor opened.

A Shulka all but fell into the room, sword in hand, blood staining his shirt and cuts all over his face. Ignoring Tinnstra's coat, the girl rushed to his side and helped him to sit on a nearby stool.

Another man followed, carrying a young girl in his arms.

'Aasgod!' Harka shouted and ran to his side.

Tinnstra stared, open-mouthed. The Lord Mage. Aasgod had been adviser to generations of royalty yet he didn't look older than forty. He was well built with broad shoulders. Sweat glistened on his bald head, like crystals on his dark skin. There was blood, too – on his face, on his clothes. He fought to catch his breath. The child in his arms was no more than three or four years old, with long, dark hair hanging over her face, and clearly petrified given how tightly she clung to Aasgod. Her beautiful dress was out of place in that room. She had to be Cariin's daughter.

Another Shulka appeared, a woman called Lira who Tinnstra knew from the Kotege. Her sword was drawn and bloodied, too. She slammed the trapdoor shut after her. There was no one else with them. No king. No queen. No other children.

Aasgod looked up, his eyes bright in the gloom. 'We were betrayed. The king is dead.'

18
Yas

Kiyosun

How could one small piece of paper weigh so much? All day Yas felt it pressing down on her, getting heavier by the second, a reminder of the danger she'd put herself in. She told herself she was just being paranoid. No one suspected a thing. Yet she still jumped every time someone called her name, imagining each approaching Skull was coming to arrest her. At the rate she was going, she'd have a heart attack before the day was out.

'What you up to?' asked Arga as they changed.

Yas's head shot up, cheeks colouring. 'What do you mean?' She didn't like the way Arga was looking at her – as if she knew something.

'What are you up to once we leave here?' Arga hung her uniform back on the rack and took a bundle of clothes from one of the lockers. 'Any plans?'

Yas nearly laughed from relief. 'Nothing. I'm doing nothing. Have to get back to my boy.' She turned away to slip the folded paper between her own clothes as she took them out of her locker, unsure of where to hide it on the way out. The guards at the gate would have a good feel when they searched her – they'd find it in an instant if she wasn't careful. She'd not thought this through at all. She'd not thought at all.

'How old is he?' Arga put on a worn shirt, patched and stitched many a time.

'What?' Yas looked over her shoulder at Arga. 'Sorry. I was miles away.'

'I asked how old your son is.'

Yas picked up her own blouse. Her skirt was on top of the paper but it still felt exposed. 'Eighteen months. He's a right little handful.' She fussed with her shoes, knowing she was overdoing it but her nerves had the better of her. She put them down next to her skirt. 'I'd do anything for my son.'

'Well, if you fancy it, a few of us are staying on for a bit in the kitchen. One of the lads has got hold of a couple of bottles of wine from his high and mighty lordship upstairs and we're going to have a drink. You can join us if you want.'

'I'd like to but I have to get home.' Yas slid the paper into a shoe, her cheeks flushed as she did it. For the thousandth time, she wondered what she was doing. 'They'll be waiting for me.'

'That's a shame. It's a good drop, apparently.'

'I don't think I'd notice the difference.'

'All I know is it's better than the rat's piss that's passed off as booze out in the real world these days. And I need a drink of something that's not been brewed in someone's back garden.'

'Next time.' Yas pulled on her skirt and slipped on her shoes. The paper crunched against her foot.

Somehow, Arga didn't notice. She finished dressing and came over to Yas, giving her shoulder a squeeze. Yas flinched. 'You should have a drop. It'll help you relax.' She wandered off to kitchen, leaving Yas alone with her guilt.

She composed herself as best she could and followed. The long table near the door was covered with the day's leftovers. Loaves of bread sat next to pies, cold cuts of meat and assorted vegetables. Arga was sitting with a few of the others at the far end of the kitchen, glass in hand. She caught Yas's eye and smiled, as if to say well done for surviving another day.

Yas filled her basket with enough food to keep Ro and Ma happy for a few days, then waved goodbye to the others and stepped outside. The light was fading and curfew would be hard behind. She had to get home and be quick about it.

The walk across the courtyard was torturous. Her foot slipped against the paper, making every step awkward. A couple of guards at the gate watched her and spoke quietly. Yas wanted to turn around and run back to the kitchen but resisted the impulse.

The Skulls searched Yas twice. A different guard each time. As she stood there with her arms outstretched, she realised she needn't have worried. They weren't really looking for anything. The examinations were just an excuse to touch her and humiliate her. They found it funny, grunting away to each other in that pig language of theirs while they squeezed and groped Yas. Well, they could fuck off. She pressed down on the paper in her shoe while they did it and she didn't care. Let them enjoy their petty little thrills. She'd got one over on them and they didn't even know it. The shoe was the perfect hiding place. They had no interest in looking there – not while they could slip a finger in somewhere else.

'Go,' said one finally as he stepped back.

Yas glared at him before remembering Arga's rules. She dropped her eyes. 'Thank you.'

Once more, the gate clanged shut behind her and Yas set off home. She stopped two streets away and made a show of adjusting her shoe. She removed the paper and placed it in her basket. With it removed, she walked faster, eager for the safety of her house, full of pride that she'd got one over on the bastard Skulls. They weren't so bloody invincible if a cleaner could fool them.

With each step, however, all thoughts of helping the Hanran slowly disappeared. She'd been an idiot. With any luck, she'd not see Kara again and Yas could just destroy the paper when she got home. She'd made a mistake. Been stupid. That's all. Once the list was gone, she could pretend it had never happened. Go back to the way things should be. She'd never risk doing something so crazy again.

Of course, she should've known better. Kara appeared by her side a street later. 'Better day?'

'No one beat me up, if that's what you mean,' replied Yas. She felt sick at the sight of the Hanran. She could still walk away, though. Kara didn't know she'd stolen the list. All she had to do was say nothing. 'I thought I told you I wasn't going to spy for you.'

'I heard you. And I'm not asking you to spy for us.'

'Then why are you here?'

'I told you I want to be your friend. I can help you, you know.'

'Help me with what? I don't need your help.'

'Not now, no. Not with your job.' Kara nodded towards the basket in Yas's hand. 'Must be nice having plenty to eat again. Not many people in the city enjoy that luxury.'

'You're not going to make me feel guilty about feeding my family.' Yas pointed to the bruises on her own face. 'I've earned that food. Bloody earned it.'

'Others might not see it that way. Might think you've gone over to the enemy's side.' Kara raised an eyebrow. 'A collaborator.'

'Are you threatening me?'

'Not at all. But I can make sure no one gets the wrong idea. Let people know you're my friend.'

'I can look after myself.'

'I know. I know.' Kara paused. 'Still ...'

'Still what?'

The woman shrugged. 'Why take the risk?'

'Oh, fuck off, why don't you?' spat Yas.

Kara took no notice. They walked together in silence for another block. The whole time, the slip of paper in Yas's basket preyed on her mind. Why didn't she just tell Kara about it? Get it all over with? Why argue with the woman? Why did the woman piss her off so much?

Yas stopped walking and Kara stopped with her. 'Please just leave me alone.'

'It doesn't work like that.'

'Why not?'

'There's a war on. People's lives are at stake.'

'You don't have to tell me that. I know better than anyone.'

'Why's that?'

Yas wanted to scream. 'Why won't you leave me alone? Why?'

'What do you know?' asked Kara. 'If you know something, tell me. I won't bother you again. Just tell me. If I can save one person's life—'

'You're too late. The Skulls are hanging thirty prisoners to-morrow.' There it was. She was a spy.

'Shit.' Kara shook her head. 'Figures. Three of theirs got killed at Hasster's so they're going to kill thirty of ours.'

'Were you behind the bombing?'

'No. No way. This was the work of some mad kid. It wasn't us.'

'A kid?'

'Yeah. We're going to have words with him.' Kara glanced around. 'Can we keep walking? Talking on the street will get us noticed.'

Yas shook her head in exasperation. 'Sure.'

'Did you see or hear anything else?' asked Kara as they moved on.

'Here.' Yas held out the list and Kara plucked it from her hand a heartbeat later.

'What is it?'

'A list of suspected Hanran. I took it from Aisling's office.'

'From his office?' There was something different about Kara's voice. It sounded almost respectful.

'Yeah.'

'Thank you. That was incredibly brave of you.'

'Incredibly stupid.'

'No. Not stupid. We need this. And I do appreciate the danger it places you in.'

'Like you care. Well, that's it. No more. I've done my part. I don't want to see you again.'

Kara smiled. 'There's one more thing I need you to do. Just one, and then I promise I'll leave you alone.'

'You already said you'd not ask anything else of me.' Yas's temper flared. Even as she said it, she knew Kara would never leave her alone. There would always be one more thing.

'I need a map of the Council House with all the rooms and who they belong to. And, most importantly, I need you to look for where they keep the Tonin. It'll be somewhere safe – hard to get to.'

'Tonin?'

'They have people who can open up windows in space, connecting one place to another, even if they're thousands of miles apart. It's old world magic but somehow Raaku's managed to bring it back and put it in humans. Once the window is established, they can march whole armies through them. That's how they got behind our lines during the invasion, moved around the country so quickly. We want to know where they are so we can work out how to destroy them. With them gone, the Skulls can't get reinforcements into Kiyosun. Then we can really hurt the bastards.'

'If they're inside the Council House, it doesn't matter where they are. They're untouchable. The Skulls have that place sewn up tight.'

'Just try and find out where they are.'

'I can't do this. I was sure they were going to arrest me today. I can't get hanged. You need to find someone else.'

But Yas was talking to herself. Kara had disappeared again.

19

Tinnstra

Aisair

'The king's dead.' Aasgod's words hit the room hard. Shock ran across every face, all their hopes turned to ash.

'What happened?' asked Harka.

'The king's brother,' replied Aasgod, still trying to catch his breath. 'He betrayed us.'

'Prince Larius?' said Majas. 'Why?'

Aasgod looked down at the girl in his arms as if he didn't want her to relive the events through his words. Someone tried to take the girl from him, but she hung on to the mage with all her might. Tinnstra's heart broke just looking at her. She was so small, so fragile.

'Hush, my dear. Everything will be okay,' Aasgod lied as he stroked her hair. Once she'd quietened down, he continued, 'Everything was going to plan. I had them all with me – the king, the queen, little Zorique here and her brother Ghent. Then Larius appeared with a cadre of Egril troops and two Chosen. They killed the king and queen before I could do anything. Prince Ghent took an arrow in the back ... we had to leave him.'

'But why? Why would Larius do such a thing?' asked Majas.

'Why does that man do anything?' Harka spat on the ground. 'Power. He was always weak and jealous of his brother.'

Aasgod nodded, still trying to catch his breath. 'He's agreed to rule Jia on the Egril's behalf. He's promised to end the Hanran.'

'Not while we still live,' said Majas.

'He dies tonight,' said Harka. 'I'll go myself.'

'What's the point? We're ruined,' said the Weeping Man. 'With the king dead, there is no Hanran.'

'Wait!' Rosina's voice silenced them all. Every head turned towards her. 'That poor girl in Aasgod's arms is now our queen and the rightful ruler of Jia. It is our duty to continue as planned. We must get her to Meigore and safety. Without her, they'll never send us aid. While she's alive, Larius will never have a legitimate claim to the throne. She's our only hope.'

'She's a child,' said the Weeping Man. 'No one will follow her.'

'You mean *you* won't,' said Harka. He stepped forward with sword raised.

Tinnstra watched in utter dismay as the room erupted with a barrage of shouting. The noise unsettled the girl and she began to cry once more. She looked as lost as Tinnstra felt. Tinnstra couldn't even begin to imagine what it must have been like for her to see her parents murdered and then find herself in this room full of madness.

'Peace,' shouted Aasgod. 'We've more—'

The far wall exploded in a ball of flame.

The blast threw Tinnstra across the room. Splinters and shards of wood flew in every direction. She lay on the ground, trying to clear her head. Her face was wet. She touched it. Blood. She wasn't sure if it was hers. Alo protect her, she hoped it wasn't hers.

Egril troops burst into their midst, white armour clearly visible through the smoke. A Chosen accompanied them, baton in hand.

The Shulka attacked, led by Harka and Majas. Swords clashed, the Shulka's straight blades ringing against the Skulls' scimitars, and then people were shouting, screaming, dying. Chaos surrounded her. Bitter smoke burned her nose with each breath. The Weeping Man lay next to her, the bottom half of his body missing. A surprised look on his tattooed face.

No.

A blast from the Chosen smashed into the wall beside her, shocking Tinnstra into action. Sobbing, she pushed herself upright, ignoring the pain and the way the room spun, and scrambled away on her knees, with her coat still in her arms.

A body tumbled into her, knocking her over. A Shulka, gutted from hip to hip, covered Tinnstra in blood. She pushed him away, crawled on towards the trapdoor. It was still clear. She could get out. *Escape.*

Then she saw Aasgod. A splinter jutted from his eyebrow. He stood in front of Zorique, protecting her, with lightning flaring from his hands. He looked invincible, fighting the Skulls. Then he turned and she saw that the back of his black robes were shredded, exposing bloodied and lacerated flesh. *How is he even standing?*

A Skull lunged at the mage but Aasgod thrust out his palm and the man stopped dead. The very air buckled, crushing the Skull's body inwards with a crunch of bone. Lifeless, he collapsed to the floor.

To her left, Harka fell under a flurry of blades. Majas killed a Skull and then immediately took on two more. The Chosen blasted one of the other Shulka, turning her to ash. Tinnstra crawled past Rosina, half-buried in rubble, eyes devoid of life. A bolt crackled past her head, singeing her hair. Blood splattered across the floor. Other Hanran fighters held the Egril back but they'd not survive much longer.

She glanced around and saw Zorique. The girl was petrified, crouched down behind the mage. Aasgod repulsed attack after attack by the Skulls, but he couldn't last much longer. Not against that onslaught, not looking as pale as he did. The girl was going to die. They were all going to die.

Tinnstra grabbed the handle on the trapdoor. *Run. All I can do is run. There's no other choice.* She opened it an inch then stopped. She looked back at Zorique. So scared, so out of place. *Just like me.* It didn't matter what her title was. She was just a frightened little girl. Zorique looked at her, eyes wide with fear and tears, pleading to be saved. *Dear Gods, I have to help her.*

Tinnstra dashed back across the room to grab the girl. As she reached for Zorique, Aasgod spun around, eyes ablaze, lightning crackling around his hands. Tinnstra shrieked and fell back but the mage stopped his attack, recognised her as an ally. 'Get her out of here.'

Tinnstra was already moving. She scooped up Zorique, wrapped her in her coat and ran while Aasgod defended their retreat. Debris now covered the trapdoor but Tinnstra found strength from somewhere, pushed the shattered wood aside and heaved the steel door open. She climbed down with Zorique, looked back, saw Aasgod following. She jumped down the last few steps to the tunnel floor. She didn't need to see any more people die. When Aasgod slammed the trapdoor closed behind him, for a second, Tinnstra felt utter relief. *I'm alive. I'm alive.* She looked down at the girl in her arms and couldn't believe what she'd done. She'd rescued the queen. Somehow, she'd done it.

There was a crack of lightning, bright in the darkness. Tinnstra screamed and covered her eyes with her hands.

'Pull yourself together,' snapped Aasgod, climbing down towards them. His face was a bloody mask. 'I've sealed the door, but it won't hold them for long.'

Tinnstra's relief evaporated. It was only a stay of execution. She lowered Zorique to the ground, untangling her from the coat. Not knowing what else to do, she put it back on. At least she still had the letters.

'Which way?' demanded Aasgod. He loomed over her, eyes full of fire and drenched in blood, as terrifying as the enemy.

There were four tunnels. She couldn't remember which she'd come through. Blood seeped into her eyes. It was hard to focus. The sounds of battle grew louder above her. *There is no time.* Her whole body shook with fear and shock as her panic continued to build.

'*Which way?*' Aasgod's eyes glowed. Smoke rose from his clothes and sparks flickered around his hands.

'This way,' she said, pointing to her left.

'Are you sure?'

'Yes, yes.' She recognised it now. She always knew the way to run.

'Zorique.' Aasgod's voice was softer but still commanding. The girl looked up, sniffing back her tears. 'We need to crawl through the tunnel to get to safety. You have to go first but I'll be right behind you.'

The girl shook her head. 'I'm scared.'

'So am I, sweet child, but in this we have no choice,' replied Aasgod, stroking her face. Someone screamed above them and a body crashed against the trapdoor. 'We must go now.'

Tinnstra had no idea where the girl found the courage, but, thank the Four Gods, find it she did. She scurried along the tunnel like a mouse.

'I won't let them take her,' said Aasgod as he crouched down. 'She means more to us than anyone knows. The future of the world rests with her.'

Tinnstra nodded, not understanding, more scared for herself than for the princess. She wasn't even sure why she'd gone back to help now. It wasn't what she did. At least she knew how to run and hide. 'May the Four Gods protect us all.'

Aasgod snorted and followed Zorique into the tunnel. Tinnstra came behind him. Zorique set the pace. *Not fast enough. Dear Gods, we need to be quicker or we're dead.*

Tinnstra listened for sounds the Egril were following. Everyone else had to be dead by now. Or captured. It was only a question of how soon the Egril would spot the trapdoor.

Blood dripped from her head as she crawled along, little red dots splattering her dirty, dusty hands. She could hear Zorique crying ahead of her, but at least they were still moving. It would all be over if they got trapped in the tunnel. Stone pushed down on her back, rough rock scratched and tore at her skin. She breathed in stale air, hot from her own panic, drying her mouth out even more.

There was a crack from behind, the sound of metal crumpling. The trapdoor breaking.

She pushed on. She couldn't stop. She didn't want to die down there, in the dark, on her hands and knees.

Voices echoed along the tunnel behind her. 'We have to move faster,' she whispered urgently. 'The Skulls are coming.'

Inch by inch, the tunnel widened, allowing them to pick up speed. 'Come on,' she urged herself.

Light filled the tunnel ahead. Aasgod and the girl were standing in the room beyond, filthy with blood and dirt. A hand helped Tinnstra to her feet. It was the Shulka she'd met earlier. She fell into his arms, needed to feel his strength. 'The enemy follow.'

'I will stop them.' The Shulka touched his head against Tinnstra's. 'Hurry.'

'Thank you,' replied Tinnstra as he let her go.

'We are the dead,' the man answered, a smile on his face as he drew his sword. He knew his fate, accepted it and found comfort in it. Tinnstra envied him, wished she'd even a fraction of his courage. She nodded at Aasgod. The mage picked up the girl once more and they set off down the tunnel.

As they ran, Tinnstra could hear the Shulka pray, his voice loud and clear.

'*We are the dead who serve all who live.*

'*We are the dead who fight.*

'*We are the dead who guard tomorrow.*

'*We are the dead who protect our land, our monarch, our clan.*'

Tears ran down Tinnstra's face. From fear and sorrow, from pain and horror. Her father used to say there was magic in the prayer, but whatever power it had, it was nothing compared to the Egril's might. How long would it be before there was no one left to recite the words?

'*We are the dead who stand in the light.*

'*We are the dead who face the night.*

'*We are the dead whom evil fears.*

'*We are the Shulka and we are the dead.*'

Aasgod suddenly stopped, pulled Tinnstra in front of him and thrust the girl into her arms. 'Keep moving. I'll close the tunnel.'

Tinnstra looked past him, back the way they'd come. 'But the Shulka—'

'He's dead already,' said Aasgod. 'Now move.' Tinnstra took a few hesitant steps forward. She didn't want to leave the mage. 'Move!' His voice shook her to the bones and she had no choice. She ran.

The explosion shook the tunnel. Tinnstra was thrown against one wall and then the other but managed to keep her feet, managed to protect the princess. The noise and fury of the blast pounded her ears. Smoke and dust smothered her and stole the light from the torches. Panic gripped her like she'd never known before. Was the mage alive? What would she do with the princess if he wasn't? She pulled the girl tighter into her arms, fighting back a sob. Then Aasgod appeared, crackling with energy. His red eyes burned with fury as he saw her standing there. Tinnstra's fear of the man grew but, when he marched past, she followed. It was safer with him no matter how much he scared her.

They moved quickly, illuminated only by the energy flaring off Aasgod, turn after turn until they were dizzy from it all. Then Aasgod stopped, thrust out a hand. Tinnstra skidded to a halt.

'It's a dead end,' said Aasgod.

Tinnstra tried to catch her breath. 'There's a hook. Pull the hook.'

With a creak and a groan, the door opened.

'There's stairs leading up on the other side of this chamber,' said Tinnstra as she returned Zorique to the mage. She took the lead, stumbling forwards, searching with her hand. Relief flooded through her when she reached the steps.

She hesitated at the top, fearful that the Egril would be waiting, although they had no choice but to go forward. A sliver of light appeared in the dark, growing wider until Tinnstra could see the inn's kitchen. She crawled in first, shaking with fear, looking for the enemy. The kitchen was clear. She grabbed a carving knife and darted across to the inn's front door. *Please let there be no one outside.* Even with the knife in her hand, she had no idea what she'd do if the Skulls were waiting.

She peered into the darkness, listened to the silence. Nothing. They were alone.

She went back into the kitchen and signalled for the others to come up. They staggered into the room, panting. Aasgod placed the girl on the ground and slumped over a counter top as he fought for breath.

Tinnstra closed the trapdoor behind them. There was no way the Egril were following – not after that explosion – but she still pushed a cupboard over the trapdoor. Better safe than dead.

'There's food here, some clothes to change into,' she said as she tried to catch her breath. 'But we need to be quick. The Egril might be on their way here.'

'Let's go,' said Aasgod. He took a step forward and stopped, and his eyes rolled back in their sockets. The mage's legs went out from under him and he smashed into the table full of crockery.

20

Jax

Kiyosun

Jax and three former Shulka sat on empty crates in the back of an empty warehouse down by the empty docks. A small fishing boat hung on ropes from the rafters in one corner. A patch of dark wood showed where it had been repaired before the invasion. Jax wouldn't have been surprised if it were the last surviving boat in Kiyosun. The Egril had taken great pleasure in destroying all the city's fishing boats after the invasion and the Shulka's warships lay sunk in the harbour.

The ocean-facing gates were open, allowing the night breeze to blow through. There wasn't even an Egril ship to be seen. The port of Kiyosun was closed to the world.

He sighed, tired after a night of little sleep followed by an even longer day. Hasster's death had affected him more than he'd like to admit. The tavern owner had been a good man and he and his family hadn't deserved their fate. And now things were about to get worse. 'Are you sure they're going to hang thirty prisoners in revenge?'

'That's what our girl inside the Council House said.' Kara held out a folded piece of paper. 'She took this from the governor's office as well.'

'What is it?' asked Bethos. A good fighter, tall, with shoulders broad enough to take on the world.

Kara handed it to Jax. 'It's a list of suspected Hanran fighters in the city.'

164

Jax scanned it. 'They haven't got a single name right.'

Kara nodded. 'I know.'

Jax sighed. 'Send someone around to a few of them – warn them that they need to hide for a while. Be clever, though. Tell too many and the Skulls will know we've got someone on the inside.'

Kara nodded. 'Will do, Boss.'

'What about the ones who are going to be hanged? The prisoners they already have?' asked Bethos. 'We've got to help them.'

'Come the morning, the Council House will be crawling with Skulls looking for any sign of trouble. It'll be a bloodbath if we try anything,' said Kara. 'To stand any sort of chance, we'd need more soldiers than we've got. More weapons.'

The last of the group, a mountain of a man, didn't say anything. Not that Jax expected him to. Greener was content to just follow orders and let his actions do the talking. There wasn't a better Shulka to have by your side when the shit came down. If Jax said they had to attack the Council House, he'd be the first over the wall. If Jax said attack the sea, then Greener would leap in. In either situation, Jax would put money on Greener coming out victorious. He always found a way.

'How many swords have we got?' asked Bethos.

'Half what we had now that the Skulls found the cache on Bleeker Street,' said Kara.

Jax rubbed at his stump, not liking what he was about to say, but there was no way around it. 'We can't do anything. Not now.'

'Don't say that,' said Bethos. 'Don't say that. We're talking thirty people. Just because that bloody kid blew up some Skulls.'

'It's a mess, there's no denying it,' said Jax, 'but you know what's in play. The king and his family should be at the gate in the next few days and that has to be our only priority.' Jax looked from one face to the next. 'I don't want anyone to die, but Kara's right – we don't have the numbers right now. We need everyone to help with the king's escape. Once he and his family are on their way to Meigore, we can start hitting the Egril again. Until then, we keep our heads down.'

Even Bethos could see the logic to that. His shoulders slumped. 'What are we going to do about Dren?'

'I've sent Monon to have a word,' replied Jax. 'Dren needs to stop. It's the only way to keep everyone safe.'

'This is no way to fight a war,' said Bethos.

Jax chewed on his lip for a moment, then turned to Kara. 'This girl. The one on the inside. How much does she know about us – if it all goes wrong?'

'She knows my name, my face,' said Kara. 'But that's it. Not enough for them to find me. We're safe.'

Jax liked Kara. The woman had no false bravado. She always got the job done quickly and efficiently. 'Tell her not to do anything that may compromise her. We can't act on anything until the king is free anyway.'

Kara nodded. 'I've told her already but I'll tell her again. I've asked her to locate the Tonin.'

'What about the Daijaku? We found a way into their roost?' Jax asked Bethos.

'We've not been able to get close. They have security sewn up tighter than Monon's purse. Tolis was the last one who tried his luck and you know what happened to him.'

Hanged, drawn and quartered for the whole city to see. *Poor bastard.* Jax shook his head. 'We still have to try. As long as the Skulls control the sky as well as everything else, we won't get anywhere. But if we can take out the Daijaku and the Tonin at the same time, the Skulls will be crippled in Kiyosun.'

A long, drawn-out whistle interrupted them. One of the lookouts. Someone was approaching the warehouse. Everyone leaped to their feet, and Jax would have reached for his sword if he had one, or even a sword-arm to reach with. Blood surged through him as his body prepared for fight or flight.

A second whistle followed. Shorter. A friend. They all relaxed, even if they didn't return to their seats.

Monon appeared a second later, entering the warehouse through a door at the back. He shook hands with the others, nodded at Jax.

'Did you see the boy?' asked Kara.

'I did,' replied Monon, not looking too happy about it.

'What did he say?' said Jax, already knowing the answer.

'He said no,' said Monon. 'Though not quite as politely as that.'

Jax sat down. 'That's all we need.'

'I told you – that kid's angry at the world,' said Monon. 'He'd be a great asset if we could control him, but we can't.'

Jax glanced at his friend, who looked just as tired as he felt. 'If he's not going to listen, then we need to keep him under control until our main business is done. Take Greener and a couple of others and pick him up.'

Monon nodded. 'What do we do with him then?'

'Bring him here,' replied Jax. 'Maybe a one-to-one chat will help him come around to our way of thinking.'

'And if he won't come quietly?'

'Do what you have to do.'

21

Darus

Aisair

Darus stood the ruins of the Hanran hideout while his troops searched the bodies. It infuriated him that Aasgod had succeeded in escaping from the castle with the child in the first place, but, it looked like Darus had just wiped out a key group of Hanran in Aisair. If Aasgod and the child were amongst the dead, the Emperor would be happy and glory would be his.

The Egril losses were barely worth noting; eight soldiers died fighting the Shulka in the room and another five in the tunnels when the explosion went off. Nothing to lose any sleep over. The fools deserved to die. No one should've escaped. They could explain themselves to Kage in the Great Darkness.

'You.' He waved a finger at a nearby trooper and the man snapped to attention. *Good.* Darus liked obedience. 'Check everybody here. I want names. And tell me the moment you find Aasgod and the child.'

'Sir. Yes, sir.' The trooper saluted before executing a sharp right turn and marching off.

Already bored, Darus found a chair that still had four legs, set it upright and sat down. He hated this part – the waiting. At least he could have some time to himself. He pulled out a slim volume of *The Trials of Kage* from his pocket, a beautiful leather-bound edition, handwritten and illustrated by a high priest from a temple in the Rolshvik Mountains. It was one of his favourite possessions – after his knives, of course.

Darus settled down to read, stretching out his legs to rest his feet atop a dead man's forehead.

The book told how Kage seized a glimmer of light lost in the Great Darkness and turned it into the world, feeding it with his blood to make it grow as a gift to his children, Alo, Xin, Ruus and Nasri.

He brought life to the world and created the five nations of Egril, Jia, Meigore, Dornway and Chongore so they all would have kingdoms to rule.

Egril was to be Kage's and Kage's alone. It was the heart of the world, the start of all creation and closest to the Great Darkness. The people who lived there were his Chosen and most favoured, made from his blood and filled with his ferocity.

Jia belonged to Alo and, as Kage's firstborn, he was given magic so he could build great temples in Kage's honour.

Xin held sway over Dornway and to his favourite daughter, he filled the mountain of Ffrilyon with eternal flames so she could forge his sword, Twilight, and sacrifice the unworthy in his name.

Ruus commanded Chongore, the most fertile land, so no one would ever know hunger.

For Nasri, his youngest and most curious child, Kage gave the islands of Meigore and all the oceans to explore so that she would never be bored.

All his children had to do was give Kage blood in return and pledge their souls to him when the time came to return to the Great Darkness.

But the four would not. Struck with greed, they wanted everything for themselves. Alo, Xin, Ruus and Nasri imprisoned Kage on a rock beside the Great Darkness and stole his powers for themselves, declaring themselves Gods in his stead. They tricked humankind into believing they were the powers behind the wonders of the world and basked in the false glory that was bestowed upon them.

The crows, however, ferrying souls to the Great Darkness, found Kage and recognised him for who he was. In return for an eye and an ear, the crows freed Kage and he returned to the world. He found that only the Egril had kept their faith with him.

Only they had rejected the False Gods. From the other peoples, he took back his gifts and left them to fend for themselves until it was time to pay for their failings. Until it was time for Sekanowari, the Last War, when the whole world would once more return to the Great Darkness.

'So, this is where you disappeared off to.'

Darus looked up and saw Skara step through the hole in the wall he had made when they stormed the room. Not who he wanted to see. Could she never leave him alone?

'Looks like you had some fun,' she said. 'But I'm rather hurt you didn't invite me along. I was all lonely in the castle waiting for you.'

Darus sighed, shut his book and replaced it in his pocket. There'd be no peace and quiet now. He smiled but made no effort to pretend it was genuine. 'Skara. So nice to see you.'

'Did you catch him?'

Darus waved a hand. 'They're checking the bodies now.'

'But he's here?'

By Kage, she pissed him off with her implications. 'Does it look like we let anyone escape?'

She raised an eyebrow, pretending she wasn't impressed. 'I hope so – after he escaped you at the castle ... I'd hate for you to lose him again. Not to mention the girl.' Skara twirled her axe.

Darus jumped to his feet. '*That* wasn't my fault. That idiot Larius moved too soon – against my explicit orders. If we didn't need him, his head would be on a spike somewhere right now.'

'Of course, brother. Of course. *Obviously* not your fault. I'm sure everyone would agree. And if they don't ... well, what does it matter? If you have Aasgod and the girl now, Raaku will be pleased.'

If. Skara didn't have to elaborate. There was nothing more lethal to a man's career than failure. He watched the soldiers check the bodies, face after face. Skara had got to him – sowed that little seed of doubt. By Kage's rage, he *hated* her. As another body proved not to be Aasgod, the seed sprouted. Raaku did not forgive. His punishment would—

Darus drew his baton and squeezed the grip as he tried to stay

170

calm. The soldiers had nearly finished checking the room.

'Perhaps his body is under the rubble somewhere?' Skara kicked a rock. 'Shall we dig?'

Bitch. Darus was tempted to use his baton on her. Put an end to his misery. But no, he couldn't do that. *Not yet.*

The trooper returned. 'Sir. I'm sorry, sir, but it would appear the mage and the girl eluded us.' This time his salute was shakier.

'Oh *dear.*' Skara giggled.

'Fuck!' He wanted to kill someone. He glared at Skara. He'd love to kill *her.*

'I've warned you about that temper of yours, Darus.'

'Don't push your luck, sister,' he said. 'They can't have gone far. Not yet.' He pointed at a trooper with his baton. 'You! Get everyone out. Start searching the streets. Tear the city apart if you have to. GO!'

No one needed telling twice. They ran from the room, eager to please him.

'They'll find him, brother,' said Skara, softer this time, with no humour. She knew her career was tied to his.

'Of course.' Darus nodded. He wasn't taking any chances, though. 'I'll request the use of the Kyoryu.'

Skara perked up. 'You'll have to say why.'

'I'll say why but not confess all.'

Skara was quiet for a moment, then placed her hand on his shoulder. 'We'll find them.'

Her sympathy was worse than her gloating. Why had Kage seen fit to punish him with such a sibling?

He stormed from the building. Night had fallen, bitterly cold, and the street was empty except for four soldiers standing guard. They jumped to attention when they saw him. *A wise move.* He felt the need for blood.

After he'd sent the request for the Kyoryu, he'd visit the castle cells, find someone to bleed. He deserved that, at least. There was nothing better than pain to lift his mood. Nothing.

DAY FOUR

22

Tinnstra

Aisair

Light fell on Tinnstra's face, waking her. For a moment, she felt confused. She didn't recognise the room or the chair she was curled up in. Then the pain from her head and her battered body hit. Even sitting up hurt. Then she saw Zorique asleep under a pile of blankets with Aasgod beside her and it all came back. The inn. The queen of Jia and the Lord Mage. Everyone dead. The fear came next, mixing with the pain.

She managed to get Aasgod upstairs, dressed his wounds with strips of cloth she'd found in the kitchen and then put him into bed. The girl had clung to Aasgod's bedside, too frightened to leave the mage and refusing to sleep but, in the end, exhaustion had given her no option. Tinnstra had tucked her up in blankets next to the mage.

Every part of her body was in agony. She touched her scalp, feeling the dried blood holding her gashed forehead together. She'd been lucky not to lose her scalp. Even after cleaning the wound last night, there was no hiding the cut. She brushed her hair over it and hoped that would be enough to stop anyone from noticing it. The sight of injuries like hers would be enough for someone to report her to—

The Skulls!

Tinnstra was on her feet in an instant. She rushed over to the window to check the street, praying that they hadn't surrounded the inn while she'd slept. *Thank the Four Gods.* There wasn't a Skull in sight. Snow had fallen during the night and settled, coating the cobbles. In another life, she'd have thought the scene looked beautiful, but now all she saw was danger and added difficulties.

The snow hadn't stopped people going about their daily errands now curfew was over. Snow would only make it harder to find food. *Dear Gods, as if it wasn't hard enough already.*

At least people out and about meant crowds to get lost in. If Aasgod could walk, he and the girl might be able to get away. If the Egril hadn't found the wagons, that is. Or if they didn't get picked up at a checkpoint. *If, if, if.* So much could go wrong just by stepping outside.

What have I got myself involved in? I should've run when I had the chance. Left Aasgod and the queen to it.

I still can.

The thought made Tinnstra feel guilty, but already the plan was forming in her mind. She'd sneak out of the inn while the others still slept. Run home. Lock her door. Pretend none of this had ever happened. No one knew who she really was. She'd done her part. She'd helped Aasgod and Zorique get away. No one could expect more of her. She'd done the job Beris had asked of her.

She made up her mind. Aasgod wouldn't expect her to stay anyway. It was the only real option.

'Are we safe?'

The sound of Aasgod's voice made Tinnstra jump. She turned and saw the mage was awake and staring at her. A rush of guilt hit her along with a sudden dread that he could read her thoughts. She dropped her eyes.

'We are for now, I think,' replied Tinnstra, unwilling to meet his gaze. Even injured and weak, Aasgod was still an intimidating man. She felt herself shrivel. 'How are you?'

'Alive,' croaked Aasgod.

She looked up. Some colour had returned to his cheeks – if grey could be called a colour. 'You have some serious injuries on your back. I cleaned up the wounds as best I could and bandaged everything, but I'm no expert. You need to see someone who knows what they're doing. Someone who can stitch them and care for them properly.' Truth was, Tinnstra didn't even believe that would make a difference. It was a wonder the mage was still alive.

'We both know that's not going to happen. What about Zorique … ?'

Tinnstra glanced down at the girl asleep beside the bed. It was hard to think of her as the queen. She was so small to have the whole country's hopes on her shoulders. 'She's doing okay. I gave her some food and water and she's been asleep since then. Poor thing. She's been through so much.'

'These are the days we find ourselves in. All we can do is our best to deal with them.'

'I still have your letters of travel,' said Tinnstra, picking up the papers from a nearby table. She'd unstitched them from her coat after she'd bandaged up the mage. 'At least you can still get past the checkpoints with these.'

Aasgod rubbed his face but didn't take the papers from her. 'As you say, I'm not in a fit state to move.'

'Harka said there was a wagon at the stable on Garrett Street. Maybe it's still there. Is there anyone I can ask to pick it up for you? Maybe someone could bring it over here for you?'

'Everyone I knew was in that meeting room last night. I doubt any of them are still alive.'

'I'm sorry.' Tinnstra sat down on a stool, her shoulders slumped and her eyes fixed on the floor. She didn't want to cry. 'I think it was my fault.'

'How so?'

'I was stopped by a Chosen on my way to the meeting. Harka thought he might've read my mind. That's how they found us.'

'Did you know how I planned to get the king and his family out of the castle?'

'No.'

'Or the location of the meeting?'

'I knew about this inn.'

'Then stop feeling sorry for yourself. Only someone intimate with all our plans could have betrayed us to the enemy.'

Tinnstra looked up. 'I'm sorry. I'm not very good at this.'

'Who is? Stop apologising.' Aasgod grimaced as he tried to sit up. Tinnstra helped him into a more comfortable position.

'You shouldn't move too much,' she said as she passed him some water before scooting back to her place by the window. He scared her, even wounded as he was. She remembered what he'd done to the Skulls with a wave of his hand – what he could do to her if he so wished.

Aasgod took another sip of water. 'However, your idea is a good one.'

'My idea?'

'To collect the wagon and bring it here.'

'But you said you didn't know anyone who could collect it.'

Aasgod's smile held no warmth. 'I know you.'

Tinnstra got to her feet, holding up both hands as if to ward off his words. 'No. I'm sorry, but no.'

'*No?*'

The room seemed to shake with the word. She wanted to crumble beneath his stare, but the Skulls scared her more.

'No,' she repeated, shaking her head, not quite believing she'd said it. 'No. I said I'm no good at this. I wasn't even supposed to be involved. It was only because of my brother. I've done my part. I'm going home. I wish you well. I really do. I hope you get away but … no. Not me.'

'There's no one else.'

'I'm not a Shulka. Far from it. I'm sorry, but I can't help you,' said Tinnstra, pulling on her coat, eager to get away. 'It's nothing personal. I would like to help you. I would, but I'm just not cut out for this.'

For a brief moment, fire flared in Aasgod's eyes and Tinnstra stepped back, as if another yard would save her from his fury. Then a sense of calm fell over the mage. 'Why were you with Harka and the others if you don't want to help?'

'My brother asked for my help, but … he died and I … I wasn't supposed to be there.' She looked to the door, to the way out. It was so close and yet so far.

'You could've escaped last night. But you came back for the girl, stayed with us. You could've left us at any time.'

'I didn't know if you were going to live or die and I couldn't leave the girl. She's ... she's too young to be on her own ... But you're alive now. You don't need me—'

'I need you to get the wagon. Without it, you might as well have left us all to die. Your brother will have died for nothing. Is that what you want?'

Tinnstra sat down and put her head in her hands. If only Beris had lived instead of her. He'd have no doubts over what to do, no fear of helping the mage and the queen. She pictured the route she'd have to take to Garrett Street. She knew where the checkpoints were and how to avoid them. Maybe she could do it. If she was quick. If she was careful. She shook her head. What was she thinking? It was madness to go. But Aasgod was right. She couldn't betray them now.

Tinnstra looked up, hating the position she was in. 'I'll do it. I'll get the wagon. But after that, you're on your own. You'll have to drive it out of the city without me.'

Aasgod smiled. 'Of course. Of course. I couldn't ask any more of you.'

'Right. Okay.' Tinnstra stood up. Took a deep breath. 'I'll be as quick as I can.'

'We'll be here, ready and waiting,' replied Aasgod.

Tinnstra headed for the door again, trying not to think too much about what she'd just agreed to do. She grabbed the door handle, turned it.

'One last thing,' said Aasgod.

'What's that?'

'I need to know the name of the person saving us.'

'Tinnstra. My name's Tinnstra.'

Aasgod's eyes narrowed. 'What was your father's name?'

'My father was Dagen of Clan Rizon. My mother was Moiri of Clan Rizon.'

Aasgod nodded. 'I thought you looked familiar. But you said you're not a Shulka?'

'I'm not.' And with that she ran downstairs.

The cold hit her as soon as she stepped outside and she pulled her coat tighter around her. It did her little good as she still shivered and shook. She cursed the snow. It was going to make everything so much harder. And what had Harka said? Something about reaching a gate? What gate was that? She hoped Aasgod knew, otherwise they'd not be going anywhere. The whole thing was a disaster.

She set off slowly, her nerves in shreds. Her eyes never stopped moving. Every window she saw held a danger, every door hid an enemy, every face concealed a threat. For once, she was glad of the fear. It made her sharp. It kept her alive. It tuned her in to the world and warned her of anything that could harm her.

The bells started to ring just after she'd passed through the Butchers' Quarter. It wasn't the curfew bell, it was too early. The sound grew and spread until the ringing filled the whole city.

'What's going on?' asked a passing man.

'I don't know,' replied Tinnstra. Nothing good, that was for sure.

The bells brought the whole street to a standstill. Everyone looked up into the skies as if the answers were going to come from the Gods. Tinnstra couldn't stop, though, and continued to thread her way through the crowd.

She crossed another street when the criers appeared. 'The king is dead! The king is dead!'

Shock, anguish and disbelief rippled through the crowd as the words spread. 'The king is dead! The king is dead!' A woman collapsed into her husband's arms while others cried and moaned. Tinnstra could see the hope die in the faces of the people around her. She knew exactly how they felt. Cariin had been well loved. A link to life before the Skulls.

She'd crossed over Alliance to Hasling when she realised she was the only one still moving. The whole city had been struck still by the news. She had no choice but to stop. To keep walking would bring undue attention and that was the last thing she wanted.

Another crier approached the corner of Hasling, ringing a small bell as he walked. 'The king is dead! The king is dead!' He stopped a few yards from her and unrolled a news-sheet. 'The king is dead. Murdered by his closest advisers. The king is dead. Murdered by Shulka traitors along with the queen and their children, Prince Ghent and Princess Zorique. Prince Larius will be crowned king with the full moon.'

Tinnstar couldn't believe it. That was only three weeks away. The Skulls weren't wasting any time.

The crier resumed ringing his bell and moved on to spread the news further.

Slowly, people woke from their shock. Tinnstra could hear mutterings and curses, blaming the Shulka for the king's death.

'Wasn't enough that they lost us the war,' said one man. 'Now they do this.'

'Bastards. They lorded it over us like they were something special before the Egril came, and now they've gone and made it worse for us,' said another. 'Why kill Gentle Cariin?'

'They were supposed to protect the king,' added a woman with a babe in her arms. 'I just can't believe it.'

'I don't think they did anything,' said Tinnstra. 'It's lies. Something the Skulls want us to believe.'

One of the men looked at her as if she were mad. 'You saying the king's not dead?'

'I don't think the Shulka killed him,' replied Tinnstra, her voice dropping to a whisper. Why had she spoken?

'Why would the criers lie? Eh?' spat the woman. 'I think they've got more important things to do than waste our time with a load of lies.'

'The Egril are just trying to turn us against each other.' Tinnstra looked from one face to another but it was as if she spoke another language. 'The Shulka have protected us for centuries.'

The man dismissed her with a wave. 'Piss off, lady. Do us all a favour and keep your opinions to yourself.'

Tinnstra's cheeks flushed but she did as she was told. Head down, she left Hasling and headed east. She couldn't believe people were so ready to think ill of the Shulka, but there was no point arguing with them. She didn't need the attention. Taking no chances, she followed the back streets and quiet roads and took detours around any areas that might be patrolled by Skulls.

When she reached Garrett Street nearly an hour after she'd left the inn, she stopped dead. No way was she going any further.

The street was full of Skulls.

23

Yas

Kiyosun

Yas carried Little Ro on her hip as she walked alongside her mother towards the Council House amidst a growing stream of people heading for the square. Hangings always got everyone out of their homes. The Skulls made sure of that. If they were going to make an example, they wanted everyone watching.

'Maybe you should take Ro home,' said Yas for the hundredth time. 'A hanging's no place for a baby.'

'He's not going to see any of it,' replied Ma. 'And even if he did, he wouldn't understand what's going on.'

'It's not safe.'

'And what if the Skulls see I'm not there? Eh? What'll happen then?'

'They won't—'

'By Alo's good bloody grace, Yas. We've been arguing about this since we both woke up. I'm tired of it. I'm sure if Little Ro could speak, he'd tell you he's sick to death of hearing you moan about it, too. I'm going and, as you're working, he's staying with me. Got it?'

'At least stand at the back so if anything happens, you can get away.'

'Just concentrate on what you need to do, all right? Make it through the day without a beating.'

Little Ro wrapped his finger in Yas's hair and gave her a smile that made her heart melt. 'I'll do my best.' Of course, she

183

wouldn't be helping the bloody Hanran if that were the case. Yas wondered if anyone had noticed the list was missing and, if they had, whether they suspected anyone – suspected her. Her mind raced with it all. She wasn't even at work yet and already she was a bag of nerves. And it was all her own bloody fault. Why had she done it? Why had she stolen the list?

She kissed Little Ro's cheek and knew why. He needed a better world than the one they had. He needed a chance in life. She rubbed her nose against his. 'Mama loves you.'

'Mama,' replied Little Ro. His answer for most things. Bless him.

Yas's stomach lurched when they reached the square, already packed with spectators. The scaffolds loomed over the crowd – five nooses for thirty necks. She stopped, clutched Ro tighter to her. 'I want you to take him home right now. No arguing. Please, for me.' Tears welled up in her eyes.

'You're being silly,' replied Ma.

'I've got a bad feeling about this. Please – take him home.'

Ma shook her head. 'I'm not gonna get any peace and bloody quiet if I don't, am I?'

'Thank you.'

'Come on, love.' Ma reached for Little Ro but the boy didn't want to let go. He clung to Yas with all his might. She lifted him off her hip as he started to cry, face red.

'Mama!' His little fingers pulled at her hair. 'Mama!'

'Stay with Grandma, Ro. Mama's got to go to work. I'll be back soon.' She pushed him away, dying inside as he screamed and thrust his arms out, trying to hold on to her.

'Hush, Ro,' said her ma, wrapping her arms around his wriggling body. Still he screamed and fought.

'Take him home, Ma,' said Yas, trying to be cold when all she wanted to do was keep hold of her child.

'I will, love. May Alo bless you.' Ma turned and headed back the way they'd come. Ro shouted and hollered, wordlessly pleading for Yas to come with them.

His crying followed her all the way to the gatehouse. The Skulls had doubled the guard because of the hangings but she got through quick enough. She barely noticed the guards groping her, already used to it and expecting it. A few people in the crowd shouted insults as she passed through the gate but she paid them no mind. Let them believe what they wanted – she knew the truth of what she was doing and why.

The mood inside was sombre, the usual banter silenced. The only sounds came from food being prepared and cooked. Bets barely gave Yas a nod as she walked through the door and she only got a grunt from Arga.

The silence continued as Yas and Arga went about their duties. They moved quickly through each room, eager to be away from a window when the condemned started to dance on the gallows. She didn't want to see anyone die. Maybe the information she'd passed to Kara had helped and the Hanran would come to save them. She hoped so.

In the meantime, Yas tried to work out where the Egril would keep the Tonin. There was that well-guarded area on the ground floor, but Yas had seen a prisoner being dragged there and Arga had confirmed it was for interrogations.

The living quarters upstairs were a mix of single rooms and dormitories, and she'd cleaned most of those. That left the kitchens and the prison cells. The Tonin weren't being kept in the kitchen and they wouldn't hold them in the prison cells ... Then she remembered the steel doors beyond the cells. What did they keep behind those?

Inside his office, the governor was dressed in his full ceremonial uniform and accompanied by three aides. Judging by his haggard eyes, he'd not slept much the night before. The group sat at the table, facing each other.

'There must be some way to stop this farce,' said Aisling. 'Something we can do.'

'We've tried everything, my Lord,' said one of the aides. 'The Egril are being quite insistent.'

'What about me?' replied Aisling. 'What if they hang me instead? Surely my death would make more of a statement?'

The aide shook his head. 'I'm afraid you're worth more to them alive. They'll never agree.'

Aisling slammed his fist on the table. 'Damn it. Damn it all. And they still demand I go and say a few words to justify the murders! Do they want me to just stand there and watch innocent people die?'

'It'll be worse if you don't, sir.'

Aisling held his head in his hands. 'I thought I could help people if I worked with the Egril, but it makes no difference what I do.'

One of the aides noticed Yas watching. 'You two. Leave. Have the kitchen send up some wine.'

Arga bowed. 'Yes, sir. Yes, sir.'

The two girls left quickly. Yas was confused by what she'd seen. She'd never have thought Aisling would give a shit about anyone other than himself, and yet there he was, nearly in tears, volunteering to be hanged in the prisoners' place.

But Yas still wore the bruises from the last time she'd felt sorry for the man. It wouldn't happen again. He deserved everything he received.

24

Tinnstra

Aisair

Tinnstra ducked back around the corner, hiding from the Skulls in Garrett Street. She could feel the bile churning in her gut. *By the Four Gods, what am I doing? It's madness. I should run while I can. Leave them. This isn't my fight.*

She took another look to make sure and pulled her head back pretty damn quick. She'd not been imagining it. Ten Skulls at least. *Shit.*

Maybe there was somewhere she could hide. Wait until the Skulls moved on. But who knew when that would be? The truth was, she didn't have time. Aasgod and Zorique needed to get out of the city as soon as possible. She checked the alleys and storefronts, looking for a way up onto the roofs, maybe she could climb across that way, but it was all too exposed and covered in snow. The Skulls would spot her before she made it two feet – *if* she didn't fall first and break her neck.

She looked again. She didn't spot any black uniforms. No Chosen to worry about, at least.

There was nothing to do except pray her forged pass would work. She leaned against the wall, filled her lungs with air. *Everything will be all right. I don't look like a Shulka. I don't look like a threat of any kind. All I have to do is stay calm and not panic. Easy – for someone else.*

She turned into Garrett Street and a Skull spotted her immediately. 'Come here.'

Tinnstra dropped her head and walked over. Obedient. Submissive. Petrified. There was no pretence on her part.

The Skull waited, hand on his sword hilt, letting her know he was ready to draw. A long knife dangled from his belt on the opposite side. 'Where you going?' He spoke Jian well, even though his accent was thick and heavy.

Tinnstra pointed at the stable. 'Just picking up a horse and cart. I'm heading down to Haslam.' Somehow, her voice didn't crack but she could feel the sweat running down her back despite the falling snow and her legs wobbled. Two Egril stood by the stable door. Another pair had stopped a man and a woman coming from Hastin's Way. The rest were moving east, towards Lenster's.

'Papers?' asked the Skull.

Tinnstra fumbled the document from her pocket. 'Sure. Here.'

'Why Haslam?' The Skull glanced over the document.

Tinnstra prayed he couldn't read. 'My father's not well. We're hoping the climate will be better for his health. His brother – my uncle – lives there.'

'What's wrong him?'

'His lungs,' replied Tinnstra. 'It's too cold for him here. We're hoping the drier weather down south will help him.'

The Skull looked her over, then checked the paperwork again. He took his time, too much time for Tinnstra's liking.

The Skull pointed at the stable. 'Is your cart there?'

Tinnstra nodded, too scared to speak.

'Open it. Everything okay, you go.'

'Thank you,' replied Tinnstra. At first, her legs refused to cooperate, but with an effort, she got them moving and walked over to the stables.

'I'll handle this,' said the Skull in Egril to the two waiting by the door. Tinnstra kept her head down, didn't show she understood. 'You go with the others and I'll catch up with you when I'm done.'

'Oh yeah?' replied one with a chuckle. 'Sure you can handle a full search on your own? Happy to lend a hand.'

The Skull slapped his colleague on the shoulder. 'I've got this.'

The others moved off, leaving Tinnstra alone with the Skull. She hesitated, unsure of what to do.

'What's wrong?' asked the Skull in Jian.

'You scare me,' replied Tinnstra.

The Skull chortled.

A spike of anger took the edge off Tinnstra's rising panic as she shoved the stable door open and stepped inside. One day soon, she hoped the Egril would get their comeuppance. One day.

The cold, dark interior stank of oats, straw and horse muck and did nothing for Tinnstra's nerves. She hoped there would be a stable-boy inside – anyone – so she wouldn't be alone with the Skull, but the stables were empty apart from a wagon and some horses.

'Any weapons?' said the Skull.

'There's nothing here. Least, nothing I know about,' replied Tinnstra, praying she was telling the truth. Only the Gods knew what the Hanran might have hidden in the wagon.

'Sit. Don't move. Understand?'

'I understand,' replied Tinnstra. She did as she was told and let her head drop to hide how nervous she was.

The Skull wandered around the wagon, checked under the tarpaulin covering the back, then headed off to the other side of the stables. Tinnstra sat with heart in her mouth, trying not to be sick. She glanced up every now and then to check on the Skull's progress, never letting her gaze linger for long.

She caught the Skull watching her, his hand resting on the hilt of his scimitar.

Fear squeezed Tinnstra's heart.

The Skull walked over.

Tinnstra thought about all the ways she could try to kill him if she had to – the ways she'd been taught at the Kotege. *Snatch his sword. Ram my fingers into his solar plexus. Smash the heel of my palm up into his jaw. Drive his nose into his brain.* All the things she'd been trained to do. All the things she could never do. Then she imagined all the ways he could kill her, and it took all her courage just to sit there and not move.

'Nothing here,' said the Skull, sounding disappointed.

Tinnstra stood up. 'Can I go now?'

The back of his hand cracked her across the jaw, spinning her off her feet.

Blood dripped from her split lip onto the floor. His boot crunched into her ribs, flipping her over onto her back. Her head spun, her vision faded in and out and every breath sent a shard of pain shooting through her.

The Skull stood over her and took off his helmet. His face was twisted with anger. 'Stupid woman. You do as told. Better that way. Better for you. Better for me.' He threw the helmet onto a pile of straw, unbuckled his sword belt and dropped it onto the floor. His chest armour followed. He loomed above her, in a white undershirt and trousers. He looked only a year or two older than her, just like a hundred other boys she'd trained with at the Kotege. So ordinary. A boy, not a monster.

Then she saw the look on his face. The lust and, *dear Gods*, the hate. He was going to rape her and kill her.

She kicked, pushing herself away from the Skull. She had to get away. *Survive.*

With a laugh, he stepped on her ankle, grinding it with his boot. She cried out, but the Skull didn't care. He undid his trousers. 'You good, you live.'

On the floor, a few inches from her hand, lay the knife, still with the sword belt. Whatever happened, Tinnstra knew she didn't want the Skull to have a blade in his hand.

'I'll be good.' It hurt to talk. Her tongue felt too large and a mouthful of blood made her gag. Her blood.

He fell on her. Pawing at her. Yanking her trousers down, hurting her. He held her by the neck as he reached into his trousers and pulled himself free. Tears filled her eyes and she sobbed as she felt his flesh on hers.

She clawed at the ground. She had to stop him. Her fingers touched the belt as he forced her legs apart.

His grip tightened on her neck. 'Don't fight.'

Tinnstra let her legs fall open as she pulled the belt closer. His breath was hot on her neck as he lay on top of her. So heavy. He got a hand under her, lifting her groin up. She could feel him. *Dear Gods, no.*

Her hand closed around the hilt of the knife as she pushed against him, trying to throw the Skull off.

His fingers dug into her throat. She couldn't breathe.

The Skull sneered in her face. 'You enjoy real man.'

'*No.*' She pulled the knife free and stabbed him, good and hard, under the armpit.

He jerked sideways, looking confused. He let go of her throat and sat back on his knees, his hand feeling for the wound. It didn't matter. Tinnstra still had the knife and she stuck it in his kidney. She could feel his blood spill over her as she pulled it free, stabbed him again. And again. '*No.*'

The Skull tried to push her hand away but there was no strength in him. She shoved him off and then it was *her* turn to climb on top. *Her* turn to watch as he stared at her, wide-eyed and petrified. *His* turn to claw at the dirt. He coughed blood as he tried to speak. It didn't matter. He couldn't stop her. There was no mercy in her. She struck again and again. Blood soaked his white shirt and bubbled in his throat, and still she jabbed the knife in again and again, stabbed him until the rage in her died and the bastard wasn't going to hurt anyone ever again.

She stopped then, out of breath, heart racing, alive. Her hands, her clothes, everything was covered in blood. *His blood. Not mine. Not mine. I'm alive. I'm alive.*

She dropped the knife and staggered to her feet, pulling her trousers up. *I killed a man.* She couldn't believe it, but there he was, at her feet. Dead. *Shit.* What had she done?

I survived. That's what I've done. Survived. That's all that matters. But if the other Skulls come back ... Shit. She ran to the stable door, opened it a sliver and checked the street. No Skulls. They'd gone. She found a bar and locked it shut.

I've killed a Skull. I have. Killed him. The body's there. Proof. They'll hang me. Dear Gods, what have I done? The Skulls would come back for him. No doubt about it. They'd seen her go into the stables with him. They knew what she looked like. They'd come looking for her. No way they'd let it go. They'd want her punished. Not stop until she was swinging on a rope. *Shit*.

As she fastened her trousers, she noticed they were covered in blood. She swabbed at them with straw, but it did little to help. She had to get away. Run.

Only a few moments had passed, but already it was hard to connect the corpse at her feet with the man who'd so terrified her. He'd seemed so powerful before but now he was ... nothing. She remembered a woman in a house in Salin Street, left to rot. She remembered her friends at the Kotege. The Skulls had murdered too many Jians. It felt good to fight back.

She dragged him to an empty stall and covered him with straw. A thorough search would find him easily enough, but maybe the Skulls wouldn't go to that much trouble. The sight of an empty stable might be enough to send them looking elsewhere – at least for a while.

She scattered more straw over the bloodstains on the floor and then washed herself as best she could with water from a trough. There'd be no hiding the split lip, but with the gash on her forehead, she was just another battered face. There were plenty of those around these days.

Tinnstra hitched four horses to the wagon. In the back were more supplies – food, water, blankets and a tent, some feed for the horses – enough for a few days' travel if they were careful. And clothes. Clean clothes.

She put on new trousers, a new shirt, a new coat. None of them fitted that well but at least she no longer looked like she'd been in slaughterhouse, and they were a damn sight warmer than her old clothes. She buried those in the straw alongside the dead Skull.

She opened the stable doors wide and a blast of cold air hit her, stinging her cuts. The street was clear of Skulls. *Thank the Four Gods. Time to go, get back to Aasgod, and then I can walk away for good.*

But walk where? I'll be wanted. Hunted. If I stay in Aisair, I'll end up swinging. She shook her head. Fate seemed to have its own plans for her.

As she took one last look around the stables, she spotted the

Skull's knife lying on the ground. She picked it up. Blood still marked the steel. Best not to leave it behind. Better to have it with her. Just in case.

Slipping it under her belt at the base of her spine, she let her coat fall over it. She could feel it as she climbed into the driver's seat. It felt good, pressed against the small of her back, like she had some power at last. And for the first time for as long as she could remember, Tinnstra wasn't scared. *Maybe there's something of my father in me after all.*

25

Dren

Kiyosun

The hangings were due to start at noon and a crowd had gathered outside the front of the Council House to witness them. Dren thought they would all have had more than enough of that over the past six months, but then folk never failed to disappoint him.

He sat on a wall on the eastern side of the square, a stone's throw from the scaffolds, watching the preparations. There was still half an hour to go. Quist and Falsa were with him, the bag between their feet. Quist smoked a pipe, as cool as could be, but the girl looked far from happy.

'Do you think the Hanran will try and save them?' asked Falsa, her voice full of hope. The silly kid probably still believed in fairy tales and heroes on white horses. Dren didn't bother replying.

The girl looked from Dren to Quist and back again, not wanting to let the matter drop. In the end, Quist took pity on her. 'No one's coming.'

'Wh ... why not?'

Quist pointed to the other corner. 'Look over there, down that street. There's a couple of squads of Skulls waiting for anyone dumb enough to show up and try something.' Falsa's mouth dropped when she saw the soldiers. Quist then pointed to a balcony. 'And see up there? The Skulls have a load of crossbowmen ready and waiting. And there'll be even more if you want to look for them. Maybe even a Chosen or two. No way is anyone dumb enough to try anything against those sorts of numbers.'

Falsa choked back a sob. 'So, no one will even try to do any-thing? Those people are just going to die?'

Dren sighed. 'Yeah, they're going to die. If you hadn't noticed, we're fighting a war, and people die in wars.'

'But they weren't fighting,' protested Falsa. 'The Skulls are hanging them because of what we did the other night. More people will die today because of us. This is our fault.'

Angry now, Dren jumped off the wall and got in Falsa's face. He kept his voice low but made sure she heard every word. 'This isn't our fault. It's the Egril's fault for invading. It's Old Fat Man Hasster's for collaborating with them. It's the Shulka's for being bloody useless and surrendering. And it is those poor bastards' fault because they didn't do a bloody thing to stop it, either. They should be fighting. Everyone should be. We're never going to win this war if most people just shrug and do fuck all except moan about how life isn't what it used to be. If you choose to be a sheep, then don't be surprised when you end up in the slaughter yard.'

'Bu ... but ...' stuttered Falsa.

'But nothing. I'm a wolf. I do the hunting and the killing,' said Dren, jabbing himself with his thumb. 'Quist's a fucking wolf, too. It's time for you to decide what you're going to be.'

Falsa looked down, cheeks as red as fire, avoiding Dren's eyes, but he was having none of it. He lifted her chin, saw her lip tremble and her eyes fill with bloody tears. There was a time, back before the war, back when Dren still had his parents, when he'd been like that, too, but not now. There was no place for weakness in a fucking war. Especially in his crew. He bunched up his hand into a fist, ready to knock some sense into her, when Falsa looked up. 'I want to be a wolf,' she said.

'Want's got nothing to do with it,' snarled Dren. 'Either you are or you're not.'

Falsa squared her jaw, straightened herself up. 'I'm one of you. A wolf.'

'Good girl,' replied Dren. He kissed her forehead, the way his dad used to kiss his. Let her feel wanted. 'If just one other person in this crowd today gets pissed off at watching innocent people hang and decides to fight the Egril, then no one's died in vain. We need people angry. We need their blood all fired up. We need them to want to do something about this fucking army squatting on our land. We need them to realise it's not enough just to survive another fucking day. We need the Egril to keep killing ours so we get more soldiers. More wolves. It's the only way we'll win.'

Falsa nodded. 'I get it now. I understand.'

Dren glanced over at Quist, who gave him a wink back. That boy definitely knew what the score was.

The crowd stirred. The Egril were bringing out the prisoners. A squad of Skulls cleared a passage to the scaffolds. They stood shoulder to shoulder in two rows, white armour shining against the backdrop of the Jians' dirty rags. The sight of them always got Dren's guts all twisted up. He wanted the bastards dead. He grinned. Soon.

Another load of Skulls arrived with the prisoners. A right sorry bunch they were, too – shuffling along, dragging their chains, all crying and sobbing, begging and pleading. If it were ever Dren's turn, he'd not give the bastards the pleasure. He'd go out with his head held high, damn fucking proud of what he'd done.

The Skulls had only erected five nooses, so they lined up six prisoners behind each one.

Next, out came the drummer, banging a tattoo on his pigskins, letting the crowd know the show was about to start. Hot on his heels was the old man, the governor, Lord Aisling himself, grey hair swept back, hawk nose held up in the air as if the smell of common folk offended him. His long, black cloak hid Raaku's hand up his arse.

Dren spat at the sight of him. If ever there was someone on top of his kill list, then Lord Aisling was it. The father of all collaborators. He'd sold out his people for a mouthful of Egril cock just so he could hold on to some illusion of power. Dren had no idea how the man slept at night. Probably sandwiched between a couple of Skulls, taking it in turns to do what they wanted to him, smiling all the while, saying thank you, yes please, please do it again.

Aisling wasn't too popular with the rest of the crowd, either. They started booing and hissing when they saw him, and Dren could've sworn he saw the governor flinch. Served the fucker right.

By the time Aisling took his place in front of the scaffolds, the mob was right riled up. You couldn't even hear the drummer rat-tatting away beside him. Dren laughed when Aisling held up his hand for silence. *Fat chance of that happening, you wanker.*

The man was so close, Dren wished he had a brick to lob at him. Watch his face pulp. It would serve the fucker right. But Dren didn't have a brick. What he did have, though, were the orbs.

He signalled Quist. It was time. Dren slipped a glove on and ducked down, reached into the bag they'd brought with them and took hold of the bomb. He stood up just as the Skulls repositioned themselves in front of the scaffolds, bristling with spears.

Quist drew a small blade, no bigger than his thumb but plenty sharp. Dren held out his other hand and Quist nicked the side of his thumb so it bled. Dren pressed the cut against the bomb's black surface, smearing it with his blood. He could feel the orb react, start to heat up straight away. There was no messing about. The liquid inside swirled around faster and faster as the blood seeped through the surface.

Quist stepped back, giving Dren some room. The scaffold was a stone's throw away, with Aisling and the Skulls all lined up in front of it. Fucking lovely. He wound his arm back, waited one heartbeat, then threw the bomb. Dren, Quist and Falsa ducked behind the wall.

Dren covered his ears but it still felt like the end of the world when the bomb struck. The blast from the explosion smashed against the wall and, for a moment, he thought it was going to fall, crushing them all. Dirt and debris, fire and thunder – nothing else existed. His ears rang with the bloody gorgeous fury of it all as they hid behind the little barrier.

Fuck knows how long it took for the world to settle back down. For the dust to lie still. For sound to return to the world. But settle it did. There was no avoiding what he'd done.

Dren heard the screams first. The cries of the wounded and dying, the pleas for help, for the Gods, for mercy. He lowered his hands and opened his eyes. Saw Quist and Falsa staring at him, both covered in dust and dirt. Bodies lay near them, and plenty of bodies, too. Blood stained the ground. A man staggered past, clutching his severed arm. A woman tried to drag her intestines back into her stomach.

He stood on shaky legs and peered over the wall. The scaffolds were splinters and smoke. The Skulls a pile of corpses in blackened armour. And Aisling? Nothing of him left at all. Dren had done it. He'd bloody well done it. He'd got the bastard.

How many had he killed – forty? Fifty? More than he'd hoped. And the fucking Shulka had tried to stop him! What fools they were. The world had changed. It didn't need the Shulka any more. It needed Dren and people like him. A new breed of warrior. Someone who could get shit done.

A hand grabbed his shoulder. Dren spun around, ready to fight, but it was only Quist. 'We gotta go. Now. More Skulls will be on their way.'

Dren nodded but stayed right where he was. He didn't want to leave. It was his moment and he wanted to savour it.

'Come on!' shouted Quist and dragged Dren towards the south exit from the square. Falsa was with them, crying again. So much for being like Dren and Quist. The girl was a fucking sheep. Soon enough, she'd be dead like the rest of them.

People fled in every direction, pushing and shoving, desperate to escape. Dren bounced from shoulder to shoulder as he fought his way along. It was easy to lose himself in the chaos. He just let himself get sucked along, feeling the energy of the crowd, riding the panic he'd caused. He was grinning like a mad man, but he couldn't stop himself. He felt so fucking alive. He'd woken the whole city up, shown it what could be done. He had. No one else. Dren from Toxten. The fisherman's son.

It was late afternoon by the time they made it back to the streets of Toxten and the sky was bruised purple. The ruined buildings offered little protection from the wind, which promised a cold night ahead. Another hour or so and the curfew bells would start ringing, but already there was no one in sight.

Quist plonked himself down on a pile of rubble. He rested his arms on his knees and let his head drop. 'I'm knackered.'

Falsa slid down a bit of wall that was still standing until she was sitting on the ground next to him. She wrapped her arms around her legs and stared back the way they'd come, back towards the other side of town, as if she could still see the carnage they'd caused.

Dren was buzzing too much to sit down or even stand still. He bounced from one foot to the other, pacing in a circle. Grinning even as his ears still rang with the roar of the explosion and his skin still tingled with the heat from the blast. 'We did it. We did it. We fucking well did it.'

Quist raised his head and managed a half-smile. 'We sure did.'

Falsa just pressed her chin against her chest and looked like she was about to start bawling again. It was the last thing Dren wanted to see.

'Oi, Falsa, why don't you just piss off back to your parents,' snapped Dren. 'Come and find me when you've grown up.'

She looked up then, little mouth wobbling. 'M ... my parents are dead.'

'M ... my parents are dead,' mimicked Dren. 'By Alo's balls, I don't need you here. I don't need a cry-baby feeling bad about everything. Do you understand? Now go.'

'Bu ... but I haven't got anywhere else to go,' she replied. 'I'm sorry. I'll try harder. I ... I ... I promise.'

'Your promises mean fuck all to me.' He flicked his hand at her. 'Go on ... do one ... leave ... get out of here.'

'Come on, Dren,' said Quist. 'Give her a break.'

'I don't remember asking for your opinion,' said Dren without looking at his friend. He kept his eyes locked on Falsa until it finally sank into her thick head that Dren wasn't pissing about. He bloody well meant it. He wanted her gone.

She wobbled to her feet, sniffing snot. 'Dren, please—'

'Fuck. Off. Now.' He slipped his hand around the back of his jacket, where he kept the knife. He wouldn't use it, but she didn't know that. He smiled as her eyes bugged out and then she was off, running for her life.

Dren laughed as he watched her go. 'Fucking hell. Did you see her scarper? She really thought I was about to stick her.'

Quist didn't reply. When Dren turned to his friend, Quist had the same look as Falsa. Dren took a step back, screwed his face up. 'You didn't think I was going to do that, did you?'

It took Quist a moment to find his voice. 'Nah. Not really. No.' He paused. 'You weren't going to, were you?'

Dren couldn't believe it. It was like he'd been slapped. 'Fuck. What do you take me for? You know me. I wouldn't hurt her. She drives me mad but she's one of us.'

Quist didn't look convinced. 'Sure. Whatever you say, Dren. You're the boss. You say you weren't going to knife her, then you weren't going to knife her.'

'Then why ask? Why look at me like that?'

'I didn't mean anything by it, all right?' Quist held up his hands in surrender. 'Don't get mad at me.'

'Why? You worried I'm going to cut you, too?'

Quist got to his feet as casual as he could, hands still in the air. 'I'm going for a walk. Let everyone cool down a bit. That okay with you?'

Dren turned his back on him. 'Go on, piss off. You're as bad as Falsa.'

'Dren, there's no need for that ...'

Dren ignored him until he got the message and slunk off.

Alone now, he stewed at their stupidity. He expected it from Falsa but not Quist. Not after everything they'd been through together. They should be out celebrating what they'd done today, not arguing over nothing. What a waste of time.

He looked up and down the street, or rather what was left of his street. Craters, rubble, destroyed homes and fuck-all else. Here and there, the odd tent or awning had been erected to keep some of the wind out, but not much else had been done to repair the Egril's damage. He could see someone in the distance but, other than that, the place was deserted. Dren was alone.

Well, fuck them all. He climbed up the stairs to the roof. Once it got dark, maybe he'd go and cause some more mischief. No way he'd be able to sleep after what he'd done.

He slumped down in the corner of the water tower alongside the pile of Skull helmets. After today, there should be a lot more joining his collection. He'd taken out two squads and the fucking governor – just like that. Forget about that old one-armed fool Jax, too scared to take a shit. People wouldn't be telling tales about the Shulka any more. No. Dren was the legend now.

He threw a stone at one of the helmets. As it bounced off the metal with a ping, he picked up another.

'Which building is it?'

Dren stopped mid-throw. A man's voice. It'd come from the street below.

'This one.' Dren recognised the voice. Monon.

Shit.

He scrambled to his feet and scuttled over to the other corner where he could see the street. Monon, the lanky bastard, was easy to spot, and he had a beast of a man with him. They were coming for him. They had to be.

Had Monon shown up alone, Dren would've been more than happy to take him on, show him how sharp his knife was, but he didn't fancy his chances against the hulk he'd brought with him. He pressed back into the shadows, mind racing. He couldn't go down. Couldn't stay where he was, either.

That just left the roofs. *Easy*. He'd be well gone before they even got halfway up the stairs. Let the fools find nothing but an empty roof.

He scooted around the side of the water tower. He'd go to the end of the street and jump the gap to the next building over.

'Evening, Dren.'

Dren pulled up quick. There was a man on the roof already. One of Monon's boys. A bloody Shulka.

'The boss thought you might be up here. Sent me to stop you leaving,' said the man, smug smile all over his face.

Dren gave him a shit-eating grin of his own. 'You'd think, after the kicking the Egril gave you, you fucking Shulka would've learned not to be so cocky.' He threw the stone he still held in his hand. It smacked the stupid fuck straight in the eye.

The man staggered back, clutching his face. 'You little shit ...' But Dren had already passed him, sprinting along the rooftops.

Dren had spent most of his life on the roofs and even now, in the half-gloom and half-ruined, they didn't hold any fear for him. He hurdled the walls, skipped over holes and weaved around the wrecks of the water towers. This was his home, his territory.

The Shulka stumbled after him, tripping and knocking into things. The roof creaked where he took a misstep, groaned when he landed in the wrong place. He didn't have a hope.

Dren reached the end of the row. He didn't even slow down, just bounced onto the end wall and launched himself across the gap.

He landed on the next roof, bending his knees to take the impact, rolled forward to kill the momentum and then he was off again, running. *Too fucking easy*. He laughed, not caring if the Shulka heard. This was exactly what he needed.

Something hit him in the chest. Hard. Knocked him off his feet. Took the air out of his lungs. He tried to get up but a boot caught him under the chin, cracking his teeth together, rattling his skull. His vision blurred. He spat blood.

Monon stood in front of him. 'Kid, you are one pain in the arse.'

'Fuck y—'

Monon kicked Dren in the head again. The world swirled into darkness.

26

Tinnstra

Aisair

Tinnstra drove the wagon towards the South Gate. She was wrapped up in an old oilskin travelling cloak she'd found in the kit the Hanran had provided. Zorique sat in the back, hidden beneath the canvas roof covering the wagon. She'd not said much since Tinnstra had picked Aasgod and her up from the inn and Tinnstra didn't know if that was a good thing or not. Hopefully she'd get some rest once they were on the road.

Aasgod sat hunched up next to Tinnstra on the driver's seat. She'd changed his bandages but the mage's wounds worried her. Men died from lesser injuries. The fact he was still alive was a miracle.

Wrapped in an old cloak with the hood pulled over his bald head, he didn't look like a man who had advised kings and queens or commanded armies, but that was the point, after all. However, Tinnstra did know and it wasn't helping her nerves. Especially now that he was relying on her to save their lives. *May the Four Gods help them all.* Whatever strength and self-confidence she'd got from killing the Skull were long gone. In truth, she wasn't sure who frightened her more – the Skulls or Aasgod. And what if he died? She had no idea. She didn't even know where they were heading – just south, he'd said. No mention of where this gate was that they were supposed to reach before the snow settled. She wanted to ask more questions but didn't have the courage, leaving her head to spin with the madness of it all.

A few Skulls watched them pass, panicking Tinnstra, but when they didn't try to stop the wagon, she felt the first fluttering of hope in her heart. Soon, only the city gate lay ahead of them. Time to find out if the Gods were with them after all.

Tinnstra tried not to tense up. There were eight Skulls at the gate. Fully armoured. Curved swords on their hips. Spears in hand. 'Are they looking for us?'

'No. They're checking everyone,' croaked Aasgod. The Skulls were taking a wagon apart while the driver stood by and argued with them. 'Look. They don't have any papers.'

The driver was middle-aged with greasy white hair. His haunted face had the air of someone gambling on one last throw of the dice, yet who knew he'd already lost. A woman, probably his wife, lay in the back of the wagon. Sick, maybe dying. A spear shaft cracked against the man's skull persuaded him to shut up and head back into the city.

Her heart thudded as they moved closer. Her brother had died at one checkpoint, she'd nearly been raped at the stables. She dared not think about what could happen this time.

She looked around. There was no way off the road now, no way to turn back without drawing attention to them.

Tinnstra took a deep breath. *Keep calm.* As if such a thing were possible.

The sound of vast wings reached her a second before the screams.

Daijaku.

They flew low over the road and along the city wall before swooping around and back. Six of them, tall and lean, the shell-like armour covering most of their bodies leaving few parts vulnerable to attack. Spurs jutted out from their elbows, forearms and knees, sharp enough to gut any man foolish enough to get close. The beating of their batlike wings was thunderous.

People scattered, looking for any sort of cover. Already frightened by the Skull guards, Tinnstra was petrified now. Memories flashed through her mind of the invasion, of what they'd done at the Kotege.

Aasgod put his hand on hers. 'Wait.'

'We can't let them take us.'

'They won't,' said Aasgod, watching the sky. 'They're not searching for us, but if you run, they'll see and come looking. Be patient. Be brave. They'll be on their way soon enough.'

Tinnstra didn't know how to tell him that she'd never been brave. Instead, she sat there and watched the Daijaku swoop down and soar back up, again and again. A man broke under the pressure and sprinted down the main street. A Daijaku split off from the pack and flew after him. Tinnstra looked away before she saw the man die.

Minutes passed. Aasgod's breathing grew more ragged and he slumped to the side, leaning against Tinnstra while she shook with fear. Then, with a shriek, the lead Daijaku took off east and the others followed. The demons were gone, leaving only the scared and the dead behind.

At the gate, the Skulls waved through the cart they'd been inspecting and then it was Tinnstra's turn. She moved the horses closer. A Skull approached her while another covered Aasgod. A third examined the back of the wagon.

'Papers,' he said, holding out a hand. His shoulder armour bore the markings of a sergeant.

Tinnstra smiled as best she could. 'Yes, of course. Here you are.'

The Skull unfolded the paper and glanced at the writing. 'Where you go?'

'We're going to Haslam,' replied Tinnstra. 'To stay with my uncle.'

The guard stopped trying to read the documents and looked them over: Tinnstra with her face all beaten up, Zorique crying in the back and Aasgod hunched in the front, his hood pulled up over his head.

'My husband's not well. We're hoping the sea air will do him good.' Tinnstra knew she was babbling but she couldn't help herself.

The guard peered under Aasgod's hood. 'He look dead.'

'The doctor says it's just a fever,' replied Tinnstra.

The Skull thrust the papers back at her. 'Go.'

'Thank you. Thank you,' said Tinnstra, shoving the papers inside her cloak. She flicked the reins and they were off, through the gate and out of Aisair. Free. Somehow, they'd done it.

Aasgod rolled over in the seat and Tinnstra barely managed to catch him before he fell off the wagon. 'Please don't die,' she whispered. 'I can't do this without you.'

Aasgod didn't answer.

A mile on from Aisair, Tinnstra pulled the wagon to the side of the road.

'Why are we stopping?' asked Zorique, her voice all aquiver.

Tinnstra smiled, trying her best to look reassuring and hide the fear she felt. 'We need to move Aasgod into the back of the wagon with you, so he can rest and stay warm.'

'Is he going to die like that man said?' the girl asked.

'No. No, of course not. He just needs some rest, that's all. Nothing to worry about.'

'Okay,' replied Zorique, sounding as unconvinced as Tinnstra.

The girl watched Tinnstra struggle to move the mage. He was a big man with little strength left to help her. Eventually, though, she had him settled in the back and covered with what blankets they had.

'Snuggle next to him,' she told Zorique. 'Help keep him warm. The weather's only going to get worse.' As if the Gods wanted to prove her right, more snow began to fall. If Tinnstra hadn't feared their wrath, she would've cursed them for it. Instead, she climbed back into the driver's seat and steered the wagon onto the road.

Tinnstra pulled the hood of her oilskin up as the snow fell heavier. Even the horses grew skittish as it whipped around them, and whinnied in complaint. Probably wanted to be back in their stable. Tinnstra didn't blame them.

As they drove down the main road, the snow continued to get worse. It cut and nipped with a vicious touch, making Tinnstra more anxious by the second.

She glanced back towards Aisair, expecting to see Skulls or the Daijaku chasing after them. But all she saw was more and more snow falling from the sky, hiding the city from sight, splattering on her face and thumping against her cloak. One glance at the skies was enough to tell her this was only a taste of what was to come.

The world around them turned white, but at least the road was reliable, made from stone and gravel. Tinnstra just had to find a decent place to shelter for the night before it got too dark to see. For now, there was nothing but frozen fields to either side and camping in the open would be the death of them.

She checked on her companions. Both looked asleep. Good. They needed the rest, especially Aasgod. If they were going to make it to wherever they were headed, she needed the mage.

The snow fell more heavily, swirling around her. Visibility shrank to less than twenty feet and the icy flakes stung her face. Her hands grew numb but still she kept the horses moving forward, despite their complaints. There was no other choice.

She thought of the man she'd killed and wondered if his body had been found yet. No doubt the Egril would give him a medal and make him a hero. People would cry over his grave, not knowing he died a would-be rapist. While Beris would end up in an anonymous pit or be shoved in a furnace. Discarded and forgotten. Her brother deserved more than that.

Tinnstra shivered. If the Skull had killed her in the stable, who would miss her? She had no friends or family left to wonder where she'd gone.

It was dark by the time it stopped snowing. The oilskin had kept off the worst of it but Tinnstra was frozen to the bone. She'd lost the feeling in her fingers and her face was red-raw. The canvas roof covering the wagon sagged with the weight of the snow caught in it. If they didn't stop soon, the cold would kill them just as well as any Skull. Tinnstra's eyes grew heavier, desperate for some sleep. She straightened up, shook her head to clear the fatigue, but a second later, she found herself fighting to stay awake once more. Sleep was all she could think of. Just a few minutes' rest. She'd feel better if she could just ...

Someone groaned from behind her and the sound made her jump. Tinnstra looked back and saw Aasgod and the girl. She'd forgotten they were in the wagon. He looked so pale. They all needed some proper rest, some hot food, some warmth.

But where could they stop? A fire on the side of the road would bring the wrong sort of attention. Anyone looking for them would spot it easily. No, she had to find somewhere hidden, sheltered. And soon. If only she could think, remember where the road went ... It was the road she used when she fled the Kotege. If only she wasn't so tired. At least the cold wasn't bothering her any more. Her eyelids drooped but she managed to force them open again. Couldn't sleep. No. Had to keep going. Find somewhere ... a fire ... but she was so tired ...

27

Jax

Kiyosun

Jax stood in the dark warehouse, staring at the sea. Meigore was out there, thirty-odd miles away, hidden by the night. Close enough to swim, if you were fit enough – and had two good arms. Close enough for the small fishing boat hanging above him to make the crossing – if you had two arms to sail it.

The boat from Meigore would arrive in three days to take the king and his family away. Three days! He prayed that Aasgod had managed to get everyone away from the castle in time. They were on a tight schedule even if everything went to plan, and the Gods knew that never happened. Two days to the gate and then a day to Kiyosun. Nothing could go wrong. They were only going to get one chance at it. Even with no moon in the sky, the Meigorians were taking a terrible risk. The Egril might not have ships to patrol the seas but the Daijaku were proving more than lethal enough in keeping the channel clear.

The last thing he needed was Kiyosun stirred up like a hornet's nest, but Dren had fucked that right up. Jax shook his head. Give him an army of Shulka and a field of battle and he knew exactly what to do, but this new warfare of magic and terror from the shadows? He didn't have a clue.

'Boss?' It was Dylar, one of the sentries. 'They're here. With the boy.'

'Bring them in.' Jax cracked his neck from side to side and pushed his feelings deep down, burying them with every other emotion and memory that might stop him from doing what needed to be done. Complacency had cost them Jia. He'd not make the same mistake again.

He recognised Monon and Greener by their silhouettes as they entered the gloomy space. They held the boy between them with a hood over his head, dragging his feet in the dirt behind them.

'Is he still alive?' asked Jax, walking over to meet them. He took a chair with him and placed it in the centre of the warehouse.

'He's okay. A bit beaten up,' replied Monon. 'He tried running. Needed a boot to the head to stop him.' They dropped the boy onto the chair and Greener retied the kid's ropes so that he wasn't going anywhere. Only then did the Shulka remove the hood, revealing the bloody mess Monon's boot had made of Dren's mouth.

Looking down at the unconscious boy, Jax was reminded how young he was. Not old enough to take the vows. Probably not even old enough to shave. And yet there was so much blood on his hands ...

He sighed. 'Wake him up.'

Greener chucked a bucket of seawater over the boy, the cold to wake him up and the salt to get his cuts stinging. Dren came to, coughing and spluttering, eyes wide and wild.

'What the fuck?' His head swivelled around, taking in his captors' faces, his new surroundings. There was a flash of panic and he bucked against the ropes, but no one ever slipped a knot Greener had tied. When Dren realised he wasn't going anywhere, he calmed down and Jax saw the 'tough man' mask slip over his face. Things weren't going to go easy.

Dren cleared his nose with a snort and spat the bloody phlegm at Jax's feet. 'Nice place you got here.' He nodded at the hanging boat. 'My old man used to have one just like it. You do much fishing?'

'How are you, Dren?' said Jax.

'How do you think I am?' said the boy, with a grin. 'I'm fucking wonderful, all tied up, with a broken tooth or two, looking at your ugly faces in the middle of the night. Fucking great. Nowhere else I'd rather be.'

'Believe me, I'd rather be at home, asleep in my bed,' said Jax. 'But you wouldn't do as you were told, would you?'

'Fuck off, old man. No one made you the boss of me. No one gave you the right to tell me what I can and can't do.' He looked at Monon as if he were a piece of trash in the street. 'I'm not one of your stupid Shulka.'

'There are no more Shulka now,' said Jax. 'We're all on the same side. All Hanran.'

'Fuck you. I'm not,' snarled Dren.

Monon went to slap him but Jax stopped him with a wave of his hand. Not yet.

Dren laughed. 'At least you've got them well trained.'

'You don't look too worried,' said Jax.

'If you were going to kill me, you would've done it by now,' said Dren. 'Reckon the worst I'll have to put up with is a lecture from you. I might get bored but I think I'll survive.'

Jax wondered if he'd ever been that confident, that cocky. 'Do you know how many people you killed earlier?'

Dren pursed his lips as he looked to the ceiling, pretending to think. He shrugged. 'I hadn't thought about it, really. I know I got the governor, two squads of Skulls. I dunno ... say ... twenty, twenty-five.'

Jax pulled up a crate and sat down so he was eye to eye with the boy. 'That was just the enemy dead. You also killed thirty of our people waiting to be hanged. *And* their friends and family who were there to support them in their final hour. That's seventy-three. Dead.'

'Seventy-three, eh? Seventy-three?' Dren chuckled, then spat more blood on the floor. 'So fucking what?'

'You killed *fifty* of your own countrymen,' said Jax. 'That's *what*.'

'Thirty of them were already dead. I just made it quicker. Some could say it was a mercy. No dance on the rope, no shitting and pissing themselves in public. Just boom – over and done with.' Dren shrugged again. 'The others shouldn't have been watching in the first place. It's the audience the Egril want. Without the baying crowd, the Skulls wouldn't hang anyone. So fuck them, too. They deserved it.'

Jax glanced up at Monon, who shook his head. His friend probably thought the best place for Dren was the bottom of the harbour. Jax was starting to agree. 'Okay. So the lives of innocent people don't matter to you. I get that. But what did you achieve today? What have you gained with all that mayhem and chaos?'

'What did I achieve? I killed the fucking governor. I showed the Skulls just how easily they could be got at.' Dren sniffed, then grinned. 'Damn sight more than you've ever done, old man.'

'The governor was a puppet we knew and understood. Someone we could work around. Now the Skulls will replace him with someone who'll have a point to prove, who'll want to make their career on the back of breaking this city into submission. And they'll have an army of Skulls ready to kick down doors and murder and maim anyone they want to.' Jax paused, hoping his words were sinking into Dren's thick head. 'You've given them an excuse to go out and murder as many of us as they bloody well wish.'

The boy laughed. 'Let them try it. The more Skulls they send, the more I'll kill. If you haven't forgotten, we're at war with the bastards.'

'You don't win a war by mindlessly killing people,' said Jax.

'What do you know about winning a fucking war?' snapped Dren. 'All you Shulka did was lose one.'

Monon's back-hander knocked the kid sideways. Boy and chair crashed to the ground. Greener picked him up as if he weighed nothing and put him back in place.

Dren smiled a bloody smile. 'Ouch.'

'Boss?' Dylar was back. 'We need a word.' The man's expression told him it was important.

'As hard as it may be, don't hurt him,' Jax warned the others and walked over to Dylar. It was only then he noticed Kara waiting by the door. Something was wrong. Something terrible. 'Kara, what are you doing here? You shouldn't be out after curfew.'

Kara scratched at her cheek and brushed the hair from her forehead. Her eyes flicked to Jax and then back to the shadows. 'Jax ... Oh, Jax.'

The old general put his arm around her shoulders. 'What is it?'

He wasn't sure he had the stomach for more bad news.

'Caster came through the gate ... He said ... The king's dead. The queen, too.'

'What?' The words hit him hard. He didn't want to believe them. Not now. Not when all their hopes had rested on the rescue attempt. How could it all have gone so wrong yet again? 'When? How?'

'While they were trying to escape. Larius has claimed the throne. His coronation takes place on the full moon.'

The world spun. Jax wanted to sit down, feeling faint, but he knew he couldn't show any weakness, not even to Kara. 'What of the children?'

Kara shook her head. 'Official reports say they were all killed but we haven't been able to confirm it.'

'Any word on Aasgod?'

'Not exactly.'

'What do you mean?'

'The Skulls hit the meeting point where Aasgod was meant to bring the king. Harka was there. Majas. Tosmer. Rosina. They killed them all.'

'Was Aasgod with them?'

'We don't know. We just don't know.'

'That's not good enough. We need information. If Aasgod and the children are still alive, we've some hope. It's not good enough to just say "we don't know".'

'I know, but it's almost impossible to get any sort of picture of what's going on. Everyone's scared and gone to ground. We were lucky the Hanran in Aisair got a bird to Caster with the information we have.'

It wasn't over. There was still a chance. 'I'll send Monon and Greener through the gate to see if Aasgod or anyone else actually managed to get away. If they have, they'll probably need all the help we can give them.'

'Okay. I'll see what else I can dig up.'

'What about our source at the Council House?'

'I've not heard anything from her since the bombing.'

'Shit.' Jax took a deep breath and tried to calm himself. 'I'm

213

sorry. I know it's difficult. Just do your best. Hopefully she'll be in touch soon.'

Kara nodded.

His head spun; the king dead, Harka, Majas. 'What a fucking mess.'

'Just tell us what to do. Me and the boys will follow you into the Great Darkness to fight Kage if you ask us to.'

Jax was going to tell her what a fool she was but stopped himself. It wouldn't do Kara any good to see him full of doubt and fear, nor any of the others. 'Start by finding out exactly what's happened. We need information.'

'I'm on it, Boss.'

'Be careful on the streets,' he said. 'It's still curfew and we can't afford for you to be captured.'

'They won't get me,' replied Kara.

'We can't afford for you to be captured,' he repeated, looking her in the eye, hating himself for what he was asking her to do.

'I understand,' said Kara. 'If things go bad, I won't let them take me.' She patted her pocket where she kept the poison.

'May the Four Gods look after you.'

'And you, sir.'

This time, Jax let her leave. He took a moment to compose himself; he couldn't let the enormity of the situation overwhelm him or he'd lose his mind. All he could do was concentrate on the matters at hand. Keep what he could under control. It wasn't over yet.

He returned to the others, feeling so very tired, and sat on the crate once more. He couldn't recall the last time he'd had a full night's sleep.

Dren still wore that smug look on his face, like he deserved a medal more than a beating.

'Look, kid,' said Jax. 'I truly believe that you, and your friends, have a major role to play in the months ahead if we're ever going to beat the Egril and force them out of Jia. And as much as it pains me to say this, your way of fighting is what we need now. It's not the time for battlefields and the world I knew. It might never be again. But I need you on my side, working with us.

Attacks like today will only turn other Jians against you – against the Hanran. You need to be better than that, better than the Skulls. If we lose the people, we've lost everything.'

'Blah, blah, blah,' said Dren. 'Don't you ever get sick and tired of hearing yourself speak? I'll never lose the people because I *am* the people. It's you fucking Shulka who are the problem, not me. So shut up and either let me go or dump me in the fucking sea because I'm so bored of listening to you harp on.'

Jax stood up, shaking his head. It wasn't what he'd wanted to hear but it was the night for that, apparently. The boy was too wild. He was a problem Jax didn't need. A problem that had to go away. He looked at Greener. 'Go on, do as he asks. Throw him in the harbour.'

That knocked the smile off Dren's face. He struggled against the ropes. 'No. *No!*' he cried as Greener picked him up, chair and all, and walked him to the edge of the warehouse dock. The water, as black as the night, waited. 'You bastards. Put me down. This isn't right.'

Greener didn't need telling twice. He tossed the boy into the water.

28

Tinnstra

The Southern Road

The wagon hit a hole in the road. Startled awake, Tinnstra's mind was woozy from cold and fatigue. What was she doing? Then it all came back in one cruel rush. Driving a wagon. With the queen of Jia and the Lord Mage in it. On the run from the Skulls. It was insane. A cruel joke by the Four Gods – the tale of the coward, the queen and the mage and how they died.

She stared into the dark night, seeing nothing, blinking herself awake as the snow fell and she tried to get the wagon back under control. Every part of her body ached with the cold that had seeped into her bones and filled her head with a fog she couldn't shake. She checked on Aasgod and Zorique, but they were hidden under blankets in the back. The bump hadn't woken them – she just hoped they weren't dead. Chances were they all would be soon, though. She had to stop somewhere, start a fire, get warm, before it was over for them all.

But there was only the dark and the snow, the cold and the wind.

Her eyes flickered as sleep tried to claim her once more. There was nothing she could do, anyway. Nowhere to run. They were all going to die but she wasn't afraid. She was too tired to be scared. So tired, in fact, she almost missed it. Flame. At first, she thought it a trick of the snow or a figment of a dream, but there it was again. A spark of light. A flash of hope.

She sat up, cracked her neck and rubbed her eyes. Looked

again. The light remained. *Not a dream, then, not a trick. A fire. Warmth. Safety. Survival.*

The horses could see it, too. They picked up their pace as the road curved around to the right. More light blossomed. Fires. Campfires. She could see wagons, horses, people moving around.

It was a campsite. Somewhere to stop.

Tinnstra drove towards the fires, feeling relief flood through her. All she had to do was hold on a little longer. She counted at least a dozen wagons in various stages of settling in for the night. There wasn't much chatter that she could hear; no doubt everybody was just too cold and too tired to waste energy on anything that wasn't essential.

A broad-shouldered man waited by the turn-off from the road. A small brazier by his feet kept him warm but the light didn't find his face, hidden as it was under a wide-brimmed hat. 'Hold there,' he called out as they drew near.

Tinnstra leaned forward. 'Evening, friend.' She tried to sound casual.

'Am I?' A northerner, judging by his accent. The man sniffed. 'We'll have to wait and see about that, won't we? You planning on staying here for the night?'

'We are, if you'll let us,' she replied, her voice shaking. She nodded to the rear of the wagon. 'My husband's unwell and my daughter's not even five.'

'All the same, we've rules that needed obeying,' said the man.

'Of course – and they are ...?'

'We don't steal from each other, we don't fight each other, and we don't bother each other. Keep to that and you can stay.' The man stepped up to the wagon, lifted his head so Tinnstra could see his face. His nose was twisted and an ear had been battered more than once. Whoever he was, he was no stranger to violence. A frightening man, but Tinnstra feared the cold more.

She nodded. 'We will.'

'Trust you do and you'll not hear another word from me. Take the path off to the right; you'll find a spot there.' The man tipped his hat and grinned, showing off a smile remarkable for the few teeth he possessed, and stepped back, allowing Tinnstra to drive their wagon onto the site.

Tinnstra followed the directions and found a quiet corner of the field where three fallen logs were laid out in a rough circle around a fire pit. She stopped the wagon, relieved that rest was at hand. For a moment, the cold and exhaustion overwhelmed her. She sagged, almost falling from her seat to the ground. *Nearly there. Nearly there. I can sleep soon. Fire first. A fire or we all die.*

She dragged the dry wood from the back of the wagon over to the pit, silently thanking whoever had packed it. Some kindling and a few strikes of a flint got a fire burning. The flames were beautiful as they leaped from to twig to log, bright and mesmerising, their sudden warmth so very welcome. She placed the flint in her pocket. Such a small thing but it could mean the difference between life and death in the wild. Her eyes drooped again but she forced herself to stand. There were things still to do. After unhitching the horses and hobbling them, she brushed their coats down before covering them with blankets and feeding them.

As she worked, she kept watching the neighbouring wagons, looking for a threat, but found only tired, haunted faces much like her own. For once, she was happy to see them. For once, it meant they were safe.

When the fire was ready and the horses settled, she helped the others.

Zorique was awake and eager to leave the wagon. 'Let's get you warmed up,' Tinnstra said as she lifted her down. The smile she received in return was almost reward enough. Zorique sat on a log next to the fire and Tinnstra draped a blanket over her shoulders. 'I'll make something to eat in a moment. Let me see to Aasgod first.'

'He's not well,' said Zorique.

'He'll be fine once he's warm again.'

That might have been true, but the challenge lay in getting him out of the wagon in the first place. Tinnstra struggled to half-lift, half-drag the barely conscious mage and nearly fell under his weight as she manoeuvred him to the fire. What little strength Tinnstra had left was fading fast.

A man from a nearby wagon noticed. 'Want some help, lass?'

'We're fine,' she lied. 'We're fine.' The last thing they needed was for someone to recognise Aasgod. They had to stay anonymous.

The man watched her struggle the last few yards and lower Aasgod onto the log next to Zorique. When she went back to fetch a blanket, she motioned to the man that Aasgod was drunk. He nodded with a sympathetic expression.

When everyone was settled, Tinnstra set up a pot to cook dinner, happy to be close to the fire and feel the cold slowly retreat from her fingers and toes.

The heat did them all good. Gradually, Aasgod came to his senses and was sitting up of his own accord. That had to be a good sign, she told herself. Perhaps he could recover, maybe work some magic on his injuries.

Zorique looked happy enough, too, now she was near the fire. She certainly didn't look like a queen. Who would follow her? Her father was well loved, as his father had been before him, and the throne was hers by right, that was true, but in such desperate times, the fate of Jia couldn't be left to a child who barely spoke. No army would follow a girl who had just learned to walk.

Aasgod caught her looking. 'Is the food ready?'

Tinnstra glanced down at the pot, feeling guilty, and gave the contents a stir. 'I think so. I'll get some bowls.'

The food didn't taste of much, but it was hot and filled their stomachs. They ate quickly and quietly, a small moment of normality amongst all the madness. After they had finished, Zorique snuggled up against Aasgod and he put his arm around her. Within a minute, her eyes closed and she was asleep.

Tinnstra wanted to do the same. Warm, fed, there was only her exhaustion left to deal with.

'We need to talk,' said Aasgod.

'What about?'

'I'm dying.'

'No. No,' said Tinnstra, trying to stop the conversation. She didn't want to hear it. 'You're *not*.'

'I *am* dying,' repeated Aasgod.

'Please don't think that. You'll be fine. A good night's rest and you'll be fine.' Even as she said the words, she knew they were a lie, but she needed to believe he was going to get better. He was their only hope of surviving whatever lay ahead.

'I'm dying and you need to know what to do when it happens,' replied the mage.

'No. No. You're not,' repeated Tinnstra. She didn't want to know. Not again. Beris had told her the same thing and he'd died.

The mage ignored her. 'In three days' time, a ship is arriving in Kiyosun from Meigore to collect Zorique and take her to the safety of her uncle's court. I need you to promise that you'll get her on board.'

'Three days? But she'll never get there in time. Kiyosun is two or three weeks by road from here. Maybe more.'

'You won't be travelling by road.'

'What?' She was so tired. None of it made sense.

'Do you know a mountain called Olyisius?'

Tinnstra nodded. 'It's near the Kotege. I was a student there ... we used to train on it.'

'There is a small temple near the summit.'

'I know it. It belongs to Ruus.' Her heart began to race as her memories took her back. She could picture the temple. Small, covered in moss, so old it looked like part of the mountain. She'd never been inside, never dared look. Some of the villagers would climb up there and leave offerings outside it before the harvest, hoping to receive the God of the Land's blessing.

Aasgod grimaced, clearly in pain. 'It's good that you know. You need to take Zorique there. Go inside.'

'But why? We can't hide there. There's no water nearby. No food.'

'Not to hide. The temple is a gate.'

'A gate?'

'Powered by magic left over from the old world. It connects to other gates in other parts of Jia. You simply step through it and you can be in a dozen other places, hundreds and hundreds of miles away.'

Magic? Tinnstra felt sick at the thought. 'But how will I know how to get to Kiyosun?'

'There will be Hanran waiting for you at the temple. They'll guide you through and take you to meet the boat.'

'You'll be with us. You can take her.' She could feel panic rising. Even if they beat the snows that would soon make the ascent to the temple impossible, Aasgod was too weak, Zorique too small, and she was too scared.

'I could be dead by the morning,' said Aasgod.

'Please don't say that.' What had she done? She should never have agreed to help Beris, never got involved. *I'm a curse. Beris wouldn't have died if not for me. Now Aasgod? It can't happen. Alo and Xin won't allow it. Please. Please. Please.*

'It's the truth. Whatever we wish can't change that.'

Tinnstra's eyes flicked from Aasgod to the sleeping girl. She was so small. If anything did happen to Aasgod, Tinnstra would be all she had. Poor thing. Tinnstra's curse would kill her, too, if she was left in her care. 'No. No. No.'

'Get her on the boat to Meigore. Stay with her.'

'Meigore? No. No, I can't do that. She'll be safe on the boat. They'll take her to her uncle, the king.'

'This isn't just about getting Zorique to her uncle.' Aasgod checked the girl was still asleep. Satisfied, he continued, 'It's more important than just keeping her safe. What do you know about magic?'

'Only what we were taught at school, stories my parents told us.' Too many tales of what had gone before. Legends and fables of battles of good versus evil, of humans who could've been Gods. They'd frightened her as a child, given her nightmares.

'Magic comes from something called a Chikara well. There was one in the caverns below the castle in Aisair, a location known only to a few of us.'

'Who's "us"?' asked Tinnstra. She didn't like the sound of that. Aasgod was talking as if he'd been alive back then but, if he was, then he'd have to be impossibly old ...

'A thousand years ago, it was the size of a lake. It permeated everything, the water we drank, the food we ate, the air we breathed.' The mage stared into the fire. 'It was a part of us, in our blood and in our genes. Everyone had a gift that appeared with puberty, and we celebrated each new wonder.' He glanced at Tinnstra, and for a moment, he looked as old as time. 'Then children started being born without the gift. We thought it strange but what did it matter when the rest of us were still like Gods? But the powerless increased with each new generation, until those who had a gift became the exception. It was only then we realised that the well was drying up. As it faded, so did our powers. Finally, magic all but disappeared from the world.'

'But you have magic. I've seen you use it,' said Tinnstra. 'Raaku has it, too. There other mages. And the Chosen.'

'It's not something that comes naturally to me. I have a gift, yes, but I need help to use it.' Aasgod reached into his pocket and produced three vials with a green liquid inside. 'This is water from the well. When I drink the liquid, I can use magic for a short time. It's the same for my other mages. I don't know about Raaku or the Chosen, how they get their power, but we rely on this.'

Tinnstra stared at the vials, at the liquid within. 'How many vials do you have?'

'These are the last three I have. The well has run dry. There is no more.'

Panic and fear battled within Tinnstra. 'But there must be more, another well, where you could replenish your supply?'

'In my life, I've done everything possible to find more Chikara wells. My own brother died trying to find another source.'

'Your brother?'

'He died over a hundred ... a hundred and twenty years ago.' Aasgod coughed and winced with the pain. 'His name was Laafien. He was younger than me but possessed a far greater talent.'

'How did he die?'

'I honestly don't know. He went searching for more Chikara wells and never returned.'

'I'm sorry.'

'It was a long time ago.'

'So, what's this got to do with Zorique?'

'Zorique has the gift.'

'The gift?'

'For the first time in more than half a millennium, two children were born with the ability to use magic without the need for Chikara liquid: Zorique and her brother Ghent. I've never seen potential like it. When she's older, there'll be no limit to what she can do. She'll be the most powerful weapon we have in the fight against Raaku.'

Tinnstra glanced again at the girl. 'How do you know she'll have these powers?'

'There's an aura around everyone who can use magic or has potential, a unique colour depending on their ability. With Zorique, there's a myriad of colours floating around her. It's quite beautiful.'

'I don't see anything.'

'Most people can't. It was only after I started drinking the Chikara water that I could.'

'And her magic – her powers – they'll only appear when she reaches puberty?'

Aasgod nodded.

'That's ten years from now. Raaku will be defeated by then.' Tinnstra paused. It was all too much to take in. 'Won't he? When Meigore join the fight?'

'I don't know if their army can hold Raaku back. Once he sets his eye on them, they'll probably fall like every other land.'

'Then why are we going there? Why not somewhere else?'

'Because it's safe for now. Dornway's fallen. Chongore's fallen. There's nowhere else that's accessible and free from Egril control, and Zorique needs somewhere to grow up, where she can be trained. If the Egril do invade Meigore before her powers manifest fully, then she'll have to be taken elsewhere until she's ready.'

'To be queen?'

'To be a warrior.'

'But how?' said Tinnstra. 'If you … if you don't … if you're not with us … I can't—'

'One of my last living mages is waiting in Meigore. Her name is Anama. She knows Zorique's potential. I need you to promise you'll get the princess to her.'

'Does anyone else know? Her uncle?'

'No. It's too great a secret. If Raaku were to find out, he would use every weapon he has, every soldier, to kill her. We've already lost her brother. We can't afford to lose her as well. If we do, Raaku will overrun the world.'

'Is he really that powerful? Is he the son of Kage like they say?'

'The Egril believe even the Four Gods were once Kage's children too so it's an easy tale to tell.' Aasgod shook his head. 'In reality? I think he's like Zorique – gifted beyond anything we've ever seen, and he's managed to harness that power to change people into creatures unimagined.'

'Like the Daijaku.'

'Yes,' agreed Aasgod, 'and far worse. He has other monsters that have yet to be unleashed on Jia.'

Tinnstra bit her lip to stifle her cry and looked down at Zorique. 'Does she know?'

'Of course not.'

Tinnstra stared at the sleeping child. Better for her not to know. Tinnstra had endured the expectations that came from having a famous father and she'd crumbled under it. The future of the world depended on Zorique. How could anyone cope with that?

And that was if Aasgod didn't die and Tinnstra could keep her safe. May the Four Gods help them all. It was all too much to bear. She wanted to scream. She wanted to run away. She'd let everyone down in her life who'd ever depended on her. She didn't want the responsibility. *Why me? Why do I have to do this?*

But she knew the answer to that. *Because I chose to go back and save the girl. I could have left her then. I could've left her since. But I haven't because I can't. She needs someone – and I'm all she's got.*

29

Dren

Kiyosun

Dren hit the water hard. It was cold, so fucking cold, but he clamped his mouth shut, every instinct working to keep him alive. Bound to the chair, its weight dragged him down, into the dark. He wriggled and strained against the ropes but nothing moved. Panic flared in his chest.

He sank fast. The chair made sure of that. Shadows flashed past his face, disturbed by his passage. He let a bubble of air escape his lips and watched it race towards the surface, taking a little life with it as he felt a buzz build in his ears.

The bottom arrived with a gentle bump, and he lay there amongst the debris and junk, the weeds and the rocks. The cold made it hard to think and he could feel the air pressing against the inside of his lips, eager to flee from his lungs back to the surface. He let another dribble go. There was nothing he could do about it. Nothing to stop it.

He didn't want to die there in the dark. Alone. Forgotten. He wanted someone to save him, drag him back, tell him it was going to be all right. He wanted his mother. He wanted ... *No.* He wasn't that boy. He was a wolf, a warrior. He'd fight till the end.

He had to get free. He had to live.

His knife. He still had his knife. The one in his boot. The one the bloody Shulka would've found if they'd bothered to search him properly. *Hope.* He dragged his heel against the chair leg,

225

felt the boot move, shuffled in the dirt, felt it move some more. Frustration mixed with anger and fought with fear as he moved his foot a fraction of an inch at a time. The edge of his vision crumbled as another bubble of precious oxygen slipped past his lips.

The darkness pressed down on him as the need to breathe overwhelmed all his thoughts, and his chest started to spasm as if he needed to cough. *I'm going to die.* More air burst from his lips, taking some of the pain with it, and he watched the bubbles float up towards the surface, so far away. *I'm going to die.*

No.

Dren forced his panic down. Whatever happened, he'd fight it. He wasn't going to die amongst the trash in the harbour. He wouldn't let Jax win. He was better than that. Better than that fucking Shulka. He'd have the last laugh. Revenge.

He wriggled his foot, felt the boot come loose, his leg slide free. The knife glinted in the silt. If only it wasn't so hard to think. His lungs burned with what little air remained, what little life he had left.

He twisted the chair, trying to get closer to the blade, his fingers desperate for it. His chest convulsed. It was all too much. More air slipped past his lips. The pressure roared in his head. He moved another inch, and another. Why not die? Who would miss him? Why was he fighting? Better to join his mother and father. Better to give up ...

... He touched the blade. Hard. Strong. *Sharp*. Wrapped his fingers around the hilt. Felt the power it held. Life and death. His life. He turned the knife so the blade could work on the rope.

The pain in his head, his lungs was beyond anything he'd ever experienced. The rope cut into him even as he cut into it, doing its best to hold him, to kill him. The roar had gone from his head. All quiet now. Only the burning in his chest remained, and the constant pressure. It told him he was still alive or that he was dying. He wasn't sure which.

His hand floated in front of him as if made from nothing. He stared at it, fascinated, seeing the cut-marks from rope and knife, the trails of blood, until he realised his hand was free. A strand of rope snapped, then another. More air escaped from his mouth. The last strand broke and his other arm was free. He clawed at the water as if the sea were dirt to dig through. Chased the bubbles of air that fled before him. Saw the light, calling him.

His head broke the surface.

Cold slapped his face. He gasped for air and then he was under again, the sea eager to keep him for its own. He flailed, got his head above the water for another second, sank once more.

Stupid, really. Living next to the ocean. Learning to be a fisherman but never learning to swim. His dad had promised to teach him. Promised – but never had.

He pushed his head up through the water. He swallowed another mouthful of air and another mouthful of water. Choked. Saw the dock. Saw a rope. Lunged. Sank. Finally, he managed to hook his arm through the rope and pulled himself up. Coughing. Spluttering. Every mouthful hurt. His lungs ached. His head spun.

He was *alive*.

He hung there until the cold said *enough*, and he started shivering so hard he thought he'd fall from the rope. He had to get out of the water, get dry. He hauled himself up with shaking arms and poked his head just high enough to see over the edge of the dock. Jax, Monon and the big brute were still sitting in the warehouse, deep in conversation. Stupid fucking Shulka. He'd show them. Big mistake messing with Dren. Big mistake. Their last.

It was good to be out of the water, but the cold stayed with him, soaked into his bones. There was no time to wait, no time to rest. He tottered onto his feet, used the wall of the warehouse to stay upright. Every breath hurt. Every step was a battle. He gritted his teeth to stop them chattering. Hugging himself to keep his body warm, he welcomed the pain, using it to fuel his anger and drive him onwards, towards his revenge.

At the far end of the alley that ran down the side of the warehouse, he saw a sentry hidden behind some barrels. He wasn't expecting trouble from behind him. Wasn't expecting Dren. No one would be. They'd drowned him, after all. Big mistake.

Dren found a rock, good and heavy. It'd do the job just as well as a knife.

The sentry didn't hear him approach, watching for trouble in the wrong place. The fool kept his eyes on the street, following orders. A good little soldier. Dren got up close. Raised the rock high above his head. The sentry must've sensed something then because he turned just as Dren brought the rock down. The Shulka's eyes bulged with surprise but he was too late to do anything – except die. The poor sod didn't even cry out as Dren cracked him around the head. He caught the sentry as he fell and lowered him gently to the ground. He gave him another whack with the rock for good measure. Then another because he felt like splitting the man's head open.

When he put on the dead sentry's dry clothes, he immediately felt better. The man's coat was thick and warm and he had a big bastard of a blade, so Dren took them both. The Shulka owed him a knife anyway. The man's boots didn't fit him, but Dren could live with going barefoot for a little while.

He hobbled out into the deserted street, leaving the body and his clothes to be found. Jax and the others would shit themselves when they realised Dren wasn't dead after all. He headed away from the docks, searching for somewhere to hide. Somewhere to get warm. He stuck to the shadows and the doorways, only too aware it was after curfew. The Skulls could kill him on the spot just for being outside. No way was he going to let that happen. Not now. Not after everything he'd been through. Jax and the others would pay for trying to kill him. It was about to get bloody.

DAY FIVE

30

Darus

Aisair

Darus watched the Daijaku fly through the snow-filled dawn sky over Aisair while he tried to control his temper. They still hadn't found the mage and the princess. Those responsible for this failure – the governor and his five useless aides – sat awaiting judgement behind him. Skara lounged in a chair, axe in hand, infuriatingly carefree.

'We have men searching all over the city,' said the governor, an insipid man with a red nose. Sweat stains under the arms marked his grey uniform. *Revolting.* 'We will find Aasgod and the girl. It's just a matter of time.'

'Of course it's just a matter of time.' Darus turned on the man. 'The question is how long will you take? An hour? A day? A week? Tell me – exactly – how much time do you need?'

The governor looked to his aides for help. They looked to the table. The man was on his own.

At the far end of the table, Skara began to tap on the wood with her axe. *Tap, tap, tap. Tap, tap, tap. Tap, tap, tap.*

Sweat appeared on the governor's brow. 'We will find him …' *Tap, tap, tap.* 'It's a big city. The population is …' *Tap, tap, tap.* '… hostile.' *Tap, tap, tap.*

'Do you even know who the leaders of the Hanran are in this city?' asked Darus.

'There is … we believe … that there are several groups,' replied the governor. 'Acting independently. However, our sources—'

Darus walked behind the governor and placed his hands on the man's shoulders. 'It's been over twelve hours since they made their escape and you've come up with nothing! He might not even be in Aisair, for all you know.'

'But ... but my Lord ...' The governor shook under Darus's touch. *Good.*

Tap, tap, tap.

'All I hear are excuses,' said Darus, walking on. 'We are the Egril Empire. We've conquered three-quarters of the known world. We took Dornway in a week and its people, famed for their ferocity, quickly accepted the new regime. Chongore fell in ten days and now they worship, as they should, the one true God without complaint.' Darus paused, allowed the fools to sweat some more. 'Our Lord and Master, Raaku, the All-Father, the son of Kage himself, has entrusted us to bring peace and stability to these lands, and yet we are incapable of doing so. Do you think he'll understand when we say we have failed? Do you think he'll be forgiving when he discovers we've let a leader of the resistance escape with the legitimate heir to the throne?'

Tap, tap, tap.

'No.' The governor looked down, flinching with every tap of Skara's axe.

'Let us all accept that time is a gift I'm not willing to give,' continued Darus. He returned to stand by the window. 'Let us accept that finding Aasgod is a matter of such importance that we're willing to raze this wonderful city to the ground if that is what it takes to force him out of whatever hole he's hiding in. Let us accept that we'll search the country inch by inch to find him. Yes?'

'Yes,' replied the governor.

Tap, tap, tap.

Darus smiled. 'Now, I would humbly suggest that you send all your men out with orders to pick up anyone they think may know where the Lord Mage is and bring them here for questioning. They are to burn any home they think may belong to any member of the Hanran or their sympathisers. I want everyone in this city to understand that their lives will be intolerable until we find this rebel. You have twelve hours to bring me results. Do you understand?'

Tap, tap, tap.

The governor was deathly white. 'W ... w ... we understand.'

'Good. Good,' said Darus. 'Now, before you go, is there anything you want to add, Skara?'

Skara uncoiled herself from her chair, stretching her back as she stood. Her axe still beat its rhythm.

Tap, tap, tap.

She looked from one aide to another until her eyes stopped on the governor.

Tap, tap—

THUNK.

Without breaking eye contact, Skara had swung the axe and decapitated the aide sitting to her right. The head hit the flagstones and arterial blood sprayed out from his neck, covering the floor, the table, the aide on the other side of him and Skara herself, yet she still didn't move. Just kept staring at the governor. It took a few seconds for the dead man's heart to stop beating and the red rain to cease. Only then did she speak. 'I hope the governor understands how serious the situation is. I would hate for any of us to be disappointed.'

No one replied. In the silence, the dead body slipped from its chair and hit the floor.

Darus clapped his hands, got everyone's attention back on him where it belonged. 'Good. You know what to do. I'll pray to Kage that you are successful. Now go.'

'Wonderfully done, dear sister. Wonderfully,' said Darus, once they were alone.

Skara flicked the blood from her axe. 'Sometimes a point needs to be made.'

One *he* had already made. But he'd not let her know she'd riled him. He looked out over the city instead. Old Town spread below them with its magic-made, multicoloured buildings created back when the Jians had an abundance of magic – before they became so pathetic. Darus wondered what it must have been like to watch it die away, generation by generation, until only old fools like Aasgod and his mages were left.

And yet, after all that, they still worshipped their False Gods. Unbelievable.

There was a rumour of a source of holy water in Aisair, but they had yet to find it. He glanced over at Skara. No doubt she'd been searching for it while Darus was preoccupied with actually trying to solve the Hanran problem. Anything to further her own personal glory. Darus shuddered. *Over my dead body.*

His revulsion must have shown because Skara was looking at him as if trying to read his mind. He gestured out of the window. 'The Jians wasted so much power on frivolities and vain statements when they could've ruled the world.'

'They thought themselves so special,' said Skara.

'Soon their legacy will be nothing more than ash.' Darus smiled. After he caught Aasgod, he'd be able to return home a hero. Perhaps Raaku would allow Darus to bathe in Egril's holy waters once more. He closed his eyes. Skara would not dare consider herself his equal then.

'It's our time now,' said Skara.

Darus didn't like that. She hoped to leech off his glory. 'Raaku's time. Kage's time,' he corrected her. *His* time.

Skara bowed her head. 'Of course.'

Darus knew her faith was just another act, a way to climb the ladder. He knew she lacked his conviction, his belief. Another reason she'd never be his equal. One day, he would send her to be Kage's slave in the Great Darkness. 'We should all remember that.'

'My Lord. My Lady.' The Monsutas turned as one. A man, another of the governor's aides, stood trembling in the doorway. His eyes darted to the corpse on the floor.

'What is it?' asked Skara.

The man bowed. 'The Kyoryu have arrived.'

'At last.' Darus smiled. 'Lead us to them.'

They took the main staircase down into the basement and walked past the cells. Prisoners darted away from them as they passed, hiding in whatever shadow they could find, no doubt praying that Darus had not come for them at last. Perhaps later he could find time for them. But not now. Work must come first, after all. *Priorities*.

They arrived at a set of iron doors protected by guards. Inside, the Tonin's chamber took up half of the basement level of the castle. When the Egril invaded Jia, the Tonin were sent in advance, disguised as refugees from Raaku's rule, to find locations that would allow the soldiers to cross over well behind any defences. Tonin were so vital that the guards were there not only to protect them from harm, but also to stop them from leaving. When the Tonin were opening a portal, the guards would stand beside them, swords drawn, ready to kill them if they tried to escape.

The Tonin assigned to Aisair was curled up in a corner, asleep. Like all Tonin, she was bald and her skin a deathly white: a symptom of a life lived without any natural light. Sores covered her face, made worse by the dirt and the grime. If the great God Kage had ever made a more disgusting creature than a Tonin, Darus had yet to meet it.

Of course, Kyoryu were another necessary evil. And they were very necessary now if he was to find Aasgod. Chained at the neck and muzzled, they prowled the room on all fours, long-limbed and gangly. Brown hair covered their bodies like fur. Darus kept his distance. A Kyoryu was more animal than human now, and he'd seen first-hand the damage they could do.

'You have magic in you,' said the handler, a southerner. Of all the Egril, they were the most devout of Kage's followers. His mask was a likeness of Kage's own face, carved from black onyx, and behind it, Darus knew the man would be missing one eye and one ear in honour of their God.

'Of course I have magic – I'm one of the Emperor's Chosen,' replied Darus. 'I hope your animals can do better than sense the obvious.'

'Magic taints everything it touches with its stench.' The handler curled his lip as he spoke. 'When it is being used, it's strong and clear and calls my children. No distance or building can hide it from them. The stench sticks to you and marks you.'

Darus nodded. 'Do you have a name?'

'Osmer.'

'How soon will your creatures be ready to go to work?'

'Now. They need no rest.' Osmer nodded towards the unconscious Tonin. 'Kyoryu aren't weak like others.'

'Good,' said Darus. 'Set them loose immediately. I want this mage found.'

'If he's not using his powers, it will be harder for my children to find him,' said Osmer.

Darus didn't like the man's indifference to him, the lack of fear and respect. He stepped forwards to strike him, but his animals reared up, growling, so he let his hand drop. 'This isn't the first time I've dealt with your creatures.'

'Then you also understand that there will be casualties. Once loose, they will need to eat.'

Darus grinned. 'There are no innocents in the city. Only Jians. Your "children" can eat as many of them as they wish. I only require Aasgod and the girl to be found and brought to me still able to talk. Other than that, everyone else is fair game.'

Osmer returned the smile. 'Very good. We'll go to work. We'll start where they were last seen and follow the trail from there.'

'Excellent.' Darus wondered if he should warn the governor but quickly dismissed the idea. The man needed toughening up.

31

Tinnstra

Tinnstra woke early, squashed in the back of the wagon with Zorique between her and Aasgod. She checked the mage and was relieved to find him still alive. That was something, at least. A sign that their luck was changing, perhaps.

It was a cold morning with frost on the ground, mist in the air and the sun not yet up, but at least it hadn't snowed during the night. Another good sign.

The campsite was quiet; everyone else was still fast asleep, as far as she could tell. There was a guard by the road but he was sticking close to his fire with his back to the camp.

For a moment, she was tempted to lie back down – she'd not slept well. Her mind had swirled with everything Aasgod had told her, with what he wanted her to do, but she knew it was better to get up and keep herself occupied.

Tinnstra rebuilt the fire and used a flint to light it. She watched the flames crackle and grow as she threw in more sticks. A fire always made everything feel better – her father had taught her that.

Thinking of him brought back the pain of his loss: a dull, hollow ache in her gut. She doubted she'd ever get over his death.

She stood up and stretched. Enough time-wasting. It would be light soon and there was no way Tinnstra could practise her Shulikan once everyone was moving around the camp.

Her feet slid into the first position. Both her arms floated up

237

and then sank down with the rest of her body. Slowly and with perfect control, she slid her left leg back, twisting her foot at a right angle to her body, then adjusted herself so both feet were positioned wider than her shoulders. Grounded, her right arm moved forward, her left behind and over her head. The Horse stance was the first position her father had ever shown her when she wasn't that much older than Zorique. In her mind, she was a child again, training under her father's watchful eye, struggling to be perfect for him.

'What are you doing?'

The voice threw Tinnstra's concentration. She stumbled and then straightened to find Aagod glaring at her from the wagon, Zorique sitting beside him. Even through the mist, she could see how pale his skin was and the dark shadows under his eyes. But he was still alive. And angry.

Tinnstra blushed, brushed some hair from her face, feeling foolish. 'Just some exercise.'

'Perhaps it's best not to show everyone what you are,' snapped Aasgod. 'We don't need that attention.'

'I'm sorry.'

'The soldiers at the castle used to do that,' said Zorique.

'They were Shulka,' said Aasgod, his tone softening. 'Great warriors.'

'Are you a Sh … Shul … Shulka?' asked Zorique.

'Tinnstra's father was a very famous Shulka.' Aasgod stared at Tinnstra as though seeing her properly for the first time.

Tinnstra felt herself buckle under his gaze. 'He was. He taught me the exercises.'

'Is he dead?' asked Zorique, looking from Tinnstra to Aasgod and back again.

'Yes.' The pain in her chest grew sharper.

'My mother and father are dead, too,' said Zorique, looking downcast.

'Ah, my dear.' Aasgod put his arm around her. 'You're a brave girl.'

'I miss them.'

'I know you do,' replied Aasgod.

Tinnstra stood there watching them, unsure of what to say. If words existed that would make Zorique's pain less, she certainly hadn't discovered them. Time certainly hadn't healed her sense of loss yet either – and Tinnstra was nineteen years old; the Four Gods only knew what it must be like for the child.

Aasgod looked up. 'As much as I hate to waste a good fire, we should get the horses hitched up. Best be on our way as quick as we can. We have far to go and time is against us.'

'Er ... of course. Of course.' Tinnstra blushed, feeling stupid. It would take them at least a day to reach the Kotege, then a day to climb the mountain – if the weather allowed it.

The camp was stirring into activity when they left and set off on an empty road. The mist hadn't lifted, restricting visibility to no more than twenty yards. They were cut off from the world, unseen, alone. The snow started a few minutes later, a gentle fall, twisting and turning in the breeze, coming from nowhere and disappearing into the mist below. It would cover their trail and slow down anyone following.

Tinnstra was in the driver's seat with Aasgod next to her. She'd offered to change his bandages before they left but the mage had waved her away, claiming there was no need. Tinnstra wasn't so sure. 'If you want, you can rest in the back. I'm happy to drive by myself. I'll wake you if there's a problem.'

'I'm fine,' replied Aasgod. He'd found a long stick at the campsite and leaned forward in his seat, resting his weight on it.

'But—'

'I said I'm fine.'

The flash of fire in his eyes warned Tinnstra not to press the matter.

'Your form this morning was perfect,' said Aasgod. 'Your father would've been proud of how well you've mastered the movements.'

'He took his teaching seriously. We didn't get any leniency just because we were his children.'

'You might not have thought so at the time, but your father was doing you a great favour.'

'I know that now. I think I even knew it back then.' Her

mind drifted; what she would give to be back there now with her father, an early start her only worry.

'So ... you come from a famous Shulka family, you went to the Kotege, you practise Shulikan and yet you are not a Shulka. I'm sure there's an interesting story behind that.'

Tinnstra kept her eyes fixed on the road. 'No. There's not.' She couldn't tell him the truth. Not now.

'Perhaps you can tell me later.' Aasgod leaned back and pulled his cloak tighter around him.

No, I won't. I want to forget all about it. Pretend it never happened.

And yet there they were, heading south towards the Kotege. Of all the places in Jia, it had to be there. Every time she closed her eyes, she could see the Skulls attacking, the Daijaku swooping down, the blood, the dead. She'd hoped never to return to the place, but the Four Gods had other ideas. There would be no forgetting.

They made slow but steady progress with an empty road. Zorique sang songs to herself in the back while Aasgod seemed content to watch the road ahead. Lost in the mist, it was almost peaceful. *Perhaps it will all be okay. We can reach the Kotege, rest there for the night and make the climb in the morning.*

Of course, the moment Tinnstra thought that, dark shapes appeared in the mist ahead, curling up to either side of the road. She pulled back on the reins to slow down, unsure of what they were approaching, feeling the fear, but Aasgod tapped her elbow with his. 'It's only Hascome Woods. We're making good time.'

Tinnstra had passed through the area on her way to Aisair after she'd fled the Kotege. It'd been a beautiful summer's day back then. It was very different now. The trees trapped the mist until it became a solid wall of cloud around them, the only sounds the creak of the wheels and the clip of the horses' hooves. Shapes appeared in the mist: debris left by travellers past, a wheel spoke, a broken bucket, a ripped cloth. Little pieces of discarded lives and shattered hopes.

They heard voices next. Whispers carried on the wind, swirling around them. More than one voice. More than a few. Enough to worry about, and that was something Tinnstra was good at. She jumped when she heard a baby cry. It was easy to imagine it as breakfast for some unseen creature.

'I'm scared,' said Zorique, voicing what Tinnstra was feeling. She clambered from the back and squeezed between Tinnstra and Aasgod.

Aasgod put his arm around the girl. 'There's nothing to be afraid of. It's just the mist.'

'I don't like it,' replied Zorique. 'There's monsters out there.'

'No monsters,' said Aasgod. 'Just trees, maybe the odd owl and fox.'

Tinnstra wasn't so sure. More debris and litter appeared out of the mist, tangled up in bushes and covered with snow. A dead body, coated with frost, lay over a fallen trunk, which the girl didn't see, thank the Four Gods. She touched the knife at her back, more out of nerves than a will to use it.

Something moved. 'There're people nearby,' she said.

'Aye,' replied Aasgod softly, eyes squinting.

Shadows moved in the mist, shifting in and out of sight, darting back and forth. Tinnstra could make out a camp with lean-tos and tents, along with a wagon or two. There were no horses, though. All long since eaten, no doubt. A boy not more than eight or nine years old watched them from the top of a tree trunk shattered by lightning, a pipe clamped between his teeth. His ragged clothes dangled off him and his toes looked blue. He growled as they passed and Zorique let out a little squeak, burying herself into Aasgod's side. Tinnstra wished she could do the same.

More people appeared, drawn by the sound of their wagon. Tired, gaunt faces, hope flaring then dying as they realised the wagon only held more refugees.

'What're they doing here?' asked Tinnstra.

'Same as us – running away from the Skulls,' replied Aasgod. 'Maybe driven from their homes for whatever reason the Egril fancy. At least there's shelter here. Some game to catch if they're quick enough.'

A man wandered towards them, covered in mud and dirt, hand outstretched, ribs showing through his torn shirt, danger in his eyes. 'Spare a coin? Something to eat?'

Aasgod shook his head. 'We've nothing to spare.'

'Come on,' protested the man. 'We've got nothing. Nothing at all. Kids are dying.' He reached for the horse's bridle, pulled a knife out from behind his back. 'You can spare something.'

Aasgod leaned forwards, becoming bigger. 'Move out of the way.' The power in his voice sent the man scurrying back. The mage leaned closer to Tinnstra. 'Drive faster. There'll be more of them and the others won't be so easily scared once they're together.'

Tinnstra wasn't going to argue. She flicked the reins to pick up speed. More people emerged from the mist, running and screaming. Men and women with ragged hair and tattered clothes. All waving knives or brandishing clubs.

There was movement in the trees. With people up in the branches as well as in front of them, they were surrounded. Zorique let out another cry of fear and it was all Tinnstra could do to stop herself from screaming, too.

The horses trotted faster and Tinnstra could feel the wagon's wheels slipping on the snow-covered ground. If she lost control, the wagon would tip, and then the mob would have them. She prayed that there was no hidden ice lurking under the snow ahead.

A man dropped from an overhanging branch and landed on the roof. The canvas ripped under his weight, showering everyone with snow, and the wagon rocked as he hit the deck. Tinnstra risked a glance and saw him rise, mad eyes fixed on them, knife ready.

Aasgod whipped his stick around and smashed it into the man's face. He fell back and tumbled over the side of the wagon.

More vagrants formed a line across the road ahead. Tinnstra cracked the reins again and again and the horses charged through the middle of them, sending bodies flying. The wheels bumped up and over something – someone – and then they were in the clear.

Tinnstra didn't slow their pace and the wagon rattled along, jolting and shaking them with every pothole and rut until eventually Aasgod placed a hand on her shoulder, indicating it was safe to slow down. If only she could get her heart to slow just as easily. She looked back, expecting to see some mad charge following, but the road was empty and already the mist was settling back down to cover the way they'd come.

There was no more chatter after that. They kept their ears open for anything lurking in the bushes and their eyes searched the trees for danger until they left the woods an hour later. But any comfort was short-lived. They passed a farmhouse, or what remained of it – four pillars charred black and some rubble left over from where a wall had collapsed and not a soul in sight. It wasn't just in the city that the scars of war could be seen.

As the mist lifted, the snow fell quicker, covering everything, pinching at any exposed skin. Aasgod rearranged Zorique's blanket so it was wrapped around all of them, and for that kindness, Tinnstra was very grateful.

They continued on, Tinnstra's sense of unease growing by the second. The world felt wrong, as if it had abandoned all natural sense. The Skulls had done that. Knocked everything off its axis. It was as if they'd taken all the goodness from life.

At midday, Tinnstra stopped at a crossroads. The left fork would take them east to Haslam, while the other led to the Kotege. It was the last place Tinnstra wanted to go to, but she had no choice.

32

Dren

Kiyosun

It might have been a new day but Dren was nursing an old grudge. And, for once, it didn't involve the Skulls. Instead, he was focused on that old man, Jax, and how he was going to make the fucker pay for chucking him in the harbour. No more playing nice. No more pretending they were allies of some sort. It was time to get nasty. Time to get bloody.

Dren had spent the night in an abandoned set of rooms. Whoever had lived there had been taken by the Skulls or fled the city, not that Dren cared either way. He'd smashed a chair up and got a good fire going and then fallen asleep, warm for once.

Now curfew was over though, Dren returned to the docks and found a nice dark alley with a good view of Jax's warehouse and a pile of rubbish in which he could hide. After all, you needed to be patient if you were going to kill a man.

Some time later, he saw Monon and Greener rush off, looking like their world was going to end, but Dren ignored them. They were just lackeys. Jax was the prize.

The old man left about an hour later, hobbling along with his stick, acting a hundred years older than he was. Dren slipped out of the alley and followed, keeping well enough back not to get noticed. Careful, careful, every step of the way.

Jax left the docks, skirted the edge of Brixta and headed into the Risenn District. The fucking Skulls were everywhere, but Dren had become a master at avoiding them over the last six months. They didn't give a shit about a gutter rat like him.

He lifted an apple from some women's basket and took a mouthful before he'd gone another step. Not that she noticed. Dren was too quick for that.

His mouth watered with every bite. Juice ran down his chin. His stomach groaned in appreciation. It wasn't much, but it would keep him going for now.

The streets grew narrower and more crowded, making it easier to stay hidden. Risenn was much like Toxten, except the Skulls hadn't bombed the shit out of the place. People there still pretended to live normal lives. They weren't eating, sleeping and shitting in piles of rubble that were once their homes. They didn't have the Weeping Men snatching bodies for the slave trade the moment their backs were turned. Dren spat. Lucky bastards. Good job they were all in this together.

Jax entered a carpet shop and Dren wandered past but couldn't see inside – fuck knows when the windows had last been cleaned. There was nowhere at street level to watch from without being noticed so he sneaked into the building opposite and ran up the stairs to the roof. It was a perfect lookout's perch, so Dren settled down to see where Jax was off to next.

Minutes passed with no sign of the Shulka leaving. Dren didn't care. He wasn't in a hurry – he was a patient man, after all.

Minutes became an hour. The sun climbed higher but the westerly wind off the ocean kept the temperature down to bloody freezing. Good job Dren had his new coat. Shame about his feet, though. He rubbed some warmth into them. Maybe he'd take Jax's boots when he was dead – only fair as Dren had lost his because of the old man.

Midday passed and there was still no sign of Jax. He wasn't coming out. His visit to the carpet shop wasn't an errand or a message drop. He was staying put. Maybe it was his home. Maybe he was having a nap. Maybe it was the right time for a visit. Dren grinned.

He stood up and stamped his feet to get the blood flowing in them again while he checked the gap between the buildings. It was an easy jump. A distance Dren had made a hundred times before.

He pulled his stolen knife out and gripped it tight. Better in his hand than risk it slipping as he jumped. Dren wasn't going to make a house call on Jax without a blade ready. That wouldn't be a good idea. He checked the street but no one looked up. Why would they? Too busy worrying about their own fucking lives. He checked the skies, but the Skulls didn't have any Daijaku out and about, either. He was good to go.

Dren backed up, made sure he had enough space for a decent run-up. Took some deep breaths. It was time. He could do this. Time for some fucking payback.

After landing on the roof opposite, he waited in the shadows while he caught his breath. His blood coursed through him and he told himself it was just from the jump. He wasn't frightened. Not of some old man with one arm. An old man who would probably shit his pants when he saw Dren walk in through the door, knife in hand. Like a ghost.

That thought got Dren smiling. He was ready.

The rooftop door popped open easily. People always worried about the front door and never thought about what was above their heads. They never believed trouble would come that way.

It was dark inside the stairwell, so he waited while his eyes adjusted. He listened for clues about where Jax might be but the house was silent. With any luck, the old bastard would be asleep. He'd wake him, though, just so Jax could see who cut his throat. No way did he want the man to die without knowing who'd killed him. No way. Dren wanted to look the bastard in the eye. If there was some sort of afterlife, Jax could spend the rest of eternity knowing Dren got the better of him.

He moved down the stairs all careful like, watching where he put his feet, making sure his weight was evenly distributed. No creaking board would give him away.

There were two doors on the third floor, leading to bed-rooms, neither of which had been used in a long time. A child's doll lay on the floor of one of the rooms, layered with dust and cobwebs. Maybe the kid who'd lived there had escaped and, wherever she was now, life was carrying on much as it had before. Dren, though? He was grateful his parents couldn't see him now.

He thought his dad would understand, but he knew his mother wouldn't.

On the second floor were two more rooms with closed doors. He held his breath as he crept to the first one. He reached for the door handle, tightened his grip on the knife and raised it, ready to strike.

The handle creaked as Dren turned it and he pushed the door open quickly. The bed was in the far corner of the room. Someone was asleep beneath a blanket. Jax. It had to be Jax.

Four steps it took to reach the bed. Dren felt his anger rise. *Payback.*

Dren grabbed Jax's shoulder so he could turn him over and stab him in his heart but his hand just sank into the blanket. No one there. Dren had been about to stab some bundled-up bed linen.

Shit. Jax must be in the next room.

He turned, retraced his steps. On the landing, he stopped when he heard a man's voice from below. Not Jax, though. This voice was younger, not so worn out.

'We don't know who the new governor is yet, but the Skulls aren't waiting. They're kicking in doors and snatching whoever they want. It's worse than it's been for a long time.'

Dren leaned over the bannister, trying to see who spoke. He'd not considered that Jax might be with someone else. He wasn't worried about taking on the old man, but if he had other Shulka with him …

'There's no logic to who they're taking,' the man continued. 'It's all so random, we can't get their targets away in time to save anyone.'

Fuck it, Dren wasn't going to risk it. Jax could wait till later. Dren was, after all, a patient man, and he wasn't about to go on a suicide mission. He backed off towards the stairs. Now he knew where Jax lived, he could come back whenever he liked. He turned around. Time to go.

'I thought we killed you,' said Jax, sitting on the stairs leading up to the next floor. A big fat grin on the old man's face and a club in his hand. 'Mind that knife of yours – you might hurt someone if you're not careful.'

Dren couldn't believe it. 'How the fuck did you creep up on me?'

Jax just chuckled and eased himself up. Now that both of them were on their feet, Dren realised how much bigger the Shulka was compared to him. Jax had to be over six foot and broad with it. He suddenly didn't look so fragile with the bend in his back gone. Dren could see the warrior in him, a body made from a lifetime of fighting.

'Now, do you want to give talking another go – or shall we get straight to trying to kill each other?' asked Jax.

Dren smiled, shrugged, tried to look sheepish, like a boy caught with his hand in the cake tin. 'Probably best if we get right to the killing.' He lunged with the knife before he'd even finished the sentence, could see in his mind's eye the blade already sinking into Jax's gut.

Except the old man wasn't there. He sidestepped out the way and, as Dren's thrust sailed past, Jax smacked his arm with the club. His arm went numb and he dropped the knife. Dren swung around, keeping his balance somehow, and threw a punch with his other hand, but Jax tilted his head out of the way and he missed again. He tried another right hook, but his arm didn't respond and Jax rammed his club into Dren's stomach. He dropped to his knees and puked a load of bile onto the floor. Anger and humiliation and hatred mixed with the acid in his stomach and he hurled himself at Jax, screaming. He'd claw the man's fucking eyes out with his fingers if he had to, rip his throat open with his teeth.

Jax cracked him in the jaw good and proper. Dropped him to the floor. He spat more puke and blood and glared at Jax, who stood there without so much as a bead of sweat on his brow.

'Come on, boy. You can do better than that. I thought you were a killer.' The bastard *laughed*.

Dren spotted his knife lying by the stairs and went for that instead of the old man. Jax waited until he had his fingers on the hilt before he stamped down with his big, heavy boots. Dren screamed as Jax's heel squashed his fingers, but another boot in the gut shut him up. He curled up in the corner of the landing, cradling his hand, trying to catch his breath.

'Got anything funny to say? Any insults you want to throw my way?' asked Jax. 'No?'

Dren knew he had no chance against Jax. Not then. Not like that. He'd been stupid to think he had. Not in a straight-up fight, anyway. He had to get away.

'Don't tell me you've had enough,' said Jax. 'I'm just an old man.' He waved his stump. 'And a one-armed old man at that.'

'Fuck you,' spat Dren and hurled himself down the stairs. He tried to roll to protect his head as he hit the landing below. He bounced off the steps and the wall before sprawling out on the floor of the carpet shop and finding himself confronted by a man in a wheelchair. They locked eyes for a second, but Dren could hear Jax coming down the stairs. Time to go. He pushed himself up and ran for the front of the shop. The door was locked, so that just left the window. He jumped up onto a pile of carpets and threw himself head first through it. Glass and wood shattered around him.

Dren hit the ground hard, cracking his head, and got showered in the debris from the window. He cut his feet on the glass as he lurched off into the crowd. He pushed and shoved his way through, ignoring the curses and the shouts. Every breath hurt. Every bloody step was agony. He still didn't know how the old man had beaten him, but Dren would be back when he wasn't looking. It wasn't over – not by a long shot. Dren would be back with a bomb in his hand and explosions to watch.

He didn't see the Skulls until he ran into them. He bounced off one and landed on his arse, leaving a bloody smear on the soldier's white armour. Two Skulls picked him up and held him tight.

The Skull with the smear looked down at the mess Dren had left on his armour, then looked up at Dren. 'You are dead.'

'Thank Kage I found you. Someone tried to kill me,' said Dren. 'I only just escaped.'

The Skull glanced down the street, past Dren. 'Why anyone want to kill you? Catch you stealing?'

'The man's a rebel. I overheard him plotting to attack some soldiers. He caught me before I could get away to warn you.'

'Rebel?' That got their attention.

Dren pointed back down the street. 'In the carpet shop. Front window's broken from where I escaped. The bloke inside – he's a top Hanran. You have to arrest him.'

The Skull backhanded Dren across the jaw. Only the soldiers holding his arms kept Dren on his feet. The Skull said something in Egril that Dren didn't like the sound of.

'I can't go back there,' yelled Dren. 'He'll kill me. I told you where to find him. Please let me go – I don't even want a reward.'

'Silence,' said the Skull. Dren saw the punch coming but there was no avoiding it.

33

Darus

Aisair

Darus had to admit the Kyoryu were a joy to watch. He'd returned to the Jian rebels' secret meeting place with their handler, Osmer, and his beasts. Once off their leashes, they prowled through the rubble like warped cats, inspecting every stone and rock. Twice they'd even inspected Darus, snarling and snapping around his horse's feet. The horse was a black destrier, a magnificent beast and bred for war, but the Kyoryu unsettled it all the same. His soldiers remained as far away from the Kyoryu as they could, hands always close to weapons – just in case.

Darus could feel his sister's eyes on him. He knew she hoped the Kyoryu would be a disaster. Any opportunity to make him look small.

He ignored her as much as possible, refusing to give her the satisfaction. His success would be revenge enough – until the day he could kill her. He smiled. That would be a moment to truly savour. It would be ... *exquisite*.

'How long before they find the scent?' Darus asked Osmer as the Kyoryu continued to dig amongst the ruins.

'As long as it takes,' replied the southerner. 'There was a battle here. Both sides used magic. The animals must work out which is the scent we seek and discard the others. It won't be long now.'

'Good. We can't—'

The creatures sprinted away. Darus had never seen anything

move so fast. Floor or wall, it was all the same to them. They sped down the street, leaping from one surface to the next.

'Now we follow,' said Osmer. The man set off, unperturbed that his creatures had already disappeared from view.

'What if you lose sight of them?' asked Darus.

'Impossible. They are connected to me as if they were my very limbs.'

By Kage's infinite wisdom, Darus hated the man's glibness. He signalled for his sister and the guards to follow and then rode off behind Osmer.

It soon became apparent that Darus didn't need the handler to follow the Kyoryu. They left a distinctive trail. First, there was the screaming. Then there was the destruction. Finally, there was the carnage. The Kyoryu stopped for nothing. Not some stupid Jian. Nor even windows or walls. They left a trail of blood and rubble haunted by the wails of the dying. Darus had to admit he was rather enjoying himself. He dismounted so he could better follow on foot while the others went via a less direct route.

'The Jians travelled underground,' said Osmer as they stepped through the front of a candle shop. Broken glass crunched underfoot. A woman lay dead by the counter, her throat ripped open. Her blood decorated the wall behind.

'Indeed,' said Darus as he pushed a dangling shard of wood out of the way and stepped into the neighbouring shop. The destruction was ... *beautiful*. And it had all been done so quickly. So effectively. 'Why don't we have more of these creatures?'

'They are the hardest of all the Emperor's creations to make,' said Osmer. 'And the most difficult to control.'

'You appear to manage well enough.'

'That is because they are my children.'

'You mean you raised them.'

Osmer looked at Darus, a sudden sadness in his eye. 'No. I mean they are my children. Born to my wife, sired by me. I gave them to the Emperor when they were a month old. He returned them to me a month later. I've raised them since.'

They crossed the street, entered another building through another hole in the wall. 'Quite the sacrifice.'

'It was my duty. When the Emperor asks, one does not refuse.'

'There is no greater honour.' *Not if one wants to live*, thought Darus. 'So, they obey you because you are their father?'

'Every handler must have a connection – father, mother, husband, wife. There has to be some bond for loyalty. Without it …' Osmer waved his hand at an eviscerated Jian. 'Of course, a blood tie is not always enough.'

Darus gazed ahead. The Kyoryu had reached an inn – the Crook'd Billet – and were prowling around outside. 'Do they have names?'

'Of course – Kage'san and Kage'sa.'

The son and daughter of Kage – how wonderfully original. Still, to give up one's children took a certain religious fervour, even more so than the eye and the ear the man had already sacrificed. Darus had to give the southerner credit for that. Would he do the same thing? If he had children? If Raaku asked? He smiled. Without a doubt. To serve the Great Darkness was the highest honour. 'It looks like they've found something.'

'Yes. But the trail moves on, I think,' said Osmer. 'Perhaps they stopped here for a while.'

'Call your children. I'll have my men search the place. Perhaps one of them is still there and I'd prefer them captured alive.'

'As you wish,' said Osmer. He took a small bell from his belt and rang it twice. The effect on the Kyoryu was immediate. On the first ring, they stopped what they were doing; on the second, they bounded back and came to heel before Osmer. Both creatures' mouths were covered in blood. Osmer stroked their heads and fed them treats from a small pouch on his belt. Such foul creatures, and yet Darus couldn't help but see them in a new light now he knew they were once Osmer's flesh and blood. Perhaps the handler would let Darus feed his sister to them before they were called elsewhere in the Empire. That would be *delightful*.

'Have you found something?' said Skara, almost on cue.

Darus had to hide his grin before he turned around. 'Aasgod may have stopped here. Send the men in and search the place.'

'As you wish,' replied Skara.

Darus watched her pass on his orders to the soldiers. At least his sister was obedient. If their positions had been reversed … The thought alone had Darus fingering one of his knives. He would've killed her by now if that were the case.

'They're not here,' said Osmer as they watched the soldiers enter the inn. 'My children are eager to be on their way again.' He held them by their collars but it looked like it was taking all the man's strength to restrain them both.

'Make them wait,' said Darus.

A Kyoryu snarled in response but the man did as he was told.

Eventually, the soldiers returned to the street, empty-handed. They reported to Skara, who in turn came to speak to Darus. 'They found a secret passageway in the kitchen that leads to the tunnels. It looks like they spent some time here but the place is empty now.'

'We can move on?' asked Osmer.

Darus nodded.

The handler released the creatures and they bounded off, heading southwards. Osmer began his slow walk after them.

Darus signalled for his horse. He'd had enough of walking.

'There's one more thing,' said Skara before Darus could mount his horse.

'What?'

'The men found a lot of blood in there, some stained bandages. One of them is injured.'

'Ah.' He mounted his horse and looked down on his sister. 'Best we try and catch them before whoever it is dies, eh?' With that, he spurred his horse on, leaving Skara behind. Where she belonged.

They reached the South Gate an hour later. Despite not catching their prey, Darus was in a joyful mood. The Kyoryu had been a delight to watch, ripping and roaring through the city. Blood always made him happy.

Osmer attached leashes to the creatures and they both curled up at his feet, licking the blood from their hands. Even though Darus knew the truth of what they were, it was hard to see any humanity in the creatures. 'Why have we stopped?'

254

Osmer nodded towards the road leaving the city. 'They've gone south.'

'Your animals can still track them, though?'

'Of course,' replied Osmer. 'But I must keep them leashed now. They would leave us too far behind if allowed to run free. If you want our prey alive, the going will be slower.'

'No matter – as long as we catch them.' Darus looked behind, saw Skara and the others approaching.

'Good of you to join us,' he called out as she got closer. 'Our prey have left the city. Send some men to get supplies and re-inforcements and tell them to catch up with us on the road.'

'As you wish.' Skara glanced up at the cloud-laden sky. 'Are you sure you want to go yourself, brother? It looks like it'll snow again. You know you like your comforts.'

Darus glared at her. 'I think we'll catch them before nightfall, but if we have to slum it in some country inn, *sister*, then so be it.'

'So be it,' replied Skara with a bow.

By Kage's fury, she was enjoying this. She knew Darus would never survive the shame if Aasgod and the girl escaped. Only their capture or their corpses would satisfy the Emperor.

And he would give Raaku one or the other.

34
Jax

Kiyosun

'That fucking kid. How much trouble can one person cause?' said Jax, staring at the broken window.

'Quite a lot, by the looks of it,' replied Kaine.

'Why couldn't he stay dead? With everything that's going on, this is the last thing we need.'

'Maybe if you'd told him what was happening, he might've listened.'

'He's like a mad dog. I can't tell him shit. He can't be trusted. He needs to be put down before he destroys everything.'

'I'm not saying he isn't in the wrong but he's not a Shulka. He's not one of your soldiers. He's shown he won't jump when you say jump, but he hates the Egril and wants them out of Jia as much as we do. Maybe if we explained to him that we're dealing with a bigger picture, he might actually help us.'

Outside, Dren's bloody footprints disappeared into the crowd. 'I'll wring his neck when I see him next. That's what I'll do. Now I'd better tidy up the mess he's made.' He snatched the broom up from the corner of the shop and marched outside, ignoring all the people watching.

He started sweeping the glass up, cursing how difficult it was with just one arm, cursing how easily the boy had evaded him, cursing the mess they were all in. Maybe he shouldn't have tried to kill him, but the kid was out of control.

The Skulls' reprisals would hit everyone hard. And how was

Jax supposed to lead the Hanran now? He could barely sweep the road. It was all going so wrong. They'd lost the war and now they were losing the resistance. If they didn't find Aasgod and the children before the Skulls did, it was all over. If they were even still alive ...

Greener and Monon had left that morning to try and find them. At least he could trust those two. If Aasgod and the children were still at liberty, they'd find them. He wished he could have gone with them – at least it would feel like he was actually doing something – but instead he just had to stay where he was and wait. Feeling useless.

They had three days before the boat from Meigore arrived. Three days before all hope was lost.

'Jax!' His neighbour Asta rushed towards him. 'The Skulls are coming. They got the boy who broke your window.'

He looked past her, up the street. Sure enough, a squad of Skulls was marching towards him, dragging Dren along with them. They weren't coming to chat about a broken window. He dived back inside the shop, tossed the broom and pushed his son's wheelchair to the back of the shop.

'Dad? What's wrong?' asked Kaine.

'Skulls,' he said. 'They've caught Dren and they're coming for us.'

There was no need to say any more. They had to get out of there, find somewhere else to hide. Fuck, he wished he had his sword or a weapon of any sort. Dren's knife was upstairs but there was no time to get that.

They went through the beaded curtain that separated the shop from the small room at the rear and Jax unbolted the back door.

'Where do you think you're going?' shouted a Skull, entering through the front of the shop.

Jax ignored him and pushed Kaine out into the courtyard, rattling him from side to side. It was so bloody difficult to manoeuvre with one arm.

'Leave me, Father,' said Kaine. 'I'm slowing you down.'

'No.' He was right, but Jax wouldn't – couldn't – leave his son.

He'd unbolted the back gate and turned to get Kaine when it exploded inwards, sending him sprawling on the ground. Three more Skulls entered the courtyard.

'Don't move!' shouted one, scimitar drawn and ready.

More Skulls rushed after them from the shop. Jax was grabbed by the arm, by the legs. A punch smacked him in the mouth. Another hand ground his head into the stone. He heard Kaine's wheelchair get overturned, heard his son fall out.

'Leave him alone. He's done nothing.'

'Silence.' A boot took the air from his lungs.

An officer appeared and spoke to his men in Egril. 'Bring them out front and someone fetch the wagon.'

'Please, leave my son,' begged Jax.

A sword was thrust in front of his face. He got the message.

They were led out. A crowd had formed outside the shop, growing in number and hostility by the second.

'Let them go!'

'Bastards!'

'They've done nothing!'

Jax smiled. There was still fight in his people. They'd not given up, they weren't content to watch others suffer. There were enough gathered to concern even the heavily armed Skulls who pushed and shoved back, shouting threats of their own. More swords were drawn when their words fell on deaf ears. Still no one backed away. The crowd moved closer. A cabbage hit one Skull on the head. They weren't used to this resistance. Jax could see that. There was confusion and uncertainty. If this were a battle, he'd have sworn the Skulls were on the verge of breaking. Routed by a crowd of street vendors – now that would be a sight.

'As good as any Shulka, eh?' said Kaine.

'Better.' Jax looked across at his son, dangling between two guards. 'You okay?'

His son nodded, tried to smile. 'Had worse on the training ground.'

Pride swelled in Jax's chest. 'Stay strong.' He tried not to think how he'd get Kaine away if the crowd surged. He could only hope someone would help. Jax spotted Dus the butcher amongst the crowd. He knew Kaine couldn't walk. And then there was Rikard, and Olhor – all good neighbours. He could count on one of them, at least.

Jax saw Dren lying unconscious five yards away. What had the fool said to bring the Skulls down on them? Well, he could bloody well stay where he was. He deserved whatever was coming.

'Where's that wagon?' shouted the Skull officer. 'We need to get out of here.'

'We could let the prisoners go,' said one of the soldiers. 'Return to the Council House.'

'Fool,' said the officer. 'If I didn't need every man, I'd kill you myself. Start killing the Jians. That will disperse them quick enough.'

'No!' screamed Jax, fighting to free himself, but he was held fast, forced to watch as the Skulls attacked the crowd with their scimitars. It was no contest. Unarmed civilians against a well-trained squad of soldiers. It was a bloodbath. Bodies fell – men, women, children, the Egril didn't care. And just like that, it was over.

The crowd still had the numbers but they weren't soldiers. They weren't to know they could still overcome the Skulls if they attacked. Instead they retreated from the whirling blades and the blood and the screams of the dying. The Skulls didn't stop. They hacked into the backs of anyone still within reach. They didn't care they were unarmed and running away.

It was over in seconds. The street was deserted except for the Skulls and their prisoners and a pile of the dead. Dus was amongst them, Asta, too. So many faces of people he'd counted as neighbours for the last six months. Good people. Innocent people.

Jax watched the blood run between the cobblestones. Deep red against cold grey. His knees went from under him. If the Skulls hadn't been holding him up, he would've fallen, and he wasn't sure he'd have the strength to get back up again.

The wagon arrived a few minutes later, drawn by two black horses. Jax, Kaine and Dren were thrown in the cage at the back. Dren was still out cold.

'Please – my son – he needs his wheelchair,' Jax called out as a Skull slammed the gate shut.

Kaine touched his arm. 'Leave it, Father. Don't show them they've got to us.'

'Bastards. *Bastards.*' Jax slammed his fist against the bars.

35
Yas

Kiyosun

Yas was going mad. The building had been locked up tight since the bombing the previous day. No one had been allowed in or out. Yas had begged and pleaded to leave but the Egril refused. When she persisted, a Skull punched her.

They were forced to work constantly. The building had suffered considerable damage in the blast and there was broken glass to sweep up and rooms to set right. The kitchen worked overtime to provide the Egril with food around the clock.

Like everyone else, Yas did as she was told, cleaned, fetched and carried, but the whole time she worried about Little Ro and Ma. One minute she thanked the Four Gods for letting her convince Ma to go home and not watch the hangings, and the next she prayed that Ma hadn't just turned right back around again and returned to the square, being the obstinate cow that she was. Yas had seen the dead – there were bodies piled up everywhere. She would kill herself if Ro was amongst them. Or worse: what if Ma had been killed and now Ro was alone – or worse still, injured and in need of help? She was going crazy thinking about all the awful possibilities.

'I have to get out of here,' she said for the thousandth time. She was sitting with Arga in the small changing room, during a rare short break. She'd tried to sleep but it was impossible. If anything, that made it worse. Without distractions, her mind magnified her fears.

'Don't be a fool, Yas,' replied Arga. 'Do they need to beat your other eye shut before you accept you're not going anywhere?'

'I need to see my son.'

'We all know you do. But *they* don't give a shit. We're getting out of here when they say we're getting out of here, and not a minute sooner. Complain all you want but it's not going to change anything – it'll only make things worse.'

Bets appeared at the door, white-faced. Scared. 'They want everyone in the kitchen.'

All the other staff were already lined up, and Yas and Arga fell into place at the end of the row. Four Skulls stood next to a Chosen. She had a thin face, with black hair that fell to her shoulders.

'This is everyone,' said Bets with a bow.

The woman stepped forwards and removed her baton from her belt. 'It's not been a good few days in Kiyosun. Yesterday's bombing was more than an inconvenience to all of us. As a result, security is being stepped up. We can't afford to have any potential traitors in our midst.' She walked down the line, examining the staff, waving her baton. Yas could hear it crackle and knew what it could do. 'We have to be assured of your loyalty.'

Yas felt faint. She recognised the woman's voice from the other day in the governor's office – she was the one who'd told Aisling what to do.

'I have a particular gift,' continued the Chosen. 'I can read your minds.' She smiled, enjoying the fear her words spread. 'By the time we're finished here, I'll know all your secrets. As long as you're loyal to us, you'll be allowed to go home. If I discover your heart belongs to another ... Well, let us say I look forward to having longer discussions with you on the matter elsewhere.'

Yas's head spun. Read her mind? The Chosen would know everything. She'd never see Ro again. She'd disappear without even a chance to say goodbye.

The Chosen began her examinations. She didn't say anything, just held each person's face and stared into their eyes. She took her time, longer with some than others, before moving on to the next in line.

Yas watched and waited. Sweat ran down her back. Kara hadn't warned her about this. The Chosen could read minds! She was going to prison. *Tortured. Killed.* Her legs nearly went from under her but somehow she managed to stay on her feet. Already the Chosen was halfway down the line.

Yas thought about confessing. Maybe they'd let her go and she could get back to Ro. Still have a life with him somewhere. Would they forgive her? She looked at the Chosen. No – there was no mercy in that woman. They'd still torture Yas. Kill her. They'd want to make an example of her to put off anyone else who might be foolish enough to help the resistance.

Why had she agreed to help Kara? *Stupid, stupid woman.*

The Chosen reached Bets. The cook squared her shoulders defiantly but Yas could see she was petrified. Was she with the Hanran? Yas almost hoped she was – perhaps finding one would be enough for the Chosen to stop and not worry about inspecting anyone else. But no, the Chosen let go of Bets's face and moved on.

Yas was next.

She closed her eyes and thought of Little Ro. He was her life. Born eighteen months ago into a peaceful world with his father, Rossi, by her side. Came out so big, they'd laughed that he was already three months old. They'd called him Little Ro ever since as a joke.

The Chosen placed her hand on Yas's cheek. Her touch was surprisingly gentle, but Yas flinched all the same.

Little Ro had kept them all busy those first few months. Always hungry, he was. Feeding till Yas had nothing left, then sleeping for an hour before demanding more. Rossi found a wet nurse to help but still there was little sleep for any of them. Yas had no idea how Rossi had found the energy to go to work all day at the docks after a night with no sleep but he never missed a shift. He did right by them.

Then the Egril invaded and it was just Yas, Ma and Little Ro. Doing their best, getting by. She'd give everything to just hold Ro in her arms once more, hear him say her name, wake her up for a cuddle in the middle of the night. She concentrated on how he felt in her arms, imagining she was with him right then.

'Look at me,' ordered the Chosen.

Yas obeyed. The woman's eyes were a startling blue. There was no warmth in them, no empathy.

'You love your child very much,' said the Chosen. 'He's all you think about.'

'I've not seen him in two days. I want to get home. Make sure he's safe,' replied Yas, her voice shaking.

'The others – their minds are a mess. A million thoughts bouncing around in their brains, fears, hopes, pleas and prayers. But not you. You just think about your son.' The Chosen's hand pressed against Yas's cheek. 'Your Little Ro.' The Chosen raised her baton and pressed it under Yas's chin. She could feel the hum of power tingle through her skin. A touch of heat. The threat of death.

'He's all I have.' A tear ran down Yas's face.

'You're lucky to have even that.' The Chosen lowered the baton and moved on to Arga.

Yas had made it. Thanks to Little Ro. He'd saved her once more.

The Chosen stepped away from Arga with a look of disappointment on her face. 'So, no spies here despite how you feel about us. Good. Let it stay that way. We don't need your love but we demand your loyalty. Before you go, let me remind you that it is your duty to report anyone you suspect of being a rebel. We will reward such information handsomely. A hundred gold aureus for any name given.'

A hundred aureus? That was a fortune. Everyone looked at everyone else, thinking the same thing. That was more than enough money to betray someone. Why, Yas would almost give herself up for that much gold.

The Chosen smiled, happy at the effect her words had on them. She turned and left the kitchen, followed by the Skulls.

The staff stood watching the door until it sank in that they were free to go.

'Oh, my sweet Gods above and below,' said Bets. 'I thought we were all done for then.'

'Why's that?' said Arga. 'You got something to hide?' There was a gleam in her eye that Yas didn't like.

Nor did Bets. 'Don't you start getting any mad thoughts in your head, young woman. I just meant that I thought they were going to do us all in. They don't need no excuse to torture and kill any one of us. What you done's got naught to do with it.'

'Not suggesting anything,' said Arga, putting her hands up. 'You know me – I mind my own business.'

'All right,' said Bets, sounding like things were far from it. 'Now listen in everyone. It's been a long, hard couple of days. There's not much food left over so share it out and then get yourselves home bloody quick and see your loved ones. Then it's straight back here in the morning so we can start the madness all over again. Now fuck off home.'

No one needed telling twice. Yas was one of the last to move, still shaken by the Chosen's examination.

Bets put a hand on her shoulder. 'You doing all right?'

Yas nodded.

'Look, you're new and you've had it worse than any of us this week,' said Bets. 'I'd like to tell you it'll get better but I ain't gonna lie to you. It's a fucked-up world and we're in the heart of it here. If you don't want to come back tomorrow, I'll understand. Take as much food as you can tonight – it'll keep you and your little one going for a while so you don't need this job.'

'I appreciate you saying that.'

'Don't appreciate nothing. Just do as I ask and stay away. You're one of the good ones and I don't want anything to happen to you.'

Yas didn't take all the food, just her share. It wouldn't have been fair on the others to take more, despite what Bets had said.

It was cold and dark outside but it felt so good. She rushed straight home. She only stopped when she reached her street and saw the candle burning in her window. She started crying all the tears she'd kept inside for the last two days as she ran up the stairs to her family.

36

Tinnstra

The Kotege

They travelled all day, stopping only occasionally to rest the horses and to eat a few mouthfuls of cold meat and dry bread. Aasgod's strength had faded with the day and he'd returned to the rear of the wagon with Zorique. Left alone, all Tinnstra's fears were magnified. She jumped at a bird flying past, thinking it was Daijaku. A rustle in the undergrowth had her looking for ambushes. The only positive thing was that she was still alive. She knew how to survive.

It was a mistake to agree to go with Zorique to Meigore. A mistake to promise to look after her. What use will I be when there's real danger? She glanced back at Aasgod. He's not going to make it. He'll die and we'll be alone and, dear Gods above and below, we'll die, too. This is awful. A nightmare.

Dark clouds rolled across the sky, threatening more snow. Judging by Aasgod's hacking cough, that was the last thing they needed. But the Kotege wasn't far and she knew the way well enough. When she was a child, she'd sat next to her father on their way to see her brothers, just loving being so close to him. He was a magnificent man, a hero to everyone who met him but even more so to her. He'd tell her tales of past times, of Usagi of Clan Rizon who fought three mountain Kojin for a day and a night, or of beautiful Kizmo who chased a Daijaku who'd stolen her child all the way across Jia. She'd loved those tales, feeling

266

scared but safe next to him, not knowing the monsters were real. They'd driven down this very road. Nothing had changed and yet everything had.

She heard movement and turned to see Zorique climbing out from the blankets.

'Can I sit with you?' the girl asked.

'Of course you can,' replied Tinnstra, moving to one side of the driver's bench. 'I'd like someone to talk to.'

The girl snuggled up beside Tinnstra as she pulled a blanket over the two of them.

'Where are we going?'

'A place called the Kotege,' said Tinnstra.

'What's that?'

'It's a school – was a school. It got destroyed during the invasion. I used to live there.'

'Oh,' said Zorique. 'Did you like it?'

Tinnstra's memories were of blood. Of fallen friends, of fear, of fleeing, of leaving everyone else to die. It was the last place she wanted to go. 'It was where they taught people to be Shulka and I wasn't very good at that.'

'Why not?'

Such a simple question, with a simple answer. 'I'm not very brave.'

'You're braver than me.'

Tinnstra looked away, focusing on the road. She couldn't let this little girl see the truth – that everyone was braver than Tinnstra. Even a four-year-old runaway princess. Especially her. 'You're the bravest girl I know.' Her voice choked as she spoke.

'I'm not.'

Tinnstra smiled. 'Believe me, you are. I know what I'm talking about when it comes to bravery and fear.'

The girl tried to return the smile, but it quivered and then broke as tears filled her eyes.

'I'm sorry.' Her voice was barely more than a whisper. 'This is all my fault.'

Tinnstra pulled her into a tight hug. 'Don't say that.'

'But it is.'

'It's not. I promise. There are bad people in the world who will always find an excuse to justify what they do. They'll blame anyone and hate everyone who isn't on their side. It's not your fault they're like that. It's just how they are.'

'I hate the Skulls.'

Tinnstra sighed. 'Me, too.' She squeezed Zorique, the way her father used to do when his stories scared her. 'Everything will be all right. I promise. We'll all be safe soon.' She didn't believe her own words.

The girl didn't look convinced, either. She just kept crying, her little body juddering with each sob.

Tinnstra stroked Zorique's cheek and kissed the top of her head. 'You're a special girl. Never forget that. It's just the world is a mad place right now.'

'I hate it. I hate it all,' sobbed Zorique.

'Don't worry. Everything will be all right. Aasgod will make sure of that.'

'What if he can't? What if he dies?' Zorique's eyes were full of tears. 'You won't leave me, will you?'

'I promise I won't leave you. We're like sisters now, aren't we?'

'Sisters.' That drew a glimmer of a smile from Zorique. 'I've never had a sister before. I had a brother.'

'Me, too,' replied Tinnstra. 'I had three brothers. I always wanted a sister.'

'Are your brothers ...'

Tinnstra shook her head. 'That's why you're so special. You're all I have now.'

'I used to fight with my brother all the time,' said Zorique. 'Now I wish he was here. My mother and father, too.'

'They're with Xin now, under her protection, but I know they'll be looking out for you from there, doing whatever they can to keep you safe. Then one day, you'll be reunited for ever.'

'And you can be with your family, too.'

'I hope so,' said Tinnstra, even though she wasn't sure what sort of reunion that would be. The heroes waiting for the coward to turn up, an eternity of disappointment ahead of her. She hugged Zorique again because she didn't know what else to do. What a mess it all was. The girl deserved someone better than Tinnstra to be her sister and protector.

There was little daylight left when they reached the Kotege. The gate hung half-off its hinges and the sentry box was a burned-out shell. Weeds had invaded the once-immaculate parade ground. Broken windows looked down on them as they drove past the main entrance, the doors nothing more than splinters. And the bones of the dead lay everywhere. She tried to hide Zorique from the worst of it but there were too many. Zorique buried her head in Tinnstra's side, her little fists all bunched up in the folds of Tinnstra's cloak. Only the Four Gods knew what effect it would have on her in the years to come – if they lived that long.

'The students gave a good account of themselves when the Egril came,' said Aasgod from the back of the wagon. His voice was no more than a whisper. 'They fought like true Shulka.'

'They were *children*,' said Tinnstra, tears forming in her own eyes.

'Alas,' said Aasgod, 'war doesn't care who it calls to fight.'

The truth of his words hit her hard. *I've done everything I can to avoid getting involved and yet here I am, up to my neck in it, with a four-year-old girl and an injured mage as my only allies, the future of the bloody world on my shoulders*. She glanced at Aasgod. *He'd better not die*.

Tinnstra halted the wagon at the rear of the barracks and un-hitched the horses. She put blankets over them and gave them plenty to eat. She didn't move them to the stables, just hobbled them, preferring the animals remain close to hand – just in case. The night would be cold but bearable.

With Aasgod using her like a crutch and Zorique holding on to the corner of her cloak, it took all Tinnstra's strength to get them inside. The moonlight coming through the shattered windows and the fallen walls provided enough light to see by. Cold clung to the stone and fogged their breath. Dark smears marred the marble floor where the dead had been dragged outside. Pieces of armour lay scattered here and there, alongside broken swords and spent arrows. It was no longer a place of honour and aspirations. It was a memorial to a lost dream. A marker to the dead.

'The barracks are in the west wing, second floor,' she said as she led them on. 'We should find beds there. We can rest and then head up the mountain tomorrow.'

'Aasgod doesn't look well,' said Zorique.

'I'm all right, my love,' replied the mage. 'I'm just tired.'

They climbed the stairs, Aasgod growing heavier with each step, and she could feel her legs shake with the effort. When he slipped on a step and stumbled, they all nearly fell.

'I'm sorry,' said Aasgod.

'Don't worry. Let's get you to a bed,' said Tinnstra.

The rooms weren't much, but Tinnstra found two at the end of the corridor that didn't have broken windows. She eased Aasgod down onto a cot in one of them. The man was barely conscious, whatever strength he once had long since spent, and Tinnstra didn't feel much better.

There was a small hearth in the room with firewood already stacked in it. She remembered the beatings a cadet would receive if an instructor found a room without a fire prepared. She tried not to think of her own room, or the knife she'd left on the floor and what she'd wanted to do with it.

Zorique watched as Tinnstra lit the fire, chewing her lip. It wasn't long before a warm glow filled the room, but it didn't seem to make the girl happier. 'Is he going to die?'

'I hope not,' replied Tinnstra, slipping the flint back in her pocket. 'The fire will help. I'll clean and rebandage his wounds, make him some hot food. Then, after a good night's rest, he'll be better in the morning.'

'You promise?' Her tears glistened in the firelight.

Tinnstra bent down so she could look the girl in the eyes. 'I promise. Right now, I want you to wait here with Aasgod. I'm going to fetch some food and blankets from the wagon. I'll be as quick as I can. Okay?'

Zorique nodded and sniffed. 'Okay.'

Tinnstra squeezed her hand. 'I'll be back before you know it.'

Out in the dark corridor, away from Zorique's sight, Tinnstra leaned against the wall, exhausted. Months hiding in Aisair hadn't prepared Tinnstra for a life on the run. An hour's Shulikan a day hadn't kept her fit enough. She was so tired, so out of her depth. Who was she to reassure anyone? She felt as scared and worried as Zorique.

To her left were the servants' stairs. They led down to the side of the house. To the woods. To her old escape path. She knew the way ...

Aasgod can look after Zorique. He'll be fine once he's had some rest. Even if he isn't, they're not my problem. I have to look after myself first. I have to survive, and that means not getting any more involved.

And yet ... I made promises. Promises I've been forced into. Promises to Beris and a dying mage. They don't count. No one would blame me for not keeping my word.

Except Zorique. Zorique would.

Tinnstra knew then she couldn't run, no matter what. Not with Aasgod so weak, not after what he'd told her. If he died, who would look after the girl? Abandoning her was as good as killing her and Tinnstra wouldn't have that on her conscience. She couldn't watch the world die because she was a coward. With a sigh, Tinnstra turned around and headed for the main stairs.

She fetched one of the food bags from the wagon along with some blankets and an old shirt she could use for bandages.

Zorique was asleep when she got back, curled up underneath Aasgod's bed. The mage was awake, though, and for that, Tinnstra was glad. 'Are you feeling better?'

'Not really,' replied the mage. 'But I'm still alive.'

Tinnstra set a small pot over the fire, filled with water and vegetables. 'Food will help.'

'It certainly won't hurt.'

'Let me look at your wounds.' Tinnstra rolled Aasgod onto his side, then used her knife to cut open his shirt and through the bandages she'd applied the day before. Even though she knew it was going to be bad, she wasn't prepared for what she saw. His back was covered in blood. Each wound looked newly acquired. And the smell ... by the Four Gods, *the rot had set in.*

'It doesn't look good, does it?' said Aasgod.

'It ... it just needs cleaning.' Tinnstra filled a bowl with water and wet a cloth.

Aasgod winced as she wiped his back.

'I'm sorry – I'm trying to be as gentle as I can.'

'I've never been good with pain.'

'You're doing fine.'

Soon the bowl of water was red and Aasgod's back was as clean as it was going to be. The smell remained undiminished.

'Tinnstra.' There was an edge to Aasgod's voice.

'Yes?' She began to wrap fresh bandages over the mage's wounds. They would have to stay at the barracks for a while, find some other way of getting Zorique to Meigore. Perhaps if she kept cleaning the wounds, the mage would get better.

'I'm dying.'

'No, you're not.'

'Don't lie. We both know the truth. Even I can smell the poison in my wounds. I can feel it burning.'

'I'm sorry.'

'Zorique is all that matters. You're going to have to look after her – get her to the boat. The leader of the Hanran in Kiyosun is a man called Jax.'

'Shhh. You just need rest. You'll feel better in the morning.'

Aasgod twisted to face her. Sweat peppered his brow. 'There's no time for us to lie to each other.'

'I can't do this without you.' Tinnstra's head dropped. Time for the truth, then. 'I'm not the right person for this. I've only come this far because of you. I'm ... I'm ... not brave enough to do this on my own.'

'You are.'

'Do you want to know why I'm not a Shulka? Why I never took the oaths? It's because I'm a coward. I was expelled from the Kotege because I ran from the enemy during my trials. I dropped my spear and ran, and I've been running ever since.'

Aasgod flopped back on to the bed, his face deathly white. 'What if I could make you brave? Could you do it then?'

'How? It's not possible.'

'Find me a weapon of some sort – a sword or a bow, whatever is your preference. I can give it powers so that as long as you hold

272

it in your hands, you'll never be killed. It will heal you of any wound. You'll survive any attack.'

'You can do that?'

'Not easily, but yes, I can.'

Tinnstra sat down, imagining having such a weapon. 'But I'd still feel pain?'

'Only briefly. The weapon would heal you quickly enough.'

She looked at Zorique – she'd not be able to abandon her. She'd already made that choice. And Aasgod might not survive the night. What choice did she have? 'I'll do it.'

'Where's the armoury?'

'In the east wing.' Where she'd stolen the knife.

'Go. Find something.'

'Will you be okay?'

Aasgod smiled. 'I will or I won't.'

'Don't die on me.' For the second time, Tinnstra left them both. This time, she ran.

The armoury was at the opposite end of the Kotege. During normal times, it would've been locked up and only opened under the supervision of Master Smade, a retired Shulka with kind eyes. It was a cramped space with rack after rack of every type of weapon imaginable. Now it was unlocked and unguarded, the racks lay on their sides, broken, and only a few weapons remained scattered on the ground.

She groped around in the dark. It took her some time to find a Shulka sword in a sheath with straps. She pulled the blade free.

Some Shulka's swords were patterned with intricate designs to reflect their owners, but the one in Tinnstra's hand was un-adorned and looked all the more beautiful for it. Her father's had been simple, too – as he said, it was what you did with a sword that mattered, not how it looked.

She resheathed it and fixed the straps so it hung on her back. Harka would've frowned at her for carrying a sword that way but it felt right to her. *Right? Dear Gods, what am I becoming?*

She ran back to Aasgod and found the mage sitting upright in bed, waiting for her. The smell of soup filled the room and made her mouth water.

'You chose a sword, I see,' said Aasgod.

'I did.' Tinnstra handed over the weapon. 'This magic to heal any wound ...'

'Yes?'

'Why not use it on yourself? You'll always be a better protector for Zorique than I could ever be.'

'It is too late for me. The future is yours.'

'No. I don't believe that.'

'And yet it is true.' Aasgod drew the sword. Light from the fire danced along the blade. He produced a vial, uncorked it, drank it. 'Now give me your hand.'

Tinnstra did as she was told and bit her lip. It wouldn't do to show how scared she was.

He closed his eyes and began the spell. His voice was too quiet for Tinnstra to understand what was said. Heat emanated from his hand, increasing quickly. Burning. She tried to pull her hand free but Aasgod held her tight. The sword glowed, throbbing in time with her heart. The heat spread up her arm and into her chest. Sweat broke out across her brow as her blood raced around her body. The sword pulsed faster and faster as her heart rate increased. The room swirled. Breathing took all her concentration. She grew faint. Her eyelids fluttered.

Aasgod let go of her hand. The heat disappeared and the light in the sword died. 'It is done,' said the mage and collapsed back onto the bed, dropping the sword. It clanged on the stone floor, waking Zorique with a start.

'What's happening?' asked the girl, eyes wide.

'It's Aasgod,' replied Tinnstra. She checked his wrist and found a weak pulse.

'Is he dead?'

'No ... but he's not well.' Tinnstra pulled the blanket over the mage. 'Best let him sleep. Are you hungry?'

The girl nodded.

Tinnstra filled a bowl with soup and handed it to her. 'Eat this.'

'Thank you.'

Tinnstra smiled. Such good manners from one so young. 'My father told me that you should always eat when the opportunity allows. You never know when you'll next get the chance.' Her stomach rumbled as she filled her own bowl. She watched Zorique take a tentative mouthful and then smile when the taste was acceptable. Tinnstra had been the same as a child, always needing encouragement or, on occasion, threats to try something she didn't recognise. It used to drive her parents mad.

Zorique looked up, soup on her chin. 'I'm scared.'

Tinnstra sat down next to her and slipped her arm around the girl's shoulders. Zorique was such a small thing, so fragile. 'So am I,' she said. 'So am I. But we've come this far. We'll stay here tonight and get some sleep, and in the morning, Aasgod will be better and we'll be on our way. It'll be hard, but we'll make it.' She glanced down at the sword and thought of Aasgod's gift. For once, her fear was gone.

They ate the rest of the soup in silence, snuggled up together. Eventually, Zorique fell asleep again and Tinnstra watched the flames dance in the fireplace, enjoying being full, warm and dry. For now, that was enough.

Noise from outside woke Tinnstra. She cursed herself. How long had she been asleep?

'What's that?' asked Zorique, stirring beside her.

'I don't know,' replied Tinnstra. It couldn't be good, whatever it was. She rushed to the window and gasped.

Skulls filled the courtyard below. A man stood in the centre with two creatures on chains. They snapped and snarled. A Chosen was next to them on a black stallion. Tinnstra recognised him as the man from the attack in Ester Street.

They all looked towards Tinnstra's window, illuminated by a fire in an otherwise darkened building.

'Oh no.'

37
Jax

Kiyosun

The Skulls dumped Jax, Kaine and Dren in a large cell beneath the Council House. The only light flickered in through the bars in the door. The kid was still unconscious, but he could rot for all Jax cared. Kaine was another matter.

'Are you all right, son?' Jax staggered over to him.

Kaine's laugh wasn't a happy sound. 'We're in jail, Father. I think "all right" is the last thing we are.' He dragged himself across the cell floor through the blood, shit and straw until he could lean back against a stone wall. 'But I'm alive. So that's something.'

Jax peered out between the bars. The faint light came from a few torches hanging on the walls. There were about twenty cells running the length of the cellar with oak doors sealing off one end and steel doors at the other, where two Skull sentries stood guard. They wouldn't be getting out of there easily. If at all. 'We've not done anything wrong that they know of. They only have Dren's word that we're Hanran. We can explain we caught him stealing and that this is his way of getting us back.'

Kaine wiped some blood from the side of his mouth. 'It might work – if we can persuade Dren to say the same thing. Not much glory in hanging two cripples and a kid.'

The kid. 'Fucking fool.'

'Leave him,' said Kaine. 'He's in the same shit we are.'

'This is the last thing we need right now. The last fucking thing.'

'Every plan goes to shit once the first punch is thrown,' said Kaine. 'You taught me that. It's what you do next that matters.'

Jax sat down next to his son. The ground was cold and damp and stank of piss, shit and blood. Bugs scuttled away into the deepest shadows. 'I'm sorry, son. I've messed up everything.'

'You've got nothing to apologise for. Nothing.'

Jax sighed. 'This isn't what I wanted for you.'

'Life is what it is, Father. It's not your fault, or my fault. It's not even Dren's fault, really. The Egril invaded. We've just been caught up in what happened next.'

'You're my son. My responsibility. I should have protected you.'

The oak doors swung open. A squad of Skulls marched in and stopped in front of their cell. 'One-arm. Come.'

Jax staggered to his feet, playing up his weakness and frailty. 'Why? We've done nothing wrong. Where are you taking me? I want to go home.'

'My father's not a well man,' added Kaine. 'We haven't done anything.'

'Shut up. Come here,' ordered a Skull.

As they manhandled Jax out of the cell, he stumbled and almost fell. 'Sorry. Sorry.'

'Kage's balls,' cursed the Skull in his own tongue. 'You Jians get more pathetic by the day.' The other Skulls laughed but Jax didn't care – let them think that. No one took any notice of the weak.

At ground level, he blinked in the sudden light. They passed Egril officers and Jian workers but no one paid them any heed – he was just another prisoner about to be interrogated. They'd stuck their bloody flag everywhere and erected statues of Kage, their bastard one-eyed, one-eared dog of a God. Jax could feel his anger building. The Egril had tried to destroy everything he loved – from his beloved Shulka to the Gods he worshipped. Let them do their worst. He could take it.

The room was no more than a small box at the end of a corridor. No windows. Just a chair chained to the stone floor, surrounded by stone walls. The only decorations were the bloodstains from previous visitors. They chained his one good hand to the armrest and restrained his feet against the chair legs.

The Skulls left him there.

He was supposed to panic once he was left alone, tortured by his imagination. Jax knew the drill. He wasn't some stupid civilian, however: if they were going to leave him in peace and quiet, he'd make the most of it.

He closed his eyes and went to sleep.

The door flew open with a bang, waking Jax. An Egril officer in a grey uniform stood watching him from the doorway, flanked by two Skulls.

Jax blinked at the sudden light. 'What's going on? Have you come to let me go? Where's my son?'

'Who's he supposed to be?' asked the officer in Egril.

Jax showed no sign that he understood.

'A member of the Hanran, according to some kid,' answered the Skull. 'A senior member.'

'What a waste of time.' The officer rolled his eyes. 'Let's get on with it.'

They entered the room and shut the door. The Skulls took positions in front of him, crowding him. Doing it by the book.

Jax looked from one face to the next. Let them see fear. Let them see weakness. 'Please. I don't understand. Why am I here?' Let them hear the tremor in his voice.

The officer slapped him. Just a sting. 'Only speak when I say.' He spoke Jian almost perfectly.

Jax nodded.

'What is your name?'

'Jax.'

'How long have you been in the Hanran?'

'Hanran? I'm not in the Hanran. I own a carpet shop. I sell carpets—'

One of the Skulls hit the side of his head.

'How long have you been in the Hanran?' repeated the officer.

'I'm not. I promise you, I'm—'

Another blow rocked him. Only the chains kept him in his seat.

'How long have you been in the Hanran?'

'I'm not. I—'

The officer's fist snapped Jax's head back. Blood flew from his nose. 'How long have you been in the Hanran?'

'Please believe me – I'm n—'

He didn't see who punched him. It didn't matter. He spat more blood onto the floor. He felt like laughing, wanted to tell them to stop pissing about and get on with it – he could take the beating – but that would give the game away. So, instead, he looked up with tears in his eyes, his bottom lip quivering as blood ran from his mouth. 'Please. I've done nothing.'

The officer bent down so he could look Jax in the eye. 'There is no point lying to us. This is only the start. If I have to go away without your confession, I'll come back with knives and cut you until you do talk.'

Jax let the tears hide the fire inside. Even with half an arm, he could kill the smug bastard easily enough. 'I'm telling you the truth. I'm just a carpet seller. I don't want you to hurt me, but I don't know anything about the Hanran.'

The officer sighed and stood up. 'You said we arrested him with his son?' he asked one of the Skulls, speaking in Egril.

'Yes, sir. He's downstairs in the cells. He's crippled, too.'

The officer shook his head. 'By Kage. Really?'

'Yes, sir,' replied the Skull. 'Can't walk.'

'Have we run out of proper people to arrest?' The officer switched back to Jian. 'Return this one to the cells. Bring the son up. And bring the knives with you. We might as well get straight to it.'

'No,' begged Jax. 'Not my boy. He's done nothing. I've done nothing. Why are you doing this?'

'Because I can.' The officer smiled unpleasantly. 'Take him away.'

The Skulls unlocked Jax and hauled him to his feet.

'Please. Not my son. We've done nothing.' He began to struggle. Not fighting. Not yet. He'd sent men and women to die before, watched while they were killed or maimed and not thought twice about it, but it was different with Kaine. It always

279

had been. If Jax'd had his way, the boy would never have followed him into the Shulka.

A punch in the stomach smashed the air from his lungs. Another clubbed him in the face. They dropped him to the floor and the kicks rained down. Jax curled up, tried to protect his kidneys, his head, but even with two arms, it would have achieved little. They pummelled him with boots and fists, relentlessly, mercilessly.

'Enough,' ordered the officer, and only then did they stop. Jax spat blood onto the floor, tried to see through half-shut eyes and winced as bruised ribs scratched his lungs.

The Skulls dragged him back to his cell.

'Father!' cried Kaine. 'What have you done to him?'

They dropped him, grabbed Kaine and were gone before Jax had a chance to even roll onto his back.

'Stay strong, son,' he whispered.

Someone laughed. The kid. Jax pulled himself upright, ignoring the pain. Dren was awake and watching him from the corner of the cell. He didn't look much better than Jax felt, but Jax had no sympathy for him. The kid should've drowned like he was supposed to.

'They fucked you up real good, old man,' said Dren.

'This is nothing. This is just the start. I have a long way to go before it gets as bad as it can get. You do, too. Remember that.'

'Fuck you. You couldn't break me. These bastards won't, either.'

'Everyone breaks.'

'Not me.'

'We'll see how brave you are when they're holding your dick in one hand and a meat cleaver in the other.'

That shut the kid up, took the smile off his face. Jax didn't feel any satisfaction in knocking him down, though. As Kaine said, they were all in the same shit.

'Listen to me, kid.' Jax came over so he could look the kid in the eye.

'What?' Dren gave him the full hard-man stare back, still acting tough.

'When it's your turn, tell them you made it all up – that you don't know anyone in the Hanran. You just wanted to cause me trouble because I caught you stealing. Maybe they'll let us go. Maybe they'll decide we're not worth bothering with.'

'Do you think that'll work?'

'Who knows, but it's the only hand we've got to play.'

38

Tinnstra

The Kotege

Tinnstra shook Aasgod. 'You've got to wake up. They've found us. They've found us.'

Aasgod groaned and his eyes fluttered but he didn't wake.

'What's wrong with him?' asked Zorique.

'I think he's dying,' she replied.

'No!' shouted Zorique. 'He can't be. You promised me.'

Tinnstra fumbled in his pockets, found the two remaining vials. She opened both and poured them between his lips. She didn't know if their magic would do any good, but she had no other ideas.

She waited, aware of how little time they had, praying to all the Gods for Aasgod to live, to move, but the mage didn't stir.

She checked the window again. The Skulls had taken up positions across the courtyard and more were heading for the rear of the Kotege. They'd have the place surrounded before too long. The Chosen spoke to the man with the foul creatures and then pointed at Tinnstra's window. They knew where they were. Of course they did – it was the only room with a fire burning.

'We need to get out of here,' Tinnstra said to Zorique, trying not to sound petrified.

'What about Aasgod? We can't leave him.'

Tinnstra took his wrist, tried to feel for a pulse but found none. He was so pale. 'He's gone. We must save ourselves – save you.'

Zorique flung herself on top of him. 'I won't leave him. I can't.'

'You must. He wanted you to be free, to get to Meigore. We must—'

Howling cut Tinnstra off. She could hear the creatures inside the building. They were coming.

Tinnstra slipped the sword into the sheath on her back. *Dear Gods, Aasgod's magic better work or we're all dead*. She grabbed the food bag and took Zorique's hand. 'We're leaving now.'

The girl yanked her hand free and clung to Aasgod. 'No!'

Fear surged through Tinnstra. She wrapped her arm around Zorique's stomach and pulled but still the girl held on. 'Let go. We have to leave. We'll die if we stay here.'

The howling grew closer, echoing along the corridors. Even with her newly empowered sword, Tinnstra had no interest in facing demons. Her fear gave her strength and she dragged the girl free. Zorique fought her every inch of the way, screaming, shouting, punching and scratching, but Tinnstra wouldn't let go.

They all but fell into the corridor. The main hall wasn't an option so Tinnstra turned left towards the servants' stairs. She'd made it three yards when howling stopped her mid-step. Zorique screamed. Tinnstra looked back and saw two sets of red eyes glowing in the darkness at the far end of the corridor.

Tinnstra scooped Zorique up and ran. The stairs were narrow, rickety things and she half-fell, half-ran down them, bouncing off walls into the railings, trying to protect Zorique as best she could.

They were almost at the bottom when something crashed into the stairs above. The impact rocked the stairs, sending Tinnstra and Zorique tumbling down the last few steps to sprawl across the landing.

Above them, one of the creatures was perched on the railing, muscles bunched, snarling and ready to pounce. Tinnstra pushed Zorique behind her and drew her sword. It was nothing compared to the creature, but it was imbued with Aasgod's magic. It had to be enough.

Instinctively, her feet slipped into a fighting stance as she readied the sword to face her enemy.

The creature leaped. It flew down the stairwell, straight at Tinnstra. Its claws stretched out, seeking her flesh. Time slowed.

Zorique screamed again. Tinnstra thrust her sword blindly and felt the impact as it bit into the creature before it hit her and knocked her to the ground. Blood pumped out over her face and body. Warm, sticky. Salty on her tongue. She kicked and punched and screamed and stabbed as she scrambled to get out from under the creature. Panic gripped her, making it hard to think.

Zorique shouted something Tinnstra couldn't hear. She kicked herself free and scuttled back from the demon, still gripping her sword. Her fingers were locked so tight around the hilt, she thought she'd never be able to let it go, but she needed its magic. It would heal her wounds. It would keep her alive.

'It's dead! It's dead!'

'What?' Tinnstra stared at the girl.

'The creature – it's dead.'

Tinnstra looked at the demon. It lay unmoving on the ground, blood leaking from its chest. 'But I ...' She patted herself, couldn't find any wounds. *The blood isn't mine. I killed the creature. The sword saved me. Aasgod's magic worked. I'm alive. We still have a chance.*

She staggered to her feet and sheathed the sword, in shock at being alive. She picked up the food bag again and took Zorique's hand. 'We've got to keep moving. There's still a second demon loose somewhere.'

Tinnstra pushed the door open and the rush of cold air brought some sense back. She peered around the door frame, looking for Skulls but seeing none, thank the Four Gods.

Ten yards of open ground separated them from bushes and trees where they could hide. Ten yards of ground covered with snow. They'd leave tracks a blind man could follow but there was nowhere else to go. No other choice. Run or die.

'We're going straight to the bushes over there. Do you see?'

'Yes.'

'Don't worry. I'll carry you.'

The girl chewed her lip, eyes wide and scared, but she nodded all the same.

'Good – let's go.' Tinnstra checked the way was still clear. No Skulls. No monsters. No Chosen. *Now or never.*

They moved quickly, feet crunching in the snow. Five yards,

six yards and still no one called out. Eight yards, nine and then they crashed into the undergrowth, twigs scratching them as they slipped through the bushes. The sudden darkness was comforting; it hid them from sight, protected them.

Tinnstra lowered Zorique, still not quite believing they'd made it this far alive and unharmed. *We can do this. We can get away.*

'We need to keep going,' she told Zorique. 'Put more distance between us and them.'

Zorique nodded and tightened her grip on Tinnstra's hand. They inched through the undergrowth. The fear was with Tinnstra once more, in her gut, but manageable now she had the sword, had its protection.

The front courtyard came into view. The Skulls, the Chosen and the strange man with the chains were all looking up at the room they'd just left, still illuminated by the fire Tinnstra had made without a second's thought. She had to be cleverer than that. She had to remember the Egril wouldn't stop their pursuit. Tinnstra and Zorique would only be able to rest properly once they were in Meigore – and that was so far away. Until then, she'd—

The upper floor of the Kotege exploded. Flames shot out across the night sky, lighting up the world. She wrapped herself around Zorique, afraid the fire would come for them next.

Rubble rained down on the courtyard, followed by the blackened corpse of the second creature. It hit the ground hard, a broken thing. The strange man ran to it, crying as if it were a lost child. A worried look crossed the Chosen's face. It was the first time Tinnstra had ever seen any sign of vulnerability.

'What's happening?' asked Zorique.

'Aasgod,' said Tinnstra. She grinned and her fear evaporated. 'He's alive.'

Zorique let go of her and tried to run back to the main building, but Tinnstra grabbed her. 'We have to stay here – it's still too dangerous to move. Let Aasgod deal with the Skulls first, then we'll go to him.' Tinnstra wanted to laugh. No one would be able to stand before Aasgod's magic.

They crept through the bushes to get a better view. The

explosion had ripped apart the upper floor of the Kotege. Flames licked the edges of the crater and smoke drifted out across the courtyard.

'Look!' said Zorique, pointing.

'I see him.'

Aasgod stood in the middle of the destruction. His shirt and coat were in tatters and there were fresh wounds on his chest, yet all signs of weakness were gone – he looked terrifying. Tinnstra could've sworn he was twice the size of the man she'd been travelling with. His back was straight and his shoulders broad. Fire burned in his eyes and sparks flew from his hands.

Skulls loosed arrows at him but Aasgod simply waved them away. He pointed and lightning flew down to strike one of the Skulls, vaporising the soldier where he stood.

Again and again, he threw lightning. Bodies were flung in every direction as the courtyard exploded. The Skulls stood no chance against his power. The air stank of burned flesh and Tinnstra's ears rang with the cacophony of violence. It was glorious. She couldn't help but laugh at the force of it all as Aasgod struck again and again. Finally, the Egril had met someone greater than them. This time, they were the ones who ran. They were the ones who screamed – who died.

Except one. Him. The Chosen. The man-demon. Tinnstra lost her smile when she saw him. He didn't care about the chaos around him or Aasgod's lightning. He simply raised his baton and fire struck at the Lord Mage.

Aasgod waved his hand and called lightning to stop it. The two energies smashed together, burning the very air around them and shattering the remaining windows in the Kotege. The building shook and crumbled as the mage and the Chosen flung all their power against each other. Fire and lightning twisted and curled around them both, seeking a way forward, hoping to bring death to the other. Wind surged, dragging the snow with it, whipping everything to a frenzy.

Light flashed so bright she had to close her eyes, and yet it still burned. When she looked again, the world was on fire. Aasgod hovered in the air as lightning arced from his hands, faster and faster. The Chosen didn't look so confident now. There was no hiding the strain on his face. The fear.

A corner of the Kotege collapsed in a shower of dust and stone. The ground burned around the Chosen's feet. The air grew thin, making it hard to breathe. The Chosen screamed something, but his words only fuelled the lightning. It grew in ferocity, overcoming the fire, and raced down towards the Chosen. He screamed as it struck and, by the Four Gods, it was the sweetest sound Tinnstra had ever heard. His baton exploded in his hands as the lightning tossed him up in the air. He writhed and kicked and burned. His scream became a wail and then Tinnstra had to cover her eyes as the lightning consumed him.

Aasgod's magic flickered away and the bastard Chosen fell to the ground, twitched and was still. Smoke drifted up from his scorched remains.

The Chosen was dead. His body was charred black, his features gone. The surviving Skulls scuttled away lest the mage's fury come for them next. It was over. Aasgod had won.

Victory.

Smoke drifted across the courtyard battlefield, shrouding the enemy dead. The snow was stained red and black. The dying cried out. It was no different from when the Egril had invaded – except this time, Tinnstra got to step from the undergrowth with Zorique instead of being chased away. They'd won. There was no need to run. Aasgod saw them, smiled as he descended to the ruined upper floor of the Kotege. Tinnstra waved back. Tears ran down her face, but they were of joy – not fear.

'He did it. He did it.' Tinnstra picked up Zorique and hugged and kissed her. They both cried with the sheer exhilaration of being alive. They'd *won*. Aasgod had destroyed the Skulls and the Chosen. This was the turning point Tinnstra had been praying for.

'What's that?' said Zorique, pointing up towards Aasgod. Tinnstra followed her finger. It was a shadow, nothing more, and yet ... it was moving. *Fast.* As it darted towards Aasgod, there was a flash of silver. An axe.

'Aasgod!' Tinnstra screamed for all she was worth.

He frowned, unable to hear, and stepped closer to the edge. The axe swept up, a blur held by darkness. It bit into Aasgod's side and carved a red path to his heart. He staggered, confused, looked down at the blade embedded in his chest. A woman materialised beside him. Another Chosen. So much like the one who'd died. A sister.

Aasgod coughed blood as the woman yanked her axe free. He stumbled over the edge and fell. There was no avoiding the wet crunch when he hit the ground, or the sight of Aasgod's body lying bloodied and broken in the courtyard.

'No!' screamed Tinnstra. She couldn't believe it. She was a fool. They'd won nothing. Aasgod was dead. She staggered as her fear returned, a punch in the gut, a hammer blow to her heart.

The Chosen saw them, smiled and pointed her axe towards them.

'Come on.' Tinnstra took a step back, towards the undergrowth, taking Zorique with her. Time to get away. Time to run.

A scream stopped them. An inhuman howl of agony. It came from the other Chosen. The dead Chosen. The scream froze them to the spot. *Dear Gods, no. How could you do this to us?*

The scream continued without pause, as if the corpse endured a pain beyond imagination. It shook Tinnstra to the core and Zorique flattened herself against Tinnstra's legs. She'd never heard a sound like it. Then the body twitched as a spasm ran through the charred remains. The howl choked off and the mouth gasped for air. His eyes popped open. He was alive.

'Run.' Tinnstra could barely get the word out, could barely stop her own scream. Struggled to make her legs obey her. She dragged Zorique with her, but neither of them could take their eyes off the Chosen as he pushed himself up. Ash flaked off as patches of skin reappeared. He snarled and grunted as he moved, cursing and swearing.

'Fucking *bitch*. *Fucking* bitch. I'm going to kill her. *Kill her*.' The Chosen clawed at the ground, his eyes wide with pain and confusion. 'Skara!' He staggered to his feet like a newborn calf. '*Skkkaaaaaara!*' Tinnstra could hear the hate in his voice. The anger.

She took a step back, pulling Zorique with her.

The Chosen saw them. A monster hungry for blood. His howl sounded like it came from the depths of the underworld. Tinnstra's scream was a desperate wail. He was only five feet away. He took a step towards them.

Tinnstra's fear found her feet. She hooked up Zorique, turned and sprinted into the undergrowth. This time, she didn't stop. She hurtled through bushes and jumped over brambles, cutting around trees. She didn't care where she went as long as it was away from the Kotege and the monsters. *Run. Run. Run. Get away. Don't stop.*

Twigs scratched her. Roots threatened to trip her. The snow crunched underfoot, betraying their path. *Everything's against us, working for the enemy. So foolish to think of victory. The Egril can never be defeated. Not while they have monsters on their side.*

On and on she ran, not even risking a single glance backward. She knew they were chasing her. She knew any second a spear or a sword could cut her down. All she could do was run. Run and pray and hope and cry.

The girl grew heavier. Tinnstra's lungs burned. She stumbled, jarring her knee as she righted herself, but the pain was nothing compared to the fear. Aasgod was the most powerful man she'd ever known and yet the Chosen had killed him. What could she do – a failed Shulka with a magic sword – when he had fallen?

Finally, she risked looking back. She couldn't see any pursuit, but they'd not come this far to give up. She staggered on, half-running, half-walking, air raw in her throat, stabbing pains in her side.

The ground dipped as tangled knots of branches overhead cut off what little moonlight there was. The world lost substance as the darkness enveloped them. She slowed with heavy legs and lowered Zorique to the ground, chest heaving, gulping at air. 'I can't carry you any more. You'll have to walk.'

'Don't leave me,' sobbed the girl.

'I won't. I promise.' Tinnstra tried to get her breathing back under control.

Zorique wrapped her arms around Tinnstra's leg. 'I'm scared.'

'So am I,' replied Tinnstra. 'So am I. But we'll be okay. We'll—'

'What is it?'

Tinnstra held out a hand to quieten Zorique. She needed to listen. She heard snapping branches and the crunch of boots in snow. 'They're close.'

DAY SIX

39

Yas

Kiyosun

Yas woke up, scared. Someone was knocking at her door.

Little Ro slept next to her. It was still night, still curfew, which meant it had to be the Skulls. *They've come to arrest me.* They knocked again. No, it couldn't be the Skulls – they would've just kicked her door in.

Still, only bad news broke curfew.

The noise woke Ma up. 'Bloody hells. Who's that?'

'I don't know,' replied Yas, her voice shaking.

'What have you done?' snapped Ma.

Yas slipped her coat on over her dressing gown. The meat cleaver lay on the kitchen table and, for a mad moment, Yas wanted to pick it up. *No.* She didn't have it in her.

They knocked again.

'Who is it?'

'Kara. Let me in.'

She slipped back the bolts and cracked open the door. 'What're you doing here?'

'Let me in before someone calls the Skulls.'

When Yas let her inside, she could see the hunted expression in the Shulka's eyes. Kara glanced at the fresh bruises on Yas's face but didn't say anything.

'Who's that?' asked Ma.

'Go back to sleep. It's just a friend.'

Ma ignored her and hobbled over for a closer look. Yas stepped

293

in between them. 'Go back to bed, Ma. Now.' Yas's expression begged her to listen for once without arguing.

Ma glared at Kara but backed off. 'All right. You know where I'll be if you need me.'

Ma returned to her bed on the other side of the room. She'd still hear nearly all that was said, but they could hardly go for a walk during curfew. They sat at the small table by the window.

'You promised me you'd never come here,' hissed Yas at once.

'Things have changed,' replied Kara. 'I need your help.'

'I can't do anything. They're watching us all. I nearly got caught tonight as it is. They had a Chosen read our minds.'

Kara went pale. '*Shit*. That's not good.'

Yas shook her head. 'They examined all of us. I still can't believe they didn't arrest me ... but I can't do any more now. I won't risk it.'

'That's no longer an option. You have to. There's too much at stake.'

'Why? What's happened?'

'The Skulls arrested the head of the Hanran yesterday.'

'What's that got to do with me?'

'We need to help him escape.'

Yas shook her head. 'That's not going to happen. They'll have him in the dungeons. No one gets out of there.'

'You said there were only two guards.'

'Two guards outside. At least two more inside, guarding another set of doors. I think that might be where the Tonin is.'

'It doesn't matter. We have to get him out. Especially if they have a mind-reader. Jax knows too much about everything.'

'Jax?'

'That's his name. Jax.'

Yas looked down at the table. It was all too much. 'I can draw you the map you wanted. Show you how to get to him.'

'I don't have the troops to attack the Council House. We need to be cleverer than that.'

'Cleverer? What do you mean?' asked Yas. She sat back, feeling sick, all too aware of what they wanted her to do.

'We need you to get Jax and his son out.' And there it was. A few words for an impossible job. A suicide mission.

Yas leaned forward. 'How am I supposed to do that? Just walk up and ask nicely? Smile at them? I'll end up in the cell next door – or dead – before I got five yards.'

Kara placed a piece of paper on the table. She unfolded it. Black powder sat in the middle of it.

'What's that?'

'Poison.'

'Poison?'

'Poison the guards. Get Jax and his son out.'

'Just like that? I'll put it in their bloody tea, shall I?' She stood up, angry, frightened. 'Get out of my home.'

Kara didn't move. 'You have access to the kitchens. Put it in their food.'

'Do you know how many people we feed from that kitchen? The whole Council House. I don't know who's eating what, and I can't go asking.' Yas shoved the paper back towards Kara. 'There's no way I can find out which meals are going to the guards. It's impossible.' She sat back down and crossed her arms. It was madness.

Kara refolded the paper but left it on the table. She looked at Yas, ice-cold as could be. 'You don't have to know who's eating what. Put it in all the food. Poison everyone. There's more than enough to do the job. It'll take an hour to work.'

'Poison everyone?'

'Yes.'

'You're mad. Bloody insane. You're as bad as they are.' Yas wanted to throw up. She tried to imagine doing what Kara asked. Kill three hundred people? Not just the Skulls but her friends as well? 'No. I won't do it. I'm no murderer. I *can't* do it.'

Kara stared at her with that bitch face of hers. 'We can't leave him there. He's our leader and we need him free.'

'No.' Yas wiped a tear from her cheek. 'There has to be another way. I'm sorry, but there has to be.'

'This is it. You're it. You're all we have.'

'I'm sorry. Even if I wanted to, with the mind-reader there, I wouldn't even get close. They suspect everyone as it is. They'll know what I'm trying to do the moment I walk through the door.'

'You beat her yesterday. How'd you do that?'

'I thought about my son. About how much I wanted to be with him. How much I loved him. It covered up everything else.'

Kara glanced over at Little Ro, then back to Yas. 'There you go. Think about your son. You can beat her again.'

'No. I can't. I'm sorry.'

Kara looked at Yas as if she was about to say something then changed her mind. She stood up and Yas did likewise. 'I'm sorry, Yas. I wish you'd said yes.'

'I'm not a killer.' Yas watched her walk to the door, her heart hammering, relieved the Shulka had finally accepted that Yas couldn't do it. It was insane she'd even asked in the first place. Then she noticed Kara had left the poison on the table. She picked it up and went after Kara. 'You forgot this.'

Kara opened the door. 'No. No, I didn't.'

Five men entered the apartment. Hard men. Armed with knives and the willingness to use them.

'I didn't want to do it this way, but you've given me no other option,' said Kara. 'You either poison the Council House and get Jax out or I'll kill your mother and your son.'

'You *bitch*!' screamed Yas and ran at Kara. She didn't even get halfway there before one of the thugs snatched her out of the air and threw her to the ground. The poison went flying from her hand as she skidded across the floor.

'Leave her alone,' shouted Ma, getting up to help, but another man waved a knife in her face. She sat back down.

The scuffle woke Little Ro and he started crying. Yas staggered to her feet but Kara reached her boy first and scooped him up.

'Don't do anything stupid,' said Kara, her knife against Ro's throat. 'No one wants to hurt you or your family.'

'Then let him go,' snarled Yas.

'I will if you do as you're told,' said Kara.

'You hurt him, and I swear to all the Gods, I'll kill you.'

Kara smiled. 'Yeah? Well, there's three hundred other people you need to kill first.'

'I'm not going to do it.'

'Don't test me, Yas. Don't test me.' Kara signalled one of her men, who grabbed Ma and pulled her arms behind her back.

'Get off me,' shouted Ma, but the man just forced her down onto a chair.

'She's an old lady,' yelled Yas. 'Leave her alone.' The man ignored her. Yas had to just stand there and watch him tie Ma to the chair. She felt so helpless.

'Say yes,' said Kara, 'or we'll kill your ma right now. You can watch her die, then think about how it'll feel when we kill your son next.'

Yas had never hated anyone as much as she *hated* Kara right then. Not even the Skull who'd killed her husband. 'You *fucking bitch.*'

'Yes or no, Yas. What's it going to be?'

'Yes.'

40

Tinnstra

Olyisius Mountain

The Skulls were everywhere. They shouted to one another as they crashed through the undergrowth, making no attempt to be quiet. Tinnstra had no idea how many men had survived Aasgod's attack but it sounded like a lot. Too many.

Tinnstra and Zorique ran as fast as they could – or rather, as fast as Zorique could go. Stumbling and staggering in the dark, slipping in the snow and slush, Tinnstra tried to remember the area from her time as a student. There had to be a way out. A way to the mountain.

There was a stream somewhere. If they could find that, she knew it headed south – but the Skulls gave her no time to think, no time to rest.

Zorique caught a foot on a branch and went down hard. Tears came thick and fast.

Tinnstra picked her up. 'It's all right. It was just a fall. We need to keep moving.'

'My leg hurts.'

'I know, my love.' Tinnstra ran her hands over the girl's ankle. Nothing appeared broken. 'Be strong for me for a little while longer. We need to go.'

Zorique shook her head, stuck her bottom lip out. 'I can't.'

'You're being so brave. We'll rest for a minute and then we can go on.' Tinnstra listened to the advancing pursuit. *We don't have a minute.*

'I'm thirsty.'

Tinnstra reached into the food bag she was still carrying for a water skin and realised she didn't have one. *Shit.* 'I'm sorry. I left the water back at the room. We'll find some soon. We just need to get moving again.'

Zorique shook her head defiantly. 'I can't.'

'You must. The Skulls are coming. We have to get away. Don't worry, there's a stream nearby. We'll be safe there.' *By the Four Gods, how many times have I told that lie to the girl? Nowhere is safe.* She tried her best to look calm, hide the fear raging away inside her. The panic. 'We can rest for a minute or two and catch our breath and then go again.'

One. Two. She held Zorique's hand and forced a smile while the girl did her best to stop crying. *Twenty-five, twenty-six.* Every second counted. The Skulls were getting closer. *Forty.* Out in the darkness, their voices echoed off the trees. *Sixty.*

'Time to go.'

'I don't want to.' The girl crossed her arms, refusing to move.

'I know you don't, but we must.' Tinnstra glanced back towards the Kotege. There was no time for argument or discussion. 'They'll kill us if they catch us.'

'No.'

'Zorique—'

'*No!*'

They were out of time. Tinnstra swung her up onto her hip, holding her tight while she wriggled and kicked, and began running as best she could. The girl was heavy and her resistance made it ten times more difficult, but there was no other choice. All she could do was stay ahead of the Skulls and pray. She left the food bag, unable to carry it and the girl at the same time. If they didn't get away, eating would be the least of their problems.

They were making too much noise, but what else could Tinnstra do? They couldn't die like this, not after everything they'd been through. She risked a look back – and the ground disappeared beneath her.

They fell, screaming and sliding down the bank. Tinnstra held

Zorique and prayed. It was so dark. The world was just a blur of trees and leaves and snow and snatches of sky.

Tinnstra's knee cracked against a rock and sent her spinning. She lost her grip on Zorique. Another stone smashed into her elbow. Pain flared but there was no time to register it properly. Tinnstra clawed at the ground, flailing at anything, but her fingers found only slush and ice. She picked up speed.

Zorique cried out in pain somewhere but there was nothing Tinnstra could do. Something cracked against the side of her head, making Tinnstra bite her tongue, and a salty tang filled her mouth.

She hit the bottom hard, jarring her knees with the impact and smashing the air out of her lungs, and then she was thrown forward once more. She landed in a pool of ice-cold water, banged her head and reared back, gasping for air. She spat blood, dirt and snow. She'd stopped moving, stopped *falling*. Still alive.

And she'd found the stream.

The water was freezing, shocking Tinnstra's senses back to alertness. She jumped to her feet. She reached behind her and found the sword still in place. She grasped the hilt, feeling its magic fight off the worst of it. *Thank you, Aasgod*. With the sword, she still had a chance. She just had to find the princess without bringing every Skull down on them.

'Zorique! *Zorique!*' Tinnstra called out as loud as she dared.

Silence. The girl must still be on the slope, caught in a tree or a bush. By all the Gods, she hoped so. Tinnstra looked back the way she'd fallen but it was all shadow and darkness. She started to climb, wincing with pain every time she moved. Her ribs were agony and her ankle sent a sliver of hot pain through her every time she put weight on it. The sword needed time to heal her; time she didn't have.

For every yard she climbed, it felt like she slipped back another two. The cold and her damp clothes stole what little warmth she had left, and soon her teeth were chattering and her limbs shivering uncontrollably. She looked all over the slope but there was no sign of Zorique. A different kind of coldness took hold of Tinnstra, a tiny knot of dread that the girl might be captured or dead. *I can't have lost her. She has to be alive somewhere.*

All she knew for certain, though, was that Skulls were nearby. She could hear their shouts and curses as they hacked through the undergrowth, but the falling snow made it so hard to pinpoint them.

'Zorique! Zorique!'

A flash of something caught her eye. She waited, still as stone, not breathing, heart racing, watching, hoping it was Zorique – praying it was – but nothing moved. Nothing.

She clambered sideways to get a better view of what she'd seen when something came crashing through the undergrowth above. She jerked back, seeking the shadows, as Skulls climbed down the side of the bank. There were three of them, no more than ten yards over. Their white armour made them hard to track against the snow-covered slope, but it didn't matter. They'd be on top of her soon enough.

Tinnstra pressed herself against the bank, too scared to move, trying to ignore the cold working its way through her soaked jacket. *Keep still. They can't see me if I don't move.* She clenched her jaw shut to stop the chattering of her teeth betraying her as the snow burned her back. *By the Four Gods. Be still. I can do it. Survive. Zorique needs me. The sword will keep me safe.* Tinnstra reached up, grasped the hilt of her sword over her shoulder. It might do nothing for the pain but Aasgod's magic could heal any damage done. As long as she had that, she could endure.

'This is a waste of time,' said one of the Skulls, speaking Egril. 'The kid's either dead or long gone by now.'

'That may be, but Monsuta said check the river, so we check the river,' replied a second. 'Unless you feel fucking brave enough to tell him you didn't feel like it.'

'No way.'

'Then stop complaining and let's get on with it.'

'Did you see the way his skin grew back?'

'I've never seen the like. The Chosen freak me out.'

'Quiet,' ordered a third soldier. 'His powers are a gift from Kage himself. What he does is Kage's will. What he orders is Kage's will. We seek the unbelievers because that is what Kage wants, and we will follow them into the Great Darkness itself if that is what we are told to do. "As you gave me life, so I give my life to you."'

'As you gave me life, so I give my life to you,' the others mumbled in reply, less convincing than their comrade.

Tinnstra watched them climb past her and reach the stream at the bottom. She kept her hand on the hilt of her sword, for the first time in her life ready – *eager* – to draw it. Anger filled her, hate for the men who chased her, for what they'd done to her life, for what they wanted to do to Zorique.

'You two take the sides, I'll take the centre.'

'Let's get this done.' The Skulls splashed through the water heading downstream, leaving Tinnstra clinging to the bank, wondering what to do. If only she knew where Zorique was.

A bout of shivers broke her grip and she slid a good ten yards before she could grab a rock and nearly pulled her arm from its socket in the process.

She climbed the rest of the way down and sat on a rock to catch her breath. She just needed some rest. Get her second wind. Gather her strength. She wasn't that cold any more. The sword had done its job. Worked its magic ... Maybe she could sleep for a moment ... Maybe sleep would see her right ... Maybe ... she would start looking for Zorique ... then. Her eyes fluttered. Her thoughts drifted into the night. Just some sleep ...

A horn blasted, startling her awake.

'Over here!'

'Don't move.'

'We've found her.'

Those soldiers had Zorique! The horn sounded again, calling the Chosen down to the river along with the rest of the Skulls.

Tinnstra staggered to her feet and drew her sword. Immediately she felt better as its power worked on her. She ran alongside the stream, making no attempt at stealth. The time for that was past.

She found them around a bend in the river. They were restraining Zorique, who kicked and scratched and punched and wriggled with all she had.

302

Tinnstra charged in without a second thought or a moment's hesitation.

Her swing caught the first Skull as he turned. The sword slipped in between shoulder plate and helm, opening up his neck. Blood gushed out, hot and red, but Tinnstra had already forgotten him and moved on to the next soldier.

The second Skull was holding Zorique's arm. His eyes widened with surprise behind his mask as he saw his friend die. *Good.* She lunged and her sword slid through his open mouth to the back of his helmet. He dropped Zorique and collapsed as Tinnstra yanked her sword free. More blood. More death.

The last Skull released Zorique and drew his weapon, one of the curved scimitars that had claimed so many Shulka lives. But Tinnstra's blade was *magic* and she couldn't be harmed. All her training, all the hours of practice with her father came alive in her now she was unburdened by her fear. The Skull moved in slow motion compared to her. He was nothing.

As he raised the scimitar above his head, Tinnstra ducked underneath his arm and slashed down with her sword as she passed, slicing through the man's hamstring. As he toppled, he threw out an arm to try and stop his fall, exposing the gap between the chest and back armour. Tinnstra's sword darted forward once more, as if it knew what it needed to do. In through the armpit and down into the heart. She pulled it out just as quick, its job done, and flicked the blood from the blade into the stream. Red against white snow. Steam in the cold air.

'Tinn!' Zorique wrapped her arms around Tinnstra's leg. She sheathed the sword and scooped the girl up, not feeling her weight.

'Are you okay?'

'I bumped my head,' replied the girl. 'Then I couldn't find you.'

'I'm here now.'

'You killed those men.'

'I did. They were bad men. They were going to hurt you.'

'I'm glad.'

'More are coming. We need to move.'

For once, she didn't argue. The soldiers were climbing down the bank in answer to the Skulls' horn. Too many to fight, even with a magic sword. They didn't have much time.

Tinnstra ran along the stream, Zorique in her arms, all her tiredness gone. Her body sang with power. Zorique held on tight as they splashed through the water. Tinnstra didn't care about the temperature of the river. She ignored the frozen needles stabbing away at her legs. The sword would protect her.

'The soldiers are coming,' said Zorique.

Tinnstra glanced back. Skulls had spread out across the river from bank to bank. Skeletons coming out of the darkness. Ten of them, maybe more. She picked up her pace as the water around her flowed faster. An angry roar grew louder, deafening in its intensity.

They rounded a bend and Tinnstra stumbled to a halt. The river ended in a waterfall that cascaded down into a valley, each side covered in pine trees. In the distance, she could see the black shadow of Olyisius. So far away. She couldn't see how they could make the summit in time but they had to try.

'What are we going to do?' Zorique had to shout to be heard over the waterfall.

Behind them, the Skulls closed in.

Tinnstra watched the water tumble down into a frenzied froth at the bottom. The drop looked about twenty feet. Not so bad, but bad enough. Plenty of rocks around the edges but the centre looked clear enough – deep enough. Just the drop to worry about.

'Can you swim?' she asked.

Zorique shook her head.

'I can, so don't worry.'

'Don't move!' shouted a Skull, a dozen yards away. They were approaching in a semicircle, weapons drawn, ready for her. No one was going to be taken by surprise this time.

'Hold on to me.' Tinnstra headed into the middle of the river. The cold took her breath away, so sharp it hurt. As she moved forwards, the river bed fell away and the water shot up to Tinnstra's neck. She held the girl's head above the surface and tried to get her own lungs working again as she waded through the water, fighting the current. Zorique's fingers dug into her neck and she could feel the girl shaking from cold and fear.

'Stop!' ordered the Skulls, but Tinnstra paid them no heed. They had no arrows to shoot or spears to throw. They couldn't hurt her.

'The sword will protect me. The sword will protect me. The sword will protect me.' She whispered the words over and over and over, allowing no other thought, allowing no fear to stop her.

The wind whipped around them as they reached the edge of the waterfall. The water rushed past, dragging at her legs. There was no respite from the cold as the wind whipped snow past them and clawed at their wet clothes.

The drop looked more like thirty feet now she was close to the edge. Too high. Every part of her screamed not to turn back, to give herself and Zorique up to the Skulls – every part of her except one. Her faith in Aasgod and his magic.

'The sword will protect me,' she said one last time and jumped with Zorique in her arms.

41

Dren

Kiyosun

Dren had always believed he was tough. His interrogators showed him the truth. Dren believed he was a man. The Egril showed him what he really was. Dren believed he wasn't afraid to die. The Skulls showed him that he was.

His first visit to the interrogation room had been simple: they'd asked questions and he'd denied everything.

They didn't believe him. Or maybe they just didn't care.

Questions followed a beating, followed by another beating, followed by more questions.

They bashed his fingers.

'What do you know about the Hanran?'

Punched his ribs.

'Are you in the Hanran?'

His face.

'What have you done for the Hanran?'

They knocked his teeth out and stamped on his feet.

And then they returned him to the cell. Left him there, suffering pain and humiliation.

The second time, they cut half of Dren's ear off because they said he wasn't listening. They wanted names. Dren didn't know any. They wanted to know about the weapons. They wanted to know who'd killed the governor. Dren kept his mouth shut for that one. All his boasting didn't feel like such a good idea now.

As Jax said, the pain was just beginning. He held on as best he could. Trouble was, it wasn't as easy as he'd hoped. This was nothing like the beating the Shulka had given him. He understood now how soft they'd gone on him.

On the third visit, they beat him harder. They knew how to hurt him, but somehow, he stuck to the story. Dren cried and begged. He was a thief. A liar. A street rat. He was *nothing*!

When they dumped him back in the cell, he lay on the floor in the stink and shit, crying like a child. What he'd give to have his mother take him in her arms once more and tell him everything would be all right. To have her kiss the pain away. But she was dead and no one was going to save him. He was going to die in that room upstairs. It wasn't going to be legendary. It was going to be slow, and painful, and then he'd be left to rot somewhere. Forgotten.

He cradled his left hand, whimpering as every breath sent shivers of agony through him. He dribbled blood onto the floor as he ran his tongue over the gaps where his teeth had once been. And he knew it wasn't over yet.

Dren must have passed out because when he opened his eyes again, Jax was back and his son was gone. The old man lay with his back against the wall, even more battered than before.

'You're awake,' said Jax.

The only reply Dren could manage was to spit some more blood onto the floor and groan.

'Don't move.' Jax staggered to his feet and stumbled over to Dren's side.

Dren flinched. He had no strength left to fight. 'Wha ... what're you doing?'

'Don't worry.' Dren was rolled over onto his back and straightened out. 'The pain'll be easier if you're not hunched up. How's your breathing?' The old man examined him.

'Hurts.'

'I can't do anything about your ribs, but I'm going to fix your nose. It'll hurt for a second but then it'll be better and you'll be able to breathe easier.'

Jax crunched and pulled Dren's nose before he could reply so he screamed instead. The old man smiled. 'You'll never be good-looking again, kid, but it'll heal well – if they let it.'

'What's the point?' Dren rubbed at his face. He hated Jax seeing him like this. He should be stronger. 'It's all over. We're never getting out of here.'

'I don't know that and neither do you. There's still hope. You need to hold on to that and take strength from it.'

'I don't want to die.'

'No one does, kid.' The old man's eyes held no pity. Just honesty. 'But it's going to happen. Sooner, later. In here or out there. Don't hide from it or give in to it. Fight it. Every breath you take is a victory. Every minute you survive is something to cherish – especially in that room.' Jax shuffled over to a bucket by the door and returned with a cup of water. 'Drink this. You'll feel better.'

The water was old, stagnant and bitter, but Dren gulped it down anyway. 'Why are you being nice to me? You tried to kill me. You hate me.'

Jax shook his head. 'I don't hate you, kid. I was angry with you and I wanted to stop you killing innocent people. It's bad enough the Skulls are murdering us without us doing it to ourselves.'

'There's a war on and I was fighting it,' said Dren, but his fire was gone, his belief. He wiped blood from his chin.

'There's a difference between being a soldier fighting a war and a murderer killing people because they hate the world they find themselves in. I tried telling you, but you didn't want to listen and there were too many lives at stake to let you carry on like you were. You left me with no choice.'

'I'm not a murderer.'

'Tell that to the families of the people you've killed because they happened to be in the wrong place at the wrong time.'

'You're no better. At least I was doing something. You fucking Shulka just sat around talking shit. You let people die, too. If you'd done what you'd promised to do ...' Dren blinked. No way was he going to cry in front of Jax. 'My mum and dad were killed by Daijaku because you couldn't stop them. My whole neighbourhood was destroyed. The city lost. Why should I trust you now?'

'I'm sorry about your parents. A lot of people died during the invasion. A lot more since. And there'll be even more before it's all over.'

'So fucking do something instead of walking around pretending you're still in charge.'

'Kid, if you knew what was going on – really going on … We're trying to free a country, not just collect a few helmets as trophies. I should be out there now trying to make things happen instead of being stuck in here because of you.'

Dren turned his head, looked at Jax and his battered face. 'Don't expect me to say sorry.'

'No one's expecting you to, but by the Four Gods, kid, I hope you start seeing things the way they really are. I could do with your help out there – yours and all your friends' – but I need to trust you. You need to follow orders.'

'To do what? You never did anything except sit around and talk.'

'Just because you don't see the city on fire, it doesn't mean we're not doing anything. We've spent the last few days getting families falsely accused of being in the Hanran to safety. We're gathering weapons, intelligence, infiltrating the enemy. Your attacks on the Skulls are nothing but flesh wounds to them. We're doing things that can really hurt them in the long term.'

The words stung Dren. He'd judged the Hanran by body count. He'd not thought of anything else. He hadn't considered a bigger picture – just what was in front of his face. 'It's too late now. We're not leaving this place.'

'Don't give up yet. You're still alive. I'm still alive. Nothing's over until we're dead.'

When Dren sat up, a thousand knives stabbed him across his chest.

Jax helped him lie back down. 'Stay still. Keep the pressure off your ribs for now.'

'I fucked up everything.'

'That you did – but you're young. That's what young people do. The question is: can you learn from it?'

'What are they going to do to us?'

'Don't think about that. Think only about now. Rest. Drink

more water. Whatever is going to happen will happen. Worrying won't change a thing. In fact, your mind will make it worse.'

The wooden doors at the end of the passageway creaked open, silencing them. Footsteps approached, dragging something with them. The Skulls opened their cell door and threw Kaine in. He was soaked from the waist up and barely conscious. Jax rushed over to him. 'Fucking bastards. Do you feel good beating up a cripple?'

All he got was a boot in the face in reply, then the Skulls snatched Dren up.

'No. No. Leave me alone.' He wriggled and tried to fight his way free. An armoured fist smashed into his chest, winding Dren and rattling his ribs. He would've screamed if he'd had any air in his lungs. Instead he collapsed and they dragged him upstairs. The sudden light hurt his eyes and pleas for mercy dribbled out of his mouth. Some big man he was. The king of fucking nothing.

The officer was waiting in the room. The floor was soaked. Behind the chair with its restraints was a large bucket of water. Dren dug his heels in to stop them dragging him inside but a club to his leg put a stop to that.

The officer smiled. 'Ah. The other young man. Tell me ... have you ever drowned?'

'Please ... please ...' begged Dren. 'This has all been a big mistake. I'm just a silly thief.'

The Skulls strapped him to the chair and took up position beside him.

'We know who you are and what you've done,' said the officer. 'The others have told us everything. All I want you to do is confirm the facts.'

'I tried to steal from their shop, that's all.' Dren looked from the officer to the Skulls and back again. 'You have to believe me.'

The officer nodded at the Skulls. Dren's chair tipped back and his head was plunged into the water. He thrashed about but the Skulls held him tight. The roar in his head grew quickly along with the need to breathe. It wasn't like when he was thrown into the sea. There was no escape here. No knife.

They lifted him out and he gasped for air. Water streamed down his face, hiding his tears.

'So,' said the officer. 'What do you want to tell me?'

'*Please*,' begged Dren. 'I was hungry. I needed food.'

The officer nodded. They tipped Dren's head back into the bucket.

Hold on to hope, the old man had said.

The water closed over his face.

What hope?

42

Darus

The Kotege

Darus and Skara stood in the grounds of the Kotege. Aasgod's body lay between them but that didn't make Darus feel any better. The bastard mage died too easy; he should've suffered more for what he did. How dare he strike Kage's blessed? And how dare his sister let him?

'You took your time,' snapped Darus. 'I bet you thought it was funny watching me burn.'

'Brother, brother,' replied Skara. 'Why do you always think the worst of me? I got there as quickly as I could. And killed him the first chance I had.'

'So you say.' Darus didn't believe a word of it. 'I *hate* dying. Do you know how much it hurts?'

Skara looked away. 'No.'

'One day, you *will*.' May Kage give him strength, but he wanted to do it there and then. Kill her. That would shut her up. Every part of him screamed in agony. If she'd been faster ... The pain was almost more than he could bear. It wasn't *right*.

And the girl had got away. He glared at Skara. She'd done it on purpose. She liked watching him suffer. She'd let the mage kill him and now she was going to humiliate him in front of Kage. *Bitch. Bitch. BITCH.*

In the distance, the sun clawed its way over the treeline. Another day stuck in this miserable wilderness. The soldiers could still return with the girl ... even dead and the night would be a success. If not ... there would be no extra gifts from Raaku, no promotions, no glory. He only hoped Aasgod's corpse would satisfy the Emperor.

Skara rested her hand on his shoulder. 'You heard the horn. The men have found her. Once they bring her to us, we can be gone from this place and return to Egril.' She glanced back at Osmer, still mourning his dead hounds. His children. 'And the loss of two Kyoryu won't matter a jot.'

He stiffened. She had to bring that up. Remind him of his failure. Was she keeping a tally? Was her lust for power so great she'd sacrifice her own brother? By Kage's fury, how he'd love to watch her bleed to death. She wouldn't be so smug then. Her list would be of no use then. 'So where are the soldiers? They should be back by now.'

'The snow makes it difficult.'

'If they haven't got her, they might as well cut their own throats before I do.'

'You're always so cranky after you come back. Is it that awful?'

'The man roasted me. Of course it was fucking awful.' He kicked the side of Aasgod's head. 'Bastard. And everything itches. I want to tear my skin off.'

Skara held up both her hands in surrender. 'Remember I'm on your side.'

Right. Skara must think he was a fool to believe that. Darus smiled sweetly. She could wait. Once he had the girl, had the glory, had Raaku's favour, then he would discuss with her whose side she was on. He would let her experience his knives. That would help her understand how painful nearly dying really was.

He focused on the woods, wishing he could set them on fire, burn the bastards out, but the snow made that impossible. Ever since he was a child, he'd *enjoyed* fires. He'd started small, with rats and mice, and moved on to stray cats and dogs. The way they'd look at him, all confused as he threw them into the fire. One mongrel had escaped, its fur aflame, and nearly set the family castle alight. Father hadn't been pleased. The lesson hadn't been pleasant but had served him well. After that, he made sure to cut their hamstrings first. No one was allowed to escape.

White dots moved in the treeline.

'They're back.' Skara stepped forward. 'Have they got her?'

They watched the soldiers approach out of the shadows. Darus chewed his lip then stopped himself, not wanting to show any sign of weakness. He forced his expression into the usual impassive yet slightly amused mask. As if he didn't care.

The soldiers appeared empty-handed. 'No. They don't.'

They stopped twenty feet away, too scared to come any closer. Eventually the captain stepped forward, dropped to one knee and bowed his head. 'The princess and the woman helping her are dead.'

'I don't see any bodies with you,' replied Darus.

'I'm sorry, my Lord. We pursued them along the river but they jumped off a waterfall and died. They're serving Kage in the Great Darkness now.'

'Serving Kage?' repeated Darus, his rage building. Quoting the one true God would not save them. 'Did you go down and check in person? Did you see the bodies with your own eyes?'

'N ... no, my Lord. The drop ... They couldn't have survived the drop. Nor the water. Not at these temperatures.'

'The drop? The temperature? I don't care if the waterfall goes straight down to Kage's kingdom itself. If you have no body, then the princess is alive. Do you understand?'

The captain's head dropped lower. 'Sir. Yes, sir.'

'Then I suggest you take your men, turn around and go back to this ... waterfall and search for her body. If you don't find it, you'll continue the pursuit until you do.'

'Yes, sir.' The captain stood up.

'Captain?' said Darus. 'Before you go ...' He walked over to the officer.

'Yes, sir?'

Darus smiled and put his arm around the man. 'I hate failure. Hate it. Won't tolerate it.'

'Yes, sir. We won't let you down, sir.'

'But you already have.' Darus stabbed the man in the side, through the gap in his armour. Once in the kidney, then the liver, and finally extra deep to get the lung. Darus wriggled the blade a little so the man could feel it. *Oh yes, Skara dear, dying does hurt. Just a little bit.*

The captain actually looked surprised. Then his legs went and he collapsed to the ground.

'Darus,' said Skara. 'Stop playing. We've been up all night and I'm tired.'

Darus glared at his sister. Always ruining his fun. 'Fine.' He knelt and placed his hand on the captain's neck. Let his power pulse out, healing the wounds. The captain's eyes popped open. Darus smiled. 'Consider that a warning. Don't let me down again.'

'No, my Lord.'

Darus wiped the blood on his hand across the man's armour before standing up and returning to Skara's side.

'Feel better?' asked Skara.

'Some,' replied Darus. At least that was true.

'Do you think they are alive?'

'I know they're bloody alive.' Darus gave Aasgod's body another kick. 'The question is, where are they going? They didn't come all the way out to the middle of nowhere for the fun of it.'

'They're trying to get to Meigore.'

'Of course they're trying to get to bloody Meigore!' By Kage's roaring fury, why did she have to state the obvious? 'But it's weeks away and I don't want to be bloody chasing them across half this fucking country for all that time.'

He tried to calm himself. They were pursuing a little girl. An inconvenience, not a failure. He turned to Skara. 'Why here? Why come to the Kotege?'

'They were looking for somewhere to rest ...'

Darus stared up at the mountain. 'It doesn't make sense. Unless ...'

'Unless what, brother?'

Could she really be that stupid? 'There must be a gate up there – one we don't know about. It's the only answer.'

'Shit.' Her confidence wavered. Finally, she saw that Darus's failure would be hers also. Perhaps even understood what harm would befall them *both* should they fail Raaku.

315

'Fly ahead to Kiyosun – that's the nearest port to Meigore. If they're trying to go anywhere, it's there. Mobilise their troops and start a search for the girl in case they've got through the gate. I'll look for it here. Whatever happens, she'll be trapped between us.'

'As you wish, brother.' Skara inclined her head and then dissipated into the shadows. Darus had been jealous of her powers growing up – disappearing and appearing at will, being able to fly – which all seemed far more fun than his own. Of course, now he was older, he accepted his healing power was a far greater gift. As long as the Emperor didn't remove his head from his shoulders. That might be beyond even his abilities to fix.

Darus followed the soldiers. There was no way a little girl would be the death of him.

43

Tinnstra

Olyisius Mountain

Down they fell. Into darkness. Down into only the Four Gods knew what.

Tinnstra let go of Zorique a moment before they hit the water. Some sixth sense warned her that they would both drown if she kept hold of the child. She plunged into the dark water, knocked about by the force of the impact. The cold attacked her instantly. She couldn't see anything except bubbles and she thrashed her arms and legs chasing after them. The sword on her back had other ideas. The weight of it pulled her down into the deep. The irony wasn't lost on her that she could be killed by the very thing keeping her alive.

But another few kicks and her head broke the surface. She gasped for air and called for Zorique. She swivelled around in the water, looking everywhere. Fear grabbed her. What had she done? The child couldn't swim.

Some bubbles broke the surface to her left. Tinnstra didn't wait. She dived down again, arms outstretched, racing into the dark, ignoring the cold. There was a flash of white and Tinnstra thrust towards it. Her hand caught hold of the child's arm. She pulled Zorique close and kicked back to the surface, then swam towards the water's edge. The girl felt small and limp in her arms. 'Hold on,' she urged. 'We're nearly there. Nearly there.'

Panic and fear fuelled every stroke, every kick of her legs, but for the first time, they weren't for her. Zorique was too cold, the shore too far. She was too late. Everything had been for nothing.

Her hand touched rock and her foot brushed ground. She stumbled out of the water, dragging Zorique with her. Her eyes were closed, and she was so white, so still. *Please no, let her live. Please Alo above, protect her. Please Xin below, stay your hand. She is all we have. All I have. Don't let her die.*

She sagged on the riverbank and lowered the girl on the ground. Zorique looked so small and fragile lying there. Like she was dead. *Please move. Show me you're alive. Please.*

But Zorique didn't move. Tinnstra knew she should check for a pulse but she was too sacred to try. She didn't want to confirm what she feared. Didn't want to lose what hope she had.

Then Zorique coughed. A small sound. Barely noticeable, but it happened. Her chest moved. She coughed again. Water dribbled from her mouth. Tinnstra rolled her onto her side and rubbed Zorique's back, relief flowing through her. 'Good girl. That's it. Get it out.'

The girl groaned, confused and scared, and then she saw Tinnstra and relief flashed across her face.

'Hey, beautiful girl,' said Tinnstra, pulling her into her arms. 'We made it.'

For that moment, they were safe.

But only for a moment. Staying where they were would kill them just as well as the water. Tinnstra could feel the cold in her bones. Aasgod's sword would protect her but Zorique had no such magic to help her – only Tinnstra. 'We need to move. Find somewhere we can get warm and dry our clothes. Do you think you can walk?'

Zorique nodded, bless her, and the two set off along the riverbank. Their wet clothes chafed and began to freeze against their skin as snow continued to fall. The sun had started to climb into the sky, but it would be a long time before they enjoyed even a little warmth. If any. They had so little body heat left. So little life left.

Tiredness swept over Tinnstra unlike anything she'd ever known. They had to find shelter and they had to find heat – otherwise the cold would get them as sure as drowning almost had.

Heat. Sleep. That's what they needed and they needed it right now.

She led Zorique into the pine trees that covered the side of the valley. They walked on for an age, snow crunching underfoot, with no end in sight. One foot after another. Deep into the woods. Cold, hungry and all but broken.

They stumbled into a hollow half-hidden by a fallen tree and protected from the snow. It would do. It had to. She didn't have the strength to go on.

'Sit down. Stay awake. I'll make a fire,' she told Zorique. The girl didn't reply – she had already succumbed to sleep. They needed fire quick or they'd both be dead. At least there was plenty of kindling. Tinnstra struggled to concentrate. She didn't have the energy to make mistakes, to do things twice. Building the fire was so simple, but every step was a struggle. Tinnstra's eyelids drooped and she felt herself falling asleep. She just had to get the fire going, and then she could rest. Thank the Four Gods, she still had her flint. She placed it next to the kindling and struck it with her knife. Small sparks jumped off but none caught in the nest of tinder. Again and again she tried, each strike becoming harder to make than the last. Then a spark landed on the flint shavings in the kindling and it fizzed into life. Beautiful little flames spread, taking hold of the twigs. Tinnstra added more kindling, blowing on the flames to help them grow. The heat from even such a small fire was glorious, countering the icy chill in her bones. Slowly and carefully, she added more sticks, increasing the size, revelling in the warmth.

Only then did she think about rest. Placing the sword within easy reach, Tinnstra wrapped her arms around Zorique and held her tight. The fire felt wonderful on her skin and was mesmerising to watch. This time, she didn't fight when her eyes closed.

'I'm telling you, they're dead.'

Tinnstra awoke to voices and reached for her sword. The sky was bright and clear of clouds. Daytime.

'Yeah? So what? Unless we've got a body, we're not going back. You saw what Monsuta did to the chief.'

Egril voices from the riverbank. She flattened what was left of the fire, smothering any smoke that could betray them. She peered through the leaves and saw Skulls no more than a hundred yards away at the water's edge. Tinnstra thought they'd walked for miles trying to find some safe shelter but they hadn't.

'We keep looking,' said another Egril.

She woke Zorique but kept her hand over the girl's mouth to stop her talking. She held up three fingers and pointed to the river. Zorique nodded and Tinnstra removed her hand.

'Just saying it's a waste of time, is all,' said the first.

'Just keep your eyes peeled and ... urk.'

'Fuck! Get down! Get down!'

'Where'd that fucking arrow come from? You see anything?'

'Fuck! Fuck! He's dead, Pole. He's dead.'

'Urgh!'

'Pole? Pole? Shit. Don't die, Pole. Don't—'

Silence.

Tinnstra looked up. Three bodies lay by the river. Arrows jutted out of them. Blood leaked over grey stone and white snow and into the foaming water.

A giant of a man, dressed in shades of green and brown and covered in leaves, stepped out of the undergrowth. In his hand was a long, curved bow, almost as tall as he was. She smiled at the sight of the Shulka weapon – a favourite of her father's. Not many had the strength required to use one properly, but that wasn't a problem for the giant. He strolled down to the river and pulled his arrows out of their bodies. Then he dragged their bodies into the bushes to hide them.

'Glad you're awake.'

Tinnstra spun around, drawing her sword as she covered Zorique with her body. A tall, lean man was watching them from the other side of the fallen log. A Shulka sword hung at his waist. Three other men and a woman stood behind him, all camouflaged to blend with the woods. Tinnstra's heart raced. Too many to fight. 'Who are you?'

The tall man smiled. 'We are the dead.'

44

Tinnstra

Olyisius Mountain

'You're Shulka,' said Tinnstra, getting to her feet. She savoured the sight: Jians, bearing weapons, her father's comrades. Definitely dangerous.

'We were. Most of us, anyway,' replied the tall man. 'Now we're Hanran.'

'And you just happened to be passing?' Tinnstra kept her eyes on him while still shielding Zorique with her body.

The tall man nodded. 'We were up in the mountains when we saw the fire and lightning at the Kotege. Thought some people we're supposed to meet might be in trouble and need our help. Then we saw the smoke from your fire.'

Tinnstra's sword didn't waver. 'And who're you looking for?'

'We were sent from Kiyosun to find Aasgod, the Lord Mage, and anyone he might be travelling with.' His eyes flicked to Zorique. 'Including a four-year-old girl. A rather special girl.'

'Who sent you?'

'A man named Jax.'

Tinnstra relaxed at the mention of the name. 'Aasgod is dead. He died last night at the Kotege. He caused the lightning.'

'You were with him?' asked the tall man, glancing back towards the ridge.

'We were,' replied Tinnstra. 'He died battling two Chosen. We barely escaped ourselves.'

'His death is a great loss to us all,' said the giant from a few feet away. Tinnstra nearly jumped out of her skin. She hadn't seen him approach – hadn't even heard him move. She had no idea how he'd done it – he looked even larger up close and all of it was muscle. His voice rumbled like thunder. His bow was slung across his back. Other Hanran stood half-hidden in the trees and bushes behind him. 'What clan are you?'

'My father was Dagen of Clan Rizon.' There was no need to tell them she wasn't a Shulka. Not now she had Aasgod's sword to protect her.

'Shit,' said the tall man, smiling. 'You're Grim Dagen's daughter?'

'I am.' And, for the first time, she felt good to admit it. She would live up to his legacy, not dishonour it. 'My name's Tinnstra.'

The tall man looked at the giant and then they both bowed to Tinnstra. 'It's an honour to meet you, daughter of Dagen. My name's Monon of Clan Huska. I fought alongside your father once, in the Syrias Pass.'

'And I,' said the giant, 'am Greener of Clan Huska. I knew your brothers – may Xin look after their souls.'

Tinnstra sheathed her sword and bowed in return, grinning as she did so. It felt so good being with Shulka. They were safe.

'And the girl?' asked Monon.

Tinnstra stepped aside. 'This is Zorique, the rightful queen of Jia.'

'Your Majesty.' The Shulka dropped to their knees and bowed so low their heads touched the earth.

Zorique looked at Tinnstra in confusion. *The girl has a lot to learn*. Tinnstra smiled. 'You can rise.'

'The Four Gods are on our side,' said Monon. 'We will get you both to Kiyosun.'

'Thank you,' said Tinnstra.

Monon looked towards Olyisius and the clouds behind it. 'We need to be quick. The paths are still clear but another snowfall and we might not be so lucky. We go now.'

'But the girl—'

'I'll carry her,' said Greener. He smiled as he bent down so he

322

was at eye level with the girl. 'I've never carried a queen before.'

Zorique giggled but she was Tinnstra's responsibility. 'I'll carry her.'

'Your choice,' said Monon as he headed into the woods, 'but it'll be quicker if Greener does it. It's hard going, especially with the snow, and we've not much time.'

'I want the giant to carry me.' Zorique held out her arms towards Greener.

'Fine,' said Tinnstra, 'but I'll be watching you.'

'Better you watch for the Skulls,' said the giant as he picked up Zorique and tucked her into the crook of his arm. 'You can trust us.'

There were ten Hanran, it turned out, and although they set a fast pace, they took no chances: any sound or sign of the Skulls and they melted into the undergrowth until it was safe to continue.

No one spoke. All communication was done by hand signals. Tinnstra recognised them from the Kotege. Training she'd thought she'd never need. She'd been one of the best at escape and evasion. Her fear had been an asset then, driving her on while making her cautious. It's easy to remain motionless, hidden in the undergrowth, when you're too scared to move.

She felt better with the Shulka around her. They didn't know she'd failed – that she was Grim Dagen's disgrace of a daughter. They saw her as Zorique's protector. She could almost pretend that she'd taken the vows. Out there in the woods, with mission and purpose, it even felt like it wasn't a lie.

They stopped to eat after two hours, only cold meat and a hunk of bread, but both Tinnstra and Zorique devoured it all. Afterwards, they set off once more, Monon leading the way, Greener behind him carrying Zorique followed by Tinnstra, while the others covered the flanks and rear. The path took them up the side of the valley through an ancient forest. Streaks of sun punched through the gnarled branches, melting the snow drop by drop. Their pace slowed on the steep slope made treacherous by the snow and ice, although Tinnstra suspected that was for her benefit more than the Shulka's.

They encountered the Skulls an hour later. Monon's hand shot out and they sank to the ground, knowing any sudden moves would draw the enemy's eye. Greener settled Zorique down and covered her with twigs and brush before pulling an arrow from his quiver.

Monon pointed down the hill eastwards and showed a closed fist before counting eight. Eight Skulls. Tinnstra crawled forward and peered over a pile of leaves. The Egril were headed straight towards them.

Monon crawled alongside Greener and whispered in his ear. The big man nodded. Monon then slithered his way down to Tinnstra and cupped his hand around her ear. 'If we move, they'll see us. If we try to run, they'll catch us or bring reinforcements and surround us. So we're going to have to fight them. Need to take them by surprise.'

Tinnstra nodded, not taking her eyes off the Skulls. It wasn't the choice she wanted but the man was right, it was the best of a bad bunch.

'Three of us will move down and to the right of them,' continued Monon. 'When they get within range, Greener and Marin will take as many of them out as they can with their bows. When the Skulls go to ground, we'll come up behind and cut a few throats. If we're quick, we'll get them before anyone utters a sound. If we're not, chances are we'll have the rest of the Skull army on us in short order. Whatever happens, you protect the girl.'

He was gone before Tinnstra could answer, disappearing into the bushes without disturbing a leaf.

Greener lay on his back, looking over his shoulder at the approaching Skulls, an arrow nocked and ready. His expression was calm, like he was resting after a long walk, not getting ready to kill someone. The other man, Marin, joined him. His bow was shorter than Greener's but no doubt just as lethal.

Tinnstra wrapped her hand around her sword hilt. Her fear had reawakened. The food she'd eaten felt like a ball of stone in her stomach. She wanted to be sick. She wanted to run. *The sword will protect me. The sword will protect me. The sword will protect me.*

Her new prayer to counter her old fear. *Aasgod's magic won't let me down. The Skulls won't be able to harm me. I'm invulnerable.*

The Skulls climbed towards them. All bunched up. Chatting like they were out on a country stroll. Tinnstra's instructors at the Kotege would've beaten them for such lax patrol skills. The Egril had forgotten what it was like to be afraid – to have an enemy stand up and fight back.

The Skulls were three hundred yards away. Tinnstra slid her sword from its sheath, carefully avoiding any reflection of sunlight that might give away their position. She looked for Monon but there was no sign of him. He'd be ready, though. Ready and waiting.

The Skulls were two hundred and fifty yards away, looking down, checking their footing. One complained about the steepness of the hill. Tinnstra smiled.

Greener swivelled up to kneel facing the enemy. Marin mirrored the action. They pulled back their bowstrings, aimed and released. The arrows hissed towards their targets. One hit a Skull in the chest, punching through his armour and straight into his heart. The other struck a Skull in the eye. They both died without a sound.

More arrows flew towards the enemy. One pierced the centre of a Skull's forehead. He managed a cry of surprise as he fell backwards and tumbled down the slope. While the surviving Skulls looked around in shock, the next arrow punctured the back plate of another soldier. Four dead in two seconds. It was only then that those remaining realised they were under attack and dropped to the ground, seeking cover.

Greener and Marin continued to shoot arrows at them, pinning them down, adding to their panic.

'Anyone see anything?' shouted one. 'Where are they fucking shooting from?'

'Up the slope somewhere.'

'I fucking know that – but where?'

A Skull raised his head and nearly got an arrow in the eye for his trouble. As he ducked back down, it skittered off the top of his helmet. 'Over here!' he screamed. 'Hanran! Over here!'

Someone blew a horn.

Not what they wanted.

Monon emerged from a bush, a moving shadow, with two Hanran close behind. They slipped past the enemy line and attacked before the Skulls even knew they were there. Three more died. Only one remained.

The last Skull jumped up and threw his sword into the undergrowth. 'Surrender!' His Jian was terrible but his intentions were clear enough. 'Please. Surrender. Don't kill.'

Monon walked up to him and cut the man's throat.

Eight dead Skulls and Tinnstra hadn't needed to do a thing. A part of her was almost angry at not getting a chance to fight, to test her sword, and the realisation of that shocked her even more. *I've spent my life running from every battle. Who am I becoming?*

Greener and Marin collected their arrows silently while Tinnstra pulled Zorique out of her hiding spot. The girl smiled, and for the first time in a long while, Tinnstra believed everything would be all right. With the Shulka to help them, they were going to make it. Escape. Thank the Four Gods.

Then she heard a noise behind her.

She swung around. The three Skulls were almost invisible against the snow-covered slope – but there was no hiding the swords in their hands.

She pushed Zorique behind her. 'Monon! Help!' she called without taking her eyes off the Skulls.

'Put the sword down, girl,' said one of the Skulls. 'It's too big for you.'

'Gut her and get the kid,' said the one next to him.

The Skull swung his scimitar high, aiming for her neck. Time slowed. Tinnstra saw it coming easily, ducked beneath it and lunged; her blade slid effortlessly through his chin into his brain. He coughed blood and fell as she pulled the sword free. She parried the second man's attack, the sound of clashing steel startlingly loud in the mountain air. Their swords slid together, bringing them close. Close enough to see his eyes. Close enough to stamp down on his knee. His leg went from under him and he tumbled to the side. Unprepared, the third Skull only managed a

326

wide-eyed look before she took his sword-hand off and reversed the cut to open his throat. Blood sprayed over snow-covered leaves.

She spun back, kicked the second one again as he tried to stand and shoved her sword into his face.

Zorique screamed as he died and Tinnstra rushed over to her. 'I'm sorry,' she said, scooping the girl up in her arms. Zorique buried her face in Tinnstra's shoulder, sobbing. 'I'm sorry. You're safe now. You're safe.'

Monon and the others reached them a second later. 'Are you okay? Are you injured?'

'We're fine,' said Tinnstra, her heart racing. Her sword suddenly felt heavy in her hand.

Monon looked around at her handiwork, impressed. 'Grim Dagen's daughter indeed.'

Tinnstra followed his gaze, shocked at what she'd done, uncomfortable with Monon's praise. Part of her wanted to confess, tell them it was Aasgod's magic that was responsible, not her, not her genes. But she didn't want them to think less of her. She liked their approval. 'It was my duty,' she said in the end. She placed Zorique back on the ground and was glad to see her tears had dried up.

'Let's go,' said Monon. 'There's always more of the bastards and that horn will get them up here as if their arses were on fire.' He flushed red and bowed to Zorique. 'Please excuse my language, Your Majesty.'

Zorique blushed in return.

'Come here, Your Majesty,' said Greener and scooped Zorique up again. The girl chuckled and wrapped her arms around the giant as far as she could.

They set off once more. The Skulls might be following close behind but the gate and freedom waited ahead of them. They just had a snow-covered mountain to climb.

45

Darus

The Kotege

'Now we're chasing a dozen people instead of two little girls?' Darus couldn't believe it. Two days stuck outside in the bloody snow with nothing to show for it other than a growing number of dead soldiers was really starting to wear his patience down.

'Yes, sir,' said the officer. 'From the tracks we've found, they met a group coming up from the south and are now returning that way via the mountain.'

The mountain in question, Olyisius, jutted up against the purple sky. The pine trees stopped halfway up. And above the treeline, nothing had the guts to grow on the exposed rock. It was the last place he wanted to slog, chasing a band of rebels. Especially now it was getting dark. But he had soldiers. They could do all the climbing that needed to be done. 'You have about another hour of light. Make best use of that time and go after them. And try not to get any more of your men killed in the process. It's embarrassing enough as it is.'

'Yes, sir.' The officer snapped to attention, saluted and about-faced to join his men.

Darus watched him, fuming and scratching at his itchy newborn skin. And he only had himself to blame for working with incompetents. Fortunately, most of the soldiers he'd brought with him were dead, otherwise he'd have killed the lot of them. The remaining thirty had better get some results or it was the hangman's rope for all of them. Returning to Aisair without the princess would not be pleasant. Dead or alive, he didn't care. In fact, it would be a lot easier to bring a corpse back.

'Sir!' One of his men pointed to the sky. 'Daijaku.'

'Signal them to come here,' said Darus.

Four of them swooped down in perfect unison. They must have spent hours upon hours drilling that landing manoeuvre alone. Darus admired their dedication. He understood the pain the men had gone through at Raaku's hands to be transformed. If only everyone was as committed, as devoted. It was hard to imagine such hideous creatures being so disciplined, though.

A Daijaku strode over. 'Darus Monsuta?' The words rasped out of its misformed mouth.

As if he could be anyone else. 'I am.'

'We were sent from the capital to check on your progress.'

Time was running short for Darus. The Emperor's patience was not infinite. 'We've pursued the girl and her associates up into the mountains. The weather is hindering our progress.'

The Daijaku glanced at Olyisius. 'It is only a small mountain.'

'Not all of us can fly,' snarled Darus. He didn't care who'd sent the creature, he wouldn't be spoken to like some common soldier. 'But you can. Go after them. Pursuit will be faster and easier for you. I believe they're heading to a gate at the top of the mountain.'

The demon nodded. 'It will be done.'

'Do not let me down. The Emperor is not a forgiving man – nor am I.'

'Daijaku always get their prey.'

'Then I will see you shortly with your prisoner.'

The Daijaku nodded once more. It'd be too much to expect a bloody salute from the creature. He watched the demon return to the others and then they took off, heading for Olyisius. He almost felt pity for the girl. Perhaps he should've remembered to tell the Daijaku to bring her back alive. *Oh well*.

46
Yas

Kiyosun

Yas stood with Kara on the corner of the square where Ma and Little Ro had seen her off only a few days before. The powdered poison was in the stitching of her coat. Such a small thing to have such power over so many lives.

'I'll be waiting for you here. The moment you appear with Jax and his son, we'll take out the guards at the gate. No one will stop you,' said Kara.

'What if I'm captured before I can use it?' asked Yas. 'What happens to Ro and Ma then?'

'They'll go free. We're not monsters. But don't think about giving yourself up. We'll know if you do and we'll kill your family. You're not the only spy we have inside.'

'Then why aren't they doing this? Why me? Why *my* family?'

'You're the only one with the access. The opportunity.'

Yas stared at Kara with utter hatred. 'Bitch.'

Kara gave her just as hard a look back, harder, in fact. 'Yeah, I am. Remember that and do what you're supposed to do.'

Yas strode away without saying another word – what was the point? The Skulls at the gate recognised her and barely looked at her papers. They still gave her a good pat down for weapons, though, groping her just as much as they usually did. Her cheeks burned as their hands brushed against her coat. The paper seemed to grow twice in size as they searched – to the point where she couldn't understand how they missed it.

'Go,' said the Skull when he'd finished, but Yas just stood there, looking at him in disbelief. How could he not realise she planned to kill them all?

'You deaf? Go.' The Skull shoved her and Yas stumbled away, her body working instinctively as her mind was filled with Little Ro, Ma, Kara and that blasted paper.

The kitchen was so *normal*. Bets at the heart of it all, organising the crew like a master conductor with their orchestra. Breakfast service was finishing while the rest prepped for lunch. She spotted Yas and gave her a big smile. 'All right, love? You came back. Good on you. Today will be better, I promise.'

It won't. Yas's heart cracked into a thousand pieces as she wandered through to the changing room, barely acknowledging everyone's greetings, avoiding their eyes.

Arga was already there and doing up the buttons on her uniform. 'By the Four Gods, you look rough. Didn't you sleep at all last night?'

Yas shrugged. 'Not much.'

'That business with the Chosen get you all worked up, did it? Don't blame you there. I thought they were gonna snatch some of us just for the fun of it.'

'I'm worried about my little boy, that's all.'

'I can understand that. Got three kids of my own at home. Drive me mad, they do, but I wouldn't swap 'em for naught.'

Yas looked up, aghast. '*Three?* I didn't know.'

'You never asked. But yeah, three. Two boys and a girl – and the girl's the wildest of the lot. They'll be the death of me one of these days.'

The knot in Yas's stomach grew, soaking up all the guilt it could. Suddenly breathing took effort. She couldn't do it. Couldn't kill Arga, couldn't kill any of them. But she couldn't let Kara kill Ro, either. Not her little boy. By the Gods, there had to be another way.

Yas forced the panic down and finished getting dressed. She slipped the wrap of poison into her apron.

'Yas?'

She froze, her hand still clenched around the paper. 'Yes?'

331

Arga stared at her. 'If you ever want to talk, you can trust me. We're family here. I just want you to know that.'

Yas nodded, heart hammering in her chest and bile burning her throat. 'Sure.'

When they started work, it was if she were seeing the place for the first time – seeing the people in it for the first time. Most of them were Egril, the enemy, but when she looked past their uniforms, they were no different from anyone else she knew. How many of them wanted to be there? How many had wanted to invade Jia in the first place? Maybe they were all conscripted. Maybe they had families they wanted to protect. She couldn't believe they were all evil. They were people just like her. And she had to kill them.

All morning, she thought of nothing else. She tried to come up with another plan, any alternative, to rescue Jax but there was no way she could see. She wasn't a bloody Shulka, trained to fight. She was just a single mother with a child to protect. *Had* to protect.

May the Four Gods forgive her, she was going to do it.

She had no choice. There wasn't anything she wouldn't do to keep Little Ro safe. Just as Kara had known.

'Hey, Arga – I forgot something. I have to go downstairs for a minute.' Her voice didn't sound like her own now the decision was made. It was as if she'd stepped out of her body and someone else was in control.

'How many times do I need to tell you? Don't go walking around on your own – and don't go leaving me on my own, either. Can't it wait?'

'It can't. I'm sorry.'

'Be quick, then. Be careful.'

'I will.' She hurried down to the kitchen, taking the paper out of her apron as she walked, unfolding it, getting it ready.

'What you doing back here?' asked Bets as she walked in.

'I'm feeling faint. I've not eaten,' replied Yas. 'Could I have a bowl of something?'

'You do look pale,' said Bets. 'Don't worry, my love. Rib over there's nearly finished the beef stew for lunch. Have some of that. It'll sort you out.'

Rib grinned. 'Help yourself. It's good and ready.'

'Thanks,' replied Yas. The world slipped out of focus as she picked up a bowl and ladle. Rib stepped back, giving her room, and she dipped the ladle into the pot, emptying half of the paper's contents and giving it a good stir as she did so. It was as easy as that. She filled her bowl, nodded at Rib again and headed to the staff dining room. Every step echoed her guilt. She stopped halfway and looked back, not believing she'd done it, expecting to be caught, but everyone was just getting on with their jobs. As if everything was normal. Not knowing she'd killed them. Of course, not everyone would eat the stew and she had to be sure.

The water barrels for the whole house were stored in the staff dining room and everyone drank water. She split the rest of the poison between them. She'd done it. There was no turning back. No saving anyone, except Ro and Ma.

She emptied her bowl of stew out of a window and wished she could climb out after it and run away, but she was in it now. Committed. A *murderer*.

Rejoining Arga, she continued her duties as though in a trance, sick with guilt. At lunchtime, she helped carry trays of stew around the castle, served the stew in the mess hall, delivered stew to the officers' quarters, poured water for them all to drink. She didn't look at any of their faces. She didn't want to see the people she was going to kill.

Each trip back to the kitchen, she watched her friends taste the food, drink the water. All condemned for something that wasn't their fault. They had one hour left. *Because* of her.

She could've said something, stopped them, saved them, but no. Their lives versus her family was no choice at all.

Yas was in the kitchen when Faul ran in with a dog sprawled in his arms. 'He's dead. My bloody dog is dead.'

Everyone except Yas rushed over. She knew why the dog was dead.

She steadied herself against a table, wanting to run and hide, but she knew she couldn't. She had to see it through.

Faul placed the dog on a table and they all crowded around.

Yas remembered the way it had greeted her on her first day, jumping up and wagging its tail.

'What happened?' asked Bets.

'I dunno,' said Faul. 'He was just lying there. I thought he was asleep. He was a lazy bugger, wasn't he? But he ... he's dead.'

Then Rib collapsed and the dog was forgotten.

The cook thrashed about on the floor, frothing at the mouth. Bets rushed over, tried to hold him still as she called his name, but he didn't respond. Couldn't. Someone screamed. It might've even been Yas. She didn't know. She just watched Rib jerk this way and that so violently she thought his spine would crack, and then suddenly he was still. As quick as that. Yas stared down at him. He was dead. Dead. She'd done that. Killed him. A friend. She didn't know if he had a wife or kids, if someone was going to be broken-hearted when he failed to come home that night. If he did, maybe he'd have understood why Yas had killed him. You protect the ones you love.

There wasn't time for anyone else to be shocked. No time for any of them to do anything except die. Georga screamed, clutching her gut. Baca went white and sat down, pulling at her collar, then vomited over her lap.

'Get help,' shouted someone. It might've been Bets or Samu. Yas didn't know.

She watched Wisder crumple, followed by Baca.

Followed by Georga, then Lucin.

Faul next.

Knocking over tables, smashing plates, gurgling as they choked on bile and spit.

They died one by one in front of her.

Because of her.

Screams and shouts came from upstairs, too. People were dying up there. She could hear the thumps as the bodies hit the floor.

Arga's legs went from under her and she grabbed Yas by the shoulders. 'Help me.' Froth bubbled from her mouth. Yas stood unmoving as her friend slid down her body to the ground. There was confusion in Arga's face. Then pain. Then nothing.

Bets was the last to die. She looked accusingly at Yas as if she knew what she'd done. Yas could see it in her eyes. Bets stumbled towards her, hand outstretched, made it three steps and then she collapsed, too, dragging a plate of food with her. The stew ran down her clothes like blood, mixed with her vomit.

Then there was silence. Eleven people dead and only Yas left standing. She knew she should feel guilty, feel *something*, but the truth was she only felt numb.

She stepped over Arga's body, picked up a meat cleaver from the counter and hid it behind her apron. There was no hesitation now. No uncertainty. Yas would do whatever she had to do to ensure Ma and Ro lived. In the stairwell, one guard was down but his companion still lived. He was kneeling over the other Skull's body.

'What's going on?' he shouted. 'You must get help.'

'Everyone's dead,' said Yas, walking over to him. 'They're all dead.'

'What do you mean, everyone? Go upstairs and get help.' He looked up just as Yas hacked down with the cleaver. It bit into the centre of the Skull mask and cut deep. Blood leaked through, staining the white. The man twitched and fell to the floor. As easy as that. Easier than the poison, in fact. Blood washed the shattered mask red. So much blood.

She walked up the stairs, the only sound the beat of her heart. At the top, she peered around. Bodies lay everywhere, all twisted and contorted. Somewhere, someone was crying but it didn't matter. Yas had done her job well.

Back downstairs, Yas took the keys from the guard's belt and unlocked the door. It was old and heavy and took all her effort to make it move. Old hinges protested, creaking and groaning every inch of the way until there was a gap big enough for her to step through.

Inside, a few spluttering torches made little difference to the gloom. The air stank of sweat, piss and fear. Groaning came from the cells. The guards were already dead, empty bowls by their feet.

'Jax!' called Yas, her voice an alien sound in the cellar. 'Jax! Where are you?' She peered through the bars of the first cell and jerked back as two hands thrust out at her.

'Help me, please,' begged a man.

'Are you Jax?' asked Yas, but she already knew the answer. She sought a man with one arm. 'I'm looking for Jax. Does anyone know Jax?'

'Over here.' A hand stuck out from a cell three-quarters of the way down.

Yas ran over. 'Jax?'

'Yeah, that's me.'

He'd been beaten badly: his nose was bent out of shape and his mouth was swollen and bloody, but didn't argue about having to prove himself. The stump of his right arm poked through the bars.

This was him. The man she'd killed so many for. What made him special? Made him worth three hundred lives? *Worth her son's?* He was just a beaten-up old man. 'I've come to get you out.'

'Open the door, then.'

Yas pulled the bolts back and pushed the door open.

There were two others in the cell with Jax, both as badly beaten as he was. One was a man not much older than Yas but the other was a kid, who scrambled to his feet.

'My name's Yas. Kara sent me.'

'This is my son, Kaine.' Jax pointed to the older one, still lying on the ground. 'And he's Dren.'

'Are we getting out?' said Dren. He cradled his left hand. 'What about the guards?'

'They're all dead,' said Yas.

'How?'

'I killed them,' said Yas. 'Let's go.'

Dren still didn't move. 'What about Kaine? How are we going to carry him?'

'Leave me, Father,' said Kaine. 'I'll slow you down too much.'

'No one gets left behind,' replied Jax. 'We can carry you between us.'

'What's the matter with him?' asked Yas. The sooner they were out of there, the sooner she could get Ro back.

'My son can't walk.'

'Then he's right,' said Yas. 'We leave him. Who knows how much time we have before the Skulls notice something's wrong and send more troops here?'

Jax bent down and got one arm around Kaine. 'Who's going to tell them? You said everyone was dead.'

'I didn't check the whole place,' said Yas. 'I came to get you out as soon as I could.'

'Come on,' said Dren. He went to Kaine's other side and helped lift him up. The boy winced in pain and looked fit to fall himself.

'We're all going to get killed,' said Yas. After everything she'd done. The stubborn fools.

Ignoring her, they dragged Kaine out of the cell. Jax paused when he saw the dead guards. 'You poisoned everyone.'

'Not by choice,' said Yas. 'Now come on. Kara's waiting outside with some more of the Hanran. They're going to attack the gate when they see us.'

'Wait,' said Jax. 'Put Kaine down.'

'What're you doing?' asked Yas.

'You and Dren free everyone in the cells. I meant it when I said no one gets left behind.'

Yas stared at him. Couldn't he see how precarious their position was? Didn't he want to escape? 'What're you going to do?'

Jax took a scimitar from one of the dead guards. 'Behind these metal doors is the Skulls' Tonin.'

'We don't know that for sure,' said Kaine. 'There could be a dozen guards in there!'

Jax shook his head. 'I've seen men come out but no one's gone in. The only explanation is that's where they're opening up gates.'

'The girl's right,' argued Dren. 'We need to run.'

'We take out the Tonin and Kiyosun's cut off from support. Think what we can do then,' said Jax. 'It's worth the risk. Especially now.'

'You won't do anything if you're dead. We need to go,' said

337

Yas. 'My son's life and my ma's depend on me getting you out of here.'

'Free the others,' said Jax. 'I'm going to kill whoever or whatever is behind that door. Then we go.'

47

Tinnstra

Olyisius Mountain

The sun sank towards the horizon but the Shulka showed no sign of stopping. They marched on and up, spread out along the mountain, protecting Zorique and Tinnstra. The giant still carried the princess, much to her delight, and Tinnstra was happy to have the responsibility taken off her.

Thank the Four Gods, there'd been no more snow. The previous day's flurry had left the route tricky enough. Any more and it would've been impassable. No wonder Monon had been insistent there could be no delay.

They'd left the Skulls far behind and ahead was the summit of Olyisius where the gate to Kiyosun waited them. Tinnstra wondered what it would be like, to leave one place and instantly be in another. Aasgod said it was magic left over from the old world – his world. It was hard to imagine such power was once commonplace.

She reached over her shoulder and touched the hilt of her sword. Within resided just a spark of his power and yet it had changed everything. The fear that had ruled her life was gone. Without its crushing weight holding her down, she could do anything. It was unbelievable to think that only a few days ago, she had been too scared to leave her home. Now she had purpose. She was part of something greater than herself. Was this how her father had felt all the time? Her brothers? Maybe when Zorique was safe in Meigore, she'd return and fight with Monon and the others in Kiyosun. Be what her father had always wanted her to be. A warrior. A Shulka.

She caught Monon watching her.

'How are you feeling?' he asked. 'It's a bastard of a hill.'

'I'm surviving,' replied Tinnstra. 'But I'll sleep for a week when this is over.'

'I can't promise you that just yet. We've got about an hour of light left. There's an overhang ahead that we should reach in that time. We'll rest there before pushing on to the gate.' Monon glanced back down the mountain, then looked at Tinnstra. 'Do you mind me asking you something?'

'That depends what it is.'

'What was your father like? He was my hero when I was coming up through the ranks.'

'I thought you knew him.'

'I said I fought alongside him. That's not quite the same thing.' He picked up a small stone. 'I was to your father as this pebble is to the mountain.'

'You were more important to him than that,' replied Tinnstra. 'My father valued everyone under his command, made a point of knowing everyone's names. I remember him passing a beggar in the street one time; he was filthy, dressed in rags, with long, grey hair and a beard that covered his face and half his body, and my father still recognised him. He was a veteran of one of my father's campaigns and had been forced to leave the Shulka because he'd lost his leg. Things had got even worse for him and he'd ended up begging in the street. The man was ashamed by how low he'd fallen but it didn't matter to my father. He fetched some food and ate with the man, talking about the war and the friends they'd lost.

'Afterwards, he brought the man home, bathed him, gave him fresh clothes and a bed to sleep in. My father found work for him and, once a month after that, if my father was home, they met for a meal and to talk about this and that. It always amazed me how he found time, but he always did. He told me a leader's first duty is to the people under his command. Their welfare and safety must be the priority. I asked how that could be so if he had to send those same soldiers out to die one day – surely one duty was at odds with the other. But he smiled and said it was the only way he could do it. Their deaths had to mean something.'

'We would've done anything for your father,' said Monon.

Tinnstra believed him. Strange that she, his daughter, hadn't been able to when it mattered. How she wished he could see her now.

'Daijaku!'

The Shulka dropped to the ground. Tinnstra wedged herself sideways against a boulder and searched for the enemy. They were easy to spot, even against the darkening sky, as they swooped down over the mountainside with the hated Niganntan blades in their hands. Flashes of light guided them: signals from the pursuing Skulls.

Once they'd passed and the skies were clear, Monon got to his feet. 'We need to pick up the pace, people. We're too exposed here to fight those bastards.'

No one needed telling twice. They ran as fast as the mountain allowed. Even with her magic sword, Tinnstra was in no hurry to face a squad of Daijaku. They slipped on loose rock and stumbled on shingle but they kept going, driving up the slope. Tinnstra's already exhausted body protested every step. Her lungs burned. Just getting to the top of the mountain was a big ask, let alone all the way to Kiyosun. She was a stupid girl for letting her mind wander too far when she should've been concentrating on the here and now.

The overhang ahead looked as if some giant hand had scooped out a chunk of mountain. It was a good stretch of stone to have against their backs and provided a roof to shelter beneath. Three sides lay open to the elements but there were enough of them to hold off the Daijaku if need be. A good place to make a stand, the best they'd get.

The Shulka didn't need orders. They dropped their kit in the centre and readied their weapons. Bows strung. Arrows nocked. Blades sharpened.

Greener placed Zorique in the heart of them. 'I'll give her back to you for now. Keep her safe – she's a good kid.'

Tinnstra nodded. 'I know.'

The giant crouched in front of the girl. 'Keep your head down, princess. We'll be on our way soon enough.'

'I'm not a princess any more. I'm a queen,' corrected Zorique.

Greener smiled. 'I apologise, Your Majesty.' He kissed her forehead and, carrying his huge bow, left to guard the approach.

Monon came over with a man and a woman. 'This is Eris and his sister Jao. I'm hoping the Daijaku won't come back and we can all move out together once it gets dark. But if they do attack before then, we're prepared to fight. If that happens, first chance you get, I want you to follow Eris and Jao. They'll take you to the gate and then on to Kiyosun and the meeting point. Greener will go with you, too.'

Eris greeted her all bright-eyed with a crop of mousy hair and the beginnings of a beard on his chin. The three knives belted across his chest looked too big for him. Another was strapped to his right hip. Tinnstra didn't want to ask how old he was.

Jao was tall and wiry. Armed with a bow, she had a weariness to her eyes. 'We were born near Kiyosun. The climb down on the other side isn't easy but we know the way.'

'You don't have swords,' said Tinnstra. 'You're not Shulka?'

'Our family have always been hunters, grew up in a small village a half-day from the coast. Jao and I were in the woods one day and we came back to find the Skulls had killed everyone. So we travelled to Kiyosun to kill the Skulls. We met Monon there and he asked us to join him.'

'I'm honoured to have you both with us,' said Tinnstra.

'I know it sounds impossible, but try and get some rest if you can,' said Monon. 'We have a long night ahead of us.'

After Monon left, Tinnstra sat down and pulled Zorique close to her so they could share warmth. It felt good after being so cold for so long.

The sun sank towards the horizon, leaving in its wake a bruised and battered sky. The wind picked up, cold and persistent, as they waited, still and silent.

'Stay sharp, people,' whispered Monon.

Nightfall was so close, maybe twenty or thirty minutes away.

Would the Daijaku come after them before the Hanran could slip away? Tinnstra urged the sun down, frustrated by how slowly it moved. She prayed the Daijaku stayed away.

'Here they come,' called Greener, answering her foolish hope.

'No one move,' ordered Monon. 'Wait for them to see us first. They still might fly past.'

Tinnstra's mouth was dry. Her hand went to her sword as she prepared to fight or take flight. She looked for the Daijaku but couldn't see them. Perhaps Greener was mistaken … No, they were out there, somewhere. Shadows spread across the slope, making it even harder to see. The darkness meant to save them now worked against them. She strained her ears and heard the beat of wings growing louder, faster with each second.

'Tinnstra …' said Zorique, her voice full of fear.

'Hush,' replied Tinnstra. 'Monon and his team know what they're doing.' She glanced over at the Shulka leader, sword in hand. Greener had an arrow nocked. Marin knelt with his back against the rock, his short bow ready. He caught her looking and grinned reassuringly.

Then she finally saw them. The Daijaku flew low and fast over the ground, weaving between rocks and shrubs, Niganntan blades ready. White dots moved behind them – Skulls. Lots of Skulls.

'Let them come closer,' said Monon. 'Arrows first. Don't waste a shot until you can see their bastard eyes.'

Tinnstra didn't know how he sounded so calm. The Daijaku's speed made them almost impossible to track. Eris and Jao covered Zorique and Tinnstra. She didn't blame them for looking petrified.

'Wait …' said Monon. 'Wait …'

Greener drew back the bowstring until his hand touched his cheek and held it ready, an astonishing display of strength. Her own father had barely been able to hold the position for a second or two.

'Wait …'

On came the Daijaku, swerving from shadow to shadow.

'Now!'

Greener released his arrow and drew another. A swipe of a

343

Niganntan blade knocked the arrow to one side. Marin loosed at another but the Daijaku rolled out of the way. It was like trying to hit the wind. And still the demons came.

'Loose!' screamed Monon as he stood, sword ready. More arrows flew down the mountain slope towards the demons.

The Daijaku spiralled up into the sky, faster than ever before, and not a single arrow hit its target. Time slowed as they curved around the resistance fighters trying to nock more arrows. The Daijaku were well drilled, slipping behind one another as they swooped back down – straight at the Shulka.

The demons flew through the heart of them, slashing with their Niganntan blades as they passed. Tinnstra, covering Zorique with her body, felt demon, sword and wing pass over her. There was a cry of pain.

'They're coming around again,' shouted Monon. 'Loose at will. And bloody well get down!'

Tinnstra drew her sword. A Shulka, someone who's name she'd not yet learned, lay five yards away, his legs no longer attached to his torso. Suddenly the Hanran didn't look so invincible.

But they didn't panic. Monon's soldiers showed their training and experience as the Daijaku closed in once more. Again the arrows flew and again the Daijaku avoided them all. Again they crashed through the resistance fighters. Again someone fell, Marin this time. His bow clattered to the ground as a Niganntan blade sliced through his gut.

'They don't get a third pass,' shouted Monon. 'It's their turn to get hurt.'

'Cover me,' said Greener as he stepped forward. He nocked an arrow, raised his bow and drew back the string. Every movement was precise, unhurried. The Daijaku raced towards such an invitingly large target.

Tinnstra held her breath as the Daijaku approached, wings beating ever faster. Greener released his arrow. It struck the lead Daijaku before it could turn, piercing the demon just below the collarbone. It tumbled from the sky and crashed into the ground with a crunch of bone and wing.

Another Daijaku screamed in rage and headed straight at

Greener. The giant drew another arrow but there wasn't enough time to nock it. The Daijaku swept back its Niganntan blade as it closed the gap between them.

'No!' cried Zorique and Tinnstra found herself moving. Three steps and she was beside the Shulka. All she could see was the Daijaku and the madness in its eyes. Tinnstra thrust out with her sword and felt the impact as her weapon slashed into the Daijaku's wing. Blood spurted over her as the blade sliced through the leathery membrane. The Daijaku's momentum carried it into Greener, pulling Tinnstra with it.

She staggered, trying to hold on to her sword. Greener punched the Daijaku with one hand while trying to stop the creature from ripping his throat out with the other. Its remaining wing beat furiously as blood poured from the stump where the other one had been. Tinnstra didn't think. She took a step forward, thrust, and her sword slid straight into the Daijaku's back, piecing its heart. It thrashed for a second more before it realised it was dead.

Greener climbed to his feet, covered in demon blood. He roared and kicked the fallen Daijaku again and again.

'Greener – pull yourself together,' shouted Monon. 'They're more of them.'

The giant nodded, taking deep breaths. 'Thank you, Grim Dagen's daughter.'

Tinnstra didn't say anything. She couldn't help staring at the dead Daijaku. It was a monster, and yet she'd stood before it armed only with a sword. It was madness. Her legs shook when she realised what she'd done. Her stomach lurched and she had to push away from the others. Bile surged up her throat and she heaved what little had been in her stomach, heaved until there was nothing left. 'I'm alive. I'm alive,' she muttered. Somehow. Thank the Four Gods for Aasgod's magic.

'Here, drink this.' Monon handed her a water skin.

Tinnstra took a slug to wash her mouth out. The world spun for a moment but settled as she sucked in cold air to soothe her burning throat. 'I've no idea why I did that – how I did that.'

'Because you're a warrior. Like your father.'

Tinnstra looked up at the Shulka and smiled. The compliment

helped calm her. 'You're the first person who's ever said that.'

Jao approached them. 'The Skulls are coming up the mountain. Eris counted thirty of them. The other Daijaku are sticking close to them.'

'Great.' Monon looked down the slope into the darkness below. The Skulls were easy to spot despite the night. 'We stick with the plan. You, Eris and Greener take Tinnstra and the queen to the gate. The boat from Meigore will be at Rascan's Point at midnight tomorrow. Get them on it.'

'What about you?' asked Tinnstra.

'The rest of us will stay and fight. Keep the Skulls and Daijaku away from you for as long as possible,' replied Monon.

'No,' said Tinnstra. 'That's suicide. Let's go together. We can all get away.'

'Bad odds, maybe.' The Shulka squeezed her shoulder. 'But this is a good position to defend and we'll make their approach a bloody task. It'll give you time. The queen is all that matters.' He paused, looked down at Marin's body, then his eyes drifted to the other Shulka, the one whose name Tinnstra didn't know. 'We are the dead.'

Tinnstra saw the pain in his eyes. Yet he was still willing to sacrifice more lives, including his own. 'My father would've liked you.'

A smile flickered across his face. 'Be off with you. We can talk more when I see you next.'

'May the Four Gods look after you,' said Tinnstra, and wondered if she'd ever see the man again.

She followed Eris and Jao up the mountainside. Greener was beside her, with the princess tucked in the crook of his arm once more. They moved as fast as they dared with only a sliver of moon to see by. At least in the dark no one could see her cry.

Tinnstra felt like she'd been running for ever, leaving behind people she cared about each time, first Beris, then Aasgod and now Monon. She reminded herself that Zorique was still alive and that the boat was on its way to take them to safety, but it was little consolation. People were paying too high a price to make that happen.

The summit of Olyisius loomed above them. The gate waited. Tinnstra concentrated on that: getting Zorique away was all that mattered.

The air grew colder, the ground more treacherous. The snow was knee-deep in places, sucking at their strength, and the wind howled around them, biting at their skin.

Then an explosion rocked the night.

They all stopped and looked back towards the overhang, listening to the shouts echo from below. They watched figures in white armour rush up the slope. The fight for the summit had begun.

'There are so many . . .' murmured Eris.

'We should go back,' said Tinnstra. 'Help them.'

'We move on,' said Greener. 'We follow the plan. They know what they're doing. Let's not waste the time they are buying us.'

Greener had to push Jao on for them to move. Tinnstra felt sick to her stomach but she, too, followed. She swore it would be the last time, that she'd not desert another friend again, but she knew that was a lie. She would have to do whatever was necessary to get Zorique to the boat and no such promises could be made.

Below, another explosion ripped a hole in the mountainside. Tears ran from her eyes as they climbed. The Hanran they'd left behind didn't have magic to keep them safe. They were giving their lives willingly – for Zorique, for her. It was a kind of bravery she'd never felt. Her new-found confidence wavered. *They are the dead who protect the living, not me. I'm just a coward with a magic sword.*

'Nearly there,' called Greener.

Tinnstra looked up, saw the summit against the night sky. She knew where the temple was. They were going to make it. Monon hadn't died in vain.

They stumbled on, inch by inch, dragging themselves through the snow. Greener led the way, unstoppable even with Zorique protected in his arms. Eris and Jao climbed on either side of Tinnstra, heads down against the wind.

Almost there. Another step. Another foot. Ignore the cold, forget the wind, push past the snow.

Suddenly only the sky was above them, vast space instead of mountain and rock. Tinnstra looked up, saw the temple, half-buried with snow. They'd made it.

48
Jax

Jax hated the feel of the scimitar. The weight was unbalanced – all in the blade and none in the hilt. A brutal weapon. He'd give anything for a decent Shulka blade instead. Even better if he still had his right hand to wield it, but he was stuck with what he had. A shit sword and one arm.

'You don't have to do this, Father,' said Kaine.

Jax looked at his son. Before he'd lost the use of his legs, his son had been worth at least five men in a fight. 'You know I must. We'll never get another chance. Free the others and then we go.'

'Better get on with it, old man,' said Dren.

Jax took a deep breath. 'Let's do this.'

Dren pulled back the bolt on the door. It protested as it slid free and the sound echoed around the cellar. Jax wasn't going to be taking anyone by surprise on the other side of that door. He hoped there was no one else in there with the Tonin.

It was dark inside and it took his eyes a moment to adjust. It stank even worse – sweat, damp, shit, piss, all mixed up with a dose of stale air. At first, he thought the room was empty, a big space full of nothing. Then he spotted a shape hidden deep in the shadows. Something – someone – was curled up in a ball, covering her head with her hands. As Jax got closer, she lifted her head, her eyes wide with fear, and she screeched for dear life.

The Tonin.

She was a wretched-looking creature with alabaster skin, all

349

covered with red sores and bald apart from a few strands of hair. A filthy robe was draped over her shoulders and did a poor job of hiding how thin she was, how malnourished. A chain was attached to a collar around her neck.

He approached her slowly, sword ready, but could feel his resolve wavering. If anything, she looked like a prisoner that needed to be freed, someone who'd been tortured as much as Jax had. If he could free her, turn her over to their side ...

'It's okay. I'm not your enemy.' Jax kept his voice soft. 'I can get you out of here.'

The Tonin skittered further into the corner.

'Don't be afraid,' said Jax. 'You're safe now. I'll set you free.'

The Tonin kept scuttling back until there was nowhere else to go. When Jax was a few feet from her, he saw her eyes. Big, hate-filled eyes. Hissing, she thrust out a hand and sparks appeared before him. Jax recoiled as the air screamed as it was ripped apart. The sound had been deafening up on the wall, but now, in the confines of the cellar, it was crushing. His knees buckled as he tried to cover his ears with his hand and shoulder.

He cursed himself for a fool. She was opening a portal. Jax staggered towards her as the air parted, lowering his sword, grimacing at the pain in his ears, the rattling of his bones. There was no time for mercy. No time for weakness. A two-foot hole revealed another cellar, another Tonin and at least a dozen Skulls. Everything he didn't need.

He swung the scimitar but the Tonin darted out of his way and the blade struck the stone floor. He chased after her, cursing his clumsiness with the unfamiliar weapon.

The Tonin danced away from him, bouncing and swerving, and somehow kept the window growing. She screeched and hollered, calling for help.

The Skulls on the other side shouted at Jax to put down his weapon and step away from the Tonin. Like he was fucking going to do that. His only hope lay in killing the Tonin.

Jax closed in on the creature, pushing her back into the corner. She hissed and slashed with one hand while the other continued to open the portal.

An arrow shot past his nose and clattered into the wall. Jax jerked out of the way as another followed. A Skull archer aimed at him from the other side of the portal.

'Dren!' he roared. 'Help!' He ducked as another arrow flew past, but he had to fall back. Arrows chased him, nipping at his feet and seeking his heart, pushing him away from the Tonin. 'Dren!'

The air cut and burned, screaming as it tore itself apart, expanding the hole to some four feet in diameter. It wouldn't be long before the Skulls could cross.

'Dren!'

The kid burst through the door.

'Get the Tonin,' shouted Jax.

For once, the kid did as he was told. Without hesitation, Dren rushed in like a wild thing, swinging, shouting, cursing.

The Tonin's attention wavered. The portal flickered for a moment as she skittered away from Dren's blade.

Straight to Jax. He swung at the Tonin's neck, putting all his weight behind it. The blade bit through white skin and muscle before hitting bone. Blood spurted across the grey floor. She cried out, a pitiful wail that echoed around the room. When she died, the portal died with her.

Jax stared at the space where the gate had been. It could've all been over because he'd been weak. Because he'd felt sorry for the enemy. He needed to be better. *Jia* needed him to be better.

'You okay?' asked Dren. 'You hurt?'

'No,' replied Jax. 'Let's get everyone out of here.'

The prisoners were disorientated at being free. Men, women, children – the Skulls didn't care who they'd arrested, who they'd beaten – but there wasn't a single member of the Hanran amongst them. Those who couldn't walk were carried by the other prisoners, just like Kaine. Jax and Dren kept their weapons at the ready as Yas led them from the cellar.

They entered the kitchen. The staff lay scattered across the floor, faces contorted in agony, foam staining the corners of their mouths. There wasn't a single Skull amongst them. Just Jians and all of them had died so Jax could escape.

When they reached the door, Yas put up a hand to stop them. 'We go left, then right around the main building. Then it's a sprint across the courtyard. Kara will attack the main guard house when she sees us.'

'Let's do it,' said Jax and led the ragtag bunch outside.

It was so brutally cold, it hurt to breathe. Every bruise and cut on Jax's body stung, but he didn't care. He was alive. He forced himself on.

They stopped by the corner of the main building. The gate was two hundred yards away – a long, dangerous sprint even if everyone was in the best condition and they weren't carrying a dozen injured. But there was no going back. It was what it was.

'I see Kara,' said Yas.

'Keep everyone here until we've secured the gate,' said Jax. 'Dren and I will take the guards.'

Dren nodded. 'Let's kill the bastards.'

For once, Jax was glad to have the kid with him. 'We've got to be fast. Before they can bring bows to bear.'

'Easy,' said Dren with a gap-toothed grin. And they began the run.

The guards saw them and started shouting, then Kara came from the other side with a dozen men and women, all carrying blades, and the Skulls didn't know which way to face.

It did Jax's heart good to see the Shulka swords again. Too long had they been hidden. They were meant for the kind of war Jax understood. Where men and women faced each other and fought with honour.

They hit the guards from both sides. Steel clashed against steel as the two forces fought for their lives. The Skulls had their armour but Jax and Kara had the numbers. For the first time in a long while, the Skulls were losing.

'What's that?' shouted Dren, pointing to the sky.

Jax hacked into a Skull before looking up. His blood ran cold. A black streak was racing towards them across the sky. 'Chosen!'

The sight spurred both sides on. Dren dodged a wild swing from a Skull. The strike left the Egril's armpit exposed and Jax slashed his scimitar into the weak area. The Skull screamed and tried to turn to face Jax. Dren moved in, chopped at the back of the man's knee. With his hamstrings gone, the Skull collapsed. Two Skulls were left, fighting Kara and her men, but they quickly fell under sheer weight of numbers.

'It's good to see you, sir,' shouted Kara.

'And you,' replied Jax. 'We don't have much time to get everyone out of here. We're going to have company soon.'

'I've seen it,' said Kara. 'Fuckers.' She clapped her hands. 'Move it, people. There's a devil coming in hot and fast, so let's be faster. Let's get everyone through the gate and away from this shit hole.' Kara's team didn't need telling twice. They rushed over to the prisoners. Even Dren went with them.

Yas was helping to carry Kaine but his weight made the going slow. Two of the Shulka took him off her and hauled him to the gate. Unburdened, Yas raced ahead, her face contorted in rage. She slammed into Kara, grabbing her by her shirt. 'Bitch! Where's my fucking son? Where is he?'

Kara shoved her aside. 'Back off! This isn't the time.'

Yas swung at her again but Jax grabbed her arm. 'I don't know what's going on but she's right. We've got a Chosen on our arses. We don't move it, then it's over.'

'She's holding my son and mother hostage,' screamed Yas.

'You need to stay alive and escape from this place first,' replied Jax. 'Everything else can wait.' Yas stared at him, all white-faced with anger, looking like she was ready for another fight, but then the two men carrying Kaine arrived at the gate.

'Get him to the safe house,' said Kara to her men. 'And take the woman with you. If I'm not back in an hour, find Gris and tell him to let her family go.'

'I'll see you there, son,' said Jax, squeezing his shoulder. Kaine gave him a nod in return. There was nothing more to be said. He turned to Yas. 'Go with them. Trust me, your family will be safe. I owe you too much of a debt.'

'This isn't over,' spat Yas, jabbing a finger at Kara, but the men carrying Kaine had already passed through the gate, leaving her no option but to follow.

Jax watched them disappear into the streets of Kiyosun. Hoped it wasn't the last time he saw his son. He looked up. The Chosen was closing in too fast.

'You should go with him,' said Kara. 'My people can handle this.'

More of the prisoners reached the gate and the Shulka ushered them through. It made Jax glad to see them free. 'You really kidnap the woman's family?'

'We had to get you out of there,' said Kara. 'I make no apologies for how we did it.'

'Damn it, Kara. We've got to ...' The black streak crashed into the courtyard twenty feet away. Dust and dirt flew up, obscuring the Chosen. Jax watched with horror building in his gut. 'No.'

A woman with silver-white hair stormed towards them with an axe in one hand and her baton in the other. Two of Kara's men went to meet her. A blast punched a hole through the chest of one while the other lost his head to her axe. She waded into the back of the prisoners, cutting them down like wheat. She laughed as bodies fell and blood spilled. For a moment, Jax was back at Gundan, watching his men be slaughtered.

No. Not again.

Jax tightened his grip on his sword and rushed to meet her.

49

Yas

Kiyosun

Yas had done everything the Hanran had asked of her, *murdered her friends*, and now she was stuck in another cellar in another part of town, with guards on the door stopping her from leaving, stopping her from being with *her son*.

They'd been there an hour or so, straight from escaping the Egril. An hour too long for her liking. She needed to get out of there. Get back home. Get Ro and Ma out of the hands of the Hanran.

She stormed over to one of the guards, a knucklehead called Hasan. 'Kara said you were to take me home if she wasn't here in an hour. It's been an hour. More than that. Let's go now!'

Hasan didn't move. 'Not yet. It's not safe. The city's crawling with Skulls.'

'But Kara said—'

'Kara isn't here.'

'I can see that!' Yas wanted to hit him, scratch his eyes out, do something, but knew it would accomplish nothing. The other Hanran fighter stood guard by the door, a man named Friid. He crossed his arms and scowled at Yas, so instead she turned to Kaine. He lay on one of three straw mattresses scattered on the floor. 'You tell him. Tell him he's got to take me home and make his thugs let my family go.'

Kaine sat up, wincing with pain. 'He will, I promise, but you've got to be patient. We're the only ones who've made it so

355

far. We don't know where my father is – or Kara. We need to wait a little bit longer.'

Yas jabbed a finger at him. '*You* wait. This mess has got nothing to do with me. Your people forced me into this. Just let me out of here so I can get my family.'

'I'm sorry, Yas. We'll take you to them as soon as we can.'

'Aaaargh!' Frustrated, Yas turned her back on all of them. When would her nightmare end? She stalked over to the other side of the room, sat down and put her head in her hands.

Kaine looked over to Hasan. 'Any news from Monon and Greener?'

'Nothing.'

The answer seemed to bother Kaine. 'It's been two days.'

'They'll be back,' replied Hasan. 'Nothing stops those guys.'

'I hope so,' said Kaine. 'For all our sakes.'

The group fell into an uneasy silence. For Yas, each minute took an eternity. Every second was agony. She wanted to tear her hair out, scream and shout, batter her way free with her fists if need be, but somehow she kept it all in. Little Ro needed her and losing it wouldn't help him. It certainly wouldn't help her.

Footsteps on the stairs jerked them all back to life. Hasan and Friid were on their feet in an instant with their swords in their hands. There was a knock on the door, a pause and then three more in fast succession. Hasan unbolted the door and the old man who owned the house stuck his head through the gap. 'Got some friends of yours.'

At last, thought Yas. They would let her go and she could see her son. Then the boy, Dren, limped through the door, followed by another Shulka. Before anyone had said a word, Yas knew it was bad news.

Dren slumped on the floor. 'They got Jax and the woman—'

'Kara,' said Yas, the name ash on her tongue.

'Kara,' continued Dren. 'Everyone else is dead. We only just got away.'

Yas's legs wobbled and she grabbed a chair to steady herself. Everything she'd done was for nothing. *Bets, Wider, Samu, Arga* – their faces contorted with surprise, horror, fear, pain. Their cries for help and mercy. All that she'd done: caused all that suffering, taken all those lives, and for what? Jax remained a prisoner and she still didn't have her son and mother back. Tears sprang up in her eyes. Everything had been taken from her – her husband, her dignity, her soul. All she had left were Ma and Ro, and these *bastards* were keeping her from them.

'We need to move from here,' said Kaine. 'Nowhere we normally use is safe.'

'They won't talk,' said Hasan. 'Not Jax. Not Kara.'

'They will,' replied Kaine. 'The Skulls went easy on us in there because they didn't think we were worth the effort. Now they know different. The escape attempt confirmed that. We can't afford to wait.'

'The Egril have a mind-reader,' said Yas, soft as a whisper.

'What?' said Kaine. All eyes were on her. Frightened eyes.

'The Egril. They have a Chosen here. She can read minds.' Yas looked around the room. 'Maybe she's dead. Poisoned like the rest of them. But maybe not. If she's alive, they'll know every-thing.'

'Right,' said Kaine. 'We move. *Now*. Friid, put the word out – everyone goes to ground. I want all our weapons moved. Assume everything is blown. If you see Skulls, run. Don't take any chances. Staying alive is all that matters. We can replace things, we can't replace people.'

'Okay, Boss. I'll get it done,' said Friid.

Kaine turned to Hasan. 'How many men do we have at Yas's house?'

'Five. All Shulka,' replied Hasan.

Kaine nodded. 'Good. You and Dren will take me there.'

'Thank you,' said Yas. 'Thank you.'

'Don't thank me yet,' said Kaine. 'And you need a change of clothes. Anyone sees you in that maid's uniform and the game's over.'

'There's some stuff upstairs that belonged to my late wife that might fit you,' said the old man.

Kaine took the old man's hand. 'I'm afraid you're going to have to find somewhere else to stay for a while, Uncle. If the

357

Skulls come, it won't matter if we're not here. They'll arrest you anyway.'

'They don't scare me,' said the old man, squaring his shoulders, 'but I'll do as you say.'

'All right, people, let's get to it,' said Kaine. 'May the Gods bless us all.'

Yas didn't say a word. She knew the Gods didn't give a shit about any of them.

In the end, it was easy getting away. The Skulls had rung the bells for curfew early. They wanted everyone off the streets and no one waited around to contest the point. The pandemonium helped conceal Yas, Kaine and the others, allowing them to move at speed as the Skull checkpoints couldn't cope with the crowds and just watched everyone pass. It was so easy, Yas could've laughed if the situation wasn't so awful.

Then there it was. Her home. Yas cried out when she saw her building and sprinted the last fifty yards and raced up the stairs. She wanted to hammer on her door but she forced herself to take her time and use the coded knock she'd heard earlier. One of Kara's thugs opened it and she barged past him before he had a chance to stop her. Ma and Little Ro were sitting on her bed at the far side of the room and her heart nearly burst at the sight of them.

'Mama!' cried Ro, and she had him in her arms a second later, hugging him and crying and laughing all at the same time. She would never let him go again.

Ma put her arm around Yas's shoulder. 'Oh, Yas. We've been worried sick about you.'

'I'm okay,' reassured Yas. 'I am now, at least.'

The Shulka thug had a knife out. He was an old man in his fifties but that didn't make him any less menacing. 'Where's Kara?'

'Ask your friends coming up behind me,' snapped Yas, not caring. 'And leave us the fuck alone.'

'The Skulls got Kara,' said Kaine as Hasan and Dren carried him through the door. 'Let the girl be. She's done everything we asked.'

The Hanran fighters snapped to attention. 'Good to see you. It's been a while,' said the old man.

'Likewise, Gris,' said Kaine as he was lowered onto a chair next to the dining table. 'Gather around. I've got something important to tell you.'

Dren took a chair next to him. Hasan sat opposite while Gris and the others crowded around them to listen.

'Three days ago, the king and queen were killed. The Skulls said we did it but you all know that's bullshit,' said Kaine. 'We were trying to get the royal family out of Aisair so they could be transported to Meigore and safety. Once there, they were going to enlist the aid of Meigore's armies in an effort to drive the Egril out of Jia. The king and queen were murdered before they even left the castle grounds.'

Yas tried not to listen but she couldn't help herself. Kaine had an easy way about him. She could tell everyone liked him and there was no question that he was in charge.

'However, we don't think everyone died,' continued Kaine. 'We hope at least Aasgod and one of the children got away. Two days ago, my father sent Monon, Greener and a small team to see if they could find them and bring them back here.'

'They're coming *here*?' asked Dren.

Kaine nodded. 'A small boat will arrive tomorrow night from Meigore, making the most of the new moon. It's going to be at Rascan's Point at midnight. The princess, if she's still alive, must be on it. Hasan, send whoever you can spare to keep the beach safe for when Monon arrives. I don't want any surprises.'

'A boat on open water?' said Dren. 'The Skulls might not have any ships but if the Daijaku go after them, they'll have no chance. It'll be easy work to sink them.'

'That's why I want you and your friends out causing as much mayhem as you can. We've already thinned their forces today at the Council House. Their Tonin is dead, so they're not getting any reinforcements. If you're setting off explosions all over the city, the Skulls won't know which way to turn. We keep the Daijaku busy in Kiyosun, they'll miss what's going on up the coast. Think you can do that?'

Dren grinned. 'Chaos is what I'm good at.'

'Your father know about this boat?' asked Hasan.

'He does,' replied Kaine.

Hasan leaned forward. 'Then if this Chosen is still alive – the one Yas told us about, who can read minds – the Skulls will know all about it. It's suicide for all of us.'

'I know that, too,' said Kaine.

'We're not going to be able to break him out,' replied Hasan. 'Not after today and not with us spread all over the place.'

'I know that, too.' Kaine glanced over at Yas. Something in his eye worried her. 'We need someone to go into the Council House, find my father and stop him from talking.'

Instantly, she was on her feet. 'I'm *not* going back in there.'

'Yas—'

She cut him off. 'No way. No. Way. Don't even think about it. I even show my face in that building and I'll be swinging in a noose a second later.' She shook her head. 'You're all mad. Every single one of you. What are you going to do to make me help you, eh? Threaten my family again? Well, you just try it. I'll take all of you on before I let you do that.'

Gris stepped towards her but Kaine held up a hand. 'I don't want you to do anything except keep your family safe.'

That took the wind out of Yas. 'Then how do you expect to get anyone in there? The Skulls won't just let you walk in.'

Kaine smiled. 'I couldn't walk in if I wanted to. I could get dragged in, though.'

Hasan rose to his feet. 'No.'

'If I get arrested again, the Skulls will take me right to my father,' said Kaine. 'And then I'll kill him.'

50

Dren

Kiyosun

'Are you sure about this?' asked Dren for the twelfth time. He felt like shit. Someone had taped his hand up, but everything still hurt. He ran his tongue across his gums and in the gaps where his teeth had been. He really hoped Yas had poisoned the fucker who had tortured him. He hoped he'd died in agony, rolling about in his own piss and shit. Dren wished he could've seen it. Maybe stamped on his head a few fucking times for good measure.

'Unless you've got a better plan.' Kaine hung between Dren and Hasan as they carried him down the stairs from Yas's apartment. Each step jarred Dren's ribs but he said nothing. A bit of pain was nothing compared to what Kaine planned to do.

'I agree with the kid,' added Hasan. 'This doesn't feel right.'

They stopped at the bottom. Kaine looked at them. 'I don't want to do this, either, but if the Chosen is alive, what alternative is there? If the princess doesn't get to Meigore, they won't enter the war, and we need their help if we're ever going to defeat the Skulls. We can't let my father give away the location of the meeting point.'

'Yeah, but ...' said Dren.

'But nothing. We don't have any choices here. We need to protect the meeting point.'

'I hate this,' said Hasan.

'So do I,' said Kaine.

Dren opened the front door and checked the street. It was

361

empty, as was to be expected after curfew. Perfect for the madness they were about to do. 'It's clear.'

Kaine took a deep breath. 'Let's get this over with.'

Stepping outside after curfew was a quick way to get arrested. Trouble was, you needed a Skull to see you do it. There was a checkpoint a few streets away at the junction with Houseman Street and Cressa Road, so they headed towards it.

'Was saving this princess what the old man was doing before I got him arrested?' asked Dren. 'He kept going on about some big thing.'

'Yeah, it was,' answered Kaine. 'We wanted the Skulls to think we were beaten and couldn't possibly be any sort of threat to them. Always appear weaker than you are – that way you can catch the enemy off guard.'

'You certainly had me fooled.' A thought crossed Dren's mind and he laughed. 'This "looking weaker than you actually are" business – you can't really walk, can you? Because if you're faking it, you can stop now. You're fucking heavy to carry around.'

'Trust me, I'm not faking it,' replied Kaine with a smile. 'I got knocked off the wall at Gundan during the invasion and fell thirty feet. I wasn't much use to anyone after that.'

'You were lucky to survive that fight,' said Hasan. 'I lost my sister on the second day at Gundan. A lot of my friends, too.'

'Where were you fighting?' asked Dren.

The big man looked at him with sadness in his eyes. 'Right here in Kiyosun – if you can call it fighting. I was at the barracks over in Toxten. I wasn't on duty. Asleep in my quarters, I was, and suddenly bombs were going off and we were in the shit.'

'I was there – at the barracks,' said Dren. 'I was going to paint some bollocks on the walls. Then the Skulls came.'

'Well, you know how bad it was, then. You saw how many of those fuckers there were. We got up and out pretty quick but by then we were already overrun,' continued Hasan. 'We were lucky. We fought our way out, but the Skulls were everywhere. The Chosen, too, blasting everything in sight.'

'It was the same across all of Jia,' said Kaine. 'The war was lost that first night. It just took us another eight days to accept it.'

Dren kept quiet. It was weird hearing about things from the other side. He'd only ever known his personal version of events where the Shulka had failed to live up to their myth. He hadn't considered what it must have been like for them, how many of them had died in the attacks. Yet the Shulka he'd met didn't seem angry – they were just getting on with the fight. During the rescue attempt at the Council House, Kara and the others hadn't hesitated when it came to facing the Skulls or even the Chosen. They'd sacrificed themselves so Dren could escape. Even now, Kaine was going to get himself thrown back in prison to try to kill his own father so some princess he'd never met before could escape on a boat. None of it made sense to him. They weren't people with nothing left to lose like the ones he'd sent to die.

They stopped at the corner of Cressa Road. One turn and the Skulls would see them. 'Last chance,' said Hasan. 'No shame in going back.'

Kaine shook his head. 'Get up to Rascan's Point after this.'

'I will.' Hasan paused. 'Look, I …'

'It's all right. We are the dead who guard tomorrow.'

Hasan smiled. 'We are the Shulka and we are the dead.'

Dren looked at them both, not understanding what was being said, but he could see the courage behind the words.

'Good luck tomorrow, Dren,' said Kaine.

'May Xin look after you,' replied Dren. It felt like the right thing to say even though he didn't believe. He'd seen little evidence of anything you could call the Gods' work in his life, but fuck it, if they existed, they all needed as much help as they could get.

They set off again. Turned the corner. The Skulls' checkpoint was on the opposite side of the street. Four of the bastards stood there in their bone-white armour. By the way they jumped, they weren't expecting anyone dumb enough to be out on the streets.

'Hey! You! Stop right there!' shouted one of them, his accent as thick as mud.

The old urge rose in Dren, quick as fire. He wanted to go over there and kill them. Gut them. Cut their fucking heads off. But that wasn't the plan. That didn't mean he had to keep quiet, though. 'Piss off! Go back to your own country!'

'Bastards!' screamed Hasan.

And as easy as that, the Skulls ran towards them, not even bothering to bring their weapons. Hasan and Dren set off, too, carrying Kaine back the way they'd come. They had to make it look good – make it look real.

It was a struggle to run with Kaine – the Skulls could certainly see that – so they dropped him at the end of the street. Dren hesitated for a second, looked down at Kaine, thinking he should say something else. Then the Skulls closed the gap too quickly and he had no choice but to run on. It was all for nothing if they got caught.

In the end, it was no contest. It'd be a long time before some Skulls in armour could outrun Dren in his own city, even beaten up the way he was. He and Hasan went in opposite directions, as planned – and just like that, Dren was on his own. He didn't look back. He jumped up onto a small wall and ran along it, leaped, hooked the fingers of his good hand on the edge of a balcony and hauled himself up and onto it. He didn't stop. He bounced onto the balustrade, reached up to the next balcony and dragged himself up and over. He was on the roof a few seconds later without breaking a sweat.

Up on the roof, Kiyosun spread out before him. He was back. His kingdom. His land to hunt. He filled his lungs with fresh sea air, enjoying the tang of salt, the promise of freedom. It made him happy to see the ocean. One day, he'd sail away. Just like the princess. One day. Until then, though, he had chaos to organise. Revenge to take.

His neighbourhood hadn't changed. No reason why it should. He'd only been away two days. But still, Dren felt different. Like he'd had his eyes opened. Like he'd grown up somehow. He'd changed and he kind of expected the world to have changed with him. But no, Toxten was still a bombed-out shit hole. As he walked down his street, he glanced up at his old building, half-expecting to see his mother watching him from the window.

One street over, Dren entered the abandoned house where Quist and the others lived. There were kids asleep everywhere he looked; in rooms, in corridors, on the balconies. All like him: just trying to survive.

Dren found his friend asleep with five others in a room on the top floor. Falsa was there, too, tucked up in the corner with a rag of a blanket over her. Dren felt a pang of guilt at how he'd treated her the last time they'd been together. His behaviour didn't seem quite so clever now. Maybe he'd apologise later, when this was all over. Maybe.

He tiptoed through the room, squeezing his feet into gaps between bodies, careful not to wake anyone until he got to Quist. Dren put a hand over the boy's mouth to stop him crying out. Good job, too, because Quist woke up with a fright, eyes bulging, body thrashing, until he saw it was Dren.

Dren removed his hand and pointed up to the roof.

'What the fuck happened to you?' said Quist once they were up top and alone. 'I've been looking everywhere for you. I thought you were dead.' The two hugged.

'I'm surprised I'm alive,' replied Dren, stepping back. 'The Hanran grabbed me, tried to drown me, then I got picked up by the Skulls and thrown inside the Council House, interrogated, escaped, and now I'm back here.'

Quist cocked his head to see Dren's face properly. 'They did a right number on you. Even took your fucking ear off! You look grim.'

'I feel worse.'

Quist sat down on a pile of rubble, shaking his head. 'Shit. Shit. You've got more lives than a bloody cat.' He laughed. 'At least you're alive, eh? It's good to have you back, cousin. No way do I want to be responsible for that mob downstairs. The little kids do my head in with their moaning – "I'm hungry. I'm hungry." Well, so am I. So is everyone. They can bloody well go out on the rob themselves if they need to eat so much instead of complaining to me about it.'

Quist always made Dren smile. He was one real mad fucker. 'It's a good thing I'm back now, isn't it? And I've got a job for us. For all of us.'

'Good, because I was getting a bit bored.' Quist slapped his hands together. 'Who're we going to fuck up?'

'The whole city. Tomorrow night.'

'Fuck, you serious?' Quist's face lit up.

'That's not even the crazy bit,' said Dren, smiling. 'We're doing it to help the Hanran.'

The humour drained from Quist's face in an instant. 'Now I know you're taking the piss.'

'I'm not. I'm really not. We're going to save a princess.'

Quist looked like he'd just eaten something rank. 'What is this? Some fairy tale? What fucking princess?'

'She's actually the queen. We have to get her out of Jia.'

'Why should I give a shit about a queen or a princess? Eh?'

'The Hanran need to get her to Meigore so they can join the war against the Skulls.'

'Again – what's that got to do with me?' Quist jumped up, his voice rising. 'Why do I care what the fucking Hanran tell us to do? Why haven't you told them to go jump off a cliff?'

'Hey, listen to me,' said Dren. 'I spent time with them, with the old man and his son. I understand now what they're doing. Why we need to help. It's important.'

Quist waved him off. 'Like fuck. You and me are important. Killing Skulls is important. Nothing else matters.'

'We need to do this if we're ever going to get rid of the Skulls. What we've been doing isn't even hurting them. But together—'

'Who wants to get rid of the Skulls?' interrupted Quist. 'I'm happy with the way things are. I'm glad they invaded. Because I'm free. No family. No job. No fucking Shulka. I'm not up at dawn, sweating my arse off on some stinking fishing boat. I get up when I want, take what I need and kill anyone who gets in my way. I'm a fucking wolf – just like you.'

'We're living in a shit hole,' said Dren. 'In ruins. What's good about that? With Skulls marching up and down the street, arresting people because they don't like the look of us. It's not right. We deserve better. All of Jia deserves better. And we can help make it happen. Isn't that something worth doing?'

Quist chuckled and gave Dren a strange look. 'Are you sure you're you? Because you sure as fuck don't sound like you. You didn't give a shit about anyone when you blew up the square or sent kids to die with bombs strapped to their chests, but now you want to do the right thing?'

'I was wrong. I was so wrong to do any of that. I see that now.'

'Yeah? Well, maybe you were right and now the fucking Hanran's got your head all screwed up? Maybe that's what's happened.'

'I don't understand. I thought you'd want to do the right thing. We can help people.'

'I help myself. Then you. Then those kids downstairs – and even that I'm easy about.' Quist ran his hand through his hair. 'What is it they want "us" to do, anyway?'

'There's a boat coming over from Meigore. A group of Shulka are bringing the princess to meet it. They don't want the Skulls or the Daijaku coming after them so we're going to keep them busy here. We're going to set bombs off all over the city so the Egril don't know which way to turn. They'll be too busy chasing us to go after the boat.'

'So, let me get this straight. You, or rather the Shulka, want us to go out and bomb stuff so we get Daijaku chasing after us, instead of them chasing the Shulka? You'd rather have them kill us instead of the fucking Shulka?' Quist wouldn't even look at Dren. He was too busy shaking his head and getting worked up. 'You're fucking mad. They knocked the sense out of you – they really did.'

The tone in Quist's voice had Dren concerned enough to look if his friend had a weapon to hand. Fights started over far less and, for the first time in his life, Dren could see the possibility of violence brewing between them. He forced himself to keep his voice calm. 'Trust me. We have to do this.'

Quist went to say something but stopped himself. He took a deep breath, glanced at Dren over his shoulder, no hiding the fury in his eyes. 'Fine. You say we do it, we do it. As I said, I've got no interest in being a leader to anyone. But don't make this a habit. I'm not in anyone's army.'

Dren held up both hands. 'Sure. I promise. Just this once.'

'Then let's go tell the others the good news,' said Quist and headed back downstairs, leaving Dren alone on the roof. He knew Quist would come round to his way of thinking. He only hoped it would be sooner rather than later.

DAY SEVEN

51

Tinnstra

Olyisius Mountain

It was quiet inside the temple, away from the driving wind and snow. The stillness was quite disconcerting. Outside, there was a war, people were dying, and yet inside, it was as if everything was well and at peace. Tinnstra felt like an intruder walking where she had no right.

There were no windows, no natural light of any sort, and yet a faint green glow illuminated the interior of the chamber well enough to see. Tinnstra couldn't find the source. It was just ... everywhere. It revealed an impossible space. 'How can this be?' she said. 'This room? It's too large! It must be over five hundred yards from one side to the other.'

Greener smiled. 'Who knows? Greater people than me created this, back in the old world. Some say it was Ruus himself who built it. All I know is what it can do, where it can take us.'

Stone alcoves lined the walls, etched with patterns from floor to ceiling. Tinnstra knelt and traced her fingers over them. Intricate carvings of words and lines in a language she didn't recognise and certainly couldn't read. A language from another world, another time. They swam before her eyes as she searched for their meaning, but it was beyond her. Was this the work of a God?

She stood up, looked at the others, but they'd all been there before – had travelled through the gate before. It didn't worry them like it did her. 'Where's the gate?' she asked, a tremble in her voice. There was no door other than the one through which they'd entered.

'Each alcove connects to another temple in other parts of Jia,' said Greener. 'The Skulls seized most of them during the invasion. We don't know how they knew about them or where to find them, but they did. Only a few remain free.' He led them to the rear and stopped before a small alcove with a carving of the sun in its centre. 'This is the one to Kiyosun.'

He passed Zorique to Tinnstra. 'I need both hands free.'

Tinnstra wrapped her arms around the girl. 'Does it hurt?'

Greener smiled. 'No, not really. It's just ... different.'

'What's happening?' asked Zorique, a little quiver running through her body.

'We're going to take you somewhere warm,' said Greener. 'Somewhere safe.' He placed his hand on the carving of the sun and the green light pulsed.

'What's—' Tinnstra didn't get a chance to finish the sentence as the pulsing spread along the walls.

The alcove grew brighter and warmer, the air tanged with a touch of sea salt. Tinnstra's stomach lurched and it was difficult to see. She squeezed her eyes shut lest the light blind her. It spun around her, making her dizzy. There was a pull and a sudden tug and the ground rolled like a ship's deck at sea. Her whole body felt like it was being stretched in ways it was never meant to be. Her fear blossomed once more. *The sword can't save me. I am nothing. Nothing. Falling apart. Drifting away. Lost. Dear Gods above and below, I am lost.* She tried steadying her feet but still the world spun, faster and faster. Green light, so bright it burned her eyes even through closed lids. She wanted to let go of Greener's hand, knew she couldn't. Her joints rolled and her bones contracted. Zorique cried out and panic flared in Tinnstra. What were they doing? She wanted to be sick. She couldn't breathe. Her body was tearing itself apart. *It's all too much. A mistake. I'm going to die. Lost. Need to ... If only I could breathe ...*

The light vanished and everything became still, except the thundering of her heart. She sucked in air as she tried to find the courage to open her eyes.

'You okay?' said Greener. Zorique sniffed and let out a little half-sob.

'Tinnstra?'

She opened her eyes. They were still in the temple of Ruus. Still standing in the same spot, in front of the same alcove. Nothing had happened.

'No.' She sighed. 'What happened? What went wrong?' She looked at the others, feeling the full weight of failure, wondering how they would escape now, but the others were smiling. They looked happy.

'Let's get outside,' said Greener.

Ahead, Eris pushed the stone door open. But the cold wind didn't rush in. There was warmth and the smell of the sea instead, a bright starlit sky free of storm clouds, a land free of snow.

'Where are we?' asked Tinnstra, not believing her eyes.

'The Ascalian Mountains,' said Jao. She pointed south. 'There's Kiyosun.'

Tinnstra blinked. The ocean was far below them, stretching off into the night. It was a wondrous sight. They'd made it. She laughed. It was impossible, but they'd done it. They'd travelled hundreds of miles in an instant.

'We've no time to rest,' said Greener. 'Let's get off this mountain.' He held out his arms for Zorique. Tinnstra was hesitant to return the queen to him. She felt safer with Zorique in her arms, but she also knew she didn't have Greener's endurance, his strength. Zorique seemed to know it, too, as she eagerly reached for the Shulka.

'I don't feel well,' said Zorique as she settled into Greener's arms.

'It's just the after-effects of the magic,' said the big man. 'We'll stop soon and have something to eat.'

Jao took Tinnstra's arm. 'It's always weird the first time you go through the gate. Watch your step until everything settles down.'

Tinnstra nodded. 'Don't worry. I'm fine.' She was tired but otherwise nothing was wrong with her. In fact, all her aches and pains seemed to have disappeared. She reached up, touched her forehead and found the cut was completely healed. There wasn't even a scab of any kind. 'How …' Then she took a step and the ground lurched under her. Jao still had her arm and held her upright. Her stomach did a flip and a rush of nausea hit her. She gripped Jao as she fought to get her breath and her guts under control.

Jao chuckled. 'See what I mean?'

'Thank you.'

'Follow me,' said Eris and headed down a path only he could see.

Two hours later, Tinnstra might've been feeling better but she was too exhausted to know for sure. The only sleep she'd had in forty-eight hours was the two hours snatched by the river. The only food she'd eaten were mouthfuls stolen on the rare occasions Greener allowed them to stop. She was still on her feet through sheer force of will alone and every rest stop became a challenge to get back up again.

Winter in the Ascalian Mountains was very different from where they'd been. There was a chill in the air but nothing her cloak and coat couldn't fend off. They walked down paths of dirt and dust instead of wading through knee-deep snow. And always there was the lure of the ocean pulling them on.

Eris led the way while Jao covered the rear, making sure they left no tracks for anyone to find.

'Can the Skulls follow us through the gate?' she asked.

'I doubt it,' said Greener, 'but we can't be sure. We've lost nearly all our knowledge and understanding of magic while the Skulls have discovered theirs. Maybe they have someone who knows how the gates work. I hope not.'

Tinnstra glanced back up the mountain, looking for the telltale specks of white armour that meant they were still being hunted, but there were none. They were safe for now.

Her thoughts drifted to Monon and the others. It was safety paid for with their blood. More lives lost so that a child might live. How many more before they got her away? How many before Jia was free? If what Aasgod said was true, it would be over a decade before Zorique would be powerful enough to face Raaku. The death toll by then would be incalculable.

They were more than halfway down the mountain when the sun appeared, crawling up over the horizon, colouring the sky red and indigo, revealing the sea properly for the first time. The sight made them all pause. Tinnstra had never seen anything so beautiful, so vast. The light glistened and gleamed across the water, full of hope and promise.

'How long does it take to sail here from Meigore?' Tinnstra asked, mesmerised. She couldn't remember the last time she'd seen the ocean. After so long in Aisair, the scale of it overwhelmed her.

Eris shrugged. 'About six or seven hours.'

'Is that all?' She gazed out across the ocean, examining the horizon to see if she could spot Meigore from where they were and failed. 'So they won't have left yet.'

'They'll be getting ready,' said Greener, 'but I doubt they'd leave before early afternoon. They'll want it to be dark before they're in sight of Kiyosun.'

Tinnstra's eye followed the coastline. The curve of Kiyosun's bay was easy to find. The city sat on a bed of rocks overlooking an empty harbour, its ochre buildings encased behind a high wall. And above it? She squinted, unsure of what she was seeing. 'What's going on down there? Looks like birds. A *lot* of birds.'

'Daijaku,' said Greener.

The word sent a shiver through Tinnstra's heart. She could see them now. They swarmed over the rooftops, the early morning sun catching the edge of their Niganntan blades.

'So many ...' whispered Eris.

'Are they looking for us?' asked Tinnstra.

'Kiyosun is an obvious destination,' said Greener. 'The Skulls could easily have sent word ahead.'

'Where's Rascan's Point?' asked Tinnstra.

'To the east,' said Jao, pointing. 'On the other side of the bay.'

Tinnstra followed her finger. 'Do we need to get close to the city?'

Jao rubbed her face as she thought about it. 'No. We go straight down the mountain, follow the main road from Anjon to Kiyosun for about two miles then cut south-east down to Rascan's. We

375

should be there by early afternoon. Then we wait and get the girl on the boat at midnight.'

'Thank the Four Gods for that.' Tinnstra had seen the horrors the Daijaku could cause. She didn't want to face a multitude of them. She doubted even her sword could protect her from so many.

'This is it, people,' said Greener. 'The last day.' He smiled at Zorique. 'We'll get you on a boat tonight that'll take you to your family in Meigore, where you'll be safe.'

Zorique didn't appear convinced. 'Will you come with me? You and Tinnstra?'

Greener hesitated before replying. 'I'm not sure. But you'll have your uncle to take care of you. And you'll be able to play with his children – your cousins.'

'I don't want to go without you,' replied Zorique, sticking out her bottom lip. 'I don't know my cousins.'

Tinnstra squeezed her hand. 'Don't worry. We won't leave you on your own. I promise. I'll come with you, whatever happens.'

They continued in silence, conserving their energy for the descent. They weaved between boulders, navigated down steep slopes, across loose shingle and jumped the occasional crevice watched by a few gnarled trees and sad shrubs.

The wind kept them moving, chasing them from the mountain-top, eager to suck the warmth from their bodies whenever they stopped. Tinnstra did her best to keep her eye on the main road, finding strength as it drew nearer.

Eris led them into a small gully and called a stop. Something had attracted his attention. Tinnstra looked around, hand on the hilt of her sword.

'Daijaku,' hissed the boy and they all dropped to the ground.

She heard it then – the beat of wings coming from behind them. Down from the peak. Movement drew her eye. Two Daijaku descended quickly. One carried a human figure in its arms. Tinnstra squinted as she tried to make out who they had ... a prisoner? No. Her blood went cold. It was the Chosen. He had followed them.

As they flew lower, closer, a familiar dread grew in Tinnstra. It

376

was the Chosen from the Kotege. The same one who'd been in Ester Street. The young one. *He'll haunt me for ever. Follow me for ever. I'll never escape him.* She pressed against the rock and closed her eyes as if that would make her invisible. But no attack came. The Daijaku didn't see them, didn't even look. They flew down the mountainside, heading for Kiyosun.

'They came from the gate,' she said, feeling defeated. 'They found a way through.'

They all looked at each other, knew what that also meant. Monon and the others must be dead.

'It changes nothing,' said Greener. 'We stick to the plan. We keep moving.'

They all nodded. What else could they do?

'How far to the road?' he asked Eris.

'There's another ravine on the other side of this gully, and then it's a straight run down to the road.'

'You and Jao go and check the way's clear,' ordered Greener.

They slipped off without another word, leaving Greener, Tinnstra and Zorique behind. The giant let the girl climb out of his arms and she went over to Tinnstra. She slipped her arms around the girl and hugged her close, enjoying the warmth of her and the pleasure of feeling Zorique hug her back. 'You okay?'

'I'm tired and hungry,' replied Zorique.

Greener handed her some cold meat.

The girl took it gratefully and immediately started nibbling only to stop. She offered the meat to Tinnstra. 'Would you like some?'

Tinnstra smiled. 'You eat it. I'm not hungry.'

Zorique didn't need telling twice. Tinnstra watched her, enjoying the moment. Part of her wished they didn't need to go on, that they could stay there, safe, hidden, together.

'How are you holding up, Tinnstra?' asked Greener.

'I'm tired, sore and about a million other things that I'm not sure I can explain,' she replied.

'It was a brave thing you did back at the overhang. Not many would've had the courage to do that.'

Tinnstra laughed. 'No one's ever said that about me before.'

'You're writing a new chapter now. The past doesn't matter. It's what you do now that counts.'

Tinnstra shook her head. 'Aasgod deserves the credit, not me.'

'Why do you say that?'

Tinnstra patted her sheathed sword. 'He gave me a magic sword. While I have it, I can't be hurt. I can't be killed. I wouldn't have done what I did without that protection.'

'I knew Aasgod well,' said Greener. 'He never—'

Eris and Jao appeared over the edge of the gully and slid down beside them.

'What did you see?' asked Greener.

'Better we show you,' replied Jao. 'The main mountain road from Anjon to Kiyosun is over there and we've got a problem.'

They followed the siblings over the edge of the gully to where the ground dipped down again into a ravine. Where once a river had flowed only a trickle now remained. A noise grew louder. A rhythmic beat from far away. Tinnstra knew it from her days at the Kotege. Marching. Soldiers on the move.

The distant rumbling intensified as they slowly weaved their way along the ravine. Eris signalled to keep low as they clambered up the other side. They stopped below the top and Greener placed Zorique on the ground, signalling her to keep quiet and stay still. The girl nodded, doing her best to look brave. Tinnstra gave her hand a squeeze and crawled to the top, following the others.

Hidden between two boulders, the road was only fifty yards away. The stretch of gravel track wide enough for two carts to pass side by side was one of the main transport routes between the city and the port. Now, it had a different use. Egril soldiers marched towards Kiyosun.

A small troop of cavalry led the way, followed by what looked to be an entire company of Skulls on foot – three hundred, at least – all armed with scimitars and spears. Combined with the Daijaku they'd spotted, the Egril were amassing a considerable force in Kiyosun.

Fortunate that they weren't going to the city itself. Let the Skulls fill Kiyosun with their men. Let the Daijaku fly overhead. Tinnstra and the others would pass them by and escape unseen.

All they had to do now was watch and wait for the Egril to pass. Tinnstra was glad for the rest. The sun was warm and the ground was, for her, as comfortable as any bed. Once the immediate fear of discovery had passed, Tinnstra found herself in a battle to keep her eyes open. In the end, sleep got the better of her.

She woke to a shake from Eris, crouched beside her. 'Time to go.'

The others were up and waiting. 'Sorry,' said Tinnstra.

'Don't worry about it. It's been a long haul for all of us,' said Greener. 'You deserved the rest.'

Tinnstra blushed as she stood. They picked their way through the rocks and boulders until they were finally at the bottom of the mountain. They had to climb down into a ditch deep enough for a man to all but stand in, and then back up the other side to reach the road.

There were ten yards of clear ground on the other side of the track before the forest and undergrowth resumed. 'Shouldn't we get off the road and travel through the woods?' asked Tinnstra. 'We're really exposed here.'

'We'll make better time on the road for now,' said Eris. 'And the Skulls should be far enough ahead of us not to be of any concern.'

They followed the road for another hour without sight or sound of anyone else, leaving the mountain behind as the road curved south through a valley and on towards the port. Dry grass covered the banks on either side and the occasional tree, bent over by the wind and desperate for water, marked the way. At a particularly monstrous-looking one, Eris led them off the road and up the slope.

From the crest of the hill, Kiyosun spread out below them with the emerald-green sea glistening beyond. She'd heard a lot about Kiyosun, how it was Jia's busiest port, but there wasn't a single ship in sight now. The city itself looked squashed into a tiny spit of land, a tight knot of ochre buildings with none of the uniqueness of Aisair.

Above the city flew the Daijaku. They swooped and soared, riding the wind, Niganntan blades in hand.

'The city will be a fortress once the other Skulls arrive,' said Tinnstra, trying to ignore the dread in her gut.

'There are still ways to get in and out that the Skulls don't know about,' said Greener. 'Old smuggling routes we still make use of. Tunnels under the walls. There was as much illegal trade being done out of the city as there was legitimate business.' He pointed to the east. 'But the main smuggling route came in through Rascan's Bay. It's hidden from sight until you're only a few yards from it, and the bay is deep enough for a frigate to sail in.'

'And that's where we're going?' asked Tinnstra.

'Exactly.'

Tinnstra looked back at the city. She was glad to be heading anywhere but there. She didn't fancy anyone's chances in Kiyosun.

52

Jax

Kiyosun

Jax lay in the dark, unable to move, eyes closed. He hurt in more ways than he'd thought possible. The Skulls had worked him over good and proper. They hadn't bothered with questions. Revenge didn't need answers. They'd come at him with fists, boots, clubs and whatever else had been to hand. Battered one way, beaten back the other. That was the price for trying to escape and failing.

Something was stuck to his face, around his mouth, under his nose. Dried blood. Jax hurt too much to try and brush it off. His mouth was parched and his lips cracked. Maybe there was water in the cell, but at that moment, looking was beyond him.

Thinking back, he knew he should have left Kara's boys to deal with the Chosen. Left her, too. Maybe it made him a bad leader but he'd never been able to walk away – not when he could stay and fight instead.

That Chosen was something else, though. The way she turned into smoke, disappearing from one place, reappearing in another. That axe of hers claiming the lives of anyone she'd missed with her baton. Jax had tried his best. He'd charged her, swinging his stolen sword, screaming his lungs out, but a one-armed old man never had a chance against that kind of power. She'd swatted him down without even breaking stride.

He thought some of the others had been taken prisoner. He'd heard the sounds of cell doors opening and cries of pain, but no one dared call out to each other. Better to be quiet and be left alone, even if it was only for a few minutes. Any respite.

He tried not to imagine what was to come next. Eventually, it would be the time for questioning again. The Skulls would be more inventive – they'd be treating Jax more seriously, for sure. No more playing the bumbling idiot. Still, he only had to hold out for one more day. If Aasgod had managed to get the prince and princess out of Aisair, if Monon had found them, they'd all be on their way to meet the Meigore boat soon enough. At least all the deaths would be worth something then. Hope could live on. *If, if, if . . .*

The bolts slid back with a clang. Rusted hinges groaned as the main doors to the cellar opened. Skulls entered with a prisoner.

The Skulls dragged the prisoner along the corridor. The door to his cell opened. A body hit the floor hard. The door slammed shut. Bolts rammed into place. *Welcome to hell, whoever you are.*

'Father.'

Jax must have drifted off, been dreaming. For a heartbeat, he'd heard Kaine's voice, thought him near. It was a mistake, though. His son had got away.

'Father.'

Kaine? No. It was the new prisoner.

'Father. It's me.'

Jax opened his eyes. It *was* Kaine. No mistake. No trick of his imagination. Jax rolled onto his knees and crawled over to his son. He reached out, pulled his son to him, shivering with the pain of it. 'Kaine. What have you done? Why are you here?'

'They have a mind-reader. A Chosen.'

'Where? Here?' He let go of his son. A mind-reader was not good news.

'Yes.'

'Are you sure?' That changed everything. There would be no torture. No resistance. The Egril would know everything instantly. *Everything.*

'Kara's girl told me.'

'*Shit.*'

Neither spoke. There was no need. Jax knew why Kaine was

there. A strange part of Jax felt a surge of pride. He'd raised his boy well, despite everything. Not many had that kind of strength.

'I'm glad it's you,' said Jax. 'But I wish it wasn't. I wish you were far from here, living a different life.'

'We only get to live the one we've been given. And it's been a good one.'

'Your mother would be so proud of you.'

'As she was of you. As I am.'

'Maybe you'd have been better off if I were a cobbler or a butcher. Following in my footsteps would've been easier then.'

'But less rewarding. We've made a difference. Good will come from all of this.'

'I always thought I'd die fighting, a sword in my hand. Even after I lost my arm. I never thought it would be in a prison cell in some shitty basement.'

'I'm sorry, Father.'

'There's nothing to apologise for. You had nothing to do with these bastards invading us. It was our fault for not anticipating what Raaku had planned. We never took them seriously. Never realised the power he had, what he could do.'

'Still …'

'Here we are.' Jax hugged his son again. One last time. 'I love you, son.'

'I love you, too.'

They held on to each other as Jax recalled a lifetime of memories; the moment his wife, Iss, told him he was going to be a father, watching her stomach swell, feeling his son kick for the first time, holding him as he came into the world, rocking him to sleep, watching him grow, into a boy, into a man, into a Shulka. He saw the life Kaine wasn't going to have as well: a wife, a child or two, grandchildren. Everything stopped here.

Kaine let go. Tears sprang in Jax's eyes as he suddenly grasped nothing but air – as if his son were already lost to him. Gone. Nothing but a memory.

'Here.' Kaine held his hand up and Jax saw the folded piece of paper. Kaine opened it and Jax saw the black powder within. Tears sprang to his eyes as Kaine licked half of it. No hesitation.

His brave boy. Dear Gods, what an end for them both.

Kaine passed the rest to Jax. 'We're in this together.'

Jax licked it. Death was bitter on his tongue but surprisingly easy to swallow. He crumpled the paper and threw it against the far wall. That was that. It was over.

'Do you remember the summer we went to the island of Craos?' said Kaine.

'When you were seven?' Jax closed his eyes. Beautiful blue skies under a warm sun. Seafood for every meal, plucked straight from the ocean. Wine. Nothing to do but laugh with Iss and Kaine. 'How could I forget?'

'I wandered off and climbed up the cliff . . .'

'And got stuck. I nearly died when I saw you up there, screaming for help.'

'You rescued me.'

'That was my job.'

'You did it well. The best.' Kaine's voice was slower, slurred.

Jax felt hot, a little dizzy. 'It was the best job.' His stomach cramped. He was going to be sick. He got onto his knees, propped himself up with his hand. 'Kaine, I—'

A spasm knocked him down. His face pressed against the cold stone floor. Bile shot up his throat, choking him. Couldn't breathe. Couldn't think. The room spun. So, this was dying.

Darkness called. He welcomed it. An end to the pain, the failure. Peace. Together with Kaine.

'What the fuck is going on here?'

Jax squinted. A white-haired man stood over him, skulls on his shoulders. Chosen. Jax smiled. 'I'm dying.'

A hand reached out for him. 'No. No, you're not.'

53
Yas

Kiyosun

Little Ro was crying and nothing Yas did could stop him. It wasn't surprising, not after the turmoil of the last twenty-four hours, but it made everyone's nerves even more frayed. Ma was trying to pack while Gris kept watch at the window. Yas hadn't wanted the Shulka to stay but Kaine had insisted and she was starting to see his point. They were in a world of trouble and a strong arm with a knife would come in handy before too long. Truth was, though, she didn't really mind. The old man had a welcome air of calm about him. He made her feel safe despite everything.

'I still don't understand why we need to leave,' said Ma, all sour-faced as she stuffed some clothes into a travel bag. 'This is our home. Haven't we been through enough?'

Yas sat on a chair with Little Ro on her lap, holding him tight. 'Because the Egril have captured one of the Hanran leaders and she knows I was helping them. If she talks, the Skulls will come here. We have to go. Hide somewhere safe.'

'So why wait? Why not go now? Before anyone turns up?'

'Because the curfew is on, Ma. We go outside and get spotted, we'll be arrested for sure.'

Ma stopped what she was doing and looked at Yas with utter disappointment written all over her face. 'Why did you have to get involved?'

'Because it felt like the right thing to do at the time.'

'You're a mother – what were you thinking?'

'I did it so Ro could have a better life – one without the Egril on every street corner.'

Ma didn't bother replying. She just tutted in a way that summed up how stupid she thought her daughter was and went back to her packing. The bloody woman would never understand.

Yas wiped some snot from Little Ro's nose. 'It's all right. Mamma's here. Everything is going to be okay,' she cooed. She only wished she could be sure. Truth was, she'd made a right mess of it all and no mistake. She shouldn't have got involved. Ma was right, Little Ro had to be her priority. Why worry about his future if she put him in danger today?

'Sun's nearly up,' said Gris from the window. 'Make sure you've got everything you need. I want to be out the door as fast as we can.'

'We'll be ready,' said Yas, and Ma tutted again.

'Have you got any weapons?' asked the Shulka.

'Does she look like she's got any bloody weapons?' spat Ma.

Yas held up a hand to keep her quiet. 'No. Not really. Maybe a kitchen knife I could use. If I had to, that is.'

'Take the knife. Take whatever you think can hurt a man. Until we're safe, a weapon's more important than food or clothes. If someone tries stopping you, kill them. Don't think about it, don't hesitate. If it's a choice between them dying or you or the kid dying, then it's no choice at all.'

'You don't have to tell me that. Especially after everything you Hanran have put me through.'

'Kara didn't have any choice about that,' said Gris.

At the mention of Kara's name, anger flared up in her gut. If not for Kara, Yas would be living a normal life – or what passed for normal under the Egril. Surviving. Not about to go on the run. 'All that for nothing.' She still took the knife, though. No way was she going anywhere without a weapon.

Gris checked the window again. 'Sun's up. We can get out of here.'

Yas put on her coat, slipped the knife inside the lining.

'I can't believe we're doing this,' said Ma.

'You can stay here, Ma. You really can.' Yas got Ro into his coat then shifted him onto her hip. 'And when the Skulls kick the door down, you lay into them with that tongue of yours and I'm sure they'll run for the hills.' She stared at Ma, daring her to say anything else. 'Good. Now let's get out of here.'

'We're only going six or seven streets down,' said Gris. He opened the door. 'A friend's place. She's got a cellar we can hide you in for a day or two, then we'll move again.'

'A day or two ...' Ma stopped herself and put on her coat instead. 'It is what it is. As you say: let's go.'

'If we see Skulls, don't panic,' Gris said as he led them down the stairs. 'We're just a family going to see some friends.'

It was quiet out in the street. After the fighting yesterday, Yas didn't blame most people for staying inside. That's where she'd be if she could. Mrs Saslis was coming out of her place two doors down with her husband and nodded a greeting, looking as scared as Yas felt. Yas caught her glancing at Gris, no doubt wondering who he was and what he was doing with Yas at that time of the morning. Probably give her something to talk about for the next few days, nosy old cow that she was.

At least Little Ro brightened up once they were outside. He even managed to find his smile again as he rested his head on Yas's shoulder.

They saw the first Skull on the next street, too far away for him to stop them. Curfew might be over but if they got searched, the weapons would be enough to hang them all. Gris set a brisk pace as they headed west.

A shadow passed quickly along the road like a cloud crossing the sun. Then another. And another. They heard the sound next – the beat of wings. Daijaku.

'I've never seen so many,' gasped Yas. She hugged Ro tighter and covered his eyes with her hand.

'Are they looking for us?' asked Ma, her voice trembling.

'They're just trying to intimidate everyone,' said Gris. 'They're too high up to be looking for anyone in particular.'

'They're doing a bloody good job of it,' said Ma. 'Let's go back.'

Yas hooked her spare arm through her mother's, pulled her forward. 'It's not safe there.'

They kept walking but their eyes were on the skies as the Daijaku swarmed above. 'Have they been here the whole time?' asked Ma.

'Must've flown in during the night,' replied Gris. 'Kiyosun only had about a dozen stationed here before.'

Yas's heart sank. 'They know the princess is coming here, don't they?'

'Yeah, I think they do.' Gris put out an arm and stopped everyone. 'Shit.'

The end of the street was filling up with Skulls. At least a dozen. They'd be no getting past them.

'What do we do?' said Yas.

A grey-haired man walked out of one of the houses opposite them. 'This way,' said Gris as he headed over. 'Excuse me.'

The man looked up, shocked and scared. He knew no good came from a stranger approaching in the street. He tried to go back inside his house, but Gris's hand was on the door, stopping it from closing. 'We're not going to hurt you. We just need your help.'

Yas and Ma followed the Shulka as he pushed the man inside, and then shut the door as quickly as she could.

The man backed away towards the stairs, hands held up and eyes wide with fear. 'Please don't hurt me. I haven't got any money.'

'Which one's yours?' growled Gris, towering over him.

'It's all right,' said Yas, letting the old man see Ro on her hip. 'We just have to get off the street for a while. The Skulls are rounding up people.'

That scared him even more. 'Can't you go to your own place?'

'Where are your rooms?' demanded Gris again.

The man glanced back over his shoulder and up the stairs. 'Sec … second floor.'

His rooms were much like Yas's own but the man obviously lived alone. A single bed, with unmade sheets, occupied one corner. The dining table was smaller and covered in stubs of candles and some empty flagons. Yas fought the urge to open the windows to let some fresh air in to replace the stale odour.

'Sit down.' Gris pointed at a chair.

'But ... but ...' The man didn't move, just looked from Gris to Yas and back again.

Yas sighed. 'Sit, please. We'll be out of here as quick as we can.' The man sank down without any more protest, and Yas gave Ro to Ma before joining Gris at the window. The formations of Daijaku still filled the skies, but more worrying was what was happening on the street. The Skulls had split up into two groups, each taking a side of the street. 'Are they searching each house?'

'Looks like it.' Gris let the curtain fall into place. 'We're in trouble.'

Yas looked at Ma holding Little Ro. The poor thing knew something was wrong, could see it in his mother's face. The old man was panicking, too. Yas couldn't blame him. The Skulls wouldn't care that he was harbouring fugitives against his will. He'd get the rope along with the rest of them.

She walked over to the man. 'What's your name?'

'H ... Hou ... Houghter.' The man had gone deathly white and was shaking all over.

Yas bent down so she could look him in the eye. 'My name's Yas. I'm sorry we've brought our problems to you but that seems to be the way the world works these days – we all have to do things that we have no choice in.'

'I won't say a word. I promise. If you go now, I'll keep quiet.'

'Thing is, Houghter, the Skulls are looking for me and that man there.' Yas pointed her thumb over her shoulder at Gris. 'Anyone with us will be arrested, too.'

'But I don't know you. I've got nothing to do with you,' said Houghter.

'The Skulls don't care. They'll hang all of us. Do you want to hang?'

'N ... n ... no.'

'Good. Because that lady there is my mother and she's holding my son and I don't want them to hang, either.'

Houghter looked at them as if seeing them for the first time. 'But what do we do? If they find you here ...'

Yas glanced over at Ma. She wouldn't like this but Yas couldn't see any other way. 'I'm going to leave with my friend over there, but my ma and my son are staying.'

'No, we're not—' said Ma, but Yas silenced her with a finger.

She turned her attention back to Houghter. 'You two can pretend to be happy families when they come. Let Ma do the talking and the Skulls will leave you alone. Once it's safe, she'll be on her way and you can carry on as normal.'

The old man nodded. 'Okay.'

'But,' said Yas, pulling the knife from her coat and placing the tip of the blade next to Houghter's eye, 'if anything happens to her or my son because you didn't play along, my friend and I will be back, and you'll wish the Skulls had hanged you. Got it?'

Houghter stared at the blade. 'Got it.'

'Right. Glad that's settled.' Yas put the knife away and went back over to Ma. She took her son in her arms and kissed him, filling her lungs with that wonderful scent of his, feeling his warmth, trying to remember every detail of her perfect boy. 'You be good for Grandma, eh?' She kissed him again. 'I love you.' She passed him back to Ma, hating having to do it.

'I'll look after him,' said Ma.

Yas kissed her cheek, grateful that she wasn't going to have another fight over what to do. It was hard enough as it was. Her heart broke a little bit more with every step she took to the door, where Gris waited.

Gris nodded at her. 'It's the right thing to do.'

Yas didn't say anything, just walked through the door into the hallway without looking back. She didn't want the sight of her crying to be the last thing Ro remembered of his mother. Once the door was shut, she wiped the tears away. There'd be plenty of time for that if they got away. 'What do we do now?'

'Can't go out on the street, so that leaves the roof,' said Gris.

'But the Daijaku—'

'If we're careful, we can move around without them noticing. They're trying to scare a whole city, not look for us. Yet.'

'I really should've told her to fuck off,' said Yas as she started up the stairs.

'Told who?'

'Never mind.' There was no point cursing Kara to her friends, especially now she was a prisoner, or dead, but if she ever saw Kara alive again, she'd kill her.

The door to the roof was unlocked and Yas pushed it open enough to see out. If the sight of so many Daijaku was petrifying from the ground, it was even worse up on the roof. They filled the sky, so alien-looking, carrying their bloody spear-swords. It wasn't hard to imagine being cut open by one of them. Yas feared she would never see her son again.

54

Jax

Kiyosun

Jax woke up. Alive. He'd taken the poison, had felt it doing its dark work, felt the world slipping away – so why wasn't he dead?

'Kaine! Kaine!' called out Jax. 'Kaine!'

No answer. Please let him be dead. Please.

He tried to move but restraints held him down. Stone walls, curved ceiling, rotten bricks were all he could see. If he lifted his head, he could see a cell door. He was still a prisoner. The Skulls had lit the room with a torch behind him somewhere. He could smell it burning, see its light flicker across the scarred walls. It scared him because he knew the light wasn't for him, it was for whoever was coming.

Footsteps. Someone was coming. Coming for him? Jax's heart beat faster. He struggled against his restraints without thinking, a primal urge to escape.

The door opened. Two Chosen stood in the doorway. A man and a woman, both white-haired. He recognised the woman from the courtyard, the one who'd flown in and stopped the escape, the one who'd killed so many of his men. Jax knew he should be frightened of her but it was the other who worried him most. The man was slight of build, but there was something about him ... The way he smiled beneath that mask of his. He held a rolled-up cloth in his hands so Jax could see the bumps and shapes in it, see the knives.

'Hello,' said the man. He walked over to a table and placed the rolled-up cloth on it.

Jax said nothing. He had enough strength to fight them. All he had to do was make it through the day.

The man looked over his shoulder at the woman. 'I think we have a tough one here.'

She smiled with no warmth. 'I knew you'd like him.'

The man addressed Jax. 'My name is Darus Monsuta, one of the Emperor's Chosen. This is my sister, Skara, also one of the Emperor's Chosen. We're going to be asking you a few questions. I won't lie – I'd rather you didn't talk. There's no fun if you do. No enjoyment.' He untied the cloth and unrolled it, letting Jax see the contents properly: a collection of blades in a variety of shapes and sizes. 'No opportunity to use some of these.'

Jax said nothing. The blades spoke loud enough. The man wasn't the mind-reader if he needed knives. Well, he could go fuck himself. Jax knew pain. And pain knew him. There was nothing the Egril could do to him that he'd not experienced before.

'Shall we start with something simple?' Darus leaned in close. Jax could see the chill in his eyes. 'What's your name?'

Jax said nothing.

'No? Not going to talk? That's good. I like the silent ones,' said Darus, grinning. He ran his fingers along his collection. The cloth was worn and frayed at the edges. The knives themselves sat inside individual sheaths but the handles were polished and well cared for and, by the way the Chosen was gazing at them, well loved. 'Which one? Which one? Which one?'

Skara leaned against the wall, looking bored as if witnessing a performance she'd seen a thousand times.

Darus pulled out a butcher's knife, the blade long and thick. Jax had seen one split a pig before. 'Now, I know I'm supposed to start off slowly – a little cut here, a little cut there, let you experience the pain without killing you. There's a routine to follow, an etiquette: cut, question, cut, question. Now, they tell me you're just a shop owner ...' He glanced at his sister. 'A carpet seller, but we all know that's not true. Your friends have gone to too much trouble for someone ordinary.'

Darus ran a finger along the edge of the blade until a line of blood appeared on his skin. He raised his eyebrows and then the cut was gone. A trick of the light somehow, meant to scare Jax.

'We know you're important, so you know there is an order to an interrogation. Everything building up to that big climax when you beg me to stop and tell me everything I want to know.'

Jax said nothing but couldn't take his eyes off the knife in Darus's hand.

The Chosen stepped closer and laid a hand on Jax's leg. He flinched, hating the sign of weakness. 'As much as I respect tradition, we don't really have time. As we chat, your lovely little princess – or should I say queen? – is on her way to this lovely city.'

Jax tried to suppress his smile. The fool had told him the princess was still free. She was going to get away. It'd been worth it. All he had to do was say nothing to this bastard. He could do that.

Darus noticed the smile and leaned in closer. 'I wouldn't look too happy just yet, my friend. I haven't started my work. All I want to know is where she's going once she gets here. Nothing more. Nothing less. One question. That's all.'

'Fuck you,' said Jax.

'Not very original. But as I said, time is of the essence, so I'm going to try something different. Instead of cut, question, cut, question, I'm going to try chop ...' Darus hacked into Jax's thigh with the butcher's knife. White-hot fire shot through Jax's body, every nerve screaming and Jax along with them. There was no holding it back. The blade had sunk deep into the meat of his leg, severing muscle, hitting bone. 'And question: where is the meeting point?'

Jax screamed and screamed. It was worse than when he'd lost his arm – that been quick, unexpected – but *this*? And dear Gods, did the mad man intend to cut Jax's leg off? The thought of that intensified the pain.

Darus jerked the knife free. He inspected the cut, and Jax could feel his fingers probing the wound, each touch another stab of agony. 'Delightful.'

The pain was too much. He felt himself fainting, the darkness calling.

'Oh no,' said Darus. 'Not yet.' Heat pulsed out of his hand into Jax, into his wound. The pain lessened, and then was gone. Just like that. The way it disappeared frightened Jax even more. It was a promise of worse to come.

Darus leaned in so Jax could see the joy on his face. 'Did you know that every Chosen has a special gift, given to them by Raaku himself? My power is to heal. Ironic, really, but it works. That's why your poison didn't kill you. That's why I can cut you up as much as I want without worrying about killing you accidently. Whatever I do, I can make it all better for you.'

Jax said nothing. He could take the pain. He could. *He could*.

The knife fell again. Harder this time. It cut through the thigh and stopped at the bone. Jax screamed and howled.

'Where?' snarled Darus, wiggling the blade against the bone. 'Where is the meeting point?'

Jax snarled and growled, fighting the pain, grinding his teeth together, spit flying out with his frenzied breathing.

Darus raised an eyebrow. 'No?' He glanced down at his knife. 'You know a human bone is a very difficult thing to cut through. You need a very sharp blade – which this is, of course – but you also need to find the right spot. Where it's weakest. Like a joint, for example. But a thigh bone? That's one of the thickest bones in the human body. Almost impossible to cut through.' He placed a hand on the back of the blade. 'But if you put enough weight behind the knife and the blade is strong enough, you don't so much cut it as break it – like this.' He pushed down, grunting with the effort. Fire shot through Jax's body. He howled, fighting the restraints as the pain grew and grew and then there was the most Godsawful snap as the bone broke.

The darkness took him, only to jolt awake a second later. He could feel the cursed magic at work in his leg.

'No respite for you, my friend,' said Darus. 'None whatsoever.' He hacked down with the butcher's knife into Jax's hip.

Jax screamed. 'No. No. No. Fuck you!'

Darus turned to his sister. 'Did you ever see such a nasty stare?'

'You think you're so special, don't you?' said Jax through gritted teeth. 'In your fancy uniform, all airs and graces. But I know better.'

'Do you?'

Jax grinned, and spat blood all over the bastard's face. So bright against his white skin. 'You Egril are just a bunch of goat-fuckers dressed up to look like normal people.'

The Chosen didn't bother to wipe the blood away. 'Really?'

Jax coughed blood over himself, grinned again. 'Goat-fuckers.'

Darus slashed the butcher's knife across his belly. Jax couldn't even scream this time. Fire and ice spread from his stomach through his body.

Darus stepped back and wiped the blood from the blade on Jax's leg, looking so fucking pleased with himself. 'Does that hurt? I imagine it does. Ten hours from now, you'll be dead, drained empty drop by drop. Not a nice way to go. But' – Darus held up a finger – 'tell me where the princess will be and I'll cut your throat right now, end it all for you as quick as that.'

'It's not the first time ... I've been cut there. I've ... survived worse,' gasped Jax. There was no getting out of that room. No survival. He had accepted that. This was about time. Let the bastard hurt him. He had to take the pain. Somehow. Or get the man to kill him first.

'Hurry up, Darus. Stop playing,' chided the woman. Darus shot her a look that made Jax think there wasn't much love between them.

'Yeah, Darus. Do what the girl says.' Jax coughed the words out as blood dribbled from his mouth. 'Then you can put a rug on her and pretend you're riding her back up in the mountains. Get her to kick you a few times to make it feel extra real.'

'Have you ever been to Egril?' asked Darus, cheeks flushed. 'Have you?'

Jax glared back at him, happy to see the man's anger flare. 'Why the fuck would I want to do that?'

'You see, long ago, as you say, we were just a bunch of mindless tribes, fighting each other, fighting you. No doubt some even, as you suggest, fucked goats.' Darus spat the last two words out, full of rage and hatred. 'But if you'd ventured from your pathetic, dying nation, you would've realised that the Egril we sent to fight you every few months were merely a distraction, a joke on our part, designed to keep you feeling superior when the truth was far different. We dressed our soldiers up in furs and chains and gave them bones to shake about, while the whole time we were laughing at your stupidity.'

'Some joke. I killed hundreds of you. You didn't seem to be laughing then.'

'You don't know the number we've sent to bleed so Kage's will could be done. Tens of thousands of us have sacrificed our lives for his glory – gone willingly to serve him in the Great Darkness. That's how kingdoms are built. On blood and bone. We've bled for him. Died for him. Sacrificed everything for Kage – the one true God. His son, Raaku, showed us the way.' The Egril's eyes widened, full of fire and fervour. 'He united us, brought order where there was chaos, built us cities in the wilderness with his own hands, and gave us one purpose – to destroy the False Gods and all those who follow them.'

'Do you really believe that shit?' asked Jax. 'That he's the son of a God? Really?'

'*I* have stood before Raaku and seen his power.' He held up his hands as if in worship. 'Raaku chose me – *me!* – to do his father's will in this world. I have bathed in his glory and I have given him my soul in exchange for the honour he has given me.'

'You're mad.'

'Just because *you* lack faith, because *you* have no purpose, do not mock those who know what they were born to do. I will send the whole world to the Great Darkness if that is what Kage requires of me.'

'You don't fool me,' said Jax. 'You're still a goat-fucker. A pretentious goat-fucker in a fancy mask.'

Darus didn't even bother replying. He swung the butcher's knife into Jax's other leg. Before he could scream, Darus took another chunk out of his good arm. Blood flew as he whipped the knife from a wound and swung it down to do its evil work once more. Again and again, he hacked at Jax. His intestines spilled out onto his lap. Jax squeezed his eyes shut and screamed and cried and prayed. The agony was unbearable. *Let death come, please*. He couldn't take this any more. The man was a monster. Evil. And Jax was just a man.

'Darus,' said Skara. 'Darus!'

'What?'

'The girl. We need the location.'

'Ah, yes. Mustn't get too carried away.' He gripped Jax's chin and felt the magic roar through him, fighting the pain like water on fire until only the memory of the agony remained. It didn't hurt any less. 'Ready to talk yet?'

Jax nodded as the world spun around him.

'Good,' said Darus. 'Now, where is the princess?'

Jax whispered something but a bubble of blood smothered the word.

Darus leaned in closer. 'Where is the princess?'

'F ... fuck ... you.'

'This just won't do. This won't do at all,' said Darus. 'I've interrogated countless numbers of Shulka since we conquered your pathetic country. So full of vim and vigour one minute and then a crying, bubbling, begging mess the next. And do you know what?'

'What?'

'There's nothing that makes me happier than when they break. That moment when their courage disappears and the hopelessness of what they face is all too apparent.'

Jax coughed blood, tried to open his eyes. He wanted to say something to show the man's words were a lie but he didn't have the strength. He was holding on to his sanity with his fingertips.

Darus leaned even closer so he could whisper in Jax's ear: 'My power doesn't just fix cuts and scrapes, you know. How would you like your arm back?'

Jax tried to pull his head away, struggling against the restraints.

'Let me show you,' sang Darus.

The magic pulsed, stronger, fiercer than before. It rode through Jax's body, wave after wave, crashing against the stump of his arm. White-hot. Shards and needles and blades of pain. Agony. Relentless. Unmerciful. He could feel it working, feel something

398

growing. Jax didn't want to look but Darus pushed his head around, dragging Jax's eyes open with his fingers.

The stump moved with every pulse, finding shape, finding form. Bones protruded through the skin, veins and arteries inched their way around, chased by blood and flesh. Jax had no words. Just pain, just horror. It was a monstrosity, an abomination, but still it grew. The pain ripped Jax apart. The magic burned his very soul. He prayed for Xin to take him, hoped his heart would burst with the strain, begged her to put an end to it all, but his Gods held no sway in that room.

The arm grew. A baby's arm, soft and pudgy. Then a child's. It grew a year every second, taking shape, gaining length. Hairs popped out and muscles developed. Twisting, turning. The fingers twitched with each spasm of pain that wracked his body. Every pulse.

Darus released him. So crazed with pain, Jax didn't even realise at first. Then his cries died in his raw throat and he looked in horror at his new arm. It moved when he willed it, the fingers obeyed his commands. Whatever the pain he'd endured, he was whole again. A man. He might've laughed through the tears, felt a small burst of joy in the misery.

'Now, where will we find Zorique?' asked Darus.

Jax looked at him with anger and hatred. He'd survived the pain and the agony and ended up with his arm back again. Even if he died in that room, he'd won. 'Fuck you,' he spat.

Darus turned to his sister. 'Hold the arm down.'

'My pleasure,' replied Skara.

'No!' screamed Jax. He pulled the arm tight to his body, struggled to keep it safe as the Chosen took hold of it, forced it back across the table. The arm was still weak, underdeveloped, and no match for Skara. She straightened it out, held it down. Darus brandished the butcher's knife.

'Please, no,' begged Jax.

Darus hacked down, through the biceps. 'The upper arm bone is nothing like the thigh bone,' he said as he worked. 'Much easier to cut through.' He hacked at the arm again. 'Not easy, of course – just easier.'

Jax hollered and screamed and cursed.

It took three more attempts before the knife stuck in the wooden table.

More blood. More pain.

Darus held up the arm. 'Shame to lose it so soon.' He threw it into a corner. 'Shall we start again?'

Blood poured from the wound, covering the floor, the table, Jax. So much of it but all Jax could do was stare at the severed arm in the corner. He'd had it back. He'd been *whole*. And now it was gone again. And the pain ... the pain ... He squeezed his eyes shut, trying to swallow the agony but it was like a fire consuming him. There was no holding it back.

'Where is Zorique going?' asked Darus.

Jax felt the darkness calling, clawing away at the edges of his vision as the flames started to fade. It was all over. His body had suffered enough. Time to join his son, his wife, his friends. 'We are the dead ...' he croaked.

'Oh no, you're not,' said Darus as he gripped Jax's skull, pouring his power into the Shulka. Jax fought it, bucking and screaming, trying to break the monster's hold on him, but he might as well have tried to stop the sun from moving. He felt the wounds healing, knitting, blood refilling his veins, the darkness retreating. His eyes snapped open to find Darus staring at him. 'Welcome back, my friend. Still feeling brave?'

'You're evil,' said Jax.

'Said the cow to the butcher.' Darus took hold of Jax's new arm.

Everyone breaks eventually.

After Darus had chopped his arm off for the third time and re-grown it for the fourth, Jax told them everything. About Rascan's Point, the time the boat was arriving, how many men he'd sent to help Zorique, every little detail he knew. He confessed through tears and sobs, a broken man. A failure. A traitor. He was covered in his own filth, his own blood, his own shame. He'd failed everyone and everything he'd believed in.

'Silence him, brother,' said Skara.

Jax looked up, saw them both staring at him in disgust. 'Please, I've told you everything. Kill me. I beg you, kill me.'

Darus laughed as if it was the funniest thing he'd ever heard. 'Kill you? Kill you? Why would we do that? You've answered but one question of the many we have. When we have Zorique, we'll be back to ask more and we can have all this fun over and over again.'

Jax screamed.

They left him in the cell in the basement. Kaine's and Kara's bodies and three freshly severed arms were with him. He cried in the dark. Alive and whole but damned for ever.

55
Yas

Kiyosun

Yas and Gris traversed the rooftops, jumping the low dividing walls, ducking under water towers and continuing to the next. They kept low so the circling Daijaku wouldn't spot them. Yas hated leaving Little Ro, even though she knew she'd had no choice. If she'd stayed, they'd all be dead. Splitting up meant everyone had a chance. Down on the street, the Skulls caused chaos as they searched house to house, but so far none had come to search the roofs. They reached the end of the block almost too quickly.

'What do we do now?' asked Yas.

Gris pointed to the rooftop on the other side of the street. 'We jump.'

Yas looked at where he pointed and the distance between the buildings. The gap was nothing. She knew she could jump that distance down on the ground easily. Hell, it looked close enough that she could almost step across the gap. But then she glanced down. A three-storey drop. There'd be no walking away from a fall like that. 'I can't do it. I'll never make it.'

'It's the only way,' said Gris. 'It's not as far as it looks.'

Yas shook her head, backed away from the edge. 'There has to be another way.'

'This is it.'

'We can take the stairs. Hide in some rooms the Skulls have already searched.'

'We'll get caught if we do that.' Gris took hold of her hand and pulled her towards the edge of the roof. 'Climb up onto the wall, swing your arms and jump. You'll make it – I promise you.'

The crashing sound of a door being kicked in echoed up the stairwell, followed by shouts and heavy footsteps. The Skulls were coming.

'Please, Yas. Don't get sacred now. Not after everything you've done.'

'You go first,' said Yas. 'Show me. If it's so easy – show me.' Anything to buy time before she had to jump.

The shouts grew louder. Another door was smashed in. A woman screamed.

'You have to follow me,' said Gris. He climbed up onto the wall, looked back down at Yas as if he was about to say something and then thought better of it. He bent his knees and launched himself across the gap, swinging his arms to build momentum.

Yas looked away, convinced he was going to fall and unable to watch him die. But there was no scream, no dull thud as his body hit the ground, just the scuff of boots on stone.

'Come on.' Gris waved her over as if that could dispel her fears. There was no way she could jump it. Even if he was over twice her age, Gris was a soldier; he'd been trained to do such things. Yas was a single mother; all she had was instinct and that told her not to jump.

A door opened at the other end of the row. Skulls were on the roof. They'd see her any moment.

'Yas, stop fucking about – jump!' hissed Gris.

Ignoring him, Yas rushed over to the door that led into the building. She stepped inside, looked down the stairs – Skulls were coming up. She was trapped.

She went back outside. Gris was still there, still waiting, but he was scared now. She could see it on his face. The Skulls would have them both if she didn't jump. She looked over the edge again and her stomach turned. She couldn't do it. 'Go! Don't wait for me.'

Gris climbed up onto the wall. 'I'm coming back. I won't leave you.'

'No! Don't be stupid. They'll catch us both. I'll hide.'

He looked at her, not wanting to leave her, not wanting to get caught. 'Fuck. *Fuck*.' He stepped down off the wall, decision made, shook his head at her. 'Don't get caught.' And then he was gone. And Yas was alone on the roof with Skulls coming at her from every direction.

'You're an idiot, Yas,' she whispered to herself. She scanned the rooftop. There were a couple of chairs lying around but not much else up there. Nowhere to hide.

The stomp of the Skulls' boots grew louder as they climbed up the stairs. The others at the far end of the terrace were out of sight for now but not for long. What could she do? She couldn't give herself up.

And then she saw it, right in front of her. The water tower. Every house in the terrace had one. She could hide inside until it was safe to come out.

She climbed the ladder that ran up the side of it, slid back the bolts to the hatch and peered into the gloom. Light reflected off the water at the bottom of the tower, but there wasn't much by the looks of it. She could jump in there and end up breaking her leg easily enough if there wasn't enough water to break her fall. And even if she didn't, how would she get back out again? There was no ladder on the inside. Nothing to use to climb out later.

Yas went to climb down but the Skulls on the roof were halfway to her and the ones in the stairwell would be out any second. She had no choice. The tower was her only option. She climbed inside and let her body dangle into the dark, holding on to the edge of the hatch with her fingertips while her feet touched nothing but air. *Shit*. She had no choice.

She let go and the hatch fell shut.

The world went dark as she plunged into the water and hit the bottom of the tank. Her legs buckled under her from the impact, but all she could think about was the cold. It burned through her, shutting off her thoughts and stealing her breath. She staggered to her feet somehow, her limbs all but frozen, and then her lungs started working overtime, breathing in and out as fast as she could, trying to get some air back in. She could feel the panic rising in her as the cold spread through her body, stabbing her.

With the hatch shut, Yas couldn't see a thing. Not even her hand in front of her face. But Yas wasn't a child, she wasn't afraid of the dark. The only thing she feared were the men in the white armour with the curved swords who *would* kill her. She had to calm down, get back in control. She was cold, nothing more. She forced her breathing to slow as the shock of being in the ice-cold water passed.

She waited in the dark, listening – wondering how she'd even know when it was safe to come out, never mind *how* she'd get out. She ran her hand over the side of the tower. The wood was smooth, coated with a lacquer that made the water run off it. Climbing wasn't going to be possible. She was stuck. She was going to die in there.

She should've taken her chances and jumped.

The cold water was already starting to have an effect on her. She couldn't feel her feet and her whole body had the shivers and shakes.

She definitely should've jumped.

Yas flinched as the door at the top of the stairwell banged open. Footsteps thumped on the roof and a voice called out. He was answered by one of the Skulls searching from the other end. Yas couldn't understand a word of it, but whatever was said got a good laugh from them all. They sounded young, like a bunch of lads messing about together. Not men set on killing innocent people.

Of course, Yas was hardly innocent. She probably had more blood on her hands than all the Skulls out there on the roof put together. Maybe more than Gris and the other Shulka she'd met.

The shivering got worse. She stuck her hands under her armpits and hugged herself, trying to keep as much warmth in her body as she could, and listened to the Skulls have a good old natter a few feet away, unaware she was freezing to death.

Yas willed them to leave, to give up and get off that roof. Her feet were numb, her body shook and her teeth chattered. It was too cold. She should've jumped.

Raised voices from outside drew her back to the present. One of the Skulls was cursing the others, judging by the tone of it. The more pissed off he got, the more the others laughed. Then Yas heard feet on the ladder, a clang every time a foot stepped on a rung. One of them was climbing up to look inside the tower. She was done for. There was no way he'd not see her white face gawping up when he opened the hatch and let the light in.

Clang. Clang. Clang.

Up he climbed, taking his sweet time.

Clang. Clang. Clang.

Her eyes tracked the sound in the dark. Not long now. A few more steps.

Clang. Clang—

The Skull stopped. He was at the hatch. The hinges creaked.

With a deep breath, Yas ducked down into the water. The cold nearly made her surface immediately, but she found a protruding beam and held herself under. Light streamed into the tower. She kept her face down and prayed there were enough shadows for him not to notice she was there.

Seconds passed like hours. Yas expected a spear in the back as she watched the sunlight flicker in the water, praying for it to disappear once more. Her lungs burned while the cold water made her want to scream. Holding on became a hard thing to do, an impossible thing. She was losing feeling and struggled to think.

Then the hatch closed and the light disappeared. Yas shot up out of the water, sucking in air. She wiped her face and squeezed her hair, tried to shake off the water without making too much noise, but the cold had seeped into her skin and found her bones – every part of her felt frozen. Her clothes were one big sodden weight pressing down on her body. She listened to the Skull climb back to the roof, grumbling at the others with every step as her legs shook. Yas tried to rub some life into her hands but even that was beyond her. Too difficult. She was too tired. Even shivering was too much effort for her. She wanted to sit down. *Sleep*.

No. She shook her head. Sleep later. The Skulls were still outside, talking. Why wouldn't they go? She wanted to scream at them, tell them to leave, leave them all alone. Tears welled up in Yas's eyes. What had she done? Why had she got involved? For what? To die in a water tower? To be hanged by Skulls? To leave Little Ro?

Eventually, the Skulls' voices faded and disappeared. Now was the time. Yas had to find some way to climb out of the tower. She groped through the darkness until she reached a wall. There had to be some handhold she could use, something to help haul herself out. She waded around the tower, running her hands up and down, faster and faster, hoping to find something. Nothing. She kept going, unsure of where she'd started or where to finish or when to admit defeat. In the end, her legs made the decision for her as one buckled under the other and Yas fell face first into the water.

The cold shocked her awake and she scrambled onto her knees, desperate to catch her breath. She was submerged to her neck. She knew she should stand, keep as much of her body above the water as she could, but she was so *tired*.

She'd get up in a minute. Just needed to rest. She leaned her head against the side of the tower. Closed her eyes. She didn't even feel the cold that much any more.

A noise and sudden light startled her. She brought her hand up to shade her eyes. The hatch had opened.

'Yas?' A man's voice. 'Yas? It's me, Gris.'

'Help.' Yas meant to shout but only managed to squeak the word out. When she tried to stand, her legs were locked up from the cold, so she only managed to splash about.

'I'll get you out of there.' Gris dropped something. It hit the water next to her. She had to squint to see what it was – a rope. 'Put the loop over you and under your arms. I'll pull you up.'

It took several attempts before Yas could even pick up the rope. She'd lost all her coordination. Flailing like a drunk, she managed to loop the rope around herself as Gris had instructed and collapsed back into it. She felt a pull, tentative at first, and then she was lifted out of the water. She rose towards the light, a square floating in black, a way out. Hands reached for her as everything went dark.

★

'Yas, don't give up on me.'

A voice in the darkness.

'Yas. Wake up. Come on.'

Gris's voice. She could feel the sun on her skin. Warmth. Her eyes fluttered. So tired still. Sleep.

'Don't you ignore me,' Gris insisted. Why wouldn't he leave her be? Someone slapped her face. It stung, hurt. Yas waved her arm at whoever it was – Gris? 'Open your eyes. I know you can hear me.'

She opened her eyes, saw the Shulka leaning over her. 'You came back for me.'

Gris grinned. A scared grin. 'Of course I did. A crazy girl like you needs saving. You won't jump a gap a few feet wide but you'll dive right into a water tower?' He shook his head in disbelief. 'Sorry it took so long but I had to wait for the Skulls to leave.'

'B … b … better late than never.'

Gris hooked an arm around her. 'We have to get you on your feet and off this roof. One of the rooms downstairs must have some dry clothes, maybe some hot water to drink.'

Yas nodded but it took all she had left to do that. Her strength was gone and the darkness threatened to reclaim her.

'Stay with me,' said Gris as he carried her into the stairwell. 'Don't sleep yet. We need to get you warm first.'

The door to the third floor had been kicked in. They went inside. The rest of the rooms matched the door. A young woman, around Yas's age, lay dead in the middle of the room. Her blood coated the floor.

'Bastards,' said Gris as he carried Yas into the bedroom. He stripped the wet clothes off her, dressed her from the dead woman's wardrobe and then wrapped her up in a blanket. Yas said nothing, was barely aware of what he was doing. He disappeared and Yas might have slept, or maybe she just closed her eyes, but then he was back with a mug of warm water. It burned as she drank but it hardly dented the pit of ice in her gut. Gris returned with another and Yas drank that, too.

'You didn't get that from the water tower, did you?' she said, and then the black took her once more.

56

Dren

Kiyosun

Nineteen faces watched Dren over the black orbs stacked up in the middle of the room, ready to be divided between them all. None of them looked happy about what he was asking them to do. Quist's sniping comments and constant eye-rolling weren't helping, and it was really starting to piss him off. They were his troops. He'd found them, given them shelter and food when they couldn't look after themselves. That should've made them more obedient.

Time to get them on board. 'It's going to be easy. Once the eleven o'clock bell rings, we start. Falsa and Buser take out the Skull checkpoint on Houseman Street. Boom. Jonnie and Hara hear that and then they go next – hit the Skulls on Market Street. Then it's Ange and Hicks over on Lockton, followed by Davos and Spelk at the barracks, Lo and Silus at the docks, Thos and Rudd hit the Northern Way, Bean and Yunis strike Lenis Square, Mirin and Garo blow up the checkpoint at the East Gate and finally Krin and Zola hit the West gate. Once you're done, get off the roofs and hide somewhere until the morning, then come back here.'

'What about you?' asked Falsa. 'What are you and Quist doing?'

Quist leaned against a wall, arms crossed and scowling. 'Yeah, what are we doing?'

Dren grinned. He'd been waiting for this. 'We're going for the big one. We're gonna hit the Council House.'

Everyone stared at him. Even Quist was stuck for something to say.

'It's untouchable, right?' said Dren. 'The Skulls strut around there like they own the place, right?'

A smile started to form on Quist's face. 'Right.'

'I want to put the shits up them. We're helping the Hanran, right? But it's more than that. Most people out there in Kiyosun won't know that. All they'll remember is that tonight was the night we showed the Skulls, and the rest of them hiding behind their doors, who really controls this city. Right?'

Quist nodded. 'Right.'

'I want the Skulls to come home to a place that's missing a wall or two, like we do,' continued Dren. 'I want the Skulls to find a load of rubble where they used to eat and drink. I want them to know that someone came into their home and fucked it up good and proper. Just like they did to ours.'

'Right.' Falsa, Mirin, Spelk and a couple of the others joined in, sharing a sense of budding excitement.

'This is the night we show them that *we* rule this city. It's ours, and we'll strike anywhere and hit anyone we want,' said Dren, his voice loud and proud. He looked from face to face, straight in their eyes. 'Right?'

Rudd, Ange, Garo, Silus, Lo and Falsa jumped to their feet. 'Right!'

Quist howled. Falsa joined him. And then they were all howling, jumping up and down, hugging each other, getting their blood good and fired up. Dren watched them – his pack. A bunch of blood-thirsty animals. He'd got it all wrong with Quist by trying to explain the bigger picture. It was all about the mayhem with this lot. The buzz of doing stuff that no one else had the balls to do.

They came to him then, in their pairs, and collected the orbs. Dren handed them out and made sure they all knew to be careful with them. Everyone got a word of encouragement, a smile, whatever he knew worked.

'Remember,' he told them, 'keep them wrapped up, in sacks, or whatever you've got, wear gloves, scarves around your mouths, if need be. You don't want to be touching these things longer than you have to. They can make you sick and none of us want that.'

That little nugget wiped away a few smiles but it was what it was.

'When it's time, you need to smear blood on it,' continued Dren. 'You'll feel it heat up, see the liquid inside start to move around. That's when you throw it. Don't fuck about or hesitate or any of that shit because all it'll do is get you killed. Just lob it at your target and get your head down.'

Quist came over once he'd finished handing out the orbs. He nodded down at the last few. 'That's the lot done, then?'

Dren grinned. 'Yeah, but we can steal more. The Skulls are keeping them somewhere. We'll find them.'

'You had me worried earlier,' said Quist. 'Thought we'd lost you.'

Dren looked at his cousin. There was something in his voice that made Dren uncomfortable. 'It's just been a mad couple of days, is all. I'm still me. We're good?'

'We're good.'

'Good.' They both stood there, looking at each other, and Dren knew, at that moment, neither of them believed it. Something had changed. Something he didn't know how to fix, and – worse than that – he wasn't sure if he wanted to.

Quist took a step towards the door. 'I gotta go out for a couple of hours. I'll be back before dark.'

'Sure,' replied Dren. 'Don't leave it too late. I want everyone in place before curfew.'

Quist pointed at him. 'The patient man, eh? Don't worry. I'll be here in time.'

Dren watched him go, saw Falsa slip in beside his cousin as they headed down the stairs. That surprised him. He hadn't thought they were that close. Seemed a few things might have changed in the last couple of days.

When he was alone, he filled a backpack with the last seven orbs. More than enough for what they needed to do. Maybe he and Quist could get inside the Council House and do some real damage. He shivered. The Skulls had really done a number on him in there. The thought of returning there made him feel sick, and that was a weakness he couldn't tolerate. He needed his strength restored – his confidence – and the only way to do that was to destroy what frightened him. Put the fear back into those bastards.

On the roof, a load of bricks and stones were piled up in one corner. After making sure he was alone, Dren bent down and wriggled one of the bricks free. He removed an oilskin from the hole. Inside were two knives, one big, one small. He'd hidden them there way back when Jia had first fallen, when the Skulls announced that having a weapon would get you the rope. Not even Quist knew he had them.

The big one was his dad's fishing knife, with a wicked edge on one side and serrated teeth on the other. It'd been his dad's favourite, the one he'd used when they were working on the boat together.

The first time they went out to sea, he was petrified being away from his mother and the streets he knew so well. Every sound had him jumping, looking in the water for monsters. His father had laughed and shown him the knife. He promised it was more than enough to deal with anything that came their way. Dren had believed him. There was nothing his dad couldn't do.

Holding that knife again, it felt like his dad was with him still. A stupid thought, but there it was. He was glad of it. Dren missed his old man, wished they could sit down and just talk about nothing, like they sometimes had. Looking back, it wasn't as often as they could've or should've. Dren had been too busy fooling around, hanging with the boys while his dad drank in the inn. Just another thing he wished he'd done differently.

He fixed the knife onto his belt, making no attempt to hide it.

He'd found the other smaller knife stuck in the back of some dead bloke down an alley somewhere. A fool who'd lost an argument with the wrong person or taken a wrong turn. The dead man had no use for it, so Dren plucked it free and made it his. It was small and vicious, just like Dren. He slipped it inside his boot, out of sight, just in case.

Feeling better now he was armed, he surveyed Kiyosun. There

were still a lot of Daijaku in the air but few bothered with Toxten. They didn't see his part of town as a threat. He searched east for a glimpse of the Council House, but it was too far away and obscured by other buildings. He wondered if Kaine had managed to give the old man the poison or if they were both still alive in there, getting tortured. Hard roads to travel either way but Kaine hadn't hesitated, despite knowing what he faced. The man had balls. No wonder his men respected him so much. When the time came, Dren hoped he could face his path with the same determination.

He hoped he could survive the night.

57

Tinnstra

Rascan's Bay

For the last hour, Tinnstra and the others had travelled in the open, surrounded by wild grass more dead than alive and no cover in sight. They were all jittery, nervous at being so exposed, jumping at every sound. If a Daijaku should come their way, they'd be spotted immediately. Thankfully, the skies above them contained nothing but the odd wisp of cloud. The open road at least let them pick up the pace as much as they could. Tinnstra didn't know how the others were feeling but she was exhausted, drawing on what little reserves of energy she had left. She could see the ocean, she could feel it on the breeze, hear the crash of waves against rock, smell the tang of the salt, and that helped pull her on, knowing the end of their journey had to be near.

Ahead lay a scattering of giant rocks and boulders. 'Rascan's Bay is on the other side of those,' said Eris.

'Thank the Four Gods,' said Tinnstra, relief flooding through her.

Then three men appeared from behind the rocks, armed with swords and bows. Everyone stopped. Tinnstra drew her sword, unsure how she'd find the strength to fight, before realising no one else had done the same.

Greener smiled. 'Don't worry. They're ours.'

Hanran.

'Greener, you bastard,' called one of them. 'It's good to see you.'

'Hasan!' The giant put down Zorique and went over to hug his friend. 'They've not killed you yet?'

'They keep trying. They keep trying.'

Greener stepped back. 'This is Grim Dagen's daughter, Tinnstra. Tinnstra, these reprobates are Hasan, Friid and Onlar. Good Shulka.'

The elder man shook her hand. 'That man was a hero to me. It's a pleasure.'

Tinnstra bowed her head to hide her blushing. 'It's good to meet you.'

'And this,' continued Greener, 'is Her Royal Majesty Queen Zorique of Jia.'

The three Shulka dropped to their knees and bowed before the girl.

Zorique giggled. 'Rise.' And then giggled some more.

'Let's get you out of sight,' said Hasan as he stood. The men led them into the rocks where they'd set up a small camp. It was camouflaged from above with netting and shrubs and well hidden from the road.

It was then Tinnstra got her first proper look at Rascan's Bay and, by the Four Gods, it was beautiful. The inlet lay at the bottom of the cliff, with a stretch of golden sand separating the ocean from a clump of wild woods. The sea shimmered in the afternoon light and it was hard to believe that, somewhere out there on the ocean, there was a ship coming to take them away from the Skulls and the Daijaku and the Chosen and everyone else who was trying to kill them. *You'd be proud of me, Beris. Father, too. We've made it. Zorique is safe. I didn't let you down. I didn't run away.* She fought the urge to smile. She wanted to look professional, a seasoned Shulka, but when she saw Greener's grin, there was no stopping it.

They settled down on rocks and Hasan passed around water skins. Tinnstra gulped down the water, grateful to wash the dust from her throat.

'Where's Jax?' asked Greener. 'I would've thought he'd be here.'

The Hanran looked at each other. It was obvious they had bad news to convey.

'He got arrested,' said Hasan. 'We tried busting him out yesterday but a Chosen appeared and put a stop to that. They got Kara, too. Since then, the city's been on lockdown.'

Tinnstra's good mood evaporated. Jax was the Shulka Aasgod had wanted her to meet. The thought of anyone in the hands of the Skulls made her feel sick and reminded her once more of the danger they were all in. Until they were safely on the ship, she couldn't relax.

'Jax knows about the boat tonight,' said Greener. 'What if he's talked?'

'Kaine got himself captured so he could deal with that problem,' said Hasan.

'His own father?'

The man shrugged. 'What can I say? It's a fucked-up world.'

'That it is, brother. We had to leave Monon up on the mountain.'

'I didn't want to ask. He was a good man.'

'Might still be,' said Greener. 'He was up to his arse in Skulls when we left but that doesn't mean he's dead. If anyone could survive bad odds, it's Monon.'

'The Four Gods love him, for sure.'

'How long have you been waiting for us?'

'A day. A dozen more Hanran will be coming from the city before it gets dark. I want to be mob-handed when the boat gets here.'

'That's never a bad thing.'

'What's the plan, then?' asked Tinnstra. 'Stay up here till the boat arrives?'

'Better to head to the beach now,' said Hasan. 'The path down is easy enough in daylight but you're more than likely to fall and break your neck in the dark.'

'There's an old smugglers' cave right underneath us on the beach,' said Friid. 'It's dry and as comfortable as it's going to get and hidden from sight. We've left some blankets, food and water, so you can wait there until the boat comes.'

'How do we get down to the bay?'

'The smugglers cut a pathway into the cliff,' said Hasan. 'You'd never find it if you didn't know it was there, but it's an easy walk down if you do. I'll take you. Friid and Onlar will keep watch up here, let us know if trouble's coming.'

'It's all right,' said Greener. 'I know the way.'

They picked up their kit and moved off from the rocks. Tinnstra checked the skies once more but they were clear – the Daijaku remained over Kiyosun.

The path down was steep, but the steps made the route passable as long as they watched their feet. They took their time, and Tinnstra held on to Zorique's hand, not wanting the girl to slip now. Halfway down, the cliff fell away on one side, leaving nothing but a sheer drop to the sea below and the crashing waves. The wind tugged at Tinnstra but Greener reached back and picked Zorique up, unbothered by the drop, and carried her down to the beach. Tinnstra followed, holding on to the rocks and the shrubs on the cliffside to steady herself.

It felt unreal to finally step onto the sand. Their journey for now was over. *Thank the Four Gods.*

Tinnstra took Zorique off Greener and hugged her. 'We did it. We did it.' It had been a long and impossible journey – so many dead, such good people lost – but they had made it. Alive. Now all they had to do was wait.

'When will the boat be here?' asked Zorique.

She put her down and kissed her cheek. 'Tonight. When it's dark. When it's safe.'

'Oh.' Zorique didn't look so happy about that. 'I want to go now.'

'Soon, Your Highness, soon.' Greener ruffled her hair. 'You'll be on the boat before you know it.'

Tinnstra looked back at the cliffs. Shrubs and bushes grew along the base where the cliff met the beach but she couldn't see any openings. 'Where's the cave? I don't see it ...'

'I'll show you,' said Greener. 'There's a reason why the smugglers liked this place.'

Leaving Jao and Eris on the beach, Tinnstra and Zorique followed Greener through the undergrowth to the rock face, where he pulled some hanging shrubs to one side and revealed the entrance. He slipped through the gap and the others followed. Enough light found its way into the cave to allow them to see. The interior stretched back some thirty feet into the cliff and the ceiling was high enough for even Greener to stand straight. More importantly, there were blankets piled up next to a basket of food and some more water skins. 'That should be enough for us until the boat comes,' said Greener.

Tinnstra settled Zorique down and gave her some bread to eat. 'I'll be back in a minute.'

Tinnstra led Greener back to the cave entrance. She glanced over at Zorique but the girl was happily munching on the bread with a blanket wrapped around her. She turned to Greener and dropped her voice. 'Will you come with us? To Meigore?'

'I'd like to,' he replied. 'She's a good kid.'

'But?'

'I have to go back and look for Monon. I need to know if he's alive or dead. If he died up on that mountain, he deserves to have his body brought back to his family.'

'He has a family?'

'Does that surprise you?'

'Kind of ... yes. He seemed too much of a Shulka to have a family.'

'Your father was the best of all of us and he had a family.'

'It *was* a stupid thing to say. Could someone else go? To find Monon?'

'Why? What's wrong?'

Tinnstra brushed some hair from her face. 'The girl likes you. You like her.'

'As I said, she's a good kid.'

'It would be ... helpful if you could join us. I don't know anything about looking after children. None of it comes naturally to me.'

'You're more at home on the battlefield, eh?'

'What do you mean?'

'As they say – too much of a Shulka to have a family. Come. We can talk about this after we've got food in our hands.'

418

They sat down on either side of Zorique. The girl smiled at them and rested her head against Greener's arm.

Tinnstra wrapped a blanket around her shoulders and leaned back against the rock. She took a bite of bread and cheese. It tasted like the most wonderful meal she'd ever had. 'I can't remember the last time I had something to eat where I could just sit and enjoy it.'

Greener put his arm around Zorique. 'How are you, my Majesty?'

Zorique laughed and looked up at the Shulka with big eyes. 'Don't call me that!'

'But that's what you are,' replied Greener. 'You're not a princess any more – you're the queen of Jia. Remember that when you get on the boat tonight.'

'I don't feel like a queen.'

'That's okay. But can I tell you a secret?'

The girl nodded.

Greener leaned in closer, so their noses were all but touching. 'You just have to pretend. It's like a game of make-believe. Just act like a queen and you'll be a queen.'

'I can do that,' said Zorique with an even bigger smile. 'That's easy.'

'I wish someone had told me that when I was younger,' said Tinnstra. 'I could've just pretended to be brave.'

'But that's what all of us do,' replied Greener.

'That's not true. My brother, Beris, was never frightened of anything. Not even when—' Tinnstra choked. She couldn't say the words.

'I served with your brother,' said Greener, 'and he was a fine soldier, but – and I mean this with the greatest respect – he got scared, same as anyone. There was this one time, it took him six weeks to pluck up the courage to ask a girl he liked to have a drink with him. Petrified that she'd say no, he was.'

'What happened in the end?' said Tinnstra, laughing.

'She said she thought he was cute, but she liked his big friend better.' Greener winked. 'He was mad with me about that, he was. Mad as—'

419

They all heard the whistle. Tinnstra and Greener looked at each other, as if to confirm they'd actually heard it. Then it blew a second time and there was no denying it – trouble was on the way.

'What's happening?' asked Zorique.

'Everything's okay,' lied Tinnstra. 'Don't worry.'

Eris appeared at the mouth of the cave, white-faced, scared. 'Hasan says there's Skulls heading this way. A lot of them.'

'Go and join the others,' ordered Greener. 'I'll follow.'

Eris nodded, then disappeared.

'They could be on their way somewhere else,' said Tinnstra. 'Doesn't mean they're coming for us.'

'We're not taking that risk. Stay hidden – no matter what.' Bow in hand, Greener ran out of the cave.

With shaking fingers, Tinnstra checked her sword was safely secured on her back. *So much for rest. So much for being safe.* Instead of an escape route from Jia, Rascan's Bay was going to be their last stand. Without a boat, the only way out of the inlet was back up the smugglers' stairs and straight into the arms of the Skulls.

Zorique watched her, huddled up in the blanket, her face full of fear but Tinnstra barely had the strength not to cry herself, let alone offer solace to Zorique. The girl had been through enough that week to understand what was going on. To know they were in trouble. 'Don't worry, my love. I'm sure it's nothing.'

Zorique pulled her blanket tighter around her as if it were a shield.

Tinnstra moved to the mouth of the cave, watched the empty beach, checked the empty skies and wondered how long it would be before the enemy reached them.

Drawing her sword, she thanked Aasgod for his gift. *It will protect me. I will protect Zorique. It will protect me. I will protect Zorique.* The words ran through her mind, over and over, as she waited, hand tight on her sword's hilt. Her eyes searched for danger, her ears straining for any sound of battle. She hated being stuck in that cave, cut off from everyone else, waiting.

Minutes passed. Her confidence wavered. The old fear niggled away. She tried to clamp it down, ignore it. There was nowhere to run to anyway. She and Zorique were trapped like pigs to the slaughter.

But it was all so quiet. Maybe Hasan had got it wrong.

She checked the sky again for Daijaku – and saw a black streak cross the blue sky towards them. She stared at it, a sick knot forming in her gut as she tried to work out what it was. Nothing good.

Then she heard the shouts, the screams, the clash of steel from the top of the cliff. Sounds she knew only too well from that day at the Kotege. The day the Egril came. She began to shake. She knew what was going to happen next.

Death.

Tinnstra looked up at the streak again – a woman. A Chosen. The woman who killed Aasgod. Coming for them. She glanced down at the sword in her hand. Suddenly it looked so small, so inadequate. How could she stop that monster? *I have to. Dear Gods, I have to.*

Greener rushed back onto the beach, followed by Eris and Jao. He'd lost his bow somewhere. 'Protect the queen. No matter what happens – don't let them take her.'

'There must be a way out ...'

Greener glanced back. 'We are the dead who serve all who live.'

Tinnstra shook her head. 'No. No. No.' Tears welled up in her eyes. They were all going to die. After everything they'd been through.

'Make your father proud.' Greener turned to face the Chosen.

The monster hit the beach. Sand, dirt and smoke mushroomed up from the impact, hiding the woman from sight for a moment. But then the Chosen emerged, death incarnate, hair flowing, eyes blazing, snarling, and marched towards them, axe in hand.

Jao loosed an arrow but the woman became smoke and it hit nothing. She rematerialised next to Eris and swung her axe, gutting him from groin to chest. Blood sprayed out across the yellow sand.

Greener yelled a battle cry. The woman turned slightly as he charged. His Shulka blade scythed down but the Chosen disappeared, only to reappear behind him. She hit him square in the spine with the back of her axe. The crack of bone echoed across the beach. He spun with the blow, flailing his sword towards her. He hit nothing and the Chosen rammed her axe into his gut.

Tinnstra watched, transfixed with horror. She'd never seen anything like it. The woman was unstoppable. A killing machine. Greener had been the best and yet he had fallen without so much as marking her. What chance did she – did any of them – have against such power?

Jao was the last one standing on the beach, trying to nock another arrow with shaking hands. She should've run. Tinnstra wouldn't have blamed her. It was the sensible thing to do. But the woman stood her ground as the Chosen came for her, holding her bloody axe, taking her time as if she was enjoying the moment, enjoying the fear.

Jao raised her bow, aimed, and the Chosen took her arm off at the elbow. Jao stared open-mouthed at where her arm had been, at the blood gushing out, then the Chosen decapitated her with a swing of the axe.

Tinnstra still hadn't moved. She wanted to run, but some part of her, some childish part, told her that if she kept still the woman wouldn't see her. She held her breath as if that, too, would help. Her sword was a dead weight in her hand. Tinnstra didn't know what to do with it. What was the point?

On the beach, the Chosen stood amongst the corpses, grinning like a mad woman, white hair flowing around her, a crazed gleam in her eye and that deadly axe in her hand. Blood dripped off the blade – Tinnstra's friends' blood. Then she saw Tinnstra. Pointed at her with her axe.

She disappeared into black smoke and, a heartbeat later, the Chosen stood before Tinnstra.

'You stay away,' said Tinnstra, raising her sword. *It will protect me. It will protect me.*

'Or what?' The Chosen laughed and stepped towards her.

Tinnstra lunged with her sword but the Chosen wasn't there. Only black smoke remained.

'Silly girl,' said a voice from behind her. Zorique screamed as Tinnstra spun around. The Chosen was in the cave. She raised her sword again.

'Do you even know how to use that?' asked the woman, bringing up her axe.

Tinnstra ran to stand in front of Zorique, a last barrier. 'The sword will protect me,' she whispered to herself. 'The sword will protect me.'

'Really? That little thing?'

'I'll never let you take the girl,' said Tinnstra.

The Chosen waved the comment away. 'Please – let's not insult each other. No one's coming to save you, and we both know you haven't got what it takes to hurt me.'

Tinnstra gripped her sword with both hands, slipped her feet into position. The sword would protect her. She had the advantage the others didn't. She had power like the Chosen. She had Aasgod's magic. She could still keep Zorique safe.

The Chosen stepped in, swung the axe overhead and hacked down at Tinnstra. She moved her sword to block the blow, ready to counter. Axe met sword and the sword shattered. The axe bit into Tinnstra's face and the world went black.

58

Darus

Rascan's Bay

Atop the cliff, Darus waited, mounted upon a fine stallion borrowed from the barracks at Kiyosun. The creature lacked the quality of Darus's personal stable, but it was more than adequate for now and far preferable to walking. Especially in all the dust and dirt of the south. At least he'd been able to get a clean uniform to wear after that old man had bled over him. He still didn't have a baton to use but his favourite knife was sheathed on his hip instead – not that he expected to do any fighting.

A soldier approached. 'Sir, the Hanran are all dead.'

'How many were there?'

'Three up here, sir.'

'It took your men half an hour to kill three of them?' Darus shook his head in disbelief.

'Yes, sir.'

'And how many of your men died?'

'Ten, sir.'

'May Kage torture their souls for eternity. No wonder we're struggling to stop this damn rebellion if they kill three of ours for every one of theirs.'

'Your sister killed four more on the beach, sir. And she has the girl.'

'Does she?' replied Darus, pursing his lips. 'How wonderful for her. Shame there aren't more like her, eh?'

'Yes, sir.'

'I'd better go and congratulate her,' said Darus. 'You're dismissed.'

The soldier bowed, no doubt grateful to still be alive. 'Yes, sir. Thank you, sir.' He scuttled off as Darus rode over to the cliff edge, where two more soldiers were searching the bodies of the dead rebels. There were only two bodies.

'I thought you said you killed three Hanran up here?'

A soldier rushed to take his horse's reins. 'One fell over the cliff, sir. His body's lying on some rocks halfway down.'

Darus sighed and dismounted. 'How do I get down to the beach?'

'The pathway is right there, sir,' said the soldier, voice quivering. Darus smiled to himself. It was the simple things in life that made him happy.

Some industrious peasant had cut steps into the rock, for which Darus was grateful as he made his way down to find his sister. Her work was very evident – three dead bodies in various stages of mutilation. Always the show-off. Skara knew how to get people's attention while Darus did all the hard work. If not for him, they'd never have known where to find the Hanran. Skara would definitely have failed to get the old soldier to talk. She needed her brother for that – not that anyone would remember. No, they'd just be praising her for capturing a four-year-old.

'Where is my sister?' he asked the soldiers on the beach.

'This way, sir,' said one, pointing back towards the cliff. He led Darus around a large boulder, revealing a cave. 'She's inside with the prisoner, sir.'

Darus waved him away and entered.

A woman lay dead on the floor. A cut ran from her eye to her chin. Despite the wound, Darus recognised her from somewhere. Or perhaps not – Jians all looked the same to him.

A few yards away, two guardsmen were tying up a small girl while Skara watched.

'Is this her?' asked Darus. 'She doesn't look like much.' The girl was filthy, no doubt infested with fleas and lice. She did her best to glare defiantly at him, but it was hard to achieve with eyes full of tears and snot running down her face.

'Hello, brother,' said Skara, looking too damn pleased with herself. 'May I present Queen Zorique the First of Jia.'

Darus looked down his nose at the creature. 'We'd best wash her before we present her to Raaku. Filthy little rat.'

Skara motioned to the soldiers. 'You heard my brother – take her back to Kiyosun and get her cleaned up. And find out where the nearest Tonin is. Have them brought to the city so we can get the girl to His Majesty as soon as possible. I'm not going to risk taking her on open roads.'

'Yes, ma'am.' Both men saluted Skara first and then Darus.

By Kage's rage, he'd had enough. He held the greater rank. How dare *she* give orders? It took all his control to wait until the men had left with the prisoner. '*I'm not going to risk taking her on open roads?* Is that what you said? When were you put in charge? I don't seem to remember being replaced. You don't decide anything – I do.'

'Darus, brother, I didn't mean anything by it,' replied Skara. 'Obviously whatever we do is by your order. Don't be so sensitive.'

Darus stepped back as if her words had been a slap in the face. '*Sensitive?* You behave like you're Kage's gift to this world and suddenly *I'm* being *sensitive*?'

Skara cocked her head, acting all confused, as if this wasn't all an elaborate plan of hers to humiliate him. 'Calm down, Darus. We should be celebrating. Raaku will reward us well.'

'He's going to reward *us*, is he? Us? Are you sure about that? After you've told him that it was you who did all the hard work? You did, after all, manage to kill so many great warriors to capture the evil queen.' He kicked the dead girl lying by his feet. 'This one looks at least eighteen years old.'

Skara stared at him but said nothing.

'Will you tell him how they led me on a merry chase across the country? How you had to step in to save the day? That without you, it would all have been a disaster? So typical of you.'

'I'm not going to talk to you while you're in this mood,' said Skara, turning her back on him. 'I'll see you in Kiyosun when you've had some rest and calmed down.'

He stepped behind her, but she didn't react. She wasn't afraid. Acting superior, as always. 'You smug little bitch.' He rammed the knife through her temple. The tip popped out of the other side of her head with a nice little spurt of blood.

'Oh,' said Skara and died. She toppled forwards and fell over the Jian.

Darus looked down at his sister. He didn't remember pulling the knife. He certainly hadn't planned on killing her. Well, not just then, anyway. Admittedly, he'd thought about it often enough, and now it was done ... well, he didn't feel any tears coming. She had needed to die. And sooner rather than later, so at least it was done now. He bent down and retrieved his knife. It was his favourite.

He wiped the blade across her chest to remove the blood. It was important to keep one's knives clean. A good craftsman looks after his tools, as they say.

Before leaving, he took his sister's baton as well. She wouldn't be needing it any more.

Feeling better, he emerged from the cave into the daylight, a great weight lifted from his shoulders. He had the girl, Aasgod was dead and, all in all, his mission had been a great success. His Imperial Majesty was a results-focused man. Raaku wouldn't care that Darus had lost two Kyoryu and he doubted Skara's death would even get a mention. Darus certainly wouldn't bring it up. He smiled, pleased with how everything had turned out. It would take a day or two to get a Tonin to Kiyosun, so there'd even be time for Darus to have some more fun. He'd so enjoyed tormenting the one-armed old man. Who knew what he could do to him in another session or two? All in all, it was quite the most wonderful day.

'Begging your pardon, sir, but what should we do with the dead?' asked one of the soldiers.

'Leave them for the gulls and the crabs.'

59

Tinnstra

Rascan's Bay

'Tinnstra, wake up.' It was Greener's voice. But he was dead. Tinnstra had seen the Chosen kill him. For a moment, she thought she was in the heavens with the Shulka, but Tinnstra wasn't that lucky. She was still alive. Her face felt like it was on fire. White-hot agony.

When she tried to swallow, all she could taste was blood and dirt.

'Tinnstra, I know you can hear me.' Greener again. A ghost, then. Come to haunt her for her failings.

She tried to open her eyes. One was stuck shut but the other opened well enough, except all she could see was a dark blur in front of her.

'That's it,' said Greener's ghost.

She tried to speak but her face was coated in something, like dried clay. She felt it crack so she stopped moving.

A hand grasped hers with a tight grip and a warm touch, gave it a squeeze. 'Good girl.'

'Greener?' she croaked.

'It's Hasan. Greener's dead. Everyone's dead.'

'Zorique?' She tried opening her other eye, needing to see the girl. Needing to know she was safe.

Hasan stopped her, gently pushed her back down. 'Take it easy. You've got blood all over your face. I'm going to pour some water over it to clean it off.'

428

She flinched when the cold water touched her skin and had to bite her lip to stop herself from crying out. It ran down her face, washing the blood away. Her blood. After the water stopped, she tried to open her eye again and succeeded. Hasan was there, looking old, looking pale, bruised. She put her hand to her own face and pulled it away quickly when she felt the open wound.

'She cut you from your eye to your chin, but it looks worse than it is. You'll have an ugly scar but that's all.'

'How did you ...'

'I got knocked off the cliff in the fight. I only fell a few feet but the Skulls must've thought I was dead. Seems like the Gods were looking after us both.'

'Zorique? Where is she?'

'They've taken the queen.'

'No.' Tinnstra sat up and looked around the cave as if Hasan were mistaken and she was going to find her sitting in the corner. But all she saw was the dead Chosen. 'I'm sorry, Zorique.'

She slumped back and sobbed. She'd failed. After everything they'd been through, they had her. Only the Four Gods knew what would happen to her now. Tinnstra could only imagine the pain and horror she'd face.

Hasan grabbed her shoulder. 'We can get her back. Together, we can get her back.'

'But you said they've taken her.'

'To the city. We can go after them, get help from other Hanran. We won't make it back here to meet the boat but at least we can rescue her from the Egril.'

Tinnstra closed her eyes. She wanted to say yes but she'd lost her sword – her power. She'd not survive the first Skull they met. 'I'm no use to you. You'd be better going without me. I'd only let you down.'

'Stop feeling sorry for yourself and come with me.' Hasan's look was one she had seen a thousand times before: a mix of disgust and disappointment.

'You don't understand. I'm a coward. I only got this far because Aasgod gave me a magic sword to keep me safe. Without it, I'm nothing.'

429

Hasan picked up the broken blade, turning it around as he examined it. 'Greener told me about this. Said it was bullshit. The mage never had that kind of power. If he did, we'd all be running around with magic swords. Do you think we'd be in this shit if he could do that?' He tossed it aside and it clattered across the cave floor.

'But I ...' The protest died on Tinnstra's lips. His words had the touch of truth about them, but she'd done so much with the sword protecting her. Had it all been a lie? She felt another strand of herself snap. *What a fool I am.*

'He told you what you needed to hear so you could do what needed to be done. I haven't got time to bullshit you. I need you. I need Grim Dagen's daughter. The woman who fought her way across the country to save a little girl's life. Now, is she here? Because she and I need to get moving!'

Tinnstra hugged her legs. 'I've given everything to get Zorique here and it wasn't enough. I shouldn't even have been with her in the first place – it should've been my brother. Grim Dagen's son could've saved her. Not me. Not the failure. The coward.'

Hasan stood up. 'Damn shame you feel that way. I wish I could get you to see things how they really are but I've no time to try and sweet talk you around. The queen needs saving.'

'It's suicide. I'll die.'

'Yeah? So what? We may succeed. We may die. But the one thing I know for certain is that if we give up on her, that girl is dead, and she'll suffer real bad before the end. So, I'm going. But you think about this life of yours – ask yourself what's so damn special about it that makes it worth putting above all else?'

Tinnstra shrank as she looked up at him, full of shame and fear. 'I'm sorry.'

Hasan sighed. 'Yeah. Me too.' He left her curled up on the cave floor, next to the body of the Chosen. A scared little girl. Too afraid to do the right thing. Crying.

Tinnstra had no idea what she'd do now. She had no life to go back to, no dream to follow, no friends, no family. By rights, she should be dead with the rest of them. The Skulls at the Kotege should've killed her or the Skull in the stables or the Daijaku on

430

the mountainside, or a dozen other times after that. She touched the cut across her face. She should be dead. She wished she were.

The only thing I have left is Zorique. There's nothing else to live for. So why am I so afraid? I've known pain and still kept going. I've faced danger and stood my ground. Maybe Hasan was right. So what if I die trying to save Zorique? No one would miss me except that little girl.

'We are the dead.' She said it without thinking, the words finally making sense. 'We are the dead who serve all who live. We are the dead who fight. We are the dead who guard tomorrow. We are the dead who protect our land, our monarch, our clan.' It tumbled out. An oath she'd known since childhood but never taken.

'We are the dead who stand in the light. We are the dead who face the night. We are the dead whom evil fears. We are the Shulka and we are the dead.' Words she knew but had never understood, never spoken. She'd never known the power in them.

'We are the dead. We are the dead. We are the dead. We are Shulka and we are the dead.' She was Grim Dagen's daughter. She was Shulka.

Tinnstra sucked in a gutful of air. *I promised Zorique I'd not leave her. I swore an oath to Aasgod to protect her. I told Beris I'd see this through – and it's not over yet.* She took a long, hard pull of water to wash the taste of blood and fear from her mouth and spat it over the Chosen. At least that monster was already dead, thank the Four Gods. She staggered to her feet, holding on to the wall as the cave spun while she found the strength in her legs. She bent down and picked up the Chosen's axe, the blade covered with Tinnstra's and her friends' blood. It felt good in her hand.

It was time to get Zorique back.

When she stepped outside, the sun was setting. A blood-red sky lay across the ocean as if the world readied for war. A cold wind drifted in from the sea, the perfect temperature for doing dark work. She collected Greener's sword. In a way, it felt like he was still there, coming along to fight the last battle with her. She didn't need magic to protect her. She had his faith in her to hold on to.

When she reached the cliff top, she could see Hasan marching ahead and ran after him. He heard her coming and stopped, allowing her to catch up. He didn't look surprised to see her.

'We are the dead,' she said in greeting.

He nodded. 'We are the dead.' And they moved off together to Kiyosun.

It was dark by the time they reached the city. A good kind of dark. The dark you needed when trying to sneak into a heavily fortified city full of people ready to see you dead. Even the moon had the good sense to hide behind some clouds.

They came up on the eastern side, flitting from shadow to shadow, crawling through dips in the ground and sheltering behind scrub and bush. The city walls loomed ahead in the darkness, still a mile away, at least. 'How are we going to get in?' asked Tinnstra.

Hasan pointed towards the sea. 'Over there.'

There was little cover on the beach, so they moved fast and no alarm rang out. They reached a smattering of rocks, where the sea crashed and churned.

'Watch your feet,' whispered Hasan as he waded into the surf. He weaved his way through the rocks with the sea lapping at his thighs and Tinnstra followed. The water was ice-cold. She nearly cried out at the shock of it, nearly turned back, but instead she gritted her teeth and surged on.

She didn't see the tunnel entrance until they were right in front of it: a black mouth yawning out of the surf and rock. Bars blocked the opening. The stink of sewage mixed with the tang of the sea. 'Ignore the smell. This leads right into the city centre – a good way to get into Kiyosun unseen.' He seized the first two bars on the left-hand side and twisted. With barely a creak, they popped out, allowing enough room for them to slip past, after which he replaced both, leaving no sign they'd been disturbed. The smell was worse inside the tunnel, trapped by the walls that curved just above Tinnstra's head, and she was glad she couldn't see what floated in the water around her legs.

The tunnel climbed gradually and Tinnstra had to keep one

hand in contact with the side of the tunnel to stop herself from slipping in the muck, while holding her nose with the other. Hasan chuckled when he saw. 'You get used to it after a while.'

'Maybe climbing the walls was a better option.' The water level dropped with every step, not that it made the journey any more comfortable. The filthy water was already inside her boots, squelching between her toes.

'We are the dead who fear no smell.' Hasan's laughter made him easy to follow.

A smudge of light appeared ahead. A shaft with a ladder leading up to a street above, covered by a grille. 'We'll take the third shaft up,' whispered Hasan. The opening brought some much-needed fresh air down into the tunnel and Tinnstra filled her lungs as she passed by.

'We're going to stink so badly by the time we get out of here, we won't be able to take anyone by surprise. The Skulls will smell us coming,' said Tinnstra.

'There's a gang of street kids in the city,' said Hasan. 'They're going to be setting off explosions later. The plan is to get the Skulls and the Daijaku chasing them all night long, so it won't matter what we smell like. Anyone still left in the Council House is going to be killed anyway.'

'The Council House?'

'It's an old government building the Skulls took over. They'll keep Zorique there.'

'But do you know where inside? We won't have time to go looking.'

'I don't, but I know someone who does. We've just got to convince her to take us there. That might not be easy.'

'She won't want to help?' Not that Tinnstra could blame her if she didn't. A part of her still didn't believe she'd joined Hasan.

'Let's just say we've put her through a lot already,' said Hasan as they reached another shaft. 'Here's number two. One to go.'

'Thank the Four Gods for that.' They moved on, splashing through the waste. Tinnstra knew how quiet the streets would be now curfew was in effect and she hoped any sounds they were making couldn't be heard on the surface above.

The third shaft appeared soon enough, its light drawing them on like moths. 'Wait here,' said Hasan. 'Let me make sure everything's safe.' He clambered up quick as a cat and then slowly lifted the grate to check all was clear. He obviously liked what he saw because the next thing, he had the grate off and was out of the shaft and above ground. He leaned back in and waved for her to join him.

Tinnstra wasn't so quick climbing up. She hadn't been doing this kind of thing all her life like Hasan had. When she got to the top, she only stuck her head up at first, despite Hasan's assurance, just in case, and was relieved to see he was alone. Tinnstra found herself in a narrow road with three-storey houses crammed next to each other along either side. All the windows were shuttered. Red Egril flags hung at intervals, just like in Aisair. The sight still sickened her, still terrified her, and after a few days out in the countryside, to have walls so close around her once more felt claustrophobic.

Hasan pointed to the end of the road. 'The safe house is two streets that way. The woman we need should be there, hopefully with some of our lads, too.' He looked at Tinnstra, sodden and stinking, and gave her a wink. 'Maybe some clean clothes as well.'

Hasan set off but Tinnstra's legs were rooted to the spot. She had to force them to move, one after the other, until the fear that gripped them had no choice but to let her go to her death.

60

Dren

Kiyosun

Dren leaped from one roof to the next, Quist following close behind. Both were dressed in black with mud smeared on their faces. It was way past curfew, but that had long ago ceased to have any meaning. There was no going back. No giving up. If they got caught, the hangman's noose awaited them. The explosives in Dren's bag would see to that. As would the knife on his hip or the one in his boot. So, best not get caught.

He wasn't wearing gloves – couldn't with his busted-up hand – and he'd be lying if he said he wasn't worried about carrying so many of the orbs at one time. Not to mention the cuts across his body. It'd be pretty fucking ironic if he got blown up because he scraped a scab off a finger. Quist had offered to take the bag but Dren refused. It was better he had it on him, just in case. Something was up between them, that much was obvious, so Dren wasn't taking any chances.

It didn't help his nerves, either, that the Daijaku were still patrolling. Not as many as earlier but enough to cause concern if they got careless or just unlucky. Clouds covered a sliver of moon, leaving little light to betray them, and the rooftops had more than enough shadows for the boys to flit between. Even so, Dren kept his ears open for the sound of wings.

Down below, the streets were empty and the city quiet. For now. The rest of his crew would be in place, getting ready to set Kiyosun on fire. The Skulls would never know what hit them.

They moved quickly along the terrace rooftops, skipping over the small walls that separated each house from its neighbour, ducking under water towers and jumping the gaps between streets. They didn't think about falling. They'd run the roofs since they were kids and knew their way from one end of town to the other as well as anyone on the ground.

Dren grinned. He was having fun. A good run and then a bombing at the end of it. The aggravation with Quist was forgotten. When it came down to it, down to the nitty gritty, the boys were of one mind.

They headed towards Coln Street, through the Risenn District. Across Bakers' Lane, along The Gate, down Link Street, over to the roofs on Kraze Road. The Council House loomed ahead, the only place where light still shone out of windows. The Egril's work there never stopped. Ruining lives took too much time. Torturing people. Just seeing it made Dren want to stop, turn back, give up. But no, he'd burn that place to the ground. He gritted his teeth and ran on.

Their pace slowed when they neared the Houseman Street checkpoint. They didn't want to risk a sound alerting the Skulls. Or spook their own crew as they approached.

They were shadows as they made their way along the row. The building had taken a pounding during the invasion and the roofs were covered in debris. Bits of broken water towers, shattered stairwells and collapsed walls made it hard going. Dren searched for sign of Falsa and Buser but they were too well hidden. Good. They'd learned something from him, then.

'Dren.' A whisper from ahead. Falsa. She appeared at the end of the row, a shadow herself against the deep blue night sky. 'Over here.'

'Get down,' hissed Dren through gritted teeth. He looked up to see if any Daijaku had spotted her, but their luck held. Falsa, though, still hadn't moved.

They quickly joined her. Dren tried to manhandle her back into cover, but she resisted, showing unexpected strength. 'Do you want to get caught?' he snapped. 'Stay like that and the Daijaku will have you.'

'Doesn't matter,' she replied. 'Ain't no Skulls down at the checkpoint.'

'What?'

Falsa pointed. 'Down there. It's deserted.'

Dren peered over the edge. There was the checkpoint but no Skulls. 'What the ...'

'All the checkpoints are going to be empty tonight,' said Quist from behind.

Dren turned to face him. 'What're you talking about?'

'I told you I weren't gonna be some stooge for the Shulka. You didn't want to listen.' His cousin had a steel pipe in his hand. Falsa was next to him with a blade.

'What's going on, cousin?' asked Dren, even though he knew.

'I'm in this for me, Dren. I told you that. For me.' Quinn's knuckles whitened as he tightened his grip on the pipe, gearing himself up for what he had to do.

'Where's Buser?' asked Dren, looking around, stalling for time, not wanting to believe what was happening.

Falsa smirked. 'Killed him hours ago. He's in an alley a few streets back.'

So, the kid was a killer after all. Dren didn't feel so proud now. 'Is that what you're going to do to me?' His hand drifted towards his father's knife.

'Don't touch it,' said Quist. 'I don't want to hurt you. You're my cousin and all, but go for that blade and I'll split your skull open.'

Dren backed up until he felt the wall against his legs. 'Are we going to stand here and chat, then?'

Quist laughed long and hard. 'No. Just waiting for some others to turn up.'

'Who?'

Falsa, looking far too pleased with herself, pointed up at the sky. 'Them.'

Dren's guts took a tumble. He followed her finger. Two Daijaku flying straight towards them. 'You dumb fucks.'

'Nah, we're rich fucks,' replied Quist. 'Did you know you've

437

got a price on your head? The Skulls gave me lots of gold for telling them about you and your plans tonight.'

The way Dren saw it, he had two options. Stick his hands up and wait for the Daijaku to get him, or show his so-called friends what a big fucking mistake they'd made in betraying him. The way he saw it, that was an easy choice to make.

Dren pulled his knife out and lunged at Quist in one quick move. Quist swerved back and brought his pipe up in time to block the blow. Metal clanged against metal, loud in the night. No matter. The Skulls were on their way by now, for sure. Silence didn't help Dren. He continued to attack, swung a left hook and caught Quist under the chin. His cousin staggered back and Falsa leaped to his aid, stabbing at Dren with her little knife. He swatted it away with his own blade and kicked down hard on her knee, putting all his weight behind it. The joint went crack and she crumpled, easy as that.

Quist came at him with the pipe, a big wild swing, trying to take Dren's head from his shoulders. He ducked under the blow and threw himself to the side as Quist came at him again. The pipe smashed against the wall.

'You bastard,' said Quist, madness in his eyes. 'Let us all down. We had it all so easy.'

Dren didn't say anything. It was a waste of breath. He risked a glance at the approaching Daijaku. They were getting close. He had to end this fight now or he was dead either way. He went for Quist, leading with his knife, jabbing, probing, looking for an opening.

Quist wasn't in a hurry. He didn't need to win, he just needed to stop Dren from leaving until the Daijaku got there. But Dren was knackered. No sleep for who knows how long and a good beating by the Skulls had left him in no state for a prolonged fight.

He stabbed with the knife. When Quist swung his pipe down to block it, Dren lunged in and smashed his elbow into the other boy's nose. It was a good strike and Quist staggered back, blood already running down his face, eyes watering. Not about to give him time to recover, Dren kicked at his groin but caught his thigh instead.

Wild and desperate, Quist lashed out and Dren retaliated, cutting a red streak across his cousin's hand. Quist dropped the pipe and Dren swept in, punching his knife into his chest.

'Oh!' said Quist in shock and surprise, his eyes wide open. Their faces touched, cheek to cheek. Dren heard Quist let out one last rattle of air and the boy's body slumped against him. When he pulled the blade free, he felt blood leak out with it. Stepping back and sheathing the knife, he let Quist's body fall to the floor. His best friend. His cousin. Gone.

'No!' screamed Falsa from the ground, but Dren was already running back the way he'd come. He hurdled the dividing walls, eyes focused on the end of the street. No time to waste. He had to get away.

Dren caught a flash of movement out of the corner of his eye and turned just as a Daijaku swept down, Niganntan spear in hand. He rolled forward and felt the blade slash past overhead. The Daijaku swooped onwards, getting ready to turn back around, but the other one was already on its way. Dren grabbed a rock, turned and hurled it with all his strength. The Daijaku swerved and Dren ran for his life.

He jumped over the street to the next block as the Daijaku came at him again. The roof was covered in trash, piled high around the water tower, and Dren grabbed a plank as he ran past. As a Daijaku dived down, Dren spun to face it, swinging the plank as he did so, launching it towards the demon. He didn't wait to see if it connected but ran on.

He hopped over another wall, ducked under a water tower and found some shadows to hide in. He paused for a moment, heart hammering away in his chest, eyes searching for a way out. He felt his bones protest, ribs jarring with every step, but he had to ignore it all. He sucked in air through his mouth, his nose all clogged and useless.

The debris on the roof gave him some cover, but he'd run out of it soon and the Daijaku would have him. He had to find a way off the roof. The creatures circled overhead, looking for him. No way were they going to make this easy for him.

Ten yards away across open space, there was a stairwell entrance that was still standing. If the door was unlocked, it was his way out. *If it was unlocked*. He didn't want to leave his shelter, but the way he saw it, he had no choice about that, either. No fucking choice at all.

With a deep breath, he ran. Above, he heard the Daijaku shriek. He reached the door, tugged at the handle. *Locked!*

A shadow loomed above and Dren half-pivoted, half-stumbled out of the way as a Niganntan slashed into the door. He scrambled back as the creature stabbed out once more, somehow avoided two more strikes and then his back hit a wall. He had nowhere else to run.

The Daijaku landed on the roof, followed by the other. The sight scared the shit out of him. The demons had him.

He looked around, eyes wild with fear, desperate for a way to escape. The end of the row wasn't far but the gap to the next block was wider than normal – too wide to jump. He couldn't go that way.

He had only one option left. A mad option. He reached into his bag with his bloody hand and grabbed an orb. He felt it react immediately, heating up, and he hoped that his blood hadn't dripped on any of the others.

He pulled the orb free of the bag and let the Daijaku see it glowing. He'd never thought the demons were scared of anything, but he saw fear then. They were off, quick as they could, wings flapping, running from *him* for a fucking change.

He threw the orb after them with all his might and ran for cover.

The blast lifted him off his feet and threw him across the roof, chased by flame and fury. He tumbled head over arse until he hit a wall, smacking his skull.

He lay there, dazed. He knew he should be on the move again, but the world was spinning and he had no idea how to get his legs to work. Ice shards of pain cut through him with every breath he took. He pressed down on his ribs and tried to swallow the agony as he looked for the demons. Half the roof was on fire, while the other half had all but disappeared. But there was no sign of the Daijaku, either. He hoped the bastards were down and dead, but even if they were, he knew there were more of the fuckers out there.

Dren wiped blood from his eyes, tried standing and fell back on his arse. It shouldn't be that hard. He tried again and made it to his knees, nearly puked. He shook his head to get some sense back into his skull.

Dren heard the beat of wings. And there they were. More Daijaku. Fear gave him the boost he needed to stand. Three of the demons flew straight towards him, Niganntan blades in strike positions. He staggered over to the stairwell. The blast had done him another favour. There was nothing left of the door except a few splinters of wood.

He tumbled inside and half-ran, half-fell down the stairs. He stopped on the second-floor landing, panting and spitting blood. He pulled his knife, still covered in Quist's blood, and stared back up the stairs for sign the Daijaku were coming after him. The knife felt inadequate in his shaking hand. What could it do against a Daijaku with a Niganntan?

Time passed. Dren's breathing steadied. He wiped more blood from his eyes. Where were they? Then he realised they didn't need to chase him. He had nowhere to go. All they had to do was wait and snatch him either from the street or from the roof.

The thought made him angry. Hadn't he shown them they weren't invincible? Hadn't killing some of them earned him a little respect? He'd give them something to think twice about.

He sheathed the knife again and wiped his hands clean of blood as best he could. He thought he had it all, but it was hard to tell in the dark. His heart hammered away, fear pummelling his gut. He just hoped his fucking luck was with him still. He reached into his bag and pulled out an orb. It was cold as death in his hand as he crept back up the stairs, his back to the wall. Through the open door, he could see the night sky. Shadows flittered past, a sure sign the Daijaku waited above.

On the last landing, he paused and spat blood on the bomb. Immediately, the orb reacted: growing warmer, the liquid glowing brighter as it churned away inside. It sparkled in the darkness as it burned in his hand. Dren had to get the timing just right.

He smiled. Time to show the Daijaku whose town they were fucking about in.

Dren stepped out onto the roof. The Daijaku circled above. Five of the bastard things. 'Hey!' he shouted. They all banked towards him, bunching together. Fucking perfect.

Dren threw the bomb up into the centre of the group and dived back through the doorway. The world ripped apart, shaking the building. The roof and half a wall disappeared from the stairwell, showering Dren with debris as he curled up, covering his ears. A Niganntan spear clattered onto the floor next to him. A torso followed with only stumps left of the Daijaku's wings. Someone somewhere screamed. But the sky was empty.

Dren had got the bastards. He was a fucking legend – the man who'd killed five Daijaku. He laughed as he took the stairs down two at a time. Five Daijaku and the night wasn't even over yet.

61

Yas

Kiyosun

The explosion made Yas jump. She rushed to the window and peered out.

'What's going on?' asked Gris. They were still in the dead woman's apartment. Her body lay in a corner, covered with a sheet.

'A rooftop a few streets away is on fire,' she replied, 'but I can't see anything else.' A shadow passed overhead and Yas darted back from the window. Daijaku flying to the scene.

'Could be Dren's lot starting their work,' said Gris, standing up.

Yas shook her head. 'It's too early for that.'

'Still … we should make a move for the safe house while they're distracted. Meet up with your ma and your son.'

Yas nodded. She glanced down at the dead woman, aware of how easily it could've been her lying somewhere with a sheet over her head – or still stuck in that water tower. 'Let's go.'

She picked up a coat she'd found. The knife was back in the lining. Easy to reach. Ready to use.

She paused for a moment as she realised she'd armed herself without thinking. The act was no longer unnatural to her, the weapon no longer alien. 'What have I become?' she murmured.

'A warrior,' said Gris from the door.

'I don't think a warrior would've got trapped in a water tower,' she replied as they stepped into the hallway.

443

'You'd be surprised.'

On the street, they stayed close to the buildings, taking their time. The Skulls were out in force and each time they had to hide, Yas's nerves became a little more frayed. She flinched every time a Daijaku flew overhead and every noise made her think they'd been spotted. The smell of smoke tainted the cold night air, adding to her fears. The city was as dry as a bone, and if the fires spread, the whole place would go up real quick. And yet, with every patrol avoided and another street crossed, she could feel a bubble of confidence growing. Maybe the plan would work.

Gris found the house and the door was unlocked. They went straight up to the second floor. Gris knocked, paused, then knocked again three times in quick succession. The door was pulled back an inch, spilling light into the dark hallway and a man's face peered out at them. A second later, the door opened and they entered.

Ma was sitting at a table and leaped up when she saw Yas. They embraced, relief holding them together. A few other members of the Hanran were in the room but Yas paid them no mind.

'You made it, then,' said Ma when they separated.

'I'm here, aren't I?' said Yas. 'Where's Ro?'

'In the bedroom, asleep. He's a tough kid.'

Yas wiped away a tear and went to check on her son.

It was dark in the room and it took a moment or two for Yas's eyes to readjust. Her son lay on a mattress on the floor, a blanket half-kicked off already. He'd always been a wriggler, even before he was born. Yas knelt down beside him and pulled the blanket back up. He looked so peaceful with his puckered lips and that little frown.

She wanted to lie down next to him, close her eyes and forget about the mess they were all in – but that wasn't going to happen. She kissed Ro and stood up. With one last look at her son, she returned to the main room.

Gris walked over. 'He all right?'

She nodded. 'As Ma said, he's tough.'

The Shulka grinned. 'Takes after his mother.'

There were six Hanran in the room and none of them looked

444

happy. She was surprised to see Hasan amongst them, slumped on the floor in the corner. Kaine had sent him to guard Rascan's Point. The man was filthy with mud and blood. Next to him was a woman Yas didn't recognise, a waif of a thing with a hard look in her eyes. A nasty-looking cut ran from her forehead down to her chin; an attempt to clean the blood off her face hadn't been too successful. An axe lay across her lap and a Shulka sword rested against her leg.

'Is this the one we've been waiting for?' asked the woman.

'It is,' replied Hasan. 'Her name's Yas.' He climbed to his feet, slowly, as if every movement was agony.

'She's done enough.' Gris stepped in front of Yas, protecting her from whatever they wanted. 'Who's the girl?'

Hasan tilted his head towards the stranger. 'Tinnstra. Grim Dagen's daughter.'

Yas didn't have a clue who this Grim Dagen was but his name carried punch, judging by the look on Gris's face. He stepped back a pace.

'She brought the queen down from Aisair,' said Hasan.

'The queen?' asked Yas.

Tinnstra got to her feet. 'Zorique. The last surviving member of the royal family and now a prisoner of the Skulls.'

'Shit,' said Yas. No need to ask how it happened. The blood and the wounds were enough. 'They've got her in the Council House?'

Hasan nodded. 'Nowhere else to take her – and their Tonin's dead, so she's not going anywhere for a while, either.'

'You can't get her out,' said Yas. 'Not if she's in there.'

'Yes, I can.' Tinnstra looked her straight in the eye. 'She's *four* years old. I'm not going to leave her in the hands of the Egril.'

Yas remembered the prisoners in the cells, the dead on the gallows, her own beatings. She nodded. There was no escaping that damned place. No matter what she did, all roads led back to the Council House. What would she do if it was Little Ro in there? She sighed. 'Let's go.'

The rest of the Shulka stood. Gris took her by the arm. 'Are you sure? You don't have to do this.'

'I do. You know I do.'

'Good.' He let go of her arm, smiling with a warmth she'd not seen before.

'You'll stay with me?'

'Wouldn't miss it for the world.'

Realisation dawned on Ma. 'Oh no. No you don't. Stay here. It's not your fight. Leave them to it.'

'It's all our fights,' said Yas. 'The Skulls aren't going to stop. They'll kill the girl, kill me, kill you. Makes no difference to them. We're all disposable. We're dead already – unless we do something to stop them.'

'What about Little Ro?' Tears ran down Ma's cheeks. Yas couldn't remember her ever crying before.

'Tell him I love him. Keep him safe as best you can.'

Yas followed the rest of them out through the door. She didn't look back. She knew her resolve would break if she did.

62

Dren

Kiyosun

Dren crouched in a doorway on the edge of the square, a hundred yards away from the Council House. A trough hid him from sight. The Skulls had cleared the bodies away but left the debris caused by his attack a few days previously. Sentries stood guard at the main gate, alert: six Skulls, spears in hand. No one talked. More waited on the other side of the iron railings that ran around the building, lined up in ranks, ready to be deployed. Looked like maybe a hundred of them. Behind them, light burned in every window in the Council House. Dren could see people moving about inside. Thanks to bloody Quist, they knew an attack was coming and were well prepared.

He shivered. Now the buzz had worn off from his fight with Quist and the Daijaku, Dren felt tired, hungry, cold and very much alone. Every part of him hurt. He didn't even know if the rest of his crew planned to go ahead with the other attacks. What if Quist had got to them, too? The Hanran needed their help – without it, the fight-back was over before it had even started.

He looked inside his bag again. Five orbs. He could do some damage with those. If he could get close enough to use them without being killed. He checked the Skulls again. Fat chance of that. It was a suicide mission, right enough.

It was funny. He'd sent others to their deaths without a second thought. Like the woman who'd bombed Old Man Hasster's place. She'd lost everything in the invasion. Her husband, her son,

447

her home. She'd been starving on the streets when Dren found her, wasting away. She'd given up, as good as dead already. He'd just made it happen sooner and got her to do some good with it rather than just rotting away in an alley. Or so he had thought. Now it didn't seem so clever. Maybe he should've helped her start something new, find her something to live for, rather than giving her an excuse to die.

Now it was Dren's turn, he found that he didn't want to die, and certainly not by blowing himself up just to take out a few Skulls. Even if the sentries didn't fill him full of arrows before he got to them, all he'd have a chance to do was kill six of the bastards, maybe ruin a bit of fencing. Hardly what he'd imagined the great last act of Dren of Toxten would be. But it was what it was. A right fucking mess.

He took several deep breaths. Maybe he was just a coward, after all. Not the big man he thought himself to be – a sheep instead of a wolf.

But no, that wasn't Dren. There had to be another way to get the bastards. Trouble was, he couldn't see it.

He spun as he heard a noise from behind him. Dren peered into the darkness, expecting to see the fucking Skulls coming for him. He nearly reached for an orb when a small group of people appeared around the corner. They ran, crouching low. Hanran.

A wave of relief swept over him. He wasn't going to have to do it alone. Maybe he had a chance to live after all.

He waved, letting them know he was there. He didn't need them killing him by accident.

Seven of them took up positions around him. Yas, the girl who had rescued him from the Council House, was there with Hasan and Gris. Dren didn't recognise the others but one of them was a ferocious-looking woman with a bloody gash splitting her face in two. Fuck knows how she'd got that, but she looked ready to start a war by herself.

He could see more Hanran further back, taking up positions of their own. They'd brought a small army with them. Things were looking up.

'Wasn't expecting to see you here,' said Dren in a hushed voice.

'It all went to shit. The Skulls have got the queen in there,' said Hasan, indicating the Council House with a tilt of his head. 'We're breaking her out.' He paused as he ran his eye over the Skulls lined up in the courtyard. 'Or we were. What are they all waiting for?'

'One of my guys told the Egril what we were planning. Tried selling me out,' replied Dren.

'I hope you cut his fucking throat,' said Hasan.

'I'm here. He's not.' It was easy to slip back into playing the big man now the others were there. It was a role he knew well, and it stopped him thinking about the reality of the situation. How he'd fucked everything up.

Hasan rubbed his chin. 'What about the rest of your lot?'

Dren shrugged. 'Fuck knows. I think they're still loyal, but I didn't see my best friend betraying me, so I'm no expert.'

'What do we do?' asked the woman. Dren could see her shaking, full of fury, clenching her fists over and over, trying to hide it. The girl looked mad keen to go and kill someone.

'We wait. See if Dren's lot come through,' said Hasan. 'If they don't, we resort to the backup plan.'

'What's that?' asked Dren.

'We go in as hard as we can and hope one of us makes it to the girl. You got any bombs with you?'

'Yeah.' Dren nodded at his bag. 'Five.'

'They'll do some damage, at least,' said Hasan. 'Get them ready. Hopefully your team will do their job and their explosions will draw the Skulls out of the grounds. If they don't, we'll blow the sentry gate. That'll get them moving our way for sure. That's when we throw two more in. If we hit them when they're all bunched up, we might do some real damage.'

They all stared at the Council House, lost in their own thoughts. Any minute, the eleven o'clock bell would ring and Dren would know whether his people were with him or not. His ears strained at the silence, eager for that first chime, praying they'd not let him down.

The Skulls on the other side waited, too, motionless in their armour. Dren wondered if they were nervous or scared. Maybe

449

they thought they were so invincible, they didn't fear a thing. With their armour, spears and scimitars, they were probably right to think that way. They'd conquered enough of the world easily enough.

Then the first chimes rang out across the city. Eleven o'clock. The first explosion rang out a second later. Dren smiled. It was fucking *on*.

63

Tinnstra

Kiyosun

The first explosion echoed out across the city. Others followed in quick succession. *Boom. Boom. Boom. Boom.* A beautiful percussion. For once, it was the Hanran striking back. The bombs were hurting Skulls – not Jians.

Tinnstra counted each one, wondered where they were in the city, how much damage done. She could see the effect on the Skulls; their neat lines wavered as another blast rippled out over the city. She clenched her fists again to stop herself from shaking, hide the fear gnawing away inside. She couldn't let them see how scared she was. She didn't belong with Hasan and the others – experienced warriors all. Even Yas looked more at home with them than Tinnstra did.

She glanced over at the kid, Dren. His eyes burned with delight as another bomb went off. He was nothing more than a street urchin and yet he'd planned a citywide assault. All Tinnstra had done was to allow Zorique to get captured. *Pull yourself together. Zorique is counting on you.*

'Come on,' urged Hasan as he stared at the Skulls. 'Move, you bastards.'

'They're not moving,' said Dren. 'They're not fucking moving.'

'Give me one of those things.'

'Be careful, man,' said Dren as he passed one to the Shulka. 'You need to put blood on them to make them work.'

Hasan grinned. 'Enough of that going around here tonight.'

Somewhere else in Kiyosun, another explosion went off.

'Get everyone ready,' said Hasan, wiping blood from his brow across the orb. He stood up, the orb glowing in his hand, and ran forward a few yards towards the guard house. The Skulls saw him as he wound back his arm. Shouts rang out, ordering him to stop. He threw the orb as a sentry threw a spear at him. Tinnstra gasped but the spear went wide, bouncing off the ground. The orb arced up in the air, glowing red against the night sky as Hasan dived back into cover.

The orb hit the ground a yard from the main gate and then the world exploded into a ball of light. Tinnstra dropped to the ground, covering her head, her ears ringing with the fury of it. Debris smacked into the trough and peppered the ground around her. She tasted the smoke and the dust and felt the heat as the air burned. For a second, she was back at the Kotege, or the house on Ester Street. The old fear tried to grab her, but she shut it off as best she could. Now wasn't the time to freeze up. Now was the time to fight back. Let the Skulls learn what fear was.

A hand grabbed her. Hasan, wide-eyed, shouted, 'You okay?' She nodded. She checked the square. There was nothing left of the guardhouse and half the fence was missing. Skulls were running towards them, swords and spears in hand.

Dren sprinted forward to meet them, shouting with rage. He stopped halfway across the square and threw another orb, dropping to the ground as the bomb detonated. Flames shot up into the sky, stealing the air. Even behind the trough, the force of both explosions pummelled Tinnstra, knocking her to the ground, singeing her skin.

Someone moved past her. Gris. She thought that was his name. There was no stopping him, nothing holding him back. No fear. He was screaming orders, telling them all to attack. The girl, Yas, ran after him. Hasan and Dren too, running towards the enemy. The others followed, shouting and hollering. It wasn't how she'd been taught to fight at the Kotege, but this army weren't all Shulka. Just Jians fighting for their queen and their liberty.

This was it. Tinnstra forced herself up and ran into the black smoke. She was dead anyway, a ghost too dumb to go to the heavens. She choked on the acrid fumes and her eyes watered, but still she went on. She had the Chosen's axe and Greener's sword. Time to put them to good use.

Dead Skulls lay everywhere, most missing body parts. Some still moved, twitched, clawed at life, but she ignored them all. She climbed over the remains of the fence and into the courtyard. The Hanran were already fighting with the remaining Skulls. Even though they were outnumbered, her friends had the upper hand, beating them back, killing them.

An Egril lunged at Tinnstra with a spear. She leaned back, saw the tip of the blade pass an inch from her nose. She swung her sword at the man's face and watched his eyes widen behind the mask, fear so very much like her own, as the blade hacked home.

Another Skull came at her, swinging wildly with his scimitar. Tinnstra checked her momentum and blocked the attack with the Chosen's axe. The Skull screamed as he slashed at her again. Tinnstra pivoted around the weapon, chopped down. The axe bit into the Skull's knee, caught him between bits of armour. A lucky strike, maybe, but he crumpled to the ground all the same. She pulled it free and buried her sword in the back of his head.

She moved on. Dren had another orb in his hand, smiling like a wild thing as it glowed. He threw it as more Skulls piled out of the front of the Council House. They never had a chance. The blast tore them apart, smashed into the building, ripping through stone and punching holes in the walls.

The woman, Yas, shouted something. Tinnstra's ears weren't working properly. All she heard was ringing, but she understood what she needed to do. Follow Yas. Hasan, Dren and Gris went with her while the others remained to fight. They sprinted around the back of the building.

Three Skulls came at them with scimitars. Hasan and Gris took two of them. The third headed straight at Tinnstra and the others. Tinnstra met him with sword and axe. Her feet slipped into a fighting stance, a move as natural as breathing. She didn't feel like herself. It was as if someone else controlled her, someone who wasn't petrified and knew what they were doing. The Skull's sword arced towards her and she countered. The two blades clashed together, sending a shock wave riding down her arm. Metal slid against metal as the swords locked guards. Sparks flew. The Skull stared into her eyes, so close she could feel his breath on her cheek as he hissed through clenched teeth. She could feel the fear – but it was his, not hers, and it felt bloody good. She pushed back with all her strength, felt him give an inch of ground. She smashed the end knob of her axe into the Skull's face, surprising him more than hurting him, but it was enough to force him back. Enough to open him up, ready to kill.

Before she could strike again, Dren drove a brick into the side of the Skull's helmet. He went down hard and Dren was on him, smashing the brick down again and again into his face mask while Tinnstra watched, panting.

He stepped back, grinning, covered in specks of blood and brain, looking as if he needed some kind of approval for what he'd done. Tinnstra nodded and that seemed good enough for Dren. He grabbed the Skull's scimitar.

Hasan and Gris had killed the other Skulls already, so Yas took them through a doorway into a long kitchen. It was empty and cold, strangely peaceful after the madness outside.

They slipped down the aisles, Yas leading the way, flanked by the Shulka. Eyes hard, weapons ready. Tinnstra wanted to be sick. They stopped at a closed door.

'The prisoners are kept at the end of the corridor,' said Yas. 'Behind locked doors.'

'Guards?' asked Hasan.

'Of course,' said Yas.

Tinnstra gritted her teeth. 'Let's do this.'

64

Jax

Kiyosun

Jax struggled to keep his mind together. Time had no meaning in the cell, in the dark, with the corpses of his son and his friend and that pile of arms. *My arms.* He could still hear the Chosen whispering in his ear as he cut each one off and the sheer joy in the bastard's face as he grew them back again.

He stared at his regrown arm, hating the sight of it even more than the amputated ones. It was evidence of his weakness, his betrayal. He wished the Chosen had chopped it off with the rest of them. If he had a knife, he'd do it himself. By the Gods, he was cursed. Why else was he still *alive*?

His tormentor was always there, too. Looking in, gloating, whispering what torments he had planned, which body part he was going to take his knife to next. All Jax could do was cower in the corner, pleading to be left alone. So far, the Chosen hadn't picked him, but his neighbours weren't as fortunate and soon the screams would begin. Jax shuddered with each howl of pain. He *knew* his own time would come soon enough. He *knew* he was being saved for further torment.

Somewhere in the real world outside, a storm roared. He could hear the thunder muffled through the stone. It was fierce enough to unsettle the Skulls on guard outside his cell. They were on their feet, moving about, whispering to each other. Something had them worried.

Jax was beyond caring though. He—

The doors imploded, chased by a ball of flame. The roar was channelled down into the basement. Even in his cell behind a steel door and thick walls, he felt it. It battered him. It was the end of the world in all its fury. Flames licked through the iron bars of his cell door and Jax laughed – the first happiness he'd felt in a long while. It was over. Let him burn. He could join his son. Beg forgiveness from Xin, the Goddess of Death.

Jax crawled to his feet, ready to die. Outside his door, the guards were dead, ripped apart by the blast. Fires burned all around and something moved within the clouds of smoke. Faces appeared. Hasan. Gris. The girl who'd tried to save him before. Even Dren was there.

It had to be a mad hallucination. No way would they have come back. Not for him. Not after Kaine.

He looked down at his poor boy, waiting for his eyes to slide open and words to come out of his mouth. When they didn't, he turned back to watch his dreams at work outside his cell.

'Jax!' Hasan saw him and ran over. 'Jax! You're alive.'

Jax smiled but he knew it wasn't real. The Chosen was playing a game with him. Some new form of torture. A cruel trick.

Hasan unbolted the door, flung it open. 'Jax! We're going to get you out of here.' He reached in, took hold of Jax's arm. His touch was warm and firm. 'Jax?' Concern flitted across his face. It was all so real, so convincing. His friend stepped back. 'Your arm? What the fuck?'

Jax laughed. A test. To break him again. He said nothing. Not to a dream. A trick.

'Jax. Come on.' Hasan tried to pull Jax out of his cell but he resisted, wise to the Egril. If he stepped outside his cell, the punishment would be severe. The pain never-ending.

The others came over. Gris. Dren. The girl. Another young woman with a scarred face hung back, watching, a sword in one hand, an axe in the other. He didn't recognise her but felt that he should.

Gris entered the cell, saw the bodies of Kaine and Kara, the arms, the filth. 'By the Gods. Let's get you out of here.'

Jax shook his head. 'No. You don't fool me. No.'

Gris took his new arm and Hasan the other and they carried him out into the corridor, Jax fighting them the whole way. They felt so real, but they couldn't be. His mind was making it all up. There was no fire, no dead, no friends.

'You'll be all right. We'll get you out this time,' said Hasan.

'No. No. *No.*' Jax struggled to break free and go back to where he belonged, but they wouldn't let him. They were too strong and he too weak.

'Any sign of Zorique?' asked the scarred girl. 'Where is she?'

'She's not here,' said Dren. The scimitar in his hand was so big. So out of place. It must be a hallucination. 'I've checked all the cells.'

'She has to be upstairs,' said Yas. 'In one of the rooms.'

Jax had been upstairs. He knew what went on in those rooms. He pulled back towards his cell, but Hasan stopped him. 'You'll be all right, Boss. I promise. We'll get you out of here this time.'

'I don't want to go up there,' replied Jax. He might've been crying. It didn't matter. He had more than enough shame already.

'Come on,' said Yas. 'It's this way.'

The men carried Jax out of the cells and into a corridor. More dead Skulls were scattered around. They took the central stairs up, the way the Skulls had taken him, stopping just before the ground floor. Hasan left Jax with Gris and went to see what lay ahead. Jax knew there would be nothing good up there. Especially if the Chosen waited for them. *Especially* if he was there.

Hasan ducked back down, looked to the boy. 'Dren, any more orbs left?'

'One.' Dren held it up.

Hasan grinned. 'That'll do. Give it here.'

Jax watched the Shulka wipe his bloody hand across the orb and it started to glow. Maybe this wasn't a trick. Not a trap.

Hasan ran up to the top of the stairs and tossed the orb onto the landing. He jumped back down into the shelter of the stairwell and covered his ears.

Once more, the world shook with the ferocity of the blast. Jax could hear the Skulls scream above them. He could picture the carnage. This wasn't a trick. His friends were *real*. They were

457

here, and they were rescuing him.

They moved quickly up the last remaining stairs. The ground floor was devastated. Paintings shredded. Egril flags burned. The dead and dying everywhere, soaking the floor with their blood. Cold air blew in through shattered windows. Broken glass crunched underfoot.

The smoke from the fires brought tears to Jax's eyes and made him cough. He thought about taking a discarded weapon but dismissed the idea just as quickly. He could barely stand, his courage gone, his self-esteem lost.

'Where'd she be, Yas?' shouted Hasan.

'I don't know,' she replied, head swivelling as she looked all around her.

'They tortured me in a room down the corridor at the far end,' said Dren, pointing. Jax knew the room he meant. Knew it well. The best parts of him had died there.

'Tinnstra, go with him. Check it out. If she's not there, look in all the other rooms,' ordered Hasan. The scarred girl nodded and off she ran with the boy. 'Gris, stay with the boss. Me and Yas will go upstairs.'

'You got it,' replied Gris. 'We'll be here waiting.'

'My friends,' a voice called out from the top the stairs. A voice Jax knew too well. His legs gave way and not even Gris could keep him standing. A man in a black uniform walked down the steps. Cropped white hair. Black mask. Baton in hand. The glint of silver on the collar. That fucking smile. Darus Monsuta. 'Stay where you are. I'd like to have a word or two with you.'

Hasan loosed an arrow. It struck the Chosen in the heart. The man's legs wobbled and wavered as he used his arms to balance himself and then he fell back on his arse. For a moment, Jax thought Hasan had killed him. Put the man down. But then Monsuta howled with pain and his arms found their way to the arrow. They watched him pull the shaft free and toss it to one side.

He sat up, eyes mad with fury.

No one did anything. They were all too shocked. The Chosen climbed back on his feet, wobbling with the effort, then he straightened and raised his baton. 'My turn.'

65

Tinnstra

Kiyosun

Tinnstra's heart hammered away in her chest as she raced after Dren. The boy had no fear, no hesitation – whereas that was all she had. Only by constantly moving could she avoid it paralysing her. Every time she wanted to give up, she thought of Zorique and how scared she must be. Tinnstra had made a vow and she wasn't going to let the girl down.

They reached the door and found it open. Tinnstra ran in, ignoring the fear in her gut.

The room was empty.

'Shit. Shit,' she said.

'Next room,' said Dren.

The crackle of an energy blast stopped them dead. Tinnstra knew that sound all too well. It had killed her brother. All but killed Aasgod.

A Chosen's baton.

She peered around the doorframe and saw the white-haired man who'd pursued her from Aisair. The monster from Ester Street.

She ducked back inside the room and pressed herself against the wall as she tried to stifle a sob.

'What is it?' asked Dren.

'A Chosen.'

Dren stuck his head out and came back looking as petrified as Tinnstra. 'What do we do?'

459

'There's nothing we can do. If we run down there to help, he'll see us and blast us before we get halfway there.'

'There has to be something. He'll kill the others if we stay here.'

The window on the opposite side of the corridor looked out over the courtyard, all the glass gone, and Tinnstra knew what they could do. It was a way out. The Chosen would kill the others but Dren and Tinnstra could get away. *Run. Run somewhere. Anywhere. Survive.*

There was another blast, and someone screamed. A man. The Chosen had got one of them. Maybe Gris. Maybe Hasan. Maybe the old man. She was too scared to look. But Tinnstra was alive for now. She could escape. If she stayed, she'd die. Of that, there was no doubt. He'd come for her after he'd finished with the others. Unless she ran.

'What are you thinking?' asked Dren. 'You got a plan?'

A bell rang over the city. Slow, precise chimes. A clock striking midnight. 'We're too late,' said Tinnstra. She could feel tears in her eyes, hated herself for them.

'What do you mean?'

'There was supposed to be a boat taking us to Meigore at midnight. It had always been a fool's hope from the beginning. It's all over now.'

The building shook from more blasts. They could hear the Chosen's laughter.

'Fuck it,' said Dren. He gripped his scimitar with both hands. 'I'm going to help them.'

Tinnstra put out her arm to block his way. 'He'll see you. You'll die.'

'I'm not going to die like a fucking sheep in a pen.' He pushed Tinnstra's hand aside. 'It's better this way. I'll show him I've got some fucking teeth left.'

'Don't leave me on my own.'

'I thought you were a Shulka warrior?'

She looked down at the sword in her hand – Greener's sword. 'I'm not. I thought I was, but I'm not.'

'Then what are you doing here?'

460

Tinnstra thought of her brother and his midnight visit, her promise to Aasgod, to Hasan. 'I wanted to save Zorique.'

'Then let's do it. Let's save her. So what if the boat's gone? There's one in a bloody warehouse down at the docks. We get the girl and take that. Nothing's over.'

That got Tinnstra's attention. 'You know where there's a boat?'

'Yeah. In the warehouse the old man – Jax – uses.'

'Can you sail it?'

'Yeah. I've been sailing all my life. I can get us out.'

Tinnstra straightened up. There was still hope. As long as she didn't give up. She could see what needed to be done. 'You get the Chosen's attention.'

'What are you going to do?'

'I'm going to come up behind him.'

Tinnstra didn't wait to see if Dren agreed. She sprinted across the hallway. It was only ten yards, but it took a lifetime to get there. Her feet pounded the marble, expecting a shout that she'd been spotted or a crack of the baton as an energy bolt flew to kill her. When she was a yard away, she dived through the shattered window into the black night outside.

DAY EIGHT

66

Yas

Kiyosun

Yas sheltered behind a marble post near the staircase. She clutched her knife, but it was useless in the battle going on around her and she was no match for the Chosen.

Gris had taken the worst of it. He had to be dead. She could see his body, all charred, not moving. After everything he'd done for her, it was no way to die. Hasan was down, too. He'd avoided a direct hit but had been struck by some falling masonry and wasn't moving. Only the Gods knew if he was getting up again.

The other Shulka, Jax, stood by the stairs to the kitchens, not moving. He had no weapon and no will left to use one. Yas had never seen a man look so defeated, so lost. The Chosen hadn't given him a second glance.

There was only Yas left and the Chosen knew it. He turned to her and smiled. 'Hello.'

Yas gripped her knife in two shaking hands and pointed it at him. 'Don't come any closer.'

'Nice knife,' he said, hooking his baton back onto his belt. 'I like knives.' He produced one of his own and walked towards her.

'No!' screamed Yas, but that didn't stop him.

All Yas's hate, all her fears, all her anguish came out in one blood-curdling shriek. She threw herself at the Chosen, hacking down with her knife. She was going to bury it in his sick heart, even if it was the last thing she did.

He punched her in the face, stopping her dead. Her nose flattened, spurting blood, as she fell backwards and went down hard. The room spun around her as her vision blurred. She'd dropped her knife and now she sat there, nose broken, crying, about to die.

He stood over her. 'You are a feisty one, aren't you? Where did they find you?'

Yas scrambled backwards, groping around for anything she could use as a weapon, anything that could keep the Chosen away from her.

'Don't run off.' He grabbed hold of her coat and pulled her towards him. As he did so, her fingers closed around a lump of brick. She swung it with all her might, cracking him across the temple. Heard the sound of bone breaking.

'Bitch.' He swiped her with the back of his hand, sending her tumbling and spitting blood. A boot thudded into her ribs before she could get to her feet. She felt something crack as the air fled her lungs. 'Bitch.' He kicked her in the jaw next and Yas went down hard. She got her arms over her head, expecting another blow there, but he went for her ribs again. Once, twice, three times, spitting curses at her with each kick. He stamped down on her back, flattening her against the ground. 'You're going to regret doing that. All you did was make your death a thousand times worse.'

She heard the crackle of his baton back in his hand.

'Leave her alone, you bastard.' The boot was removed from her back and Yas rolled onto her side to see Dren standing by a smashed-up window, scimitar in hand.

'Do you even know how to use that sword, boy?' said the Chosen.

'Come and find out,' replied Dren.

67

Tinnstra

Kiyosun

Tinnstra ran as fast as she could to the other side of the building. As she turned the corner, she could see the Chosen through a row of shattered windows. She could see Dren heading towards him. Now it was up to Tinnstra.

She climbed through one of the windows, sword in one hand, axe in the other. She moved as carefully as she could, cringing as broken glass crunched underfoot. Her legs trembled. Her hand shook. Sweat dripped off her brow despite the cold wind flowing in through the window. *What am I doing? I'm going to get killed. Stupid, stupid girl.*

She watched the Chosen draw his baton.

'Little boy, little boy. Put down the sword,' said the Chosen, 'or I'll burn the flesh from your bones.' He was five feet away, focused completely on Dren. Yas lay on the ground but there was no sign of the others. More dead, no doubt.

'And then you'll let me go?' Dren said, laughing.

Tinnstra took another step closer, tightened her grip on her weapons.

'No one's leaving here. You know that.' The Chosen raised his baton.

'You bastard. This is our country. We don't want you here,' snarled Dren.

Tinnstra heard the crackle of the baton getting ready to fire. There was no more time left. She had to strike. She took another

467

step, shifted her weight. The Chosen was almost close enough to touch.

Then Dren looked at her, over the Chosen's shoulder, his eyes beseeching her to make her move. The Chosen saw the glance, too, turned. His eyes narrowed as he brought his baton around. Energy danced at its tip, buzzing like a swarm of angry bees. Images of Beris dying flashed through her mind.

Tinnstra slashed down. A perfect strike. Just as her father had taught her. Her sword – Greener's sword – cut through the Chosen's wrist. There was no resistance to the blade as it sliced through flesh and bone. His hand and the baton fell to the ground. The Chosen cried out in shock and pain. She brought the axe up and rammed it into his chest. She could see the surprise in his eyes as a howl of pain died on his lips.

Dren ran in, brought his scimitar down and hacked into the Chosen's shoulder. The Egril's legs went from under him. He fell onto his knees, coughed blood, then tumbled onto his front. Blood poured out over the white marble. His head twitched once, twice, and was still.

They stood over the body. 'Is he dead?' she asked, panting.

Dren kicked the Chosen. He didn't move. He looked up and grinned at Tinnstra. 'We did it.' She bent down and pulled her axe from his chest, hardly believing that the man who'd chased her from one end of the country to the other was dead. Aasgod was avenged.

Tinnstra helped Yas up off the ground. 'The Chosen's dead. Dren and I need to go and look for Zorique – can you check on the others?'

Yas nodded. 'Leave them with me. Get Zorique.'

Tinnstra and Dren took the sweeping stairs up to the second floor. Neither spoke. Tinnstra had neither the breath nor the thought for words.

Grey wisps of smoke drifted in through broken windows. Fires burned across the city, red glows in the darkness. Dren stopped, his attention drawn to the view. 'Shit. We may have another problem.'

'What do you mean?' asked Tinnstra.

'We didn't start a lot of those fires.' Dren pointed out across Kiyosun. 'It's not rained for a long time and the wind's carrying sparks and flames all over the place. You can see the fires are growing, spreading across the city.'

'And?'

'If it carries on like that, we could get cut off from the docks, or the warehouses might go up in smoke and our boat along with them.'

Tinnstra stared out through the window. As if they needed any more problems. 'Let's be quick, then.'

Dren kicked open the door to the first room. A bedroom with a Skull cowering behind the bed. His helmet was off, revealing the face of a young man perhaps no older than Dren. He held up both hands in surrender. Tinnstra slammed her axe into his head. Fear offered no more protection for him than it did for her and the world was no place for mercy. The Egril had taught her that.

They moved on as quickly as their tired bodies allowed, checking and clearing each room, concern growing as they moved down the corridor without finding Zorique. Tinnstra kept checking the windows, too, watching the fires, watching them spread.

They reached the third room from the end. The door was partly open and Dren pushed it all the way with his foot. Zorique stared at them with tear-filled eyes, bound to a chair and gagged.

'Quick, untie her,' ordered Tinnstra as she rushed over. She pulled the gag from her mouth as Dren set to work on the bonds. 'It's all right. You're safe now. I'm here. I'm here.' She stroked the girl's face as tears ran down her own cheeks. She'd never been so happy in her life.

'You came back,' said Zorique through her own tears. Her arms wrapped around Tinnstra's neck as soon as Dren cut her free.

She returned the hug. 'I promised, didn't I?'

Dren placed a hand on Tinnstra's shoulder. 'We need to move.'

Tinnstra sheathed her sword and picked Zorique up. The girl felt so light in her arms as they moved back down the corridor to the stairs. 'I'm never going to abandon you,' she whispered.

'I was so scared,' confessed Zorique. 'There was a man in black—'

'It's all right. He's gone now. He can't hurt you.'

They moved quickly down the stairs, Dren leading the way once more. As they reached the turn in the staircase, he suddenly came to a halt, putting a hand out to stop Tinnstra, too.

Yas and Hasan knelt on the floor. The Chosen stood behind them with his baton aimed at their heads.

'Did you think killing me would be that easy?' he said, smiling. 'Come down and join us.'

68

Jax

Kiyosun

Jax stood and watched it all. He'd frozen when the Chosen first appeared. The sight of his tormentor had rooted him to the spot. The memories of what Darus Monsuta had done to him – of what he'd made Jax do – held him tighter than any vice. Fear, shame and guilt swirled around inside him. He wanted to be sick. He wanted to run away. He wanted to hide. He wanted to die. And yet he did none of those things. Instead, he just watched. Watched as Monsuta attacked. Watched as he murdered Gris. Watched as the scarred girl and the boy returned and fought back. Watched as they struck Monsuta down.

He knew the Chosen wasn't dead and yet he did nothing. Even when Yas got Hasan back on his feet, he said nothing. As Monsuta rose behind them, he did nothing. As he beat them and forced them to their knees, Jax did nothing. As the scarred girl and the boy returned with the queen, he did nothing. Shouted no warning, made no pleas for their lives to be spared. He knew there was no point. The man was evil and unstoppable. And now, when Monsuta had them all in his power, Jax still did nothing.

He watched as Monsuta gloated over his prisoners. 'Did you really think you'd killed me with your little swords and my sister's axe? One of Raaku's Chosen? All you did was hurt me.' He held out his arm – already, a new hand was growing. It was small and red, like a newborn babe's. 'Pain is good. Kage taught me that. And I will teach you.'

Jax looked down at his new arm. He knew the truth of Monsuta's words. Better the others die now than fall into the bastard's hands. Better that than be destroyed like Jax. He was nothing more than a ghost of a man, a spectre watching over the end of days. Was that his punishment? To bear witness to the final fall of Jia and all he held worthy?

The small girl was crying. The queen. He'd promised to protect his monach, once, taken a vow to give his life if necessary. And yet there he was, a broken old man who'd failed at everything he'd ever set out to do. At least Kaine couldn't see him now. If only he were dead with his son.

Dead. Dead. Dead.

'We are the dead who serve all who live.' The words were but a whisper on his lips, so quiet he could almost believe he never said them. 'We are the dead who fight.' He could remember the day when he'd first uttered the words, young and invincible and without a care in the world. 'We are the dead who guard tomorrow. We are the dead who protect our land, our monach, our clan.' He looked at the queen. The scarred girl had her arms around the child, covering her face, her eyes. She didn't want her to see what came next. She wasn't a Shulka and yet she was doing a Shulka's duty.

Jax's voice grew louder. 'We are the dead who stand in the light. We are the dead who face the night.' He'd been born into a Shulka family, raised in their ways. Taught to fight the moment he could hold a sword and spear. Raised his son the same way. He believed in honour and the glory of the battlefield. The Egril had other views. All they cared about was conquest and death. They had no honour, sought no true glory. Victory and the destruction of their enemies were all that mattered.

Gris's sword lay on the floor not a foot from Jax.

'We are the dead whom evil fears. We are the Shulka and we are the dead.'

As the words left Jax's lips, Monsuta stiffened, glanced back from the corner of his eye. He turned, grinning. 'Found some life at last, have you? Don't worry. I've not forgotten you. Your time will come again. Perhaps I'll cut your arm off again, or maybe a leg or two. Do you think you'd enjoy that?'

He picked up Gris's sword. It felt good in his hand, his right hand, where it belonged. He looked up at Monsuta. 'We are the dead.'

The Chosen laughed. 'I couldn't have said it better myself.'

The blast hit Jax. Sent him flying. Burning, burning, burning. Every part of him screamed in agony but he focused on the sword in his hand. Put his belief in that, a Shulka's weapon. He stood up. Faced Monsuta. 'We are the dead,' he said once more and staggered towards him.

'I heard you the first time,' replied Monsuta. He fired again.

Jax went down again. Fire danced across his skin, his clothes. Even his thoughts were aflame. 'No.' Smoke drifted off his flesh. He picked up the sword, got to his feet, took another step closer. 'We are the dead.'

Monsuta raised the baton once more.

The scarred girl threw herself on Monsuta before he could fire. Screaming, punching, clawing. He stumbled off-balance as he tried to knock her away. The boy joined her and hooked an arm around Monsuta's neck. Pummelled blows to the Chosen's head.

Jax staggered towards them, his skin blistered and cracking.

Hasan got to his feet and picked up a discarded sword from the floor. He walked over to the struggling mass of bodies and stabbed the blade through Monsuta's chest. The Chosen went limp as blood trickled from the wound. They dropped him to the floor with a thud.

'He's not dead,' shouted the scarred girl. 'He'll heal.'

The boy looked at Jax. 'Cut his fucking head off.'

Every step hurt. Every movement was agony. Every breath torture. But Jax didn't stop. He stood before Monsuta, gazed down on his tormenter. Already the Chosen's body was twitching as his magic healed it. It wouldn't be long before he was a threat again. He lifted the sword. Monsuta's eyes opened.

'We are Shulka and we are the dead.' Jax hacked down. Monsuta's head rolled away.

'Let's burn this place to the ground and get the fuck out of here,' said the boy.

Jax said nothing.

69

Tinnstra

Kiyosun

Tinnstra pulled off the Chosen's mask, revealing the face of a young man. If not for the white hair, he would've been quite ordinary-looking. Someone you wouldn't look twice at on the street. She should've been glad he was dead, but instead, she only felt numb. She knew for every victory, there would be another danger to face.

'We should go,' said Hasan, cradling his arm. One eye was swollen shut and cuts covered his face. 'Get Zorique out of here and somewhere safe.'

'We're taking her to Meigore,' said Tinnstra.

'We missed the pickup. No one's going anywhere.'

'Dren said there's a boat in the warehouse where you used to meet.'

Hasan glanced at Jax and then a flicker of a smile appeared. 'He's right. It's small, but it'll do for the queen and maybe two or three others.'

'Let's go,' said Tinnstra.

Yas and Hasan supported Jax while Tinnstra held Zorique's hand with Dren walking alongside. He'd swapped his scimitar for a Shulka blade. The boy had a wild look to him, as if he couldn't believe they'd succeeded. Tinnstra knew how he felt.

They stepped outside – into chaos. The streets and the market square were full of people shouting and cheering against the backdrop of a burning city.

Curfew was forgotten. Tinnstra couldn't remember when she'd last seen so many people gathered together, day or night. Not since the invasion, at least. Maybe it was the explosions that had brought them out, or the fire, or word of an attack on the Council House. Whatever it was, it looked like the whole of Kiyosun was up and out. Fighting back.

Tinnstra glanced at the dead Skulls littering the courtyard. May the Four Gods help her, but it felt good to see them lying there. Tinnstra and the others had achieved a victory at last after so many defeats. Really given the Egril a bloody nose they'd remember. And if they got Zorique away, it would only be the start.

As they made their way across the courtyard, people were racing into the Council House's grounds. Some came to loot the dead, while others threw torches through the broken windows. Tinnstra watched as the building quickly caught light. Pockets of fire appeared in window after window. Each time a room went up, the crowd cheered, encouraging the next person to add fuel to the blaze. There were so many happy faces, coloured red from the flames, watching the building go up.

'Good riddance,' spat Dren. 'The world's a better place without it.'

'By the Four Gods,' said Yas. 'It looks like half the city's alight. I need to get back to my family.'

'Go,' replied Hasan. 'You've done more than enough. We'll be forever grateful.'

Yas frowned. 'No offence, but don't ask me for help again.'

'We won't,' agreed Hasan. 'Go to your family.'

Yas turned to the others. 'Good luck. Especially to you, Your Majesty.' She didn't wait for a reply but ran off into the crowds and was quickly lost from sight.

Hasan adjusted his weight to support Jax better.

'Do you need help?' asked Dren.

The Shulka shook his head. 'Better you keep your hands free, just in case we find more trouble.'

Dren nodded, but they all knew they wouldn't get far that way. The strain showed on Hasan's face with every step he took, and Jax ... She had no idea what kept him on his feet. His skin was red-raw and every breath he took sounded like his last, a wheeze and a cough away from death.

At the end of the street, Jax stumbled, almost pulling Hasan down with him. They all stopped as Hasan lowered Jax to the ground. 'This isn't working,' said the Shulka.

'We're doing all right,' said Dren. 'We'll get there.'

Hasan shook his head. 'No, we won't – not with me and the boss holding you back. We carry on like this and the fire will get to the warehouse before we do.'

'We're not leaving you,' said Tinnstra, even though she knew he was right. She'd left too many people behind.

'You are,' replied the Shulka. 'We've done our part. We've got you here. Now you finish it. Take that girl to safety and give us all some hope again.'

Hasan and Jax were great men, like her father and her brothers, but they were right. They'd done their part. It was now up to her, Dren and Zorique. Their turn to lead the fight. 'May the Gods look after you.'

A flash of pride passed over Hasan's face, a look she'd never seen on her father's. 'And you, Tinnstra.'

Dren bowed to the old man. 'Sorry I caused you so much trouble, Jax. I … I'm honoured to have fought beside you.'

Jax nodded. 'You are Shulka now. You are Hanran. The honour is mine.'

Tinnstra took Zorique's hand. 'Come on, Dren.'

The boy nodded. 'This way.' He moved off quickly and Tinnstra and Zorique followed. Tinnstra tried not to think about whether she'd see either man again.

The streets grew more packed by the second, the delirium around the Council House replaced by concern and fear the further into the city they went. The temperature rose, bolstered by the press of bodies and the heat from nearby burning build-ings. A woman was knocked down, and Dren had to push others out of the way to stop her getting trampled. Mothers carried crying children, neighbours helped rouse neighbours while others pushed carts or carried bags, eager to get away from the flames.

The narrow streets channelled the fire and the smoke, making it hard to breathe, and forced them to change direction too many times trying to find a way around.

They passed a checkpoint where dead Skulls lay, killed by the mob. The tattered Egril flags drifted along the ground, chased by the wind.

There was a crack as a nearby building broke in half, spilling fire out across the street and into other buildings, blocking their way yet again. The water tower from its roof smashed into the other side of the street, spilling water everywhere, knocking people over and adding even more confusion to the turmoil. Steam sizzled when water met fire but there wasn't enough to extinguish the flames.

Tinnstra picked up Zorique, protecting her from a shower of sparks and ash. Dren grabbed her other hand and pulled her back the way they'd come. Thirty yards on, he led them through a sliver of an alleyway into the next street. The crowd wasn't as heavy there, and they moved faster with more space around them. Even so, flames danced across the rooftops, keeping pace.

'How much further?' asked Tinnstra.

'Two more streets,' replied Dren.

Tinnstra could smell the sea, even over the smoke and ash in the air. They were close, so close.

They cut down another alley, turned right, pushed past more scared people and then turned left. There was nowhere else to go: the sea was in front of them, stretching off into the darkness, warehouses at either end of the dockside. The ones to her left were already on fire. 'Is that ... ?' she asked, too scared to finish the sentence.

Dren pointed the other way. 'The second one down there.' Those warehouses were untouched for the moment.

Thank the Four Gods. They ran.

The main warehouse door was locked but Dren led them around the side and through the back.

The boat hung from the ceiling on some ropes. They stood and stared at it, as if not trusting their eyes, but there it was. Then Dren laughed. The sound took both of them by surprise, but it was infectious. Tinnstra and Zorique joined in.

'We did it. We bloody well did it,' said Tinnstra as she lowered Zorique to the ground. She walked over to the boat, staring at it. It was real. It existed and it seemed sturdy enough. There was a patch of different-coloured wood at the front on one side where it must've been repaired at some point, but it looked seaworthy as far as she could tell.

The ropes were fixed to a pulley system, but Dren had the workings of it and manoeuvred the boat down and into the water. He clambered in and fixed the oars into rings on either side of the hull. 'We'll row out of the harbour and then put the sail up once we're clear. If we get a good wind, we'll be in Meigore before you know it.'

'Okay.' Tinnstra took a deep breath. 'Let's go. Let's do it.' She passed Zorique down to Dren and he helped her settle at the rear of the boat. The girl didn't say anything, but after everything she'd been through, that wasn't surprising. She was a tough kid.

Tinnstra stepped into the boat next, felt it wobble under her foot, but Dren held out a hand and steadied her. 'Don't worry,' he said with a grin. 'You'll get used to it. If you're going to be sick, make sure you do it downwind.'

'I'll try to remember that.' Tinnstra sat next to Zorique and Dren took up the oars. She slipped her arm around the girl as she watched the darkness. Somewhere out there was freedom.

Dren worked the oars hard, setting a good pace despite his strapped-up hand. The boat moved quickly over the calm water, bobbing up and down with each stroke. Even the din from the city started to drop away and the vivid red glow from the fires dimmed. Tinnstra looked back, happy to see Kiyosun from a new angle. The fires raged across the city, some greater than others. Only the Four Gods knew what would be left by morning.

Dren pulled the oars inside the boat. 'I'm going to put the sail up now, and then we'll have to swap places. The tiller is behind you and I'll need that to steer the boat.'

Tinnstra looked towards the back of the boat and saw a handle she'd not noticed before. 'Oh, right.'

Dren shook his head. 'Have you never been on a boat before?'

'No.' Tinnstra laughed. It felt so good to laugh. 'Good job you're here, eh?'

They felt a kick of speed as Dren hoisted the sail, a triangle of white in the night. It made changing places awkward as the boat swayed when they shifted their weight. In the end, Tinnstra all but fell down on the bench. She sat up, facing Dren and Zorique, facing the city. The smile fell from her face.

'What is it?' said Dren, turning to see whatever had caught Tinnstra's eye.

'Daijaku.'

70

Dren

Kiyosun

There were five of them. Wings picked out against the night sky by the firelight. Moving in fast. They still had some time, but time to do what? They were in a small boat in the middle of the sea with nowhere to hide.

Tinnstra pulled the girl away from the stern and made her lie down under the benches. 'Don't move,' she said. 'We'll deal with this.'

Dren had to admire Tinnstra's confidence because he was shitting himself. How he wished for more orbs to throw at them. He pulled the Shulka sword free.

'Stay sharp,' said Tinnstra, gripping her sword and axe. 'You've got to make every strike count.'

Dren looked back at her, face set all grim with that gash red-raw. 'There are five of them. Five.' He didn't mean to sound scared, but he knew he did all the same.

'Hold it together. We've come this far. We'll deal with this. Now keep your eyes wide and bright. They're nearly here.'

Dren turned back, knelt down behind his bench and held his breath. The Daijaku were fucking close. He could see their faces now and the bloody Niganntan blades in their hands.

'Drop down as they pass over, aim for their guts,' said Tinnstra, voice calm.

The Daijaku dropped low to skim over the surface of the water, coming straight at them. The one in the lead bared his teeth as he pulled back his Niganntan, ready to strike. He was ten yards away, nine, eight, seven. Dren's heart threatened to punch its way out of his chest. Five. Four. Three. Dren swung as he fell back into the boat, watched the Daijaku and the Niganntan blades whistle past.

Tinnstra must've got lucky because a Daijaku went down, crashing into the sea at speed and sending up spray that soaked Dren. One down.

He sat back up as the next Daijaku landed in the boat and slashed out with his Niganntan spear. The blade passed over Dren's head and took a chunk out of the sail, but then Tinnstra attacked from behind. She rammed her sword through the demon's back and slammed her axe into its neck. Its corpse fell over the side after his friend. Two down. Fuck, she was good.

'Stay down!' screamed Tinnstra as she swung again. This time, she wasn't lucky. The Daijaku dipped and swerved out the way, looping back up high in the sky. Dren got to his feet, sword in hand, Tinnstra by his side. The Daijaku buzzed around them, waiting for their opportunity.

'May the Four Gods look after you,' she said.

'Fuck the Gods,' said Dren. 'Let's look after ourselves.'

And the three Daijaku dived down towards them.

A volley of arrows zipped out of the darkness to starboard, striking the Daijaku. Another volley followed, tearing bloody holes in them and knocking them from the sky. They plummeted down, hit the sea hard and sank.

'What the—' said Tinnstra as a ship, a square-rigger, loomed out of the darkness. It was near impossible to see, with painted black sides and black sails. Soldiers manned the deck, bows ready for any more surprises. It came in close and sent Dren's boat rocking violently with its wake. Whoever they were, Dren was damn happy to see them.

'Beware the rope,' someone called from above before the rope itself dropped down to land on their deck. Dren grabbed it and used it to pull the boat even closer to the rigger.

A ladder came down next.

'I suppose we should go up,' said Tinnstra.

'Don't see as we've got much choice,' said Dren.

She helped Zorique up from the bottom of the boat. 'Tie her to my back, Dren,' she said. 'I don't want any accidents on the way up.'

'Sure.' He did as she asked, the girl watching him all the while with a defiant look in her eyes. She was a tough kid. He liked her.

Tinnstra reached for the ladder but Dren stopped her. 'Wait a minute.'

'What is it?'

He glanced back at Kiyoson. *His* city. 'I'm going back. I've got people that need me there.'

Tinnstra nodded, understanding. 'Good luck.'

'To you too.'

Dren watched Tinnstra climb the ladder and disappear over the side of the boat, Following her was probably a better idea but a wolf didn't abandon its pack. He pushed the boat from the rigger. It was time he did the right thing.

71

Tinnstra

The Meigore Channel

Tinnstra found a full crew waiting for them on deck. Two men came over and helped release Zorique from the rope binding her to Tinnstra. They lowered her to the deck and the girl immediately wrapped an arm around Tinnstra's leg as she looked at all the faces staring her.

A man stepped forward, with a full black beard and long hair tied back into a ponytail and a silver crane on his tunic. 'I'm Captain Ralasis of His Majesty's ship the *Okinas Kiba*. Welcome aboard.'

'Thank you for your help, Captain,' replied Tinnstra. 'You saved our lives.'

'We were already nearby when we saw your boat,' said Ralasis. 'We were supposed to pick up some passengers from elsewhere, but we missed each other.'

'No, you didn't.'

'What do you mean?'

Tinnstra smiled. 'There's a brave, young lady I'd like to introduce to you. A queen, actually ...'

Acknowledgements

It was always my dream to be published by Gollancz and it's been a wonderful experience so far, full of 'pinch me' moments that I'll never forget. I owe the whole team so much for all the help and support they've given me. Thank you one and all.

In particular, the wonderful Craig Leyenaar led the charge at Gollancz from the beginning. He was the first to say yes (and, for that alone, I owe him champagne) and then proceeded to shape the book from what it was into what it should be. His advice has always been spot-on, pointing out the weak bits, praising the good and inspiring me to push beyond what I thought possible.

Rob Dinsdale, agent extraordinaire, is just the best human being I know. His belief and encouragement over the years have been incredible. I love working with him and thank my lucky stars every day that I have Rob in my corner.

To Mark Stay and Mark Desvaux, thank you for providing me with endless entertainment, education and inspiration. I think people come into your life just when you need them and you guys did just that. Here's to dancing naked in the rain.

My father, Arthur Shackle, has always been full of encouragement and support. He's always been my first reader and biggest cheerleader. He was the one who sat next to me in the cinema as I watched *Star Wars* for the first time (and second and third ...), he took me endless times to Forbidden Planet to buy crazy comics and never complained when I wanted him to drive me across the country so I could meet my heroes at another smelly comic-con.

No doubt my sister, Suzie, is crying as she reads this. Yes, your brother has a book in the shops. Maybe one day you'll read the story (but I understand it's probably not your thing). I'll try and get a love story in the next one if that helps. Thanks for putting up with such an annoying brother all these years.

I wish my mother was still here to see what her boy has done. She loved a good novel and always encouraged her children to read. Not many families need a suitcase just for their books when they go on holiday but we did. No doubt, she's raising a glass from up above and getting annoyed she's missing a party. I love you, Mum.

My children, Dylan and Zoe, are an endless source of love and delight to me. They are my everything and I'm a lucky man to be their daddy. Thank you.

Finally, to Tinnie, without whom I'd still be a long-haired, overweight ad guy, mumbling about the book I'd never write. Everyone needs a partner in life and I couldn't ask for a better person to stand beside me. She is a warrior with a dragon's heart and my one true love. Never give up, never surrender, baby.

ABOUT GOLLANCZ

Gollancz is the oldest SF publishing imprint in the world. Since being founded in 1927 Gollancz has continued to publish a focused selection of bestselling and award-winning authors. The front-list includes **Ben Aaronovitch**, **Joe Abercrombie**, **Charlaine Harris**, **Joanne Harris**, **Joe Hill**, **Alastair Reynolds**, **Patrick Rothfuss**, **Nalini Singh** and **Brandon Sanderson**.

As one of the largest Science Fiction and Fantasy imprints in the UK it is no surprise we have one of the most extensive backlists in the world. Find high-quality SF on Gateway written by such authors as **Philip K. Dick**, **Ursula Le Guin**, **Connie Willis**, **Sir Arthur C. Clarke**, **Pat Cadigan**, **Michael Moorcock** and **George R.R. Martin**.

We also have a strand of publishing in translation, which includes French, Polish and Russian authors. Gollancz is home to more award-winning authors than any other imprint, with names including **Aliette de Bodard**, **M. John Harrison**, **Paul McAuley**, **Sarah Pinborough**, **Pierre Pevel**, **Justina Robson** and many more.

The SF Gateway
More than 3,000 classic, rare and previously out-of-print SF novels at your fingertips.
www.sfgateway.com

The Gollancz Blog
Bringing you news from our worlds to yours. Stories, interviews, articles and exclusive extracts just for you!
www.gollancz.co.uk

GOLLANCZ
LONDON